Praise for the Novels of Beverly Connor

"Calls to mind the forensic mysteries of Aaron Elkins and Patricia Cornwell. However, Connor's sleuth infuses the mix with her own brand of spice as a pert and brainy scholar in the forensic analysis of bones. . . . Chases, murder attempts, and harrowing rescues add to this fast-paced adventure."

—*Chicago Sun-Times*

"Connor combines smart people, fun people, and dangerous people in a novel hard to put down."

—*The Dallas Morning News*

"Connor grabs the reader with her first sentence and never lets up until the book's end. . . . The story satisfies both as a mystery and as an entrée into the fascinating world of bones. . . . Add Connor's dark humor, and you have a multidimensional mystery that deserves comparison with the best of Patricia Cornwell." —*Booklist* (starred review)

In Connor's latest multifaceted tale, the plot is serpentine, ne solution ingenious, the academic politics vicious . . . hock-full of engrossing anthropological and archeological etail."

—*Publishers Weekly*

continued . . .

"Connor's books are a smart blend of Patricia Cornwell, Aaron Elkins, and Elizabeth Peters, with some good Deep South atmosphere to make it authentic."

—*Oklahoma Family Magazine*

"Crisp dialogue, interesting characters, fascinating tidbits of bone lore, and a murderer that eluded me. When I started reading, I couldn't stop. What more could you ask for? Enjoy."

—Virginia Lanier, author of the Bloodhound series

"Beverly Connor has taken the dry bones of scientific inquiry and resurrected them into living, breathing characters. I couldn't put [it] down until I was finished, even though I wanted to savor the story. I predict that Beverly Connor will become a major player in the field of mystery writing." —David Hunter, author of *The Dancing Savio*

"Fans of . . . Patricia Cornwell will definitely want to rea Beverly Connor . . . an author on the verge of supersta dom." —*Midwest Book Revie*

"Connor's breathtaking ability to dish out fascinating fo rensic details while maintaining a taut aura of suspense is real gift." —*Romantic Times* (top pic

Also by Beverly Connor

SCATTERED GRAVES
DEAD HUNT
DEAD PAST
DEAD SECRET
DEAD GUILTY
ONE GRAVE TOO MANY

DUST TO DUST

A DIANE FALLON FORENSIC INVESTIGATION

BEVERLY CONNOR

AN OBSIDIAN MYSTERY

OBSIDIAN
Published by New American Library, a division of
Penguin Group (USA) Inc., 375 Hudson Street,
New York, New York 10014, USA
Penguin Group (Canada), 90 Eglinton Avenue East, Suite 700, Toronto,
Ontario M4P 2Y3, Canada (a division of Pearson Penguin Canada Inc.)
Penguin Books Ltd., 80 Strand, London WC2R 0RL, England
Penguin Ireland, 25 St. Stephen's Green, Dublin 2,
Ireland (a division of Penguin Books Ltd.)
Penguin Group (Australia), 250 Camberwell Road, Camberwell, Victoria 3124,
Australia (a division of Pearson Australia Group Pty. Ltd.)
Penguin Books India Pvt. Ltd., 11 Community Centre, Panchsheel Park,
New Delhi - 110 017, India
Penguin Group (NZ), 67 Apollo Drive, Rosedale, North Shore 0632,
New Zealand (a division of Pearson New Zealand Ltd.)
Penguin Books (South Africa) (Pty.) Ltd., 24 Sturdee Avenue,
Rosebank, Johannesburg 2196, South Africa

Penguin Books Ltd., Registered Offices:
80 Strand, London WC2R 0RL, England

First published by Obsidian, an imprint of New American Library,
a division of Penguin Group (USA) Inc.

First Printing, August 2009
10 9 8 7 6 5 4 3 2 1

Printed in the United States of America

To Robbie.
This one's for you.

Acknowledgments

Thanks to Charles Connor, as always, for his unlimited support and patience.

Thanks to Kristen Weber for her hard work, expertise, and kindness.

Prologue

Marcella Payden straightened the silverware beside the two cobalt blue dinner plates, then lit the fat cinnamon-scented candle in the middle of her small oak dining table. A breeze from the open window carried the tinkling sound of ceramic wind chimes and made the candle flame dance. Nice, she thought as she surveyed the table, smiling at herself and the giddy feeling in her stomach. How long had it been since she'd had a date?

Marcella smoothed her cotton Navajo-style skirt and ran a hand over her hair, tucking stray tendrils back into the beaded barrette that loosely bound her graying locks. She felt like a teenager. It felt good.

She looked at her calloused hands—deeply tanned, a few wrinkles. Much like her tanned and lined face. It was a good face. She liked the way she looked—the roughness was the mark of what she was.

The woman next door back in Arizona had smooth, unlined skin and soft, manicured hands that Marcella's husband had found more to his liking. It hurt, of course, when he left her, but the strongest emotion was surprise. She was astonished that her husband would find someone who sold lipstick for a living more interesting than an archaeologist.

"No accounting for taste," she muttered to herself. That was what she got for marrying a philosopher. It would serve him right if he had to drive around in that lilac convertible for the rest of his life.

The wind picked up and the napkins fluttered on the table. Marcella walked to the window to close it. Outside was already dark, even though it was still early by her reckoning. Along with the rustling of leaves and the ringing of wind chimes, the wind carried a chill. She stood for a moment, taking in the cool fresh air. North Georgia was so much cooler than Arizona. It was very pleasant.

But the chill . . . or something else . . . brought a sudden shift in mood. Marcella's hair stood up on the back of her neck and her heart beat faster. She clutched at her silver squash-blossom necklace.

What brought that on? she wondered, squinting and looking out into the darkness through the open window. She saw nothing but the silhouettes of trees moving in the wind, and heard no sound but the rustling leaves, wind chimes, and distant road noise.

It was a Lewis moment.

Lewis was a cognitive archaeologist in Arizona, a colleague and intellectual sparring partner. He had a keen interest in how Paleo-Indians managed to survive among lightning-fast saber-toothed tigers and other giant predators of stealth and speed. His research into the functioning of the human brain led to the interesting discovery that the subconscious can perceive a movement or a threat and the body can respond several seconds before the conscious mind even becomes aware. A nice little brain function that helped early humans survive at a time when animals were bigger, faster, and had way sharper teeth.

Marcella agreed with this idea because she had experienced the phenomenon firsthand. It happened while she was walking through an overgrown field surveying for signs of prehistoric inhabitants—looking for arrowheads, actually. She found herself suddenly breathing rapidly, her heart pounding . . . and inexplicably she was standing more than three feet to the side of where she had been a moment before. She had no idea what had happened or why she had jumped to the side. But her eyes were fixed on the spot where her next step would have been. There, hidden in the grass, lay a rattlesnake. Subconscious awareness and involuntary response had kicked in. A prehistoric survival function had saved her from harm.

Marcella called such moments of subconscious wariness "Lewis moments." She looked through the open window again but saw no sabertooths in the shadows. She wondered whether such automated responses could really have been that effective. With snakes maybe, but tigers?

Silly woman, she thought. *It's probably all those towering trees waving in the wind.* Marcella missed the desert colors: earth tones, red rock. There was just too much giant, vivid green here.

She closed the window and walked across to the living room to turn on the light. Her eye stopped on the desk where the light sat and she realized that it was the desk—or rather what she had found in it—that was nagging at the back of her mind. That must be it.

Marcella had cleaned out the ramshackle potter's shed behind her house. Among miscellaneous pieces of broken furniture and weathered plywood, under a piece of old linoleum long ago ripped up from the kitchen floor, with myriad items littering its top, she had found the old desk. A rough pearl constructed of distressed maple, it had three drawers down each side and one long drawer in the middle. Although it was not an extraordinary desk, she liked its solid promise.

When she was cleaning the layers of dust and grime from the desk, she found writing on the bottom of the middle drawer. The house had been a treasure trove of nice surprises, but this surprise was disturbing. It was also old; too old to do anything about. Still, she intended to speak with Jonas about it and ask him to mention it to Diane Fallon.

Marcella partially pulled out the drawer as she turned on the banker's lamp on top of the desk. The fluorescent bulb had a second's delay before the light came on. Just as it brightened, she felt another Lewis-moment shiver and the world went black.

Another bright shining light appeared and Marcella wondered whether she should crawl to it. It shouldn't be this hard, she thought, as she struggled to move across the floor.

Chapter 1

Diane Fallon parked her car well out of the way alongside the narrow drive. She closed her car door and stood looking at the old farmhouse illuminated by the headlights of a police car and the forensics van already there. Diane was director of the RiverTrail Museum of Natural History and director of the Rosewood Crime Lab, which was housed in the museum. It was in her role as crime lab director that she was here, but she suspected on this occasion she would be wearing both hats. That was because the house belonged to Dr. Marcella Payden, whom the museum's archaeology curator, Jonas Briggs, had hired to create a reference collection of prehistoric potsherds for the museum's archaeology department.

It was an old house, perhaps from the early 1900s, set among trees that looked old enough to be original to the place. The two-story white wooden structure had a blue tin roof and long open porches on the first and second floors that stretched across the front of the house. There was a redbrick chimney on each end. At one end of the house a metal carport contained a light-colored SUV. Large square-cut stones lined the gravel driveway.

The yard was mainly dirt with rock-bordered areas that had once been flower beds. Broken concrete yard ornaments—statuary, fountains, vases—littered the yard. From its appearance, the place could have been an archaeological dig. In reality, it was just an old farmhouse yard containing an odd assortment of disused items.

Diane changed from her heels to comfortable loafers and slipped a flannel shirt over her dark metallic burgundy cocktail dress. She held the shirt tight around her as she walked toward the house to shield herself from the wind, which was becoming chilly.

Neva Hurley and Izzy Wallace were taking their kits from the crime scene van as they spoke with a patrolman. Diane waved to them.

"What do you know?" asked Diane as she got within earshot.

Neva and Izzy were police officers with the Rosewood PD and two of the four crime scene investigators who worked for Diane. Neva was energetic, slim, and in her late twenties. Izzy, the newest member of the crime lab, was a fiftysomething, sturdily built guy. They grinned at her when she approached.

"You know Officer Daughtry?" asked Izzy, with a tilt of his head to indicate the patrolman.

"Diane Fallon," she said, shaking the officer's hand.

"Good to meet you, ma'am," he said.

He seemed a little green. *Must be a rookie*, Diane thought.

"Nice outfit," said Neva. "I like the way your dress matches the burgundy in the plaid of your shirt. Very lumberjack chic."

Diane smiled. "I've been to a benefit at Bartrum University."

Neva looked at her watch and up at the sky. It was close to dawn.

Diane gave her a weak smile. "Frank hasn't given up on teaching me to dance. We went out afterward."

There was a gust of cool wind and Diane folded her arms across her middle to keep the chill out. She thought she heard the faint ring of wind chimes in the distance. She nodded toward the house.

"David called me about this. What's going on?"

David Goldstein was assistant director of the crime lab. This evening he was on duty handing out assignments while he worked in the lab.

"David called you?" said Neva. "He didn't have to. We've got it covered. Ol' Izzy here is doing pretty good." Neva punched him affectionately in the shoulder. "Rosewood PD said a woman was attacked here earlier tonight."

"Attacked? She survived?" Diane asked. Her body relaxed.

"Yes, but I don't know how bad off she is," said Neva. "The lead detective's on his way. I think he's been questioning someone. That's all I know."

Neva looked at Patrolman Daughtry as if he might have more information. He shook his head and shrugged.

"I was told to wait here for Detective Hanks," he said.

Neva squinted, observing Diane. "Is there something special about this case?"

"Marcella Payden is an adjunct professor of archaeology at Bartrum and a consultant for the museum," said Diane.

"Oh," said Neva. "I'm sorry. I didn't know."

The crunch of gravel and two blinding headlights heralded an approaching car. Diane stepped closer to the van with Izzy, Neva, and the patrolman, and they watched the car pull in behind the police car.

Detective Hanks, she thought. She recognized him, but she hadn't worked with him before. He took a step in their direction just as gunfire cut the ground at his feet.

Chapter 2

Loud bursts of gunfire exploded one after another. Diane ducked beside the van, pulling Neva down with her.

"What the hell?" she heard Izzy shout, ducking for cover himself.

The shots were coming from the woods beyond the drive where they were parked. Bullets dug out plugs of dirt from the ground. One ricocheted off a rock and hit the van; some hit the piles of lawn sculpture; others flew over their heads. The gunman didn't seem to be aiming at anything in particular, or he was aiming at everything. It sounded to Diane like a rifle, but she wasn't an expert on guns.

Izzy, his gun out, eased to the rear of the van. Neva took out her gun and followed him. Patrolman Daughtry moved toward the front of the vehicle and peeked out at the dark woods. A bullet struck the side of the van and he pulled back.

"Shit," he hissed. "Hey, you crazy son of a bitch, what the hell do you think you're doing? Lay down your gun and come out with your hands—"

His reply was cut short by a hail of bullets.

Keeping low, Diane climbed into the van through the sliding side door. She crawled to the driver's seat and cut off the inside lamp and the headlights. As she called for backup on her cell phone, a bullet zinged through the driver's window and exited on the passenger side. Diane jumped and hit her elbow on the gearshift.

"Diane, you hurt?" called Neva and Izzy together.

"Fine. Just startled—and pissed." Diane crawled out of the van, cursing herself for being in a cocktail dress. *What kind of idiot comes to a crime scene in fancy dress?*

Kneeling on the ground, she could see that Detective Hanks was down. Because of the positions of the parked vehicles in the drive, he was open to the woods when he got out of the car.

"Hanks is down," Diane said. "Keep the shooter occupied long enough for me to get him to cover."

"What?" said Izzy. "Well, hell."

He fired in the direction of the shooter. Daughtry fired a couple of shots blindly across the hood of the van in the general direction from which the bullets seemed to be coming.

Diane dashed out in the open to Hanks, only a few feet away. He was already struggling to his feet just as she reached him. She slipped an arm around his waist and helped him take cover beside the patrol car. A bullet would have to go through the van and the police vehicle to get to him. It was a safe place to wait.

Diane examined the wound in his thigh by what little illumination his headlights provided to their position. It was bleeding, but blood wasn't pulsing out, nor was it profuse. The bullet hadn't hit his femoral artery. It had only nicked him.

"My leg is fine. It's my shoulder," he said. "Damn it. I fell and landed on my bad shoulder. Who the hell is that?"

"I don't know," said Diane. "Is your shoulder out of joint?"

Hanks rolled his shoulder, stretched his arm across his chest, and rolled the shoulder again, wincing the whole time. "No. Just hurts like hell. I'm fine. What's this about?" He stood halfway and peered over the hood of the police car.

"I have no idea. I just got here," said Diane.

"How's Hanks?" shouted Izzy.

"I'm fine. Just mad as hell," he shouted back.

"Backup should be here soon," said Diane.

Diane eased the police car door open, intending to turn off the headlights and use the radio as a link to the police who were on their way. As she reached to cut the lights, she thought she saw a shadow cross a window of the house. It was quick, just a roundish shape passing one of the lower windows.

"That's why the random shots," she whispered.

She cut the lights. Now only light from the first-quarter moon illuminated the area. At least the shooter would have a harder time targeting them.

"What are you talking about?" said Hanks.

He was shifting his weight, trying to look around the patrol car toward Neva and Izzy at the van.

"They're trying to keep us pinned down. Someone is in the house," she said. "That's why they're just spraying bullets around, not targeting anything in particular."

Hanks looked over at her sharply, then turned his head toward the house. "Now? There's someone in the house now?"

"I'm not certain, but I thought I saw someone inside the house." Diane stared at the windows again, squinting, as if that would give her better night vision.

The shooter fired two more shots that dinged off the detective's vehicle and a tree beyond the car. Diane listened for the distant sound of sirens. She heard none.

"I'm going to ease over in the direction of the house," she said. "Do you have a second gun?"

Hanks lifted his pant leg and gave her the Chief's Special he had strapped around his ankle.

Diane weighed the gun in her hand. It wasn't a particularly heavy gun, and she was strong, but it felt heavy in her hand, as if its lethal potential had a weight all its own. She didn't particularly like guns, but it would be foolish to be without one now.

She put her cell in her shirt pocket and moved a couple of steps in the direction of the house and woods, away from the shooter.

"I'll go with you," Hanks said.

"I'm just going to watch," she said. "I have my cell phone to keep in touch. If there's someone in the house, I can tell backup when they come."

"Fine. I'm still going with you."

Hanks stood halfway, keeping the vehicle between him and the shooter. He leaned with his good side against the car.

"Are you sure you can walk?" asked Diane.

"My leg was just grazed and my shoulder's been worse. I'm fine," he said. "I'm thinking I'd like to get inside the house and see if I can spot the shooter from the second-floor windows."

Diane didn't think that was such a good idea, but she didn't say anything immediately. She called Neva on her cell and, speaking in a whisper, told her what she and Hanks were going to do.

"Gotcha," said Neva. "We'll be here at the OK Corral hanging out."

"Backup will be here soon," said Diane. She listened again for distant sirens, but still heard none.

"If we stay near the trees and outbuildings," said Diane, "I don't think the shooter will be able to see us."

She hesitated a moment. She had been trying to make nice with the detectives ever since Izzy told her they thought she interfered in their investigations a bit too often. But Hanks was about to interfere with her crime scene.

"Detective Hanks," she whispered, hoping a soft voice would make her words sound soft as well, "if you go into the house, you will contaminate the crime scene."

"That's not the priority right now. We have a shooter and maybe someone in the house," he said.

Diane stared at him a moment, weighing how to respond. Hanks was maybe in his late thirties, she guessed. His sandy hair was roughed up by his fall. She couldn't read his expression in the dark and she didn't know very much about him. He was new to the department. And he wasn't making a good impression on her.

"Backup will be here any moment," she said. "You're bleeding, your arm's hurt, and there may be someone on the second floor—who is armed."

"And if there is, I'll nail his butt to the wall. Come on, if you're coming." Hanks rose to his feet, keeping his head down.

Diane's plan of simple reconnaissance had turned into something that she really thought was a bad idea. But even in the dark she could see the tight set of his face.

Well, damn.

"If you are determined to go in," she said, "take Officer Daughtry inside with you. He has more police training than I have for that kind of thing. I'll watch your backs from outside the house. We don't know how many may be in the house and we don't know whether they have more friends than just the shooter out in the woods. Izzy and Neva can keep an eye on the front door from where they are."

She glanced at the house. It looked more foreboding than it had just five minutes ago. In the darkness without the headlights shining on it, she could barely make it out. It was a shadowy giant looming in the night and Diane didn't really want to approach it.

Hanks stared at Diane a moment, nodded, and called for Daughtry to come over. Diane watched the patrolman race the few feet between them in a half-crouched position and dive next to them beside his car. Diane thought he was a little too dramatic. Daughtry looked wide-eyed and just a little scared—and he seemed very young. Diane called Neva again and updated her on the plan as Hanks gave the policeman a quick briefing.

Diane was satisfied to let the two of them take the lead. With Hanks wounded and Daughtry looking rather green behind the ears, she didn't want them behind her with guns. As they crept among the large grove of ancient pecan trees, Diane heard Izzy trying to talk the shooter down, and getting only gunfire for his trouble. From the direction of the shots, the shooter seemed to be moving about.

This was not a good idea, Diane thought. The sound of pecan shells crackling underfoot was too loud. She slowed her pace, being careful where she put her feet, careful of tripping over unseen objects that might be on the ground. Weeds scratched at her legs and briars grabbed at her dress. She should have taken the time to change into jeans.

Her foot hit something hard at the base of a tree. In the dark, its shape looked much like a gargoyle leaning against the trunk, nestled between roots. *Guarding the pecan trees from evil spirits, no doubt*, she thought. The wind picked up and blew open her shirt, bringing in chilly air. She pulled it close around her.

It didn't take long for the three of them to reach the first outbuilding—a one-room shack.

Hanks stopped under its eaves, massaging his shoulder. "Daughtry and I'll go from here to the back door," he whispered.

"And if it's locked?" asked Diane.

Hanks studied her for a moment. "Then we'll check the windows," he said. "They got in some way."

"It's a big house," said Diane, looking at the structure looming in the darkness. "It probably has a side door too, maybe a cellar door."

"We'll look. You stay close to the house and watch," Hanks added.

Though his features were in darkness, Diane thought he was trying to stare her down. Was that what this was about, Hanks controlling the investigation? wondered Diane. Standing out in the chilly wind, she was growing increasingly irritated.

"Please remember that the house is a crime scene and take as much care as you can not to touch anything, and remember where you walked," she said.

Hanks nodded. Diane thought the movement looked rather noncommittal.

"Keep a line open with me," he said. "And try not to shoot us."

Diane took her phone out of her pocket and keyed in the number he gave her. She heard his phone vibrate in his hand and put hers back in her pocket when he answered. With that, Hanks turned and made his way to the house with the patrolman close behind.

Diane followed but walked more slowly, carefully picking her way through underbrush to the backyard. Ahead, she heard someone stumble and curse. She thought it was the patrolman. She stopped a moment and watched their dark figures making slow progress toward the house. Hanks hadn't wanted to use a flashlight. No sense in making yourself a target. But it was dark and the thin layer of clouds that drifted past the quarter moon only deepened the darkness, making Marcella's backyard look like a piece of grisaille artwork. The trees were deep black silhouettes against a black background. Diane made out a willow tree near the edge of the yard, its vinelike, black leaf–covered branches moving in the wind.

From what she could see in the dim moonlight, the yard had the familiar patchwork of the rock-bordered flower beds she had seen in the front. At the edge of the yard the trees became more numerous and gradually became a forest.

Diane waited near a stand of box hedges. She didn't have the automatic fear response to darkness that many people had. She was a caver and she enjoyed the dark. Sometimes in a deep cave she liked to sit down and turn off her lamps and let the absolute blackness surround her. Perfect darkness had a kind of beauty to her, so she didn't mind the darkly waving trees or the black forms that dotted the yard. Her gaze shifted from what looked like a birdbath to a bench, to a planter, and to several things she couldn't identify.

She lost sight of Hanks and Daughtry. They'd gone around to the opposite side of the house looking for entry. It grew quiet. The only sound was the breeze. She stood staring at the house, watching. She became aware of the sound of breathing.

Chapter 3

Diane wasn't afraid of the dark, but she was afraid of people lurking in the dark. A chill went down her spine with the realization that the steady, faint whisper easing into her awareness was the sound of someone breathing. She gripped the gun firmly as she reached with her other hand for the phone in her pocket. Trying not to look like she was fleeing, she started walking toward the house.

She had taken only a few steps when she heard the sound of footfalls behind her crunching on the forest detritus. The sound was too close. Some unexpected instinct rose in her and instead of running, she dropped low to the ground and sprang back hard with her shoulder into the knees of the approaching figure, knocking his legs from under him. He fell forward across her and landed hard with a loud groan as Diane rolled away. The voice sounded male.

Being tripped over didn't hurt as much as Diane had feared. She didn't get kicked in the side or flattened and was on her feet quickly. As she stared at the prone figure on the ground, she heard someone calling her name. The phone. She'd dropped it and it lay a couple feet away, too far to pick up. It was Hanks' voice shouting through the receiver.

"Hanks," Diane yelled as she brought up her gun and pointed it at the figure rising slowly to his feet.

He was taller than she—about six feet in height, she guessed. He was dressed in black and wore a ski mask. He stood frozen in front of Diane's gun. It was too dark to make out any details at first, but a sudden shift of the clouds away from the moon illuminated him enough that she saw his gaze move to the right and behind her.

What came next was a blur of dark shapes and sounds. She spun around in time to see a clublike weapon swinging toward her. She jumped out of the way and was only nicked by the tip. But it was enough, along with her own sudden movement, to propel her down an embankment that bordered the box hedges. It was not steep and she almost didn't fall. Her first few steps were a forced run down the slope before she tripped and rolled to the bottom. She'd held on to the gun for those first few steps, but dropped it when she fell. Diane glanced up the embankment and saw a figure at the top. He reached out his hand to hold on to one of the slim tree trunks, preparing to climb down toward her.

Damn.

Diane searched the ground for her gun. She saw a glint in the moonlight about halfway up the slope. Not good. If she went for it, she'd meet the intruder halfway. She picked up a nearby thick piece of limb to use as a club. Not nearly good enough. She'd go for the gun.

Just as she started to move, she heard shouts and a gunshot. The gunfire was very close, just a few yards from her. The figure at the top of the bank turned and disappeared from her sight. Diane lunged for her gun and picked it up. As she ran her shaking hands over it, she discovered the safety was on. Good thing the first guy hadn't been able to see in the dark either. She felt for dirt or debris and tapped the side of the gun against her hand, hoping nothing had lodged in the barrel.

Diane scrambled up the embankment, her heart beating hard in her chest. At the top she heard two more gunshots and more shouts. She crouched to catch her breath and pick up her phone. It was no longer connected to Hanks. Her thumb started keying in his number, then stopped. No use distracting him. Diane scanned the backyard from her vantage point, hidden in the box hedges. It was now strangely quiet except for rustling in the woods and distant sirens. The sirens were the backup finally on its way. But the sounds in the woods, the rustling and crunching of leaves—*Are the intruders retreating?*

Diane was hesitant to step out into the open. She clicked the safety off with her thumb.

"Diane," Hanks' voice shouted from across the yard.

She saw a flashlight come from somewhere.

"Here," she shouted, and cautiously started for the house, scanning the area as she walked, watching for movement.

As she neared the house, she saw Hanks and Patrolman Daughtry both limping to the steps. Daughtry sat down and was holding his leg, whimpering. Hanks, holding his arm, sat down beside him. Both seemed to be in considerable pain.

The three of them automatically turned their heads toward the sound of a distant car engine starting up. Hanks groaned.

"They're getting away," he said. "Hell."

"What happened?" asked Diane. She clicked on the safety and gave Hanks back his gun, relieved to be rid of it—though having it probably saved her.

"What didn't happen?" Hanks took the gun from her and put it in his ankle holster. He turned his head to look at the back door and winced again in pain. "Damn it, I've got to quit doing that."

He took a deep breath. "We found a side door that was open and we went in. Some kind of mudroom, I suppose. We heard someone moving in the next room and saw his shadow pass by the door. Daughtry clicked on his flashlight, identified himself, and called out for the perp to stop. The bastard bolted before we even got a good look at him. It looked like he was carrying a box or something. When Daughtry ran after him, his leg went through the boards on the porch and he broke his flashlight. But he kept on after him and managed to get off a shot. I followed and almost caught up with the perp, when someone blindsided the two of us, knocked us down, ran, and shot at us. To tell you the truth, it got kind of confusing." He tried to shrug and winced in pain. "Daughtry's leg is skinned up pretty bad."

"Skinned?" said Daughtry. "It hurts like hell. I'm going to sue that damn woman. Why didn't she fix her damn porch?"

Diane frowned at him. "Marcella just bought the house. She was in the process of fixing it up," she muttered, and almost added her thought, *Let's not forget that she is the victim here.*

"The son of a bitch hit me in the leg with a bat or something," Daughtry said. "He just about killed me."

Diane took Hanks' flashlight and examined Daughtry's leg.

"Oh jeez," he said, "holy shit . . . my leg . . . oh God." He looked away and groaned.

The broken boards had torn a deep gash in the side of his left leg from his ankle to midcalf.

"It looks worse than it is," said Diane. Lame, she thought, but she wanted to give him some comfort. It looked terrible. She diverted the flashlight beam from the wound.

"I don't know why the damn backup took so long," said Hanks.

Diane noticed that Hanks' breathing was off—more labored than it should have been, even considering the exertion—and it obviously hurt him to turn his head.

"Are you all right?" she asked him.

"I fell on my damn shoulder again," he said. "It's kind of hard to move and hurts like hell."

Diane shined the beam from the flashlight on Hanks' shoulder. His clothes were covered with leaves and dirt from the tumble he took. She moved the collar of his shirt aside and shined the light on his throat and collarbone area. As she suspected, there was a lump under his skin on the clavicle.

"Your collarbone is broken," she said.

"Yeah, I know," he said, rubbing his eyes and forehead with his good hand.

"Look," said Diane, "both of you stay—"

The three of them jumped when a beam of light flashed in their direction. Daughtry put a hand on his gun.

"It's me—Izzy," said the voice behind the light. "Neva's waiting out front for backup. We heard the shooting back here. Is everyone all right?"

"More or less," said Hanks.

"The shooter in the woods seems to have got away," said Izzy. "He hasn't fired any more rounds at us." Izzy stopped in front of them, letting his light play from one to the other. "The three of you look terrible. What the hell happened?" he said.

Hanks gave him a brief version of events. "We lost them," he finished. Hanks looked at Diane for a moment. "What happened to you? I heard some commotion right before we went in after the intruder."

"There were lookouts in the woods. I happened upon them," she said. "At least two that I saw. We had a little scuffle."

"Are you all right?" asked Izzy.

"Fine. Tore my dress," she said.

"Great," said Daughtry. "You tore your dress and we get maimed for life."

Diane smiled. "I knocked one down and got the drop on him. The other one tried to brain me with a club. I very cleverly fell down an embankment to get away from them. I feel your pain."

"So that means there are between five and three people," said Izzy, counting on his fingers.

"Probably four," said Diane. "The shooter in the woods who ambushed us, the one carrying the box, and the two I met near the box hedges. They left when the shooting started. They may have been the same ones who attacked the two of you."

"Could be three," added Izzy. "The shooter in the woods could've left his post and come back here. That might be why he stopped shooting at us."

"So, no less than three," said Hanks. "What is this? Some kind of gang robbing houses when the owners are out?"

"How would they know that the owner of the house wasn't here?" asked Diane. "It was early evening when Marcella Payden was attacked, wasn't it? It's almost sunrise now." She could see the sky had gone from black to dark blue. Dawn was coming. "Unless they were the ones who attacked Marcella, how would they know?"

"I don't know," said Hanks. "But why would they wait hours before coming back?"

Diane was relieved to hear police cars come to a stop in the driveway and the sirens die down. She, Hanks, and Daughtry had botched it, she felt. The two of them were hurt. It was just dumb luck that she wasn't. She wanted to leave the whole mess to Neva and Izzy—as she should have in the first place—go home, and get some sleep.

"The two of you need to get to the hospital," she said.

"I won't argue," said Hanks.

Diane sensed that he was embarrassed. She understood. So was she—standing in a ruined cocktail dress at a compromised crime scene where she had let at least three perps get away.

"I can take you in my car," she said. "Neva and Izzy can work the crime scenes."

As she spoke she looked around the yard. She could see more of it now in the approaching dawn. Some of the shapes decorating the yard that she couldn't identify earlier were evident now—a boulder carved into a bench, a galvanized metal tub containing a dead plant, and . . . there at the end of the yard near the trees . . . a body.

Chapter 4

The body lay facedown in the grass. He was dressed in black pants and a leather jacket, a ski mask over his head—and a bullet hole in his back.

Diane was kneeling beside the body. She'd put on the jeans and T-shirt she kept stashed in her SUV—what she should have done before she reduced her dress to a ruin of dirty tatters.

The paramedics had immobilized Hanks' arm, bandaged his wounded thigh, and given Daughtry first aid for his leg wound. The paramedics wanted to take the two of them to the hospital, but Hanks insisted on staying until the coroner showed up. He was standing beside her.

Whit Abercrombie, the coroner, was sitting on his haunches on the other side of the body. He had straight black hair, dark eyes, and a short black beard that made his white teeth look very bright and his face look rather rakish.

An ambulance had arrived to take the body. The driver and paramedic were standing back with a stretcher, waiting for Whit to give his okay. The sun was just below the horizon, providing only enough light for the growing numbers of personnel from the police department, the crime scene lab, the coroner's office, and the ambulance services to not stumble over one another or the numerous yard ornaments. Whit shined his flashlight on the bullet wound.

"That would definitely result in his death," he said.

"I'd like to see his face," said Hanks.

Whit nodded. He and Diane turned the body over and Whit rolled up the ski mask. The beam from the flashlight cast angled shadows across the contours of the lean face. He was young, perhaps early twenties, with a pale face showing a scattering of whiskers that he had hoped would make him look more rugged. He had a black eye that was fading to yellow. Diane didn't recognize him. Neither did Whit.

"Don't know him," said Hanks.

Whit and Diane rose and stepped away from the body. Whit nodded to the paramedics. They transferred the corpse to the stretcher and rolled the gurney to the ambulance for transport to the hospital morgue in Rosewood.

"What happened here?" Whit asked.

Hanks explained in a brisk, no-nonsense way the night's events leading up to the discovery of the body.

"I don't know how he was shot," he said. "There was a lot of gunfire."

Whit nodded and eyed Hanks. "Looks like you need to go along to the hospital."

"Yeah, I suppose so," he said, shifting his weight from one leg to the other.

Hanks looked to be in considerable discomfort, but he sounded reluctant. Diane thought he would have welcomed the chance to receive some painkillers. After a few moments' thought and with what appeared to be some regret, he left with the others, walking at a brisker pace than Diane thought she could have mustered under the same circumstances.

Whit watched Hanks a moment, then turned back to Diane. "How are things in your life now that you have control of all the museum operations again?" he said.

"So far, things are running smoothly," she said.

Diane walked with Whit around to the driveway where he was parked. Hanks' car was there, and the patrolman's. So were two other police vehicles. They watched the ambulance leave with its cargo.

"What are you doing here?" asked Whit. "I was under the impression you didn't do on-site crime scene work much anymore. Someone told me you had finally learned to delegate." He gave her a wide grin.

"I'm trying," said Diane. "Marcella Payden is a consultant to the museum."

Whit's eyebrows went up. "Dr. Payden? The archaeologist? Is this her home?" He glanced over at the house and back at Diane. "Sylvia and I heard her give a talk a few days ago on the analysis of pottery in archaeology. Not exactly my idea of a hot date, but Sylvia wanted to go. Dr. Payden was entertaining. She can make a dull topic sound interesting, even to us archaeology dummies."

He paused. "What happened? Is she—" He stopped and let the question hang between them.

"I'm told she survived the attack, but I don't know her condition. It happened early last evening," said Diane. "I'm not sure why it took so long for my crew to be called in."

"I can answer that," said Neva, who was coming from the van with a case, heading for the house. "One of the policemen was telling me and Izzy about it. Dr. Payden was unconscious when she was brought in. At first, the doctors thought she had fallen accidentally and hit her head. It wasn't until they did a thorough exam and took some X-rays that they came to the conclusion she might have been attacked. That's when they called the police."

"How was she discovered?" asked Diane.

Neva shrugged. "That's all the policeman knew." She motioned toward the house. "Izzy and I have a path cleared if you want to come have a look around."

Diane nodded. "Thanks, Neva."

"How's your dress?" Neva asked, eyeing Diane's change of clothes.

"About what you would expect after a trek through a briar patch, a little hand-to-hand with a thug, and rolling down a hill in it. Not good. It's what I get for wearing a cocktail dress to a crime scene," Diane said.

Neva grinned and went on her way.

"It must have been some exciting night," said Whit.

"More so than I would like," said Diane.

"About this Detective Hanks," said Whit, nodding in the direction the ambulance had taken him. "Do you know him?"

"Not really. He was one of the hires during the previous Rosewood administration. He was cleared of any involvement in the misdeeds involving the mayor or the chief of police, but I think he feels he has to be overly competent in order not to be suspect. You know how it is in Rosewood these days. After the destruction left by the mayor and his gang, everyone is a little on edge."

Whit grinned happily, nodding his head in agreement about the state of anxiety in Rosewood. Like all those who lived outside the city limits of Rosewood itself, Whit was a little smug and self-righteous about the recent Rosewood corruption. After all, Rose County residents weren't the ones who voted the mayor and his cronies into office. That was Rosewood City folks' doing.

He took his leave, wishing Diane luck as he got in his jeep and drove away. She wanted to yell after him that she hadn't voted for the scoundrel either. He was no friend of hers, and she had the scars to prove it. Instead, she just waved.

Diane proceeded toward the house. At the edge of the front yard there was a picket fence that might have been white at one point in its life but was now weathered to a dusty gray. In the middle of the fence was a trellised archway with no gate. There were remnants of dead vine intertwined in the wood slats, signs of recent attempts by Marcella at clearing the growth.

Behind the fence, the front yard contained more cement ornaments—birdbaths, more broken statuary. From the fresh dirt stains on most of it, Diane guessed that Marcella had dug the pieces up from the yard. Must be interesting for an archaeologist to have things to dig up in her own yard.

Diane climbed the steps to the newly refurbished front porch. The light was now on and the porch and surrounding area were well lit. She looked up at the bottom of the second-floor balcony. The wood looked new there too. Unfortunately for Officer Daughtry, Marcella's renovations hadn't yet gotten to the dilapidated back porch.

The house had four tall windows across the front. Through one of them Diane could see Neva inside using electrostatic lifting film to collect a footprint off the floor. Diane donned the plastic head and foot coverings she'd retrieved from the van earlier and slipped on a pair of gloves. She started to enter the front doorway, stopped, and stepped back.

Her eye was caught by glints of light reflecting from

something embedded in the wood frame around the door. Sparkling from underneath flakes of peeling white paint were what looked to be the broken sherds of ceramic inserts inlaid in the wood frame. Diane tried to think what the inserts might have been before they were apparently vandalized, but there was nothing identifiable left. They had all been shattered. *How odd*, she thought.

She moved to just inside the threshold and looked around at the room. There was an aroma of Mexican food in the house.

"We've found some good boot prints," said Neva. "Several sizes larger than what Dr. Payden would wear." She nodded toward the door. "I think she took her shoes off in the house."

Diane looked down at a pair of leather sandals sitting on a wooden stool near the door. "Could be right," she said.

The floor was dark, wide-plank hardwood with a satin sheen—another of Marcella's renovations. A few rugs were scattered around. They were mostly decorated in geometric patterns that looked Southwestern.

The walls were a cream color and the furniture was mostly leather with chenille throws and pillows decorated similarly to the rugs. There was no television in the room and no place for one. Against one wall was a large, dark wood hutch that was open and empty.

Under the window just to the left of Diane was an old wooden desk that had seen better days. There was a lamp on it and the middle drawer was half open.

"Have you looked in the desk?" she asked.

Neva nodded. "All the drawers are empty. I haven't yet dusted for prints there or on the hutch."

Just in front of the desk, surrounded by small flags that the forensics crew used to mark notable features at the crime scene, was a dark stain on the floor, almost invisible because of the dark wood. Blood, Diane realized. Marcella's blood. There wasn't a large pool of it. The stain was about the size of a large dinner plate. This was where Marcella was felled, thought Diane, about the time she and Frank were at the benefit at Bartrum listening to a speech about funding for the arts.

Neva and Izzy had marked a clear path through the

house with flags. This was the walk zone they examined first so they could move about the house without contaminating evidence. Diane walked into the dining room. The odor of food was stronger here. Marcella had been cooking a Mexican dinner. She was expecting company. The table was set for two. The candle in the center of the table had burned down and the pool of wax around the wick had hardened.

Diane heard Izzy working in the nearby room, probably where the most recent intruders had entered. She didn't like two crime scenes—the attack on Marcella, and the recent deadly trespass—intertwined with each other. It confused things trying to distinguish one crime scene from the other. Jonas Briggs, her good friend, chess partner, and archaeology curator, wouldn't be quite so daunted. Archaeologists are accustomed to working sites that are one on top of the other and that leave the archaeologists to make sense of the layers.

Jonas Briggs, she thought. He was probably the one having dinner with Marcella. They were good friends. He may have found her. That would make Jonas a suspect to Hanks. Diane fished her cell from her pocket.

Chapter 5

Diane started to key Jonas Briggs' number, but stopped and retraced her steps to the living room. Neva was rolling up the film of the boot print and sliding it into a tube.

"Neva, you said the policeman didn't know who found Marcella. Is that right?"

Neva looked up and nodded. "That's what he said. The two policemen are with David, searching the woods for evidence. You could call him."

"I didn't know David was here. I didn't see his car," said Diane.

"He arrived a little bit ago. It was getting crowded near the house, so he parked on down the drive," said Neva. She gestured out the window in the direction of the driveway. "Did you find something?" Neva put away the film tube and picked up the case with the electrostatic lifting device.

"No, I just thought of something. Jonas might have been the one who discovered Marcella," began Diane.

Neva opened her mouth in surprise, wrinkled her brow, and looked in the direction of the dining room. "She was having someone for dinner. And they were . . . It could be Jonas. I didn't think about that."

"I'll call him," said Diane.

She punched in the number of his cell. No answer. She tried his home. No answer there either. She called his cell again and left a message asking him to call her.

"No luck?" Neva, still with the anxious expression on her face, stood with the electrostatic device under her arm.

"He may be at the hospital," said Diane. "His cell may be turned off. I left him a message."

"Of course," said Neva. "That's where he would be."

Diane didn't know why she was so worried, but she was. She called David's cell.

"Hey, Diane. Hear you've had one of your usual evenings out," he said.

"It has been interesting. Found anything?"

"Shell casings. Maybe we'll get lucky with them. One of the policemen tells me there's an old road back behind the house. That's probably where they parked. We'll be looking there next."

"Do you know who found Marcella Payden?" asked Diane.

"No. When the call came I recognized the address. I did some computer work for her out here," he said. "Hooked up a scanner system for her. Nice lady."

"I'm probably just being paranoid," Diane said, "but it bothered me the way Hanks seems sure the attack and the theft were unrelated incidents. They may be, but we don't know. It was as if he already has a suspect for her attacker. If Jonas found her, Hanks might have him at the head of the list of suspects. Jonas is so far removed from things like crime. I hate to think of him going through an interrogation."

Neva held the lifting device close to her chest, staring at Diane in alarm. Everyone at the museum and the crime lab was very fond of Jonas Briggs. He had come to work for the museum after he retired from the faculty at Bartrum. With his white hair, bushy white eyebrows, toothbrush mustache, and crystal blue eyes, he was everyone's grandfather, or mentor, or maybe wizard.

"Jonas is pretty tough," said David. "You know that."

"In academics," said Diane.

"In city council meetings. Hell, you know they are all scared of him."

Diane laughed. "You're right. All this is just speculation anyway. I have no idea whom she was planning to have dinner with."

"Speaking of food, maybe we can have some breakfast after this," David said.

"Good idea—Waffle House?"

Neva was nodding. She loved their pecan waffles.

Diane called the hospital to check on the condition of Marcella Payden. She got only the words "critical but stable" from them because she was not on the list of people authorized to receive information about the patient. But that didn't matter. Diane was just looking for the word *alive*, and she got that.

Diane went up the stairs to look over the rest of the house. The first room she entered was the bedroom. It was a simple bedroom with a double bed made from cherry wood and covered with a plain tan chenille bedspread. A dresser stood on one wall. It held a comb, brush, perfume, and lotion. A chest of drawers opposite the bed had a large-screen TV on top. A stuffed chair sat by the window with a floor lamp beside it. Marcella's nightstand had a picture of a young family. She had a married daughter. Diane guessed it was a picture of the daughter and her family.

The bedroom was neat and uncluttered. The adjacent room was a different matter. It was a study in clutter. Long library tables flanked by bookcases lined three of the walls. Additional bookcases stood on each side of the door. All were overflowing with books, journals, and papers. More books were stacked on the floor, in corners, and on chairs.

On the table to her left sat a computer, printer, and scanner—probably the one David installed. Scattered across the table near the computer were printouts of potsherds she had scanned, many annotated in her own handwriting.

The wall above the table and every available wall space were covered in an amazing collection of maps: satellite maps of canyons, deserts, and terrains with oxbow rivers, topographical maps, road maps, and maps of archaeological sites showing postholes and other ground features. Many of the maps had numerous red dots scattered across them in clusters. After a moment Diane realized each dot probably represented a location where a potsherd had been found. As in crime scene investigation, the location of items reveals much.

The table on the opposite wall had several reconstructed pots and boxes of sherds. One box looked as if it might be part of the reference collection Marcella was creating for the museum. At one end of the table, relatively clear of clutter, were a microscope and a box of slides.

But the star of the room was on the center table. In a box of sand stood a face being reconstructed from broken pieces of ceramic pottery. Diane walked over to it. The piece appeared ancient to her eyes. It had the look of tempered American Indian ceramic. Its dark tan surface was sprinkled with white inclusions of the tempering material. But Diane had never seen any Indian artifact like this—a mask, not stylized, but with refined, realistic features. It was quite beautiful.

It was a reconstruction in progress, a broken three-dimensional puzzle being reassembled. The sand allowed the pieces to stand on edge as Marcella worked with them. Several sherds lay on the table waiting to find their place in the emerging form. So far almost half the face had been reconstructed—most of the chin, the nose, one cheek, an eye, half a forehead. In the sand behind the larger piece was a smaller reconstruction. It looked as if it was going to be the ear and the other cheek. Several sherds were glued together in clusters but still lacked the links that connected them to the main piece.

Beside the box of sand were drawings of the face. One was an extrapolation of the finished work. Diane wondered where the mask was from. She was lost in thought when Marcella's phone rang.

It startled her for a moment—a phone ringing in a house whose owner was gone. Diane walked over to the computer table and answered it with a simple "Hello."

"Who is this, please?" It was a female voice, possibly young. Sometimes it was hard to tell. The accent seemed Midwestern, but Diane wasn't good with accents.

"Whom are you trying to reach?" Diane asked.

"Someone in my mother's house . . . I mean, are you a detective? I'm Paloma Tsosie. Marcella Payden is my mother."

"Mrs. Tsosie," said Diane, "I'm very sorry about what happened to your mother. I'm Diane Fallon. I'm with the police looking over the house." Diane didn't like to say "crime scene" to relatives. It was too harsh, too scary.

"Are you one of the crime scene people?" Marcella's daughter asked.

"Yes."

Paloma Tsosie paused a moment. "That's a coincidence," she said almost absently. "Mother does contract work for a museum director named Dr. Diane Fallon."

"Same person," said Diane. "I have several jobs."

"How odd," she said.

"It is, a little. How can I help you?" asked Diane.

"My husband and I are flying out to Georgia. We're in Arizona now." She paused. "We would like to stay at the house. Is that possible?"

Diane thought of the blood on the floor. Marcella's daughter couldn't see that.

"We have a lot of fingerprint powder, equipment, and lights all over the house," said Diane. "But I think I can have it cleaned up for you by this evening. I'll have to ask the lead detective, of course." Then, as an afterthought, she added, "The museum can put you up in a hotel in Rosewood. It would be closer to the hospital."

"Oh, that would be very kind. Thank you," said Paloma, clearly liking the idea.

"Do you have someone to pick you up at the airport?" asked Diane.

"Jonas Briggs. He's a family friend. He's going to meet us," she said.

"Fine. I'll let him know your hotel," said Diane.

"This is very kind of you," she said.

"I wish you were visiting under better circumstances," Diane said. She paused a moment. "I'm in your mother's workroom. She has a lot of work in progress and the house just had a break-in," said Diane.

"A break-in? You mean after Mother was attacked? No."

"Yes, several hours after. I don't know what they took. But they didn't get her computer equipment. I was wondering if you would allow me to take her work and her computer to her office at the museum?"

"That would be good. Mother's work is really important to her, and I know she has a lot of it on the computer. She does all kinds of three-dimensional scans of her pottery sherds. She would want it kept safe."

"Good. I'll give you an inventory of what we take," she said.

"She just bought a big-screen TV that she loves. Did they get it?" asked Paloma.

"No. It's in her bedroom," said Diane.

"That's a relief. Could you take that to her office as well?" she asked.

"Certainly," said Diane. "I'll see if the police will keep an eye on the house too."

"Thank you—for everything," said Paloma.

Diane stood for a moment after the call and looked at the computer equipment, then at the television in the bedroom. None of this was taken. Did they not have time? They seemed to have cleaned out only a hutch and an old desk in the living room. That was odd.

"Diane," called Neva from the lower floor, "can you come down here? I've found something strange."

Chapter 6

Downstairs in Marcella's living room Neva was standing over the desk with a magnifying glass in her hand. She had removed the middle drawer and set it upside down on the top of the desk.

"What you got?" asked Diane.

"I'm not sure," said Neva. "The drawer doesn't have a handle or knob, so I thought there might be prints under the bottom rim where you have to grab to pull the drawer out, and, well, what I found is just really weird. I don't think it's important—I mean, it's old. It looks old. It's just really strange."

Diane looked down at the desk to see what had Neva all tongue-tied. The back of the desk drawer was raw unvarnished wood discolored with age. Nothing noteworthy about it except there was small handwriting in one of the corners.

Neva gave her the magnifying glass and Diane moved the desk lamp to view the writing. It was in a small, clear hand, a combination of cursive and printing, composed into simple declarative sentences and phrases. It was odd, poignant, and a little chilling.

> *They want to make me disappear. I don't know what to do. There is no one I can trust, no one to call for help. If I disappear, they have taken me. To where, I don't know. I'm afraid. Please look for me if I disappear. Please. MAG*

"Well," said Diane, straightening up. "What do you make of that?"

"I have no idea," said Neva. "Is it a joke? Is it Marcella's handwriting?"

"No," said Diane. "I've seen hers, and it's nothing like this."

"Then what? Where did the desk come from, I wonder? Did she buy it in some antiques shop, get it at Goodwill, a family heirloom?" asked Neva.

"That's something we can ask when we can talk with Marcella," said Diane.

"I wonder how old the message is?" said Neva. "Is someone in trouble? I suppose if they are, it's too late to help them now. It looks to me like it was written a long time ago."

"It does to me too, but we'll let David take a look at it. I'll get Korey to have a look too."

Korey Jordan was Diane's head conservator at the museum. She frequently called upon him for various jobs where his expertise would be useful.

"Questioned Documents might have some insight," said Neva. "Couldn't they?"

"Yes," said Diane, "but I doubt this has anything to do with what happened to Marcella. It looks too old—a kid may have done this years ago as some kind of play. We can't devote many resources to it."

"I know, but, well, it's spooky," said Neva.

"It is. How about the other drawers?" she asked. "Anything on them?"

Neva shook her head. "I don't know yet. I'll let you know."

"You might want to look at the back of the desk too," said Diane. "Maybe something is written there. People often tape notes on the back of furniture."

"I will. Maybe Jonas knows were the desk came from. It's kind of shabby compared to the rest of her furniture. Maybe it is some childhood piece she's never been able to part with—you know, fond memories. But that message is not quite the stuff fond memories are made of," observed Neva.

"Could've just been a game," said Diane. "I used to stuff secret spy messages in my dolls that some people might have found creepy if they read them."

"I heard about that," said Neva, smiling.

Diane smiled back at her. "Marcella's daughter called. Her name's Paloma Tsosie. She's coming in from Arizona. She may know something about the desk."

"Tsosie?" said Neva. "I've never heard of that name before. What is it, do you think?"

"I'm not sure. There's a picture of her and her family upstairs. Her husband looks American Indian. Could be a Navajo or Zuni name, maybe. Anyway, I'm going to put them up in a hotel, but she's going to want to see the house. I'd like there not to be a bloodstain on the floor. Call the cleaners when you finish."

"Sure," said Neva.

"Mrs. Tsosie is allowing me to take Marcella's work to her museum office, so I'm going to pack it up. Do we have boxes in the van or do I need to go get some?"

"We have a few in the van. They need to be put together," said Neva.

"I'll pack up her work . . . ," began Diane.

"Not her whole office?" exclaimed Neva. She had seen the overflowing shelves.

"No. Just her computer and the pottery she was working on. I don't think I could tackle all those books."

Diane left Neva with the enigmatic desk and went out to the van to find the packing boxes and foam peanuts they kept for occasions when they needed to transport fragile objects. She carried them up to Marcella's workroom and surveyed the task. Even without packing all the books and journals, the job looked daunting.

A little searching in the office revealed more boxes of various sizes stored under the tables. She located a linen closet outside the bathroom and took several pillowcases and towels.

Diane carefully packed many of the loose sherds in the various smaller boxes and labeled them. There were seven whole pots, some reconstructed from sherds and some never broken. She wrapped them in towels and packed each in a separate box.

She gathered only the paperwork on the tables, ignoring all the papers stuffed in the bookcases, and packed it in a single box. She started to leave the microscope because it would be more easily replaced, but it was small, so she packed it and the slides amid a cushion of towels.

Then there was the mask. It would be harder to pack. She experimented first by gently testing to see if the pieces were glued fast. They were. Diane wrapped the larger reconstructed piece in a pillowcase and packed it in the middle of the peanuts. She did the same to the smaller section of glued-together sherds.

The single sherds, presumably more pieces to the puzzle yet to be fitted together, lay on the table next to the mask. They presented a bit of a challenge because she thought she might need to keep the integrity of their position in respect to one another. When she began to pick them up, she discovered that each one was outlined on the paper underneath. She put the paper with the pottery pieces in place in a box and filled the box with folded towels over the sherds. There were four boxes she had to pack this way to accommodate all the single sherds in this set. It was in one of the transfers that she noticed another page under the paper holding the sherds. It contained drawings Marcella had made of the mask. From the drawings it appeared not to be a mask at all, but the front of a pitcher of some kind. An odd pitcher. Water, or whatever liquid it might have held, would have been poured out through the eyes. Not practical. It must have been simply an art piece, or as archaeologists often categorized puzzling things, a vessel meant for religious ritual. *Interesting.* Diane had never seen anything like it.

She was taping the last box closed when David and Izzy came in. David Goldstein was a good friend of Diane's. She had known and worked with him for many years and they shared a common tragedy. While they were working as human rights investigators in South America, many of their friends were massacred. It had made her and David close. Other than Frank, the man Diane lived with, David was the man she trusted most. He was in his forties, balding except for a fringe of dark hair around his head. He had dark eyes and an interesting, paranoid view of the world.

Izzy Wallace had been a policeman on the Rosewood police force and a good friend of Frank's. He hadn't liked Diane much at first, but with the unexpected death of his son came a change in his priorities. Observing how Diane and her team collected evidence that actually put criminals behind bars, he decided he wanted to join their team. Neva said he was learning forensics very quickly. Diane noticed he did seem, if not happier, more involved and satisfied with life.

"What are you doing?" David asked.

"I'm taking Marcella Payden's work to her office in the museum. David, I need you to pack up her computer equipment. And, Izzy, would you mind figuring out a way to pack up her television?"

"Her TV?" said Izzy. "You're taking her TV? Can you do that?"

"Sure," said David. "Diane's powers would let her come into your house and take things away if she wished. Besides, the crime lab could use a large-screen, high-definition television."

"Seriously," said Izzy, frowning at David.

"I spoke with her daughter," said Diane. "She asked that we take Marcella's work, her computer, and the TV to her office in the museum for safekeeping because of the break-in."

"Just checking," said Izzy.

"What have you found?" Diane asked them, making a fruitless effort to dust off particles of Styrofoam peanuts that clung to her clothes.

"I found several bullet casings," said David. "The road in back of the house is paved, even though it's a pretty old road—no tire marks. I did trace their getaway through the woods and collected some fiber evidence. That's about it. One odd thing. I found two broken pottery sherds on the road. Looked kind of archaeological. I collected them. I don't know if they're connected to our suspects, but since Marcella is an archaeologist . . ." He shrugged. "Who knows?"

Diane raised her eyebrows. "I wonder if they were looking for Indian artifacts? If they were, I don't think they made it to this room."

David shrugged again. "Maybe that was what they were after, but . . . I don't know. It doesn't feel right. That many guys for some Indian pottery? Is it that valuable?"

"I don't know either," said Diane. "Some is, I think. But you're right. It doesn't feel quite right. What about you, Izzy? Find anything?"

"I took a couple of casts of shoe prints outside in the dirt. Like David, I found fibers where they rolled around on the ground. I found lots of sequins." He grinned. "You must have rolled all the way down to the bottom of the bank."

Diane smiled. "I did. Good work. What's your sense of what's going on?" she asked Izzy. "Do you think the attack on Marcella and the break-in early this morning are two separate events or part of the same crime?"

"I don't know," said Izzy. "Like David said, it feels strange, but hell, guys will break in to steal just about anything these days. I'm thinking they would've been interested in the electronics up here. But maybe they didn't get this far. I'm with you on the problem of how they knew the house would be empty—maybe they didn't care. Maybe they knew that just one little old lady lived here. Maybe they saw activity here earlier and her being carried away." Izzy shrugged. "There's also the problem of there being no sign of forced entry. Did she leave her doors unlocked? Did she let the attacker in and he left without locking the door behind him? I know some people leave their doors unlocked, but usually not older women living alone away from neighbors, like this house is."

"I agree," said David. "Too many questions and not enough information for answers."

"Besides," said Izzy, "it's Hanks' job to figure this stuff out."

Izzy had told Diane that some of the Rosewood detectives thought she insinuated herself too many times in their cases. Diane thought it was an unfair accusation. She never interfered in cases unless she was brought in by the detectives themselves. Or in some cases, the perpetrators made sure she was involved.

Since Izzy joined her team, he had become her conscience in that regard—trying to make sure the Rosewood detectives had a good impression of Diane and the crime lab. She started to tell him that the county sheriff didn't have any problems with how she did her job, but her cell rang. She looked at the display. It was Garnett, Rosewood's chief of detectives. Diane answered.

"Hey, Diane. Just giving you a heads-up. Hanks is bringing Jonas Briggs down here for questioning. Thought you might want to observe."

Chapter 7

Diane, still in the change of clothes she kept in her car for emergencies and still with Styrofoam packing peanuts clinging to her, stood in the observation room looking with some apprehension at Jonas Briggs on the other side of the glass in the police interrogation room. Douglas Garnett was standing next to her.

Garnett was his usual well-dressed self: dark charcoal suit, crisp white shirt, and light blue silk tie. He was a tall man, fiftyish with thick, graying, well-styled hair and dark eyes. He hadn't called Diane because he was personally concerned for Jonas Briggs; his concern fell more under the heading of protecting the museum from bad publicity and political repercussions. The crime lab, a really big jewel in Rosewood's somewhat thorny crown, was housed in the museum building. Garnett and the mayor knew if anything bad happened to the museum because of the crime lab, Diane would move the crime lab out. And having the museum house the lab worked out so well for the city that it was worth the little extra political trouble to watch out for the museum's welfare. Plus, Garnett owed Diane for pulling him out of hot water. And Diane did have a personal interest in the welfare of Jonas Briggs.

Jonas was sitting there alone, his forearms resting on the table. He was dressed in a light denim jacket, white shirt, and Dockers. He looked worried, but Diane guessed he was worried about his friend Marcella, not the circumstances he found himself in at the moment. Garnett told her that Jonas had waived his right to council. She didn't think it was a good idea, but Garnett's help stopped at allowing Diane to talk to Jonas before Hanks did.

Diane's fears had been correct. Jonas had discovered Marcella Payden, which made him an automatic person of interest.

Diane heard the rattle of the door and Detective Hanks walked into the interrogation room. He didn't look particularly threatening, with his arm immobilized and his neck in a brace because of his broken collarbone.

Jonas raised his eyebrows at Hanks but didn't mention Hanks' condition. He waited for Detective Hanks to speak.

"How well do you know Marcella Payden?" asked Hanks.

"Very well. She is a fellow archaeologist and a friend. I know her family," replied Jonas.

"Did the two of you get along?" Hanks asked.

"Of course," Jonas said.

"Were the two of you dating?" asked Hanks.

"Dating? That sounds like such a young term. We went places together and had a good time. Is that what the young do on dates these days? There is an element of romance that goes along with dating, so I guess you could say we were dating," said Jonas.

"Were you intimate?" asked Hanks.

"Now, young man, that's a very private question. However, I will answer. No."

"Did that make you frustrated?" asked Hanks.

Diane felt uncomfortable for Jonas. She wanted to bang on the window and tell Hanks to be more respectful.

Garnett must have felt her frustration. He leaned toward her and said, "He has to ask these questions."

Diane nodded. But she didn't have to like it.

Jonas chuckled. "Do I look like I'm nineteen? What kind of question is that?"

"You may have wanted to go faster in the relationship than Dr. Payden," said Hanks. "Take it to the next level."

Jonas shook his head. "Next level? Where do you young people come up with these phrases? And go faster? Son, at my age, I'm happy just to go at all. You know, you haven't analyzed your target audience in forming your assumptions and questions. You're targeting a different age group from mine."

"Did you and Dr. Payden have a lot of arguments?" Hanks asked.

Diane had a desire to pound on the window again. *These are trick questions*, she wanted to shout.

"A lot of arguments? As in getting mad at each other? No."

"What if I told you I had witnesses who heard you and Dr. Payden arguing heatedly just two days ago?"

Diane watched Jonas raise his bushy eyebrows and frown. "Then I would say you had a witness who couldn't tell the difference between spirited scholarly discourse and arguing," said Jonas.

"Is that what you call it, 'spirited scholarly discourse'?" asked Hanks.

"Yes," said Jonas.

"What did Dr. Payden call it?"

"Marcella called it spirited scholarly intercourse," said Jonas.

Diane smiled.

"Intercourse?" said Hanks.

"Yes. Communication between individuals, organizations, or nations," said Jonas. "You'll find it's the first definition in the dictionary. It's kind of overshadowed by the second definition. Marcella likes the surprise aspect of using the first definition."

"I see," said Hanks. "What was the argument about?"

"Let's see. I believe the topic of discourse was the *definition* of archaeology and how it relates to the proper subject matter of archaeology," said Jonas.

"That seems pretty basic. Are you telling me you couldn't even agree on a definition of your own subject matter?" said Hanks.

"It's an academic thing," said Jonas.

Diane could see he was getting annoyed with Hanks.

"It's a common issue with all us archaeologists, one that will never be resolved because we will never completely agree. However, if you think this or any discussion I've had with Dr. Payden in any way would drive me to attack her, you're just being plain silly. Marcella loves academic discussions of all kinds." Jonas looked at his watch. "I'll have to leave soon to pick up her daughter at the airport. She and her husband are flying in from Arizona today."

"Do you know who might have done this to her?" asked Hanks.

"No. Marcella is a nice person whom everyone likes. I can't imagine anyone doing this to her."

"There is a large hutch in her living room. Do you know what was in it?" asked Hanks.

"Several pieces of pottery," said Jonas.

"Indian pottery?" asked Hanks.

"Hanks didn't go into the house," said Diane. "How does he know about the hutch?"

"He said he was going to call David Goldstein to see what kind of things your crew found," said Garnett. "I'm sure he called before he began the interview."

Diane wondered why Hanks hadn't called her, but she didn't say anything.

". . . pottery she made herself," Jonas was saying. "It does look very much like pottery from archaeological digs. She experimented with various clays and tempering material. She always signed it to be sure no one ever acquired one of her pots and tried to pawn it off as an authentic prehistoric artifact."

"Did she have any valuable artifacts in the house?" asked Hanks.

"Valuable to archaeologists as objects of study. She had a few vessels, but as to monetary value . . . to tell you the truth, I really don't know what the market is for stolen artifacts."

"There's a desk in the living room that had been emptied. Do you know what was in it?"

"Nothing. She found the desk in one of the sheds out back of her house and was going to refinish it," said Jonas.

"You said that when you found her she spoke," said Hanks. He looked down at his notes. "I believe you said she said, 'Tiger after all loose moment.' Is that right?"

"Yes," said Jonas. "That's what it sounded like she said."

"Do you know what that means?" asked Hanks.

Jonas shook his head. "I don't have any idea."

"When you drove up, did you see anyone else there or anything out of the ordinary?" asked Hanks.

Jonas shook his head and looked as if he were trying to remember. "I stopped at the gate—or that arch thing. My headlights shined in the house and I could see the paintings on the wall over the sofa, but I didn't see her, or anyone. I went up to the door and knocked. She didn't answer. I waited and knocked again. She didn't come to the door. I knew she was expecting me. The door was locked, but she'd given me a key to look in on her place when she was away. I opened the door, called her name, and went in."

He stopped and closed his eyes for a moment and took a deep breath. "She was there on the floor and there was blood. I thought she had fallen and hit her head. I called 911 and stayed with her. I talked to her and she came to briefly. That's when she spoke. It was hard to hear. I may have gotten it wrong." Jonas hesitated a moment. "Later when I found out someone had attacked her, I tried to remember if I saw or heard anything. I just don't remember. Everything was fine until I found her on the floor."

"Thank you for coming down. Please don't leave town," said Hanks.

"I have to go to the Atlanta airport to pick up her daughter, Paloma, and her husband," said Jonas.

"Just make sure you come back," said Hanks.

Hanks ended the interrogation. It wasn't as bad as Diane had feared. And it was informative. She found out what was in the empty hutch. If the thieves thought they were valuable artifacts, then they were bound to be disappointed. It was interesting to discover where the desk came from too. Apparently, Hanks didn't find the note on the back of the drawer important, for he didn't ask about it. It was also interesting that Marcella had spoken. Diane couldn't imagine what the words meant either.

Jonas stood up, then sat down again. "I just remembered, Marcella told me earlier she found something she wanted to talk to Dr. Fallon about. She didn't say what it was. I don't know whether it is related to what happened to her. What with Diane being the museum director and the crime lab director, it could be something about museum business or something from the dark side."

"The dark side?" asked Hanks.

"It's what we in the museum call the crime lab," he said.

Hanks' back was to Diane, but she could see the round of his cheek change. Apparently he had smiled.

"Would she have mentioned it in a note or diary?" asked Hanks.

"Most of Marcella's notes were about her work. I don't know if she kept a diary," said Jonas.

"Tell the daughter I would like to speak with her when she is up to it," said Hanks.

"I will," said Jonas. He rose again and walked out the door.

Hanks turned around and stared at the two-way mirror for a moment. Diane thanked Garnett for allowing her to watch and hurried out to catch up with Jonas. On the way to the police station she had called her museum assistant, Andie, and asked her to make hotel reservations for Paloma and her husband. She needed to tell him.

"Jonas," said Diane when she caught up with him at the door.

"Diane. I'm glad you're here," he said. They walked out together. "Were you behind the mirror? Do they really do that? It's not just a TV thing?"

"Yes. I was there," she said.

"Then you heard the questions he asked. Does he really think I had anything to do with this beastly thing?"

"If I had been the one to find her, I would be the one answering questions," said Diane. "It's not uncommon that whoever finds a victim becomes a person of interest. It's just procedure."

"It's not pleasant," said Jonas.

"It's not supposed to be. It's just the way it is. I wanted to tell you that I made Paloma reservations at the Latimeer."

"That's pretty expensive. Paloma and her husband aren't rich," said Jonas.

"The museum is picking it up. I spoke with her today. She called the house. She wanted to stay there, but I thought with the blood on the floor and all the fingerprint powder, it would be easier if they stayed closer to town. It's also near the hospital."

"That's good of you," he said, taking her hand and squeezing it. "I'm sure Marcella will appreciate it," he said.

"Drive safely," said Diane.

Jonas nodded and got in his car. It wasn't until he drove away that she realized what he had said in the interrogation room about seeing the paintings over the sofa. When she and her crew were in the house, there weren't any paintings over the sofa.

Chapter 8

Diane walked back into the police station, past the reception area, past the detectives' desks, to Garnett's office. She could see through the window in the door that he was meeting with Detective Hanks. She knocked and entered when Hanks opened the door.

Douglas Garnett had a no-nonsense, no-frills office. The chairs were faux leather and chrome; his desk was gray metal. A long, wood conference table surrounded with wooden chairs sat off to the side. The tan walls were decorated with an array of diplomas, awards, framed newspaper clippings, and photographs of Garnett shaking hands with many politicians from around Georgia.

He rose when she entered and waved her to a chair opposite Hanks. The two of them sat back down when she did. Hanks stared at her. It wasn't exactly daggers coming out of his eyes, but his gaze wasn't particularly friendly either. Despite what he may have felt, he was having a hard time looking aggressive in his neck brace and with his arm in a sling.

"I was just telling Chief Garnett I don't want you interfering in my case," said Hanks.

"Have I interfered?" asked Diane.

"You're here. What's the purpose of that?" he asked.

"Just observing," said Diane. "Comparing witness testimony with evidence gathered from the crime scene. I came back in because of something Jonas said during your interview that may be of importance."

Hanks sat up straight and leaned forward. "What was that?" he asked.

At least he was eager for any information he could get from her. Diane was glad of that.

"Jonas said that when he arrived at the house, his headlights shined in the window and he could see paintings over the sofa. When my team and I were in the house, there were no paintings over the sofa. I only just a moment ago realized what I'd heard or I'd have mentioned it before he left for the airport."

Hanks' expression changed to one less suspicious of her intentions. "Were the paintings stolen? When? I wonder if Briggs remembers if they were there when he was in the house. Can you call him? Do you have his cell number?" asked Hanks.

Diane fished her cell from her pocket and called Jonas.

"Diane, what's up? Nothing else happened did it, this soon?" Jonas asked.

"No. Just a question. When you were in the house with Marcella, did you notice anything about the paintings over the sofa, the ones you saw in your headlights a few minutes before?"

"Not that I remember. Let me think." Jonas was quiet for a long moment.

Diane thought he might have entered a dead zone in cell service; then she heard him whispering to himself, going over the evening's events, refreshing his memory.

"I remember my headlights shining through her front window, lighting up the back wall. The pictures stood out for me because I had not seen them before. I got out and walked across the yard and up on the porch. I knocked on the door, but there was no answer. I looked in the window, but didn't see her. I knocked again, then unlocked the door and went in, started to call out for Marcella, but there she was on the floor. I stayed with her there on the floor. I didn't know what to do for her."

There was another long pause. She heard him breathing.

"Yes, I can see it now as I stood on the porch and looked in the window. The paintings were not there! I'll be damned! The paintings were gone. You mean her attacker was there in the house stealing the paintings as I was walking from my car to the house? The absence of the paintings hadn't registered until you mentioned it. Damn."

"What kind of paintings were they?" asked Diane.

"Portraits. Three of them. But I didn't see them clearly from my car—too far away."

"You'd not seen them before?" asked Diane.

"No, I'm sure of it. Marcella had a tapestry hanging over the sofa the last time I was there. The paintings were a new addition."

"What about the hutch?" asked Diane. "Was the pottery in it when you were with Marcella?"

"Yes, it was there. I remember looking at the pottery and thinking how it looked just like authentic artifacts . . . and what a good potter she is. Are you saying the pottery is gone too? That young fellow, Hanks, asked me about it. I didn't think about the implication until now. Was her attacker hiding in the house while I was there—waiting for me to leave so he could rob the place? You know, Marcella had a lot of work on her computer. If it's gone . . ."

"No, we have her computer. We'll talk when you get back," said Diane. "Thanks for the information. You've been very helpful."

"I'll call you when I get Paloma and her husband settled. I'm sure she'll want to get to the hospital right away," he said.

Diane had the phone's speaker turned on as she spoke with Jonas so that Garnett and Hanks could hear. When she hung up, Garnett spoke first.

"You see why I've found it's a good idea to have someone from the crime scene listen to the interrogations," he said. "They often hear things that are important."

Diane knew he had made that up on the spur of the moment to mollify Hanks. It was effective. Hanks nodded. After all, she *had* noticed something that probably was important. They had also made some progress in separating events that belonged to the attack from events that occurred later in the morning with the intruders.

She also realized Hanks was off his game. He should have asked if the hutch still had its contents when he asked Jonas what was in it. He must have been very uncomfortable, not thinking at his best. He didn't strike her as a man who liked to load up on painkillers.

"David Goldstein found pieces of broken pottery on the

road behind the house," said Diane. "That's where the thieves had their vehicle parked and made their getaway this morning."

"When Marcella Payden was attacked," said Hanks, "the perp or perps took some paintings. Then the guys we ran into early this morning took the pottery from the hutch, I'm guessing. So, are we looking at art thieves?"

"Maybe," said Garnett. "But I don't know. I wouldn't expect them to be geniuses, but these guys seem pretty incompetent as art thieves. The stolen pottery isn't even authentic Indian artifacts, if I understand correctly. Is Dr. Payden's pottery valuable?"

Both Hanks and Diane shrugged.

"She made pottery more for research, I believe," said Diane. "She tried to re-create methods used by prehistoric American Indians. And she experimented to replicate past phenomena."

Garnett and Hanks both raised their eyebrows at this and traded glances.

"For example, one experiment she did was to make vessels with different-colored glazes, put them on a shelf as they may have been arranged in an aboriginal shelter. She'd tip over the shelf and analyze the breakage pattern of the pottery fragments on the floor."

"And this tells her what exactly?" asked Hanks.

"When excavating a site, you find a lot of broken pottery. Mapping the location of the pieces and then reconstructing them back into a whole vessel tells you something about how it got broken in the first place. In the example I gave, would the patterns of breakage that have been found at many archaeological sites result if the early people had pottery on shelves or racks in their houses? I know it seems like a lot of work for useless information, but archaeology is a lot like crime scene reconstruction—you keep adding pieces to the puzzle and after a while you have the whole scene. They are trying to reconstruct the past in as much detail as they can discover."

Diane didn't think she told it as clearly as Jonas did when he spoke with students or tour groups, but Hanks' and Garnett's expressions weren't entirely glazed over with confusion. Then again, neither had she enthused them to become archaeologists.

"So she didn't take a lot of care making the pottery pieces if she was going to break them," said Hanks. "They probably weren't valuable."

"I think she did take a lot of care," said Diane. "She wanted to get as close as possible to matching the kind of vessels the Indians used. I doubt her pots were valuable enough to steal. But it may be the thieves thought they were real. Perhaps someone working on her house saw them, knew there was some money to be had in trading in antiquities, and came back with some of his buddies to steal them. Just a thought," she said. "Do we know who the body in her backyard was?"

Hanks nodded. Apparently he felt more comfortable sharing, at least in the company of Chief Garnett.

"His name was Ray-Ray Dildy. He was a high school dropout, a day worker, and petty thief. Not much on the ball, so I'm thinking he wasn't the mastermind, just the muscle. I'm looking into his associations now."

"Could he have worked on Marcella's house?" asked Diane. "I noticed her front porches are new, as is the floor in the living room."

"Could have. I'd like to get her daughter to go through her mother's receipts," said Hanks. "They might tell us something."

Diane had been hesitant to ask. Afraid of the answer. But, she had to know. "How is Marcella?" she asked.

"The doctors have her in an induced coma," said Hanks. "Something about her brain swelling."

That was what Diane was afraid of. She didn't know Marcella well, but to a person of intellect like Marcella the possibility of brain damage could be of greater fear than the possibility of death. Diane needed to find out who did this to her.

No one said anything for a moment. Finally Hanks broke the silence.

"You believe Jonas Briggs is innocent of involvement in the attack, don't you?" Hanks asked Diane.

"Yes," said Diane.

"Why?" asked Hanks.

"The same reason I believe Chief Garnett wasn't involved. I know them both," said Diane.

"That's hardly a reassuring answer," said Hanks. "No offense, sir."

"It is if you trust my judgment," said Diane. "But you don't know me."

"Is your judgment that good?" he asked.

"I think it is most of the time," she said.

Hanks actually started to smile.

"Other than the fact that he discovered her and called for help," Diane continued, "there is no reason whatsoever to suspect Jonas. You might as well suspect me."

"There is the matter of the arguments that were overheard," said Hanks.

"That's nothing," said Diane. "That is the world they live in. Many academics revel in debate. Marcella is one of them. You might as well use breathing as evidence."

"The witnesses said they were pretty heated," said Hanks.

"They may have been perceived that way from an uninformed observer's perspective, but I'd have to have witnessed it myself to put any value on it," said Diane.

"Are you that rigid with all eyewitness testimony?" asked Hanks.

"I don't really deal in eyewitness testimony," said Diane. "I collect empirical data. But when confronted with eyewitness accounts, I don't automatically believe them without corroboration. In this case it would take a lot of corroboration because I've known Jonas long enough to be able to judge his character."

"Interesting perspective," said Hanks.

Diane wasn't sure what he meant. No one seemed to have anything else to say at the moment, so she stood and the two of them stood with her.

"We'll have a full forensics report for you as soon as we can," said Diane.

Hanks thanked her and Diane left the police station. Hanks followed her out to her car.

"I had been told that you are prone to take over a case," he said. "I didn't want that happening with this one."

Diane supposed he was trying to explain his hostility, but he still sounded defensive.

"I don't know where that rumor came from exactly," said Diane. "Those times when I have been more involved in a case than my position as a director of the crime lab would dictate that I should, I have been either asked by detectives—here"—she gestured toward the station—"or the perpetrators themselves have pulled me into it by coming after me. I have never just showed up and told a detective that I was taking over his case and would he please hand me his file."

"I got the impression you were more subtle than that," he said, almost smiling again.

"There are reasons Garnett occasionally invites me to observe interrogations, and they have nothing to do with any personal interest I might have in the case itself. And he only allows me to observe, nothing else. Today, for instance, I would have advised my friend not to answer your questions without a lawyer present. Not because he was guilty, but because we all know why detectives want to interview people without an attorney present. But Garnett wouldn't have allowed me to interfere—just observe."

"That's very cryptic. Why does he extend that courtesy? He doesn't to anyone else. Do you get to observe the questioning of all your friends?" asked Hanks.

Diane smiled. "Well, my friends don't often find themselves in this situation. But the answer is no, not all my friends. Just certain types of friends. After you have been here longer, you'll figure out why."

Diane got in her car and left him with a puzzled look on his face. Sooner or later he'd figure out it was not so much about her as it was about the museum and its relation to the crime lab. Garnett and the mayor didn't want her to tell them to leave and take their crime lab elsewhere.

Diane drove home—home to Frank's house. She'd left him early this morning when David called and she hadn't talked with him since. And it was Sunday, the day they usually spent together. She should have told Hanks she was very content to leave his case to him. Did they all think she just went around making work for herself?

Diane parked the SUV in the driveway behind a car she

did not recognize. It had Atlanta plates. As she passed by she felt the hood. Warm. It hadn't been here long.

Frank was a detective in the Metro-Atlanta Fraud & Computer Forensics Unit. It must be for him. She hoped they didn't want him to go in to work. She walked up to the door of the familiar, old Queen Anne–style house and went in.

Chapter 9

Diane was greeted with the aroma of hot coffee when she opened the door. She walked through the small entry into the living room, where she heard talking. She was going to pass by, let Frank know she was home, go take a shower, and let him get on with his business. Then she recognized the voice.

It was Ross Kingsley, an FBI profiler friend of hers. He and Frank were drinking coffee and laughing over something.

They rose when she entered holding her dress over her arm and clutching her evening bag and heels in her hand.

"Diane," said Frank, his blue-green eyes sparkling as he spoke, "look who dropped by."

Something was up. Diane could tell by the way his eyes crinkled at the corners as he smiled at her.

She hadn't seen Ross in several months. When she first met him, she didn't think he looked like an FBI agent. She still didn't. He looked like a college professor, with his neatly trimmed beard and tweed sport coat. She noted some small changes since she last saw him: His brown hair was a little longer, and he looked tanned. He must have been on vacation.

"Ross, this is a surprise. How are you?" said Diane.

"Quite well, thank you. I hope this is not inconvenient. I should have called—you might have been in a cave somewhere—but I had to be in Rosewood anyway, so . . . anyway, here I am."

Frank looked at the distressed dress over her arm, arched an eyebrow, and looked back up at her.

"Long story," she said.

"Did you have to go to the hospital?" Frank asked.

Diane knew he was only half joking.

"No," she said, smiling sweetly at him. "I was lucky. It was a short drop."

She noticed Kingsley had a briefcase. It was sitting on the floor near his feet. This was business. The last time he came to her about business hadn't turned out well. Actually, it eventually turned out well, but the journey was hell. He followed her gaze.

"I have something I would like to talk to you about," he said.

"Okay. Would you mind if I hop in the shower and change into some fresh clothes first? I've had an eventful morning that began long before dawn. It won't take me long," she said.

"Sure," said Kingsley. "Frank is being a very entertaining host."

Diane went into the bedroom, stripped off her clothes, and got into the shower. The warm water felt good on her sore muscles and she would have liked to stay longer. But she hurriedly washed her hair, soaped up her body, and rinsed off. Frank came in as she was dressing.

"You all right?" he asked.

"Fine. I'll tell you about it in a minute." She smiled and kissed him. "Really, I'm fine this time. I only rolled down an embankment."

He laughed and left the room. Diane finished dressing in slacks and a sweater and combed back her short wet hair.

Frank had her a cup of fresh, steaming coffee sitting on the table next to her favorite chair when she came back into the living room. It felt good to get comfortable in the cozy room with its stuffed chairs, polished wood, and sunny, cream-colored walls. There was no fire in the fireplace, but its presence in the room dialed up the cozy factor. Ross Kingsley certainly looked comfortable.

"So," said Kingsley, "what happened this morning? I've had interesting mornings myself, but I don't think they ever quite reach the same level of interest that yours do." He grinned and took a sip of his coffee.

Diane told them about the early morning's events, leaving out details of the case. Kingsley listened with a combination of openmouthed disbelief and amusement. Diane tried to make it more of a comedy of errors than the real danger it was. Frank had his usual, I-can't-let-you-out-of-the-house-can-I expression on his face.

"As I said, my mornings aren't nearly as interesting," said Kingsley. He paused for a moment as if looking for another excuse not to get down to his business.

"How's the FBI?" asked Diane.

"I'm not with the FBI anymore," he said.

Diane hadn't expected that. Ross had seemed so comfortable there. "I wasn't aware," she began.

"I had an identity crisis. I discovered I wasn't wearing clothes; I was a fraud," he said.

Diane glanced over at Frank. He looked as puzzled as she felt.

"You're going to have to explain," she said.

"I came to the realization as I was working on my book on profiling that it was all smoke and mirrors. I was a con, no different from those psychic-astrologer folk you visit at carnivals for a psychic reading," he said.

"I'm not sure I understand," said Diane.

"I'd been regarding profiling as if it were a science," he said.

"You have repeatedly told me it isn't an exact science, that it's a tool," said Diane.

"I know I said that, but down deep I believed it was something more than that. I thought it rested, at least, on good psychological models that were verified by empirical studies, hard data, statistics, and probabilities."

"What changed your mind? How did you come to your epiphany?" asked Frank.

Frank, Diane knew, was a critic of profiling, so he probably approved of this turn of events.

"Looking at some of the research done in the UK on profiling and case histories. Looking back at my own work and seeing in reality how fuzzy some of my profiles and those of my colleagues were."

"Like . . . he's someone you wouldn't suspect of being violent," said Frank.

Diane smiled and Kingsley nodded. "You know, before

now, I never really realized how that statement fit most people." He shook his head. "So many descriptions are like that—'He's someone who tends to be a hermit, but sometimes enjoys being with friends.' You know, when I read my profiles in hindsight, I am astounded at how hazy and contradictory many of them were. They would be concrete enough to point to particular individuals, and yet vague and general enough to fit a lot of very different people. I mean, the profiles sounded good, but what did they really say? I don't know how detectives got anything worthwhile out of them. And the lack of consistency. You have two profilers evaluate the same case and their profiles point in completely different directions. You remember the BTK killer?"

Diane and Frank nodded.

"A little," said Diane. "The serial killer in Kansas?"

"I didn't work on his profile, but I studied it. He was profiled out to be basically lower class, an outsider, probably unmarried, and uncomfortable with women. When he was caught, he turned out to have been married for thirty years, a father of two children, president of the congregation council of his church, a Cub Scout leader, and a right-upstanding member of his community." Kingsley shook his head again. "They got some things right, but only because so many of the descriptions were so general, they would have fit about anyone."

"How did they catch him?" asked Diane.

"Old-fashioned detective work and a little trickery on the part of detectives," said Frank. "The killer was sending the police taunting messages. They got him to send a message by floppy disk, telling him there was no way to trace it. There is, of course, and they traced it back to him." He grinned.

Diane could see that it pleased him that computer technology had played a part in the apprehension.

"There was a lot more to his capture, but that's the Cliffs Notes version," said Frank.

"It was a research report that first tested my faith," said Kingsley. "A British study analyzed a couple hundred criminal cases in which profiles were used by the police. Profiles led detectives to the guilty party in fewer than three percent of the cases," said Kingsley. He straightened up in his chair and leaned forward for emphasis. "That statistic is what got me started on my own reevaluation of profiles."

"Is that what made you give up on profiling?" asked Diane. She was a little puzzled by Ross and wondered whether he was having more of a burnout than a career crisis. But then again, she had been a skeptic of profiling too. On the other hand, she did believe there were observable patterns of behavior that could be traced back to the psychology of the person, and those behaviors were predictable.

"I think the final straw was a case that several of us profilers were assigned to." Kingsley gestured with his hands, then put his fingertips together. "We were called in on a series of rapes. There were nine of them. In each case the victim was tied with her hands behind her and had a hood put over her head or a large blindfold over her eyes. The rapist used a condom and bathed the victim in the shower or bathtub afterward, so there was little forensic evidence." Kingsley settled back in the chair again and relaxed. He took another sip of his coffee.

"Want me to warm that for you?" asked Frank.

"No. This is fine," he said. "Not all the rapes took place in the same city. Five were in a college community and four were in a suburb about forty miles away. The rapist was never seen by the victims. We went back and forth on the profile. We were throwing out ideas left and right. But most of us decided he worked at the university and lived in the suburbs and was raping in his comfort zone. We had an elaborate profile that I won't go into except to say that when unsubs do things like cover the victim's face, it has meaning. We'd look at the other elements of the crime and decide which set of meanings made sense. We had it figured that he was young, not experienced with women, and didn't want them looking at him, either from inadequacy or to hide his face, et cetera."

He paused a moment. "See, that's the problem. Different unsubs do the same things, but for different reasons," he said. "Anyway, we were pretty sure of our profile."

"And?" asked Frank.

"The case was broken by two detectives working separately: one from the suburbs and one from the campus police. It turned out there were two rapists who had no relationship to each other, but who had more or less similar MOs, but different motivations for their respective methods. One blindfolded the women because he didn't want to be identified and washed them because he wanted to get rid of any trace evidence. He chose his victims from the university because there were lots of young women there and they were easily available. He did not work at the university. He worked at a car repair shop.

"The other rapist started out as a stalker. His stalking victim committed suicide and he was overcome with grief. He made an iron-on transfer from a photograph of her and attached it to a hood. He fantasized about her when he was raping his victims. The washing of his victims was part of his 'romantic evening' with them. He was a delivery guy and actually lived somewhere else. He delivered in the area and chose victims from there because he was familiar with all the streets and houses. Both of the rapists tied their victims because they didn't want them pulling their blindfolds off. Not one of us guessed there were two unsubs, because the rapes were so similar. We were driven by our profile. The detectives who ended up solving the case had more open minds."

Kingsley paused. "We had actually been encouraging the detectives to look at another guy who came up on the radar because he fit our profile. Fortunately, the detectives didn't get around to pursuing our suspect before the cases broke in both locales." Kingsley shook his head. "First, do no harm," he said.

"Remember the guy accused of the Atlanta Olympic bombing? Turns out he was innocent. But just because he had wanted to be a policeman and failed, it looked like he fit a classic profile and was made out to be the perp. His life was turned upside down and just about ruined. Terrible. Anyway, it all just fell apart for me." He took a sip of coffee. "So here I am."

"What are you doing now?" asked Diane.

"I work for a detective agency in Atlanta—Darley, Dunn, and Upshaw," he said.

"I've heard of them," said Diane. "Big firm. They do a lot

of client defense work. What do you do? Tear down profiles in court?"

He grinned. "As a matter of fact, I have, but that's not my goal. What I would like is for profiles to be used as a simple tool, a guideline, and not to drive the case."

"What brings you here?" asked Diane, staring at the briefcase that Kingsley put his hand on.

"I have a case I'm working on. It's pro bono. The firm likes to do a few freebies when they can. Makes them look good. It's a case where I think the police misused profiling techniques we taught them. I was hoping you would help."

Chapter 10

"This is going to need more coffee," said Diane. She took their cups and disappeared into the kitchen and returned with a tray of cups of fresh coffee.

Frank had cleaned off the coffee table to make room for the files Kingsley pulled from his briefcase. Diane put the tray on an end table and passed around the fresh cups of still-steaming coffee. Ross Kingsley took a sip, then another one, and Diane had the fleeting impression he was numbing his tongue against the upcoming narrative contained in the folders he'd set on the table.

"This isn't pleasant," said Kingsley.

"When you find murder that is pleasant, please come and share it with me," said Diane. "You are talking about murder, aren't you?"

"Maybe. That is why I've come to you. The firm I work for—although they like and encourage pro bono work, they don't put the entire staff on it. That's why I need to consult. How do you feel about pro bono?" he asked, looking up at her with a thin smile.

"I've done my share," said Diane, smiling back.

Kingsley pulled a file off the bottom of the stack and opened it. "I have to start with a murder that took place nine years ago. That's where the story begins."

Diane looked down at an eight-by-ten mug shot of a man who looked to be in his mid-twenties. He had straight blond hair and brown eyes. His face was thin. He had a narrow, crooked nose and full lips. He looked frightened.

"This is Ryan Dance. He's serving a life sentence for the murder nine years ago of Ellie Rose Carruthers. El, as her friends called her, was fifteen years old. She was reported missing on a Saturday. She had been left alone at home in an upper-middle-class neighborhood while the rest of the family visited her grandmother in a nursing home. When the family returned, El was not at home. They called all her friends, drove to all her favorite spots looking for her, and finally called the police. She was discovered two days later when an anonymous caller reported a possible body on the side of the road near I-85. She had been strangled and there was an attempted rape. She apparently fought and was killed before the assailant could complete the rape. At least, that was the analysis."

Kingsley stopped speaking and took another drink of coffee.

"Who was the anonymous caller?" asked Diane.

Kingsley shook his head. "Don't know." He set down his coffee cup and continued the story.

Diane looked at the stack of folders and sensed it was going to be a long one. She stared at the picture of Ryan Dance.

"This is not a cold case. They made an arrest," said Diane.

"Yes. They found cigarette butts near the body and matched the DNA to Ryan Dance," said Kingsley.

"He stuck around and smoked cigarettes after he dumped the body?" asked Diane.

"I found that a little odd too, but it was an out-of-the-way place, and God knows, perps do strange things," he said. "Besides, as I was told, the cigarette butts could have been carried there when he carried the body."

"Is there more evidence?" asked Diane.

"The police searched his car and found strands of her hair, a button from her dress, and a smear of her blood in the trunk," Kingsley said.

"Then this was a slam dunk," said Diane.

"Ryan Dance's sister, Stacy, didn't think so. Stacy Dance was fourteen years old when her brother, Ryan, was arrested, tried, and convicted. She always believed him to be innocent. When she turned twenty-one, she started an investigation on her own. Four weeks ago, Stacy Dance, age twenty-three, was found dead in her apartment over her father's garage. Her father came to see me last week, and that's why I'm here." Kingsley closed the file and picked up another one. He started to open it, then stopped. "As I said, it's not pleasant." He opened the folder.

"Stacy's death was ruled an accident by autoerotic asphyxiation. The father believes it was murder. The police won't listen to him. Understandably, their position is that the father simply does not want to believe his child would do what it appears that she did."

Kingsley handed the detective's report, the autopsy report, and the crime scene photo to Diane.

"Most cases of autoerotic asphyxia are male," commented Diane as she read the police report.

"I know," said Kingsley. "One thing that attracted me to his case was the profiling. The detective in charge had taken basic profiling courses the FBI offered to local law enforcement departments—I was the instructor. I should be jailed for malpractice."

Diane glanced up at him. He sounded bitter.

"The detective first suggested that because she was a little overweight, and *homely*—his word, not mine—that she was dateless and therefore frustrated. That led her to practice this form of *entertainment*—again, his word, not mine."

"I imagine her father had a reaction to that," said Frank.

"He did," said Kingsley. "He pointed out that his daughter had a boyfriend, and many other friends, she was enrolled in the local community college, and she and a couple of her friends had a band. They practiced in his garage. He was sure she was not into anything kinky."

"What did the detective say about the boyfriend?" said Diane.

"He revised his original 'profile' to suggest that since she was a college student and involved in a band, the autoerotica was probably something kids in her group were trying out. He made it sound like sniffing glue or taking drugs. When his first profile hadn't panned out, he revised it to fit his conclusion of what happened. First she did it because she was unpopular; then she did it because she was popular." Ross Kingsley threw up his hands as if in surrender. "Anyway, tell me what you think. I promised Mr. Dance I would look into it. In the space of nine years he has lost both his children. He is a devastated man with no other recourse. He was going to give us his life savings to open an investigation. I talked my bosses into letting me work on it pro bono."

Diane read the report twice and handed it to Frank when he reached for it. She took a breath and looked at the photograph. It showed a young adult woman, nude, with a rope around her neck. She was in a kneeling position on a bed. One end of the rope was tied to a bedpost and she was leaning forward into the noose. There was a towel half under the rope and half falling out. There were clothespins attached to each of her nipples.

"Her father didn't find her, did he?" said Diane.

"No. How did you know?" asked Kingsley.

"He wouldn't have left her this way. No father would, even if it meant disturbing evidence," said Diane.

"She was found by a friend, who called 911," said Kingsley.

Diane put down the photograph and picked up the autopsy report. She read it several times, picked up the photograph again, and looked at it. She rose from her stuffed chair and went into the kitchen and came back with a magnifying glass.

"Is this the only crime scene photograph?" asked Diane.

"Yes," said Kingsley. "Have you found something?"

Diane didn't answer; she continued examining the photograph with the magnifier. After a minute she put the picture and the magnifying glass down on the table.

"There are two things that make me question the finding," she said. "The first is the knot in the rope. Do you have the rope?"

"That's right, you do forensic knot analysis," said Kingsley. "How could I forget that? What about the knot? Oh . . . no, we don't have the rope."

"Anyone who is into this form of self-gratification would use some variation on a slipknot to hold the rope around the neck so that when pressure is released, the rope loosens. This is a granny knot—an incorrectly tied square knot. Granny knots are known for their difficulty in untying. Look at this." Diane handed the photograph to Kingsley along with the magnifying glass. "The rope is tied tight around her neck. No way did she do this. Frankly, I'm surprised the forensics people didn't notice it. Did any forensics person work it as a crime scene?"

"No, just the detective assigned to the case," said Kingsley. "I see it now. Of course. She would never have been able to get out of this. In fact, as tight as the rope was around her neck, she would have passed out before she could even arrange herself in this position. Funny, I never noticed how the rope was tied, and I studied crime scene photographs of autoerotic asphyxia. They contained elements much like this one—accessories to aid in arousal, rope around the neck, a towel to prevent ligature marks. . . ."

"But that's the second thing," said Diane. "She does have ligature marks on her neck."

"Are you saying . . . What exactly are you saying?" asked Ross Kingsley.

"Ligature marks are briefly mentioned in the autopsy report, but only that they are present. They are not described in any detail," said Diane. "But look at the photograph. Look at the marks on the neck where the towel has slipped. See this ligature mark?" She pointed to a clear linear bruise on the victim's neck and looked up at Kingsley. "It's an inch lower on the neck than where the tightened rope is cushioned by the towel. If I could see autopsy photos, I believe they would show two ligature marks. One made perimortem, and the other made postmortem."

"You're saying she was strangled; then this was staged after her death?" said Kingsley.

"It looks that way. What I believe is the second ligature mark looks very deep and appears to extend under the towel—at least, the mark is deep right up to where the towel covers the neck. The rope should have made a lighter impression on the skin at the edge of the towel."

"The towel at that point would start to hold the rope off the neck," said Kingsley.

Diane nodded. "I think this makes the manner of death worth a second look." Diane looked at the signature of the medical examiner—Oran Doppelmeyer. "I'm not familiar with this medical examiner. Is he new?"

"I believe so," said Kingsley. "So, does this mean you will help me?"

"You have enough here to get the lead detective to reopen the case," said Diane. "The father would probably give permission to exhume the body."

"Yes, well, I'm sure we could do that. But it would be really good for my firm if we could get the credit for solving the case." He raised his hand when Diane opened her mouth to speak. "I know we will have to hand it off to the police eventually, but I, on behalf of the firm that so graciously hired me, would like to hand the detective a truckload of evidence along with the solution. After all, it's a closed case and we would not be interfering in an ongoing investigation. Besides, they might botch it up again."

Frank had been quiet the whole time Kingsley and Diane discussed the case. He eyed Kingsley.

"You think Stacy was killed because of her investigation into her brother Ryan's murder conviction," said Frank. "But you're afraid the detective will ignore that angle and try to hang her death on the boyfriend, or some other friend. You think he's a man who likes to take shortcuts."

"You're pretty good at this profiling thing yourself," said Kingsley.

"Why do you believe her death is connected with her brother's case?" asked Frank.

"Because Stacy's father told me that in her room she kept a thick folder filled with documents, clippings, interviews, and notes on her investigation into the case against her brother. Now the folder, along with all her findings, is missing. It's too much of a coincidence," said Ross. "I felt it before. And now, with what you've found in the evidence, I'm convinced there is a connection, and her death was no accident."

Diane was quiet for a moment. She understood what Ross wanted; so did Frank. It wasn't so much that he wanted credit for his firm. He wanted to control the investigation against people he believed were incompetent to carry it out—or wouldn't carry it out.

"Is her room still intact?" Diane hoped that Stacy's father had kept the room as it was.

"Yes," said Kingsley. "It is. And I've got an appointment at the prison for tomorrow to talk with Ryan Dance. I know how you love to visit prisons and would want to get it over with first thing."

Chapter 11

Diane hated prisons. They were drab, depressing, and they smelled bad. Prisons were places people wanted to leave. The last time she visited someone in prison was when she came to interview Clymene O'Riley, a black widow she had put away. It was more or less an official visit then and, although not pleasant, it was bearable. This time she almost decided to just forget about it and leave. She would have if Ross Kingsley hadn't been with her.

She filled out the mandatory forms that, among other things, gave the guards permission to search her person and allow the drug dog to sniff her up and down. The papers must also have given them permission to be ill-mannered. The prison personnel probably didn't like being there either. Once she passed the sniff test, she was allowed to go into the visiting room. Ross went to see the warden on his own mission.

The visiting area wasn't a bad room. It was painted salmon pink, and she wondered whether the color meant anything—perhaps that it sapped your strength or something, kind of aroma therapy for the eyes. On the back wall was a row of cubicles with telephones. Each cubicle contained a stool screwed to the floor. The communication stalls resembled those small doorless phone booths you used to see everywhere, except for the window in the wall that separated visitors from the prisoner on the other side.

Diane sat down on the stool in cubicle three, as she had been instructed. In a few minutes Ryan Dance came into the room on the other side of the window, sat down, and picked up the phone.

He looked older than the young man in his mug shot. Of course, the photograph was taken nine years ago. He was thirty-one now. He looked older. His once gold-blond hair was now brown, dull, and stringy. His nose looked even more crooked. He had a front tooth missing and prison tats on his arms and fingers.

Diane picked up the phone, introduced herself, and told him she was sorry about his sister.

"Thanks," he mumbled.

"Your father believes Stacy was murdered because she was getting close to discovering who framed you," said Diane.

Ryan nodded his head and looked away for a moment. "She is a neat kid—was a neat kid" he said.

Diane saw his eyes sparkle with moisture.

"I told her not to do anything dangerous. Dad doesn't have anybody now."

"I'm working with someone your dad hired to find out what happened to her. The police ruled her death an accident," said Diane.

Ryan's face transformed into a cruel mask. "I know what they said and they're full of shit. Stupid bastards. They were stupid then. They're even stupider now." He spat out the words as if they were bitter seeds. "She don't deserve none of this. None of us do."

More visitors came in and filled the cubicles, and the noise level rose. Most everyone spoke in low voices, but Diane could pick out sniffling, sobbing, whispered anger, and laughing among the low cacophony of sounds. She wanted to finish this, get the hell out, and go home.

"Would you mind telling me what you think put you here?" said Diane. "From your point of view."

He was quiet for a moment and his face went back to the emotionless mask it had been before she'd mentioned the death of his sister.

"Don't you think I've been laying awake at night for nine years trying to figure that out? I don't know. I didn't know that Carruthers girl. Never knew her. I was twenty-two years old, for Christ's sake; she was in fucking high school. I never went driving by her house like they said I did. I never went into that neighborhood."

"Start from the beginning and tell me what you do know," said Diane.

"The beginning was me sitting watching the Atlanta Braves on TV and the police coming in with a search warrant. That's the first I ever heard of that girl."

"A witness reported seeing your car in the neighborhood, and took down your tag number," said Diane. She tried keeping her voice even and calm.

"Don't I know it. She was at my trial. I never saw that bitch before and I wasn't in that neighborhood. A lot of rich folk live there. What would I be doing there?"

"She said she recognized you in your Atlanta Braves cap, your gold Chevrolet, and your license plates," said Diane.

"Maybe my car was there, maybe my hat was there, but I wasn't there. Somebody put the frame on me."

"You have any idea who would do that?" asked Diane.

"No damn idea whatsoever. I've never hurt nobody bad enough to do this to me," he said.

"Sometimes people overreact to something hurtful. Is there anyone you can think of who might have a small grudge, something that got blown out of proportion in their mind?"

"I've broke up with girlfriends, but none of them would do this. Like, they'd have to be crazy to kill somebody and blame it on me. What kind of maniac would do that? I never went with no girls that crazy . . . or that mean."

Diane wasn't getting anything useful out of Ryan. It was a wasted trip. He genuinely seemed clueless, or he was a really good actor. On the other hand, many criminals were really good actors.

"Did you have your car stolen or used by anyone else around that time?" asked Diane.

"No, not that I know," he said.

"How would you not know?" she said.

"Well, I wasn't in my car all the time. Somebody could've borrowed it and brought it back while I was working or watching TV or . . . sometimes I'd go out drinking and, well, somebody could've borrowed it then," he said. "I might not know about it."

"Did you always take your car keys with you?" said Diane.

"I left the keys shut up in the sun visor, you know, like in *Terminator 2*," he said.

"I understand you were a truck driver at the time," said Diane.

"Dad got me the job. He was a loading dock foreman at Walker Ace. They transport all over. But I only drove local," said Ryan.

"Where was your car when you were working?" asked Diane.

"Sometimes at my apartment, when I rode to work with Dad. Sometimes in the lot at work. They keep the lot locked so nobody can steal stuff out of your car."

"Did Stacy tell you what she was working on?" asked Diane.

"Just that she was going back and talking to witnesses and stuff. I told her to be careful. I told her to get a detective to do that, not do it herself. But she was stubborn."

"Did she tell you any details about what she found?" asked Diane.

He shook his head. "She had a hard time getting people to talk to her, but . . ."

"But what?" prodded Diane.

"Last time we talked she seemed, well, happy. She never wanted to get my hopes up, but I know she felt good about something," he said.

"When was that?" asked Diane.

"About a week before she . . . before she died," he said. "She should have left it alone. Maybe she could've found some detective real cheap to do the legwork for her. She shouldn't 'ave done it by herself. You find out who killed her. It's not right for her to be dead and me stuck in here. None of us did nothing to deserve this."

Diane saw movement of the guards in the background and looked at her watch. *Time to go.*

"Thank you for talking to me," she said.

"Thanks for helping my sister and my dad."

He spoke as if there was no hope for him. Diane watched him leave before she rose from the stool.

She didn't wait for Ross inside the prison. Instead, she left and waited outside by the car for him to return. It didn't take long. Within five minutes he came walking out of the gates and over to the car.

"How was it?" he asked.

"Waste of time," said Diane. "Either he knows nothing or he's a good liar. I don't know which."

They got into Kingsley's Prius and he started the engine. Diane felt relief when they pulled out of the prison grounds and into traffic toward Rosewood.

"He did seem genuinely sad about his sister," she said. "How did you do?"

"Interesting, in a way. No information, but he had some pinups under his mattress. All were more mature and voluptuous ladies than Miss Carruthers. Judging from that, his tastes don't seem to run to high school girls."

"He was closer to her age back then," said Diane. "Besides, maybe those were the only kind of pictures he could get hold of."

"I know the pictures don't mean anything. But if he had pictures of younger girls hidden in his cell, that would have meant something," said Kingsley.

"Anything else in his cell?" asked Diane.

"Books about sports, a Bible, hygiene stuff, letters from his father and sister," he said.

"How did you get the warden to let you in his cell?"

"You'd be surprised at how many career employees would like to retire from criminal justice and take a job with a private firm—and take home two salaries, as it were. To that end, they can be awfully accommodating to firms such as the one I work for," said Kingsley.

"Interesting," said Diane. "Did you read the letters?"

Kingsley nodded. "Nothing there that contributes to our purposes. His sister didn't keep him apprised of what she was doing."

"That's what he told me. He said she didn't want to get his hopes up. But he did say that about a week before she died, she was optimistic about something. She didn't tell him what."

"Well, I'm glad we got the prison visit over with." Kingsley grinned at her. "I'm sorry. I know you hated it."

"It's so depressing. Surely there must be a better model for a penal system," she said.

"I'd like to go to Stacy's apartment. Are you up for it?" he asked.

"I need to check in at the museum for a while, then the crime lab. I'll pick up a crime scene kit and meet you there. We need to process her apartment the right way, even though it's been trampled all over."

Chapter 12

When Ross Kingsley dropped Diane off at the museum, the first thing she did was go to her office suite, take a hot shower, and change clothes. Relieved to have the smell of prison off her, she went to her desk and checked in with Andie Layne, her administrative assistant, and Kendel Williams, her assistant director.

The museum had been running so smoothly lately, it almost scared her. And today hadn't brought any emergencies either: no fires to put out, no problems to solve, no large shipments overdue, no displays to put on hold, no cranky curators, no lost children—and the number of visitors to the museum was still on the rise. They were making money. So far, so good.

After her meetings, Diane spent an hour doing paperwork. Most of the time she didn't mind the budget reports, the requests, the letters, or even cutting through the red tape that frequently accumulated in the course of business. Doing paperwork was like oiling the machinery of the museum. Paperwork kept things running; it gave her staff what they needed to do their jobs; it kept the museum on the cutting edge. Less paperwork meant the museum was getting static. Diane particularly didn't mind it today. It was so far removed from the world of prisons. The moment she walked into the old Gothic building, she welcomed the smell of the museum, the smooth wood walls, brass fixtures, polished granite floors—and most of all, the happy people. She finished signing the last report and headed upstairs to archaeology to see Jonas Briggs.

Jonas had a two-room suite on the third floor, across

from the archaeology exhibits. One room was his office; the other was a small lab where he did most of his work. His office was wall-to-wall bookcases and was filled with as many books and papers as Marcella's. He did have a couple of blank spaces on the walls where he had hung enlarged photographs of archaeological excavations from the thirties. In another space he'd hung an abstract painting with bold, bright slashes of color, which he said was done by an elephant. A table flanked by two stuffed chairs sat in one corner of the room. A Staunton sandalwood chessboard was always set up on the table and he and Diane played when time would allow.

Jonas was sitting at his desk. A young couple Diane recognized from a photograph as Paloma Tsosie and her husband, Mark, sat in the two stuffed chairs.

"Diane, come in," said Jonas. He rose from behind his desk and introduced Marcella Payden's daughter and son-in-law. Jonas had said they were both teachers on the Navajo reservation. They looked younger than Diane had imagined. They also looked younger than their pictures. They must have both been just out of college.

"I wanted to thank you for the hotel," said Paloma, rising to shake Diane's hand. "It's so nice, and so convenient to the hospital."

Paloma looked like an early version of her mother. She was petite, had an oval face, honey blond hair, large blue eyes, and full lips.

Her husband, Mark, had short black hair, dark eyes, and light brown skin. He had a lean face, a slender nose, and sharp cheekbones. They were an attractive couple. Mark stood with his wife and shook Diane's hand, reiterating the thanks his wife had offered for Diane's hospitality. Diane felt sincerity from both of them. They were grateful for her kindness and it showed in their eyes and their firm, lingering handshakes.

"You're welcome. I'm fond of your mother and it's the least I could do," said Diane. "She has done some wonderful work for the museum. We're very excited about the collection she is putting together."

Mark offered Diane his chair, but Jonas shoved a stack of journals off a chair and brought it around for her. Paloma and Mark sat back down. Jonas rolled his desk chair around so he wouldn't be behind his desk.

"How is Marcella?" asked Diane.

Paloma grasped her husband's hand. "She still has swelling in her brain. The doctors are hopeful. I'm not sure what that means." She looked at Mark and Jonas, and back at Diane. "They won't say much."

"They probably don't know much," said Jonas. "We just have to wait. Marcella's a fighter."

Paloma smiled briefly. "She is that. We have an appointment to speak with the detective this afternoon. I'm worried he's off in the wrong direction," she said. "Jonas told us how he was questioned."

"It's just the way the detectives do things," said Diane. "Don't read too much into it."

"This arguing thing—Mother loves scholarly debates and her friends love to argue with her. She never bothers debating people who don't have intelligent ideas. It's just the way she is. It's obvious to me it was those hooligans who attacked you and that detective—Hanks—who also attacked Mother. What's wrong with him that he can't see that?"

"He's just getting the obvious interviews out of the way first," said Diane.

It wasn't exactly true, but she could see Paloma getting herself worked up, and she doubted Hanks would interview Jonas again.

"I hope so," said Paloma. "Unless they find out who did all of it, Mother will never feel safe in that house again, and she loves her house. She said it needs to be on *If Walls Could Talk*, you know, that home-and-garden show about old houses."

"I'm sure Dr. Fallon is right," said Mark. "The detective has to understand her world before he can understand what happened to her. When he sees she's not a woman who brings enemies around her, he'll look outside her circle." His wife smiled at him.

Diane asked Jonas, "Did you ask Paloma what her mother's words that night might have meant?"

Jonas looked blankly at Diane for a moment. "Oh, I clean forgot. There's just so much going on," he said.

"What?" asked Paloma.

"When I found . . . While we were waiting for the ambulance, Marcella was conscious for a few moments. She said what sounded like 'tiger after all loose moment.' I don't know if I heard it right. Her voice was faint," said Jonas. "We couldn't make anything out of it."

"She said, 'Tiger after all. Lewis moment,'" said Paloma, nodding her head. She looked over at her husband, who agreed. "If she could make sense right after she was hurt, then there's a chance she'll not be permanently damaged. Don't you think?" She gazed at all of them, as if looking for agreement.

Mark nodded. "I think you're right." He put a hand on her shoulder and squeezed. "That's hopeful."

Diane and Jonas glanced at each other, shrugged slightly, and focused back on Paloma.

"That makes sense to you?" asked Jonas.

"Lewis Blaire is one of her colleagues at Arizona. He's a cognitive archaeologist. His work is about—"

"Perception," said Jonas, nodding.

"He has the idea we perceive things subconsciously before we do consciously, and that ability gave early man an edge to deal with fast predators like the saber-toothed tiger," said Paloma.

Diane cocked an eyebrow and looked at Jonas.

"The idea is that you perceive a predator subconsciously and act instinctively before it has a chance to jump you. Kind of an early-warning system." Jonas wiggled his hand. "I have my doubts, but the idea is supported by some brain-function research. I just don't think it could help you outrun a sabertooth."

"Mother liked the concept because it happened to her," said Paloma. "She was surface collecting in an overgrown field—I was with her—and suddenly out of the blue, she jumped way to the side and almost knocked me down. She scared me. I asked her what was wrong, why had she done that, and she said she didn't know. Well, we looked down and saw there was a rattlesnake lying in the grass, and if she had taken another step forward, she would have stepped on it. If you believe Lewis' concept, her subconscious perception had caused an instinctive involuntary physical reaction that saved her from the snake before she could even think about it. She calls those kind of phenomena 'Lewis moments.' "

"Interesting," said Diane. "That means she probably had one of those moments before she was attacked."

Paloma nodded. "But the sabertooth got her anyway."

"So what does this mean, really?" asked Diane. "Marcella saw or heard something that didn't register, but caused her to react in some way and—what?"

They were silent for a minute, looking at each other in turn. Jonas spoke first.

"I think that's exactly what happened. She subconsciously detected some threat and reacted in some way, but no threat appeared immediately. That's what she meant by 'tiger after all.' There was a sabertooth in the bushes after all and it attacked her."

Chapter 13

Diane suggested they all go to the museum restaurant for lunch. As they stepped into the elevator just outside Jonas' office, Paloma wrapped her sweater tight around her and gave a little shiver. She looked fragile and frightened and very young. Mark put an arm around her shoulders.

"I had to buy a sweater when I got here," she told Diane. "I'm not used to it being so chilly this time of year."

"It's a little colder than normal here," said Diane. But what she thought was how vulnerable the young couple looked. He in his loafers and jeans and blue T-shirt, and she in her sandals and jeans and peasant blouse, they were innocents.

"I've been trying not to turn my heat on at night," said Jonas, "but in a few days, I'm going to have to give in."

The restaurant had a medieval atmosphere with its vaulted ceilings and rough-hewn wood tables. It was cozy, especially in the evenings when each table was lit by candlelight. At the time of day they were there, it had sunlight streaming in from the wall of windows and French doors leading to the trellis garden. The restaurant was full of diners. The waitress showed them to a booth in the corner and left them with tall menus written in calligraphy.

"Suddenly, I'm hungry," said Paloma, her eyes darting over the menu.

"If you like steak, I suggest the filet," said Diane.

She was convinced that high-protein foods and chocolate were medicine, and the two of them looked as if they needed some strong medicine. The very idea of losing someone you love is the scariest, most helpless feeling in the world. She hoped Paloma wouldn't have to face the loss of her mother, especially to such a mean cause.

"I agree," said Jonas, "the steaks here are great." He closed his menu without looking at it. "You've talked me into it."

They all ordered steak, salad, and baked potato, with Paloma ordering a baked sweet potato with her meal.

While they waited for their food, Diane talked about the museum and its holdings, inviting them to take a look around when they had the time. Mark commented that he wasn't used to so much green and it would be fun to bring his students there on a field trip if the school ever got a windfall for traveling.

"We won't hold our breath," said Paloma, smiling.

The waitress brought their food and the four of them were well into their lunch before anyone brought up Marcella. Diane told Paloma about the beautiful work her mother did and described the reconstructed mask-pitcher in Marcella's workroom.

"That was one of the pieces she dug up in the backyard," said Paloma.

"I'm not that well versed on pottery," said Diane, "but to me it didn't look Native American."

"It isn't," said Paloma. "It's modern, but Mother didn't know how old. One of the things that excited Mother about the house is all the stuff she found. One of the previous owners must have been an artist and a potter. Best of all, whoever it was used a bonfire kiln, like Mother uses. Mother found a pit in the backyard where the pots were fired. She excavated hundreds of broken sherds from the fire pit. For my mother, that was like finding a yard full of gold. Whoever the potter was, he used natural clays and tempers like she uses."

"I wonder if the artist could have been someone from the university?" said Diane.

"Mother thought they might have been an archaeologist," said Paloma. "But she knows practically every archaeologist who's ever worked with pottery and she said there isn't anyone from Bartrum in the literature. Mother told me a lot more about all the pottery finds, but I have to confess, at a certain point I kind of glaze over." Paloma smiled. “I didn’t get bit by the archaeology bug the way she did.”

“The mask she was reconstructing in her workroom is so beautiful. Did she have any clue who the artist might be?” said Diane.

Paloma shook her head. “She’s been trying to find out. The house was empty for several years. You may have noticed it got a little run-down. The guy she bought it from had inherited it from an uncle. He didn’t know any owners before that. She talked to some of her neighbors. They didn’t know anything either. Evidently there is a large turnover in the area because of all the students from Bartrum.”

When they had finished eating, Diane talked them into dessert. Paloma and her husband ordered pecan pie. Diane and Jonas had chocolate cake. Both were specialties of the restaurant. Mark asked Diane how they pronounced pecan here. Diane told him it was like *puh-CON*. That a *pee-can* is a receptacle. He laughed. It took Jonas and Paloma a second for the joke to register. It was good to see Paloma laugh.

“I saw a lot of pieces of broken garden ornaments when I was at the house,” said Diane.

Paloma and Jonas both nodded.

“Mother found a lot of modern artifacts in the yard,” said Paloma. “All kinds of pieces of statues, birdbaths, gargoyles. Someone at some point liked to decorate the garden in all manner of statuary. Mother said it was impossible to tell if they were in the same time frame as the pottery, but she was having a great time.”

Paloma’s eyes were suddenly moist. She blinked and took a drink of water. “Why would anyone hurt her so cruelly?” she asked.

Diane didn’t think she expected an answer. There was never a good enough answer to satisfy that question.

“She had some paintings on the living room wall that were stolen the night of the attack,” said Diane. “Three portraits. Do you know anything about them?”

“She didn’t have them when I was over at her house a couple of weeks ago,” offered Jonas.

Paloma nodded. “She called me last week, so excited. They were hidden inside a wall in one of the upstairs rooms.

She found them when she tore out the wall for a doorway. She thought they might have been done by the same artist who did the pottery."

"Inside a wall? Interesting. Were the paintings signed?" asked Diane.

"I don't know," said Paloma. "I couldn't talk to her very long that evening; I was late to a meeting." She started to cry and her husband pulled her over to him and hugged her.

Diane wished she had something comforting to say.

After a minute Paloma straightened up and took another drink of water. "Sorry. It's just so unfair."

"Yes, it is," said Diane.

"She told me one of the sheds out back was a potter's shed," said Paloma. "It was mostly filled with a lot of junk, but she found some pieces of furniture there that she wanted to refinish. She was like a kid in a candy store with all the stuff she was finding." Paloma smiled. "Most people would have thought it all junk and trash. Archaeologists have a different view about old things."

"Yes, we do," said Jonas.

Diane almost mentioned the odd note on the bottom of the desk drawer, but decided not to say anything. It seemed, at this particular moment, a little too disturbing. Instead, she changed the subject to the mummy the museum inherited a year ago and all the surprises that came with it. By the end of dessert, Paloma seemed to be feeling better.

Mark glanced around the restaurant. "I don't see our waitress," he said.

"Would you like something else?" asked Diane.

He grinned. "Oh, no, this will last me well into next week. I was just looking for the check."

"She won't be coming with a check," said Jonas. "It's a little-known secret that when Diane brings a guest to the restaurant, the waitstaff don't bring the check to the table. See, in the museum, Diane is queen. Really, it's true." Jonas chuckled. "We have a herpetologist who is terrified of Diane and hides when he sees her coming. Afraid he might be banished or something."

"He lost a snake in the museum," said Diane. "It turns up at odd times and scares the staff. He can't seem to catch it or tell me why it's still in the building. It should have made its way outside by now."

Paloma and Mark both laughed. "We appreciate all this," said Mark. "It's comforting to get to town and not be strangers."

"I'm just sorry your visit is for this reason," said Diane. She paused. "I really think Marcella will come out of it." *I'm hoping*, she thought.

"She has a very hard head," said Jonas.

"She does that," said Paloma.

When they got up to leave, Diane spotted Ross Kingsley at another table. She took her leave of Jonas, Paloma, and Mark and walked over to his table.

"Diane," he said when she sat down, "I'll be ready to go to Mr. Dance's house when I finish. Couldn't resist the cake here."

"I had a piece too. I'll go up to the crime lab and get a kit. You want to pick me up outside the lab?" asked Diane.

"Sure. Look, I really do appreciate your help in this. I don't know where else I'd get free forensic expertise." He grinned at her.

Diane laughed. "I don't know where you'd find a sucker as big as me. I'll see you in about thirty minutes. Enjoy your cake."

Chapter 14

The crime lab, all shiny glass and chrome, was an agency of the City of Rosewood, which didn't pay the museum any rent for the space. In exchange for housing the crime lab, the city forgave the museum all its city taxes—taxes they had raised in order to entice Diane into housing the lab. Despite the city's less than scrupulous way of getting the space, Diane liked the idea of having the crime lab in the museum, and so did the museum board. Otherwise, she would have resisted Rosewood's little blackmail scheme.

The city's great deal was compounded for them when they discovered that if they dragged their feet on approving the funds for the purchase of new pieces of expensive forensic equipment requested for the crime lab, Diane would have the museum purchase the equipment and lease it back to the lab, thus avoiding the need for large cash outlays by the city. At least they thought it was a great deal until they realized Diane could indeed pull the plug on the arrangement, boot the lab out of the museum, and keep the sexiest and most expensive pieces of state-of-the-art equipment. It was a sometimes-uneasy alliance, but it worked, and Diane and the city had a great crime lab.

David was in deep conversation with Deven Jin when Diane entered the crime lab. Jin came to the Rosewood Crime Lab from New York where he was a criminalist. He had persuaded Diane to establish a DNA lab in the museum and she had put him in charge. Jin was the youngest member of Diane's forensic team and the most energetic. He was half Asian, adventurous, and loved his job. It turned out that the DNA lab was one of the more lucrative departments in the museum.

"How are the investigations coming?" said Diane. She pulled out a chair at the round debriefing table and sat down with the two of them.

David ran down the current cases, which were fortunately few. Fewer cases meant less mayhem and murder was going on.

"We have a collection of fibers from Marcella Payden's place. Mostly collected outside from the second event, the one you were involved in. The fibers are dyed black wool, which we suspect came from the ski masks. There are also several Manila hemp fibers in association with the wool, which may have come from a rope. That may mean the masks and rope were stored together, since there was no report of a rope in connection with the fracas." David smiled at Diane. "We also have quite a collection of maroon-colored sequins."

"I'll bet you do," said Diane.

"We have several boot prints that are noteworthy," said David. "A soft-toe work boot from Cherokee, size eleven—about thirty dollars and available at discount stores; Garmont men's hiking boot, size ten—about two hundred dollars; and an Oliver steel toe safety boot, size ten and a half—about a hundred and fifty dollars. All have wear patterns that will allow us to identify them if we find the boots themselves. Notice the differences in price."

"I did," said Diane.

"Ray-Ray Dildy had the cheap boots," said David. "It looks like his partners had a little more money to spend on footwear."

"Good evidence," said Diane. "I imagine Hanks was pleased."

"He was . . . with the boot prints," said David.

Diane raised her eyebrows. "Oh?" she said.

"The description Daughtry and Hanks gave of the events doesn't fit with the findings on the dead guy."

Diane closed her eyes a moment. "I don't like this," she said. "What doesn't match?"

"Well, first of all, it was Officer Daughtry's gun that killed Ray-Ray Dildy," said David. "I don't know if you knew that."

"I feared it might be, but—is there a problem?" asked Diane.

"Daughtry and Hanks both stated that Daughtry had just stepped, or rather, limped off the porch when Daughtry fired his gun," said David.

"And?" said Diane.

David steepled his hands in front of his face, a gesture he sometimes made when he was trying to explain a point.

"Dildy was found almost at the edge of the woods, a good forty feet from the porch, and there was gunpowder residue around the entry wound on Dildy's clothing," said David.

"I see," said Diane.

"There are two explanations at the moment. Dildy was closer to Officer Daughtry when he was shot than Daughtry and Hanks remembered. And Dildy survived long enough to walk or stumble forty feet across the yard."

"Did Lynn think that was possible?" asked Diane.

Lynn Webber was the medical examiner for Rosewood and a couple of the surrounding counties. Budget shortfalls had led to a consolidation of medical examiners' offices in the area. With Diane's recommendation, Lynn Webber had been brought in from the neighboring county to serve as the multicounty ME. In the process, she had dislodged Rosewood's ME, who had been tainted by association with the corrupt leadership of the City of Rosewood's previous administration. It was one small win for the good guys. Diane and Lynn worked well in collaboration when death and crime brought them together.

"She said he could have lived long enough to get a few feet ," said David. "She wasn't sure about forty feet."

"You think Daughtry ran him down and shot him?" said Diane. "His leg was injured, but he was pumped full of adrenaline."

David shook his head. "No blood trail to the body, and Daughtry was bleeding freely from his wound. We do have a trail that more or less matches his and Hanks' tale, but with a small detour into one of the little rock gardens, or whatever those rock-bordered spaces are that are all around the yard," said David. "What I think is, Daughtry lost his gun for a time, most likely when he fell through the floor of the porch. One of the other perps picked it up, shot Dildy, and threw the gun down. I think Daughtry then retrieved it, and isn't admitting that he ever lost it. The chief of police is pretty strict about knowing a gun's whereabouts at all times. He doesn't like it when an officer loses track of his gun, even for a few minutes."

"What does Daughtry say?" asked Diane.

"Don't know. Don't want to know. I just deliver evidence, sometimes along with scenarios when appropriate. I explained things to Hanks. He tried to argue with me about what the evidence says and didn't like it when I stuck to my analysis. But it's his problem now."

"Naturally, he's going to try and protect his own," said Diane.

"We're in the same tribe," said David. He rubbed his balding crown down to the dark fringe around his head where his hair was making its last stand.

"We are on the same side, but that's a little different from being family," said Diane. "Your obligation is over now that you've told Hanks, so don't worry about it. My sense is, he may not like it, but he won't ignore it. Besides, that's better than having shot a fleeing perp in the back at forty feet. So, anything else I should know about?"

"That covers it as far as the evidence goes. We didn't get any fingerprints other than exemplars, and Jin tells me that all the blood belongs to Dr. Payden."

"How did you get Marcella's fingerprints? Did you take them at the hospital?" asked Diane.

"Didn't have to," said David. "She's on file." He grinned. "Dr. Payden has a record."

"What?" said Diane. "For what?"

"Seems that when she was a student many years ago, she protested a construction project that was about to start building on top of a Native American prehistoric site. Archaeologists were trying to get an injunction so they could excavate the site and save the remains from destruction, but the construction contractor was hell-bent on leveling the place before the court order could be issued. She sneaked into the construction site in the dead of night, revved up one of their heavy front-end loaders, and ran over all their smaller equipment, shed and all," said David, still grinning from ear to ear. "She got community service and a fine."

Diane shook her head and smiled. "Who knew? She seems so harmless. We all did things in our youth. Where are Izzy and Neva?" she asked.

"Izzy's out on his own, working a break-in. I'm sending him out by himself on some of the smaller things. He's doing well, by the way," said David. "Neva is in the museum at Document Analysis. She's curious about the handwriting on the desk."

Diane looked over at Jin. "What are you doing up here?" she asked.

"Visiting. You know, you always say that when I visit you guys up here. Like I'm never supposed to take a break."

Diane looked at Jin a moment. "Touchy today?"

"His two new employees—the ones he went through such a long process of finding—are driving him crazy," said David. "They're as obsessive-compulsive as he is."

"Being detail oriented is not OC," said Jin. "It's simply doing a good job. There's a reason that, as young as we are, we are one of the most reliable labs in the country. You have to admit, the DNA lab pays for itself many times over."

"I admit all of that," said Diane. She stood up. "I'm taking a kit out to do some private work. Call if you need anything."

"I can go with you," said Jin. "You might need help."

"It's a freebie," said Diane.

"I do pro bono," said Jin.

"Why would you want to go?" asked Diane.

"My new employees are driving me nuts," he said.

Chapter 15

They rode toward Gainesville with Ross Kingsley driving, Diane in the passenger seat, and Jin in the backseat talking a blue streak about his new lab technicians.

"I thought you liked Elvis," said Diane.

"I do," said Jin, "but I don't come to work dressed like him, and I can't recite all of his songs in chronological order."

"But your technicians are doing a good job?" asked Kingsley.

"Oh yes," said Jin, "they are great. I wouldn't trade them in or anything. I just need a little break from them once in a while."

"Both are quirky?" asked Kingsley.

"Well, they are twins," said Jin. "And I have to say, they work well together. Very efficient. Very low error rate—amazingly low."

They drove into the working-class neighborhood Stacy Dance had lived and died in. Many of the houses were empty, with foreclosure signs in the yards. It was a neighborhood that had seen better days. At the same time, many of the occupied homes were neatly kept, if a little worn around the edges. The neighborhood spoke of hard times and pride.

Harmon Dance's house, the home of Stacy and Ryan, was backed up against a small copse of trees on a corner lot. The yard of the empty house next door was overgrown and the curtainless windows reminded Diane of dead eyes. She felt a chill.

Diane saw the second-story garage apartment right

away. The garage sat a few feet away from the main house, with a dogtrot between the structures. A steep stairway on the side away from the house led up to the apartment. It was a short distance, maybe thirty feet, from the stairs to the road.

"He's expecting us," said Ross as he drove up the short drive and stopped in front of the closed garage.

They got out of the car and looked a moment at the single-story home. It was a white house in need of paint. On one end was a porch with square wooden columns and a swing. Two mailboxes attached to the side of the house next to the door were numbered 118 and 118½, one for Mr. Dance and one for his daughter.

"I'm going to start a ground survey of the property outside," said Jin. "I'm wondering. You think we can go into that empty house?"

"We'll talk about that later," said Diane.

"Sure, Boss," said Jin. With the carrying case containing his evidence bags slung over his shoulder, he left them on the porch and started a perimeter search of the area.

Diane missed having Jin along with her doing crime scene work. Since his focus was now on the DNA lab, it had been a while.

Kingsley knocked on the front door of the house. After only a few seconds, the door opened and Harmon Dance appeared. He stood in the threshold for a moment, nodded at Kingsley, and looked at Diane.

Harmon Dance had a rugged, deeply lined face. Creases around his mouth gave him a perpetual frown. Diane wondered whether he would ever smile again.

"Hello, Mr. Dance," said Kingsley. "This is Dr. Diane Fallon, the forensic specialist I told you about."

Dance nodded. "Thanks for coming." He held the door open for them to enter, stopped, and looked beyond the two of them. "Not now," he said under his breath.

Diane followed his gaze. A woman was walking with determination across the street toward them, her arms swinging in her hurry to get across ahead of an approaching car. She was middle-aged, portly, and had thinning, frizzy brown hair. Her jaw was set in a determined clinch.

"What is it, Mrs. Pate?" Dance said.

Mrs. Pate stopped at the foot of the steps with her hands on her hips and glared at the three of them. The skirt of her blue flowered housedress moved gently in the light breeze; her square-lens frameless glasses slipped on her nose.

"You gonna rent your girl's apartment to that China-man?" she said. She nodded her head toward where Jin had walked into the woods.

"How is that your business?" Dance said, his own face settling deeper into granite.

"I won't have it. Things are bad enough. Who are these people?" She looked as if she also disapproved of Diane and Ross standing on the porch. You real estate people? I want you to know this is a nice neighborhood, or it used to be before people started losing their homes. She glanced over at the empty house.

Diane saw that Kingsley was holding back a laugh. For herself, Diane felt a little irritated at the woman's racism. Diane had to dig deep to find her compassion. The woman was probably scared. She was getting older and her neighborhood was changing . . . and there had been an untimely death just across the street. Trying to have some control in what must have felt like an out-of-control world probably bedeviled the poor woman and a belligerent demeanor was her only shield against it. But, then again, Diane was probably overanalyzing.

"These are not real estate people and I'm not renting out Stacy's apartment. You can go back home now, Mrs. Pate."

As irritating as Mrs. Pate was, she was a gem for investigators—a person who was always on the lookout.

"Mrs. Pate," said Diane, "I'm Diane Fallon. May I ask you a few questions about the day Stacy died?"

The woman suddenly looked startled, as if a loud noise had gone off beside her. Her paranoia had focused on the possibility of new neighbors, not an investigation.

"What kind of questions?" she said, her hands suddenly clasped against her stomach.

"Where I live, in Rosewood, we have a Neighborhood Watch. Do you have one here?" asked Diane. She wanted to start out by making sure Mrs. Pate knew she was going to be judged well on her nosiness.

"Police ain't much good here," she said. "No use getting them to put up signs. We have to keep an eye out ourselves."

"Did you see any suspicious people here that day?" said Diane.

"You people here to investigate her death?" Mrs. Pate darted a look at Mr. Dance. "I thought it was something else that killed her."

"Did you see anything that made you uneasy?" asked Diane.

"That was a month ago. . . ."

"Mrs. Pate," said Harmon Dance, his voice raspy, "Stacy was good to you. She was good to everybody here in the neighborhood."

"Yes, she was," said Mrs. Pate. "You think somebody kilt her?"

"We're looking into the possibility," said Kingsley.

The woman was quiet for several moments. Diane thought she was trying to remember. Mrs. Pate scratched the back of her hand and put a palm on her cheek.

"Not that day, but one or two days before, there was a car, an SUV kind of car. I noticed it 'cause it circled the block a couple of times"—she gestured with her hand, moving it in a circle—"and slowed down here when it went by. It stopped for a time—maybe a few minutes—on the cross street there above your house," she said, nodding to Dance. "The windows were dark and I couldn't see inside. It was a black car. No good comes from a black car with dark windows like that."

"Did you see a license plate or a window sticker?" asked Diane. "Anything that might help to track down the vehicle?"

"No. I tried to get a fix on the license, but couldn't. You think it was them? Somebody in that car did something to poor Stacy?"

She looked alarmed. Diane guessed that the thought of perhaps having laid eyes on a murderer—or his vehicle—was frightening to her.

"Have you seen it since?" asked Diane.

She shook her head. "No, I haven't."

"Why didn't you tell the police?" said Dance.

"They never come talk to me, did they?" she said.

"Thank you, Mrs. Pate," said Kingsley. He handed her a card. "Please call me if you remember anything more."

She studied the card a moment and looked up at him. She put the card in the pocket of her dress and nodded her head sharply. "Glad you ain't renting to that Chinese guy."

They watched her cross the street and go back into her house.

Dance invited them inside. His home was sparse, neat, and smelled like vegetable soup. Diane sat down on a blue corduroy sofa. Kingsley sat beside her. Harmon Dance sat in a mission-style rocking chair with matching blue cushions opposite them. It creaked with his weight as he rocked.

"So you think my little girl was murdered by somebody?" he asked.

"We don't know," said Kingsley. "But Dr. Fallon has examined the photographs and thinks it may be a possibility."

Dance nodded his head up and down and seemed to shiver. "I told the detective. He had this idiotic idea that because Stacy wasn't a beauty queen, nobody would fool with killing her, or some such notion. I'm not sure what he thought; he kept changing his mind. He said she did this shameful thing to herself. Well, Stacy may not have been Miss Georgia, but she was a good girl and lots of people liked her. You could go up and down this street and find a lot of older folks who liked her. She was good to them. Took them shopping if they needed to go. Stacy was a decent girl, not what he tried to make her out to be."

"Mr. Dance," said Kingsley, "we would like your permission to have her exhumed. I know that's painful to think about, but we need to have someone else look at her."

Dance was nodding his head as Ross spoke. "You do that. I want everybody to know that Stacy was a good girl."

"Mr. Dance," said Diane, "I would like to take a look at her room. Dr. Kingsley here said you left it as it was?"

He nodded. "I haven't touched it."

"I need to take a look," Diane said.

Harmon Dance nodded his head. "Do what you have to do."

"Examining her room can be a little destructive," said Diane. "I have fingerprint powders and—"

"Do whatever you have to do," he said again. "Whatever it takes." His chair creaked as he rocked in it.

Chapter 16

Diane opened the door to the garage apartment with the key Mr. Dance had given them. She reached around to the light switch on the inside wall and turned on the lights without stepping inside.

"Wow," said Kingsley softly. "The crime scene photo doesn't do this room justice."

"No," said Diane, "it doesn't."

Stacy's apartment was charming. There was an efficiency kitchenette in one corner with a small round oak table and four chairs. The living room held a love seat sofa, two stuffed chairs, and a coffee table. Her bedroom area was half hidden by curtains. The small bathroom was across from the bed. The walls were painted a light dusty rose. One wall was covered in matching shades of striped wallpaper. The curtains were a complementary pink, as were the pillows on the cream-colored sofa and chairs. She had découpaged her chest of drawers with prints from a book of rococo art. A vase of flowers in the middle of the dining table had dried out, the water evaporated.

Stacy had enjoyed her life. Diane saw it in the room. Everything was carefully chosen, pretty, much of it handmade.

Kingsley started to walk in, but Diane stopped him.

"Wait until I examine the floor," she said. Diane slipped covers over her shoes. "I'm closing the door. I'm afraid you'll have to stand out here until I clear you a place to stand. It'll take a while."

Kingsley nodded. "As Mr. Dance said, whatever it takes. I'll make some phone calls."

Diane left most of the crime scene kit outside and stepped

in, closed the door, and turned off the light. The room smelled like death. She set her crime lamp on the floor, turned it on, and squatted so she could see what it illuminated. She began systematically looking for shoe prints the low-angle light would show up. There were many. She began the painstaking process of lifting the prints from the floor with electrostatic film. Most of the prints would be from the police and the coroner's people who carried Stacy out, and most would be overlapping. But she might get lucky.

She cleared the floor around the door and let Kingsley come in out of the chilly air to stand inside in the dark.

"You'll get used to the smell," she said.

He made light conversation as she went from print to print, placing the Mylar-coated silver foil over each print, lifting it using static electricity, rolling up the film, and putting it in a tube.

Most of the shoe prints were on the hardwood floor around the bed where Stacy was found. But there were a few in other locations on the floor.

"I didn't realize this is such time-consuming work," said Kingsley.

"And we're still on the floor," said Diane. "We've got the furniture and ceiling to do."

"Ceiling? You expect to find something on the ceiling?" asked Kingsley.

"Expect it? No, but it's standard protocol to look. Could find some kind of spatter, for instance, that might give us critical information."

When Diane finished, she took the tubes of rolled-up film and put them in a carrying case beside the door. There was a gentle knock from outside.

"It's me, Boss. Can I come in?"

"Come on in, Jin," said Diane. "Carefully."

The door opened slowly and Jin stepped inside. He was holding his digital SLR camera, his newest toy.

"Hey, Boss, I finished outside. How's it going here?" he said.

"I'm starting with the black light," she told him.

"The ultraviolet light detects organic stains from body fluids such as blood, saliva, semen, and urine," Jin said to Kingsley.

They watched as Diane again systematically examined the floor.

"I can do that, Boss, and you can . . . ," Jin began.

Just as he started to speak Diane stopped. On the floor near the dining table, a large area luminesced.

"What is it?" asked Kingsley.

"Perhaps where she was killed," said Diane.

"What do you mean?" Kingsley said. "How do you know? She was strangled, wasn't she? Is that blood someone tried to clean up?"

"More likely urine and maybe feces that someone tried to clean up," said Diane. "Often during a death like Stacy's, the bladder and colon relax and evacuate. Murderers usually don't count on that."

"You want me to take the samples?" said Jin.

Diane nodded. "Get some shots of this first, and let me go over the rest of the room."

Jin took multiple photos of the luminesced image in rapid succession from several angles.

"Nice camera," said Kingsley.

"Yeah, you bet," said Jin, a big grin on his face. "Don't know what I ever did without it."

Diane worked her way around the small apartment and finished with the bed.

"There's very little on the bed. You would expect urine to be here if she died here," said Diane. "Particularly if she was left in an upright position for an extended period after death. Jin, go ahead and collect samples, photograph everything, and do the bathroom."

"Sure thing, Boss," he said.

Armed with evidence bags, Diane began a search of the apartment. She used the same systematic procedure she had used with the floor to make sure she covered every spot. Just under the bed she found the towel that was around Stacy's neck in the photo, along with the knotted rope that had been around her neck and anchored her to the bedpost. Evidently the coroner's people had cut it off and dropped it on the floor and it got kicked under the bed. She put the items in evidence bags.

Diane went around the room and searched the tops of dressers, tables, and door frames for prints. She lifted several. She enlisted Kingsley's help in searching all the drawers in the apartment for any items that might shed light on Stacy's life up until the time she died.

In a small desk Kingsley found a tablet of yellow legal-sized paper. It was about half used up. Perhaps Stacy used it for notes. Diane bagged it. They could bring out the indented impressions in the paper using the electrostatic detection apparatus at the lab and see at least what had been written on the page before it.

Diane and Kingsley searched the pockets of the clothes hanging in Stacy's closet and came up only with movie ticket stubs from several months before. They searched all the trash cans, the clothes hamper, and the kitchen cabinets. Diane felt under the drawers and tables for anything that might be taped under them. She looked behind the pictures on the walls. She slid photographs out of their frames and looked for anything Stacy might have stashed behind them.

It was almost dark when they finished. Kingsley gave the key back to Mr. Dance and they left for Rosewood.

"So you think she was murdered," said Ross Kingsley.

"A good possibility," said Diane. "I'll analyze the evidence when we get back to the lab."

"So, then, to find out who did it, you'll have to find out who framed the brother," said Jin. "Unless it was her boyfriend, or a girlfriend, or a member of her band, or a neighbor, or someone from her job. What was her job?"

"She was a student," said Diane, "and the next big thing we need to do is get the body exhumed and have a new autopsy."

"Whom can we get to do it? The autopsy, I mean," said Kingsley. "I have some funds I can use."

"Good," said Diane. "There is only so much you're going to be able to get for free."

"Did you find anything outside?" Diane asked Jin.

"I found a few cigarette butts at the side of the road nearest the steps to her apartment. I don't expect much from those. Most look too new. Could be from anybody before or since. I searched the wooded area in back of the house. Didn't find anything. Took a lot of pictures. But there is an empty house just beyond the woods. There are a lot of empty houses in the neighborhood. I kind of wanted to see if I could get in, but I figured you wouldn't want me to."

"I think if we find enough to get the police to reopen the case, they can call the GBI in to do a search," said Diane.

They stopped at the museum to drop Jin off. Diane had called ahead and a member of museum security was waiting at the door with a cart to transport the crime scene gear inside.

"I'll start analyzing the evidence for you, Boss," he said, unloading the crime scene equipment and a duffel bag filled with the bags of evidence they had collected.

"Do you have time?" she asked.

"I'll do it in my free time. We're doing good in the lab. Don't worry," he said. "Am I ever not on top of things?"

"I never worry about the DNA lab," said Diane. "Thanks, Jin."

"Sure thing, Boss. We'll have to do this again sometime. It was fun."

"Where to now?" said Kingsley. "Shall I take you home?"

Diane shook her head. "Let's arrange for a medical examiner. I have someone in mind." Diane made a call on her cell to see if it was a convenient time for a visit, and directed Kingsley to the home of Lynn Webber. She lived in an apartment complex close to the university.

"Hey," said Lynn when she answered the door. "This is a surprise. What are you doing in this area?" She looked at Ross Kingsley as Diane was about to introduce him. "I know you. You're the FBI profiler, aren't you? I worked on those hanging victims. That was just terrible."

"That's right," said Ross. "I'm not with the FBI anymore. I work for a private firm."

"Well, come in and tell me about it," she said.

Lynn Webber's home was clean, neat, and modern. There were a lot of white- and cream-colored fabrics, shiny chrome, crystal fixtures, and modern art.

Lynn was about five feet five, shorter than either Kingsley or Diane. She had short, shiny black hair that always looked as if it had been done at an expensive salon. Her eyes were dark and her smile bright. She wore turquoise silk slacks and a white silk shirt and silver jewelry. Many men who met her fell in love with her. Diane could see Kingsley found her interesting. But she wasn't particularly worried about him. Kingsley's wife, Lydia, was pretty interesting herself and more than a match for Lynn.

"Please sit down. You have me intrigued. Can I get you something to drink? I always have fresh coffee."

Diane and Kingsley accepted and had several sips of hot coffee before Diane began her request.

"By *intrigued*, what Lynn means is, what am I trying to get her involved in now?" said Diane. "She knows I have a habit of coming to her with, uh, interesting problems."

"Oh, dear, what are you up to?" said Lynn, smiling over her cup of coffee.

Diane let Kingsley explain his job at Darley, Dunn, and Upshaw. When he got to Stacy's file, which he had brought with him, Diane took over.

"I'd like you to look at the autopsy report and the photograph. It's the only one we have of her. If there were any autopsy photos of her, we don't have them," said Diane. She handed Lynn the photograph and the report.

Lynn examined them carefully for several minutes. "I see your concern," she said, tapping them with her polished fingernails.

"We have the father's permission to exhume her and were wondering if you would perform the second autopsy," said Diane. "I don't know the ME who did the first one, but I don't imagine he will be pleased."

"He won't," said Lynn. "I know Oran Doppelmeyer." She looked at Kingsley and then at Diane. "He won't be pleased at all, which, I'm so ashamed to say, is the main reason I'd be happy to do it."

Chapter 17

Both Ross Kingsley and Diane looked at Lynn Webber with raised eyebrows. Ross had his coffee cup halfway to his lips, about to drink the last sip. He held it there.

"There must be a story here," he said.

"There is. It's a two-cups-of-coffee story," said Lynn.

She poured them each another cup.

"About seven years ago, Doppelmeyer was the medical examiner in South Carolina and I was assistant ME to him. One evening I was called to the apartment of a young couple after neighbors heard a gunshot and alerted the police. She was on the couch, gun in hand, with a bullet entry wound in her right temple and a big exit wound in the left side of the head. It was messy. She had been dead only about fifteen minutes by the time I got there. She held the gun so tight in her hand, it took me and two paramedics to pry it loose.

"The neighbors said she and her husband had been arguing. The arguing stopped. A few minutes later there was the gunshot. The husband was an accountant and said he left the apartment following the argument and went to his office to work. That's where the police found him."

She took a sip of coffee and set down her cup, almost spilling it on the glass coffee table.

"I did the autopsy, determined the manner of death to be suicide, and released the coroner's report. Well, you would have thought I had just given national secrets to the Russians. What I didn't know, but wouldn't have changed anything if I had been aware, was that her parents were well connected. They hated the son-in-law and were convinced he shot her and left her there with her brains spattered all over the white couch they had given the couple. The district attorney liked that story better than mine and he had the police arrest the young man."

Diane and Ross were quiet during her story, Diane because she knew Lynn and knew better than to interrupt her with questions, and Kingsley because he was enjoying watching her tell it. Lynn also talked with her hands and was quite animated.

"To make a very long story a little shorter," she said, "Doppelmeyer changed my report to say the manner of death was homicide. It went to trial and the defense called me. I testified that it was suicide. I explained about cadaver spasm and how we had to pry, with great difficulty, the gun from her hand. The prosecution, the family, and Doppelmeyer all came down hard on me. Doppelmeyer took the stand and told the jury I was incompetent and he had to constantly check my work—a blatant lie. He told them that what I called cadaver spasm was simply early onset of rigor mortis and the rigor caused her to hold on to the gun that her husband had placed there. He intimated that I had been out drinking before I got the call—I had been out to dinner, but not drinking. It was just awful. I was fired. Me, fired!" She frowned and shook her head.

Diane half expected her to stamp her foot.

"The poor husband was sent to prison. He did get out three years later because the prosecution had made several other errors in the trial and the defense attorney gave the new prosecutor a ton of information about cadaver spasm. But you know, there are people in South Carolina today who think that poor fella killed his wife."

Lynn's cheeks had turned pink during the telling of the story. Diane could see it still stung.

"I can tell you this," said Lynn. "I'm willing to bet that when Doppelmeyer saw this photograph, he made up his mind this girl was trash. Not only is he a pig, he is a self-righteous pig."

"That is a terrible story," said Diane.

"It is, isn't it?" said Lynn. "My parents wanted me to leave forensics and become a pediatrician. I told them no one was going to bring their children to me with this cloud over my head. I got a job in Atlanta, where I built my reputation back up. Let me tell you, that's why, when I go to court now, I have every kind of documentation you can think of."

"So," said Kingsley, "you aren't going to mind the fallout caused by a redo of his autopsy?"

"Mind?" said Lynn. "Honey, I welcome the fallout. I'm older now and have had a lot more experience in court."

Diane called Frank to tell him she was on her way home. He said he was ordering Chinese and to ask Kingsley to stay for dinner. The delivery arrived at the same time she and Ross pulled into the drive. Ross waylaid the delivery man and paid for the food.

"You didn't have to do that," said Diane.

"Oh, it's one of the perks of your being my consultant," he said, and they carried it inside.

"Ah, it's good to eat," said Kingsley, sitting down at the table. "Sometimes when I'm working, I tend to forget to eat." After a few bites and a drink of hot tea, he said, "Lynn Webber likes to have her ego stroked a bit, doesn't she? I noticed that you're a little shameless at it." Ross grinned at Diane as he helped himself to some sweet and sour chicken.

"She does good work, she's not afraid of politics, and she's honest," said Diane. "She also is good to her dieners. Yes, she likes people to notice her work. It's a small price to pay." Diane smiled back at him. Lynn was also supersensitive to even the most gentle slight, but Diane didn't mention that.

"So, is she going to be reliable?" Kingsley asked.

"Yes, she'll be fine," said Diane.

"She seemed a little too eager to give Doppelmeyer the shaft," said Kingsley.

"I'm sure she is very eager, but she won't lie, nor will she exaggerate. What you will get is more corroborating information than you will know what to do with—and plenty of photographs. Of course, you realize her findings could agree with Doppelmeyer's. In which case, Lynn will be very disappointed, but she won't fudge the data," Diane assured him.

"I got the impression she can be vindictive," said Kingsley.

Diane nodded. "Perhaps. But as I said, she won't lie. And

she won't get caught putting dead rotting fish under his house or frozen shrimp in his curtain rods."

Kingsley put a hand over his mouth to keep from laughing and spraying his hot tea. "Touché," he said, when he was able to talk.

Frank rolled his eyes.

"Today was a fruitful day," Kingsley said. "I knew it was a good idea to ask for your help."

"I'll process the evidence we collected, but you'll have to interview the army of possible suspects Jin pointed out," said Diane.

"Perhaps the evidence will point us in a direction," said Kingsley.

"Hopefully, the evidence and the new autopsy will give you enough ammunition to get the lead detective to reopen the case," said Frank. "I've heard of the detective you said handled the case. He's a little lazy and pigheaded, but I don't think he is dishonest."

"For the father's sake, I'm hoping the solution will clear Ryan Dance of the murder that seems to have started this whole chain of events," said Kingsley.

"Maybe you need to start retracing the steps of the young woman, Stacy," said Frank. "If she was trying to clear her brother, she probably talked to the witnesses and to the family of the victim. They might point you in the right direction."

"Oh," said Diane, "I just had a terrible thought. From what you said, Ellie Carruthers' family were certain it was Ryan Dance who killed their daughter. What if they were afraid Stacy might be successful in getting Ryan released from prison? They still think he's guilty. It would be awful if it was someone in Ellie's family who killed Stacy to stop her."

"That's an unpleasant thought," said Kingsley, frowning. "I hope it's not that."

"There's going to be some blowback with the new autopsy," said Diane. "Is that going to be a problem with your employers?"

"No. The firm handles blowback. It's usually good publicity. It shows potential clients that when we take a case, things get done. I think my bosses will like it. The more, the better. Our biggest clientele is defense attorneys." Kingsley took another helping of sweet and sour chicken and rice. "So, what's the thing with Jin's technicians?"

Diane and Frank chuckled.

"As you heard, they're identical twins and a bit eccentric," said Diane, "and big Elvis fans. They're also very detail oriented. Their reputation for accuracy was the reason Jin hired them—and the fact that they work very efficiently together. Jin's extremely picky where the DNA lab is concerned."

"Do they really dress like Elvis?" asked Kingsley.

"Not exactly," said Diane. "If you saw them, you wouldn't say to yourself, 'Those guys are dressed like Elvis.' You might think they look like they would make good Elvis impersonators. They're more subtle than Jin portrayed them. I think the main reason they drive him crazy is they are constantly telling him how he could improve the efficiency of the DNA lab, and Jin doesn't like anybody trying to step into his shoes."

"Ah," said Kingsley. "I see."

Kingsley left not long after dinner. Diane promised to get him a report on the evidence as soon as she could.

"He seemed very pleased," said Frank after they had cleared the table and put away the food. Diane poured Frank and herself each a glass of wine.

"It was very sad, but it went well. We'll see how it goes from here. How was your day?"

He slipped his arms around her waist and danced her a few steps around the living room floor. "My day was fine. But why don't we leave the topic of crime aside for the rest of the evening?"

Diane spent most of the next day working at the museum. She heard from Kingsley midday that the exhumation of the body of Stacy Dance was scheduled for the following day. Diane was about to go home when Andie forwarded a phone call to her.

"Hello, this is Archaeo-Labs," said a voice. "We've been trying to get in touch with Dr. Marcella Payden without success. Your number is a backup number she has in her file."

"Yes, Dr. Payden works here. I'm Diane Fallon, director of the RiverTrail Museum. How can I help you?"

"She uses our labs to identify species-specific protein antigens in bone-tempered pottery sherds."

"Yes," said Diane. "I'm familiar with her work on Texas pottery."

"Well, she sent us some pieces from Georgia. Actually, she said it wasn't archaeological, but relatively modern. And as in the archaeological samples, she wanted to know the species of animal used in the pottery. To tell you the truth, we don't quite know how to proceed."

"How do you mean?" asked Diane. "You don't do analysis of modern samples? I'm not sure I understand."

"No, it's not that. We did the identification, but . . . well . . . the protein antigen is human."

Chapter 18

Diane was dumbstruck for a moment. The caller must have thought she would be, because he waited patiently on the other end.

"Human?" said Diane. "Did she give you any information about where in Georgia they came from?" But Diane knew. Marcella dug them up in her yard.

"No," he said. "She just labeled them *Georgia*."

"I'm sorry, I didn't get your name." said Diane.

"Oh, I'm Justin Ambrogi. I'm the technician who runs the samples in the lab." He cleared his throat. "What I'm wondering is, that is, some of my coworkers think the sherds, because of the human bone in them, constitute a body—legally, that is—and must be reported. I suppose it could be old bones that were used, but don't the laws about the use of humans and their body parts apply to ancient ones too?"

"Yes, they do," said Diane. "You couldn't have known, but in addition to being director of the museum, I'm also director of the crime lab here in Rosewood, Georgia, and those items will fall under our jurisdiction, at least until we sort out exactly where they came from."

"Well, this is convenient, then. I called the right place," Justin said.

"Yes, you did. I'll also give you the name of a Rosewood police detective you can send a copy of the test results to. That way, your lab can be assured you followed proper protocol," said Diane.

"Yes. Thank you. To tell you the truth, we ran the tests several times. The first time we thought it had to be an error."

"I can see why it would give you pause," said Diane. She fished in her purse and pulled out Detective Hanks' card and read off his name and address.

Diane gave Justin her fax number so he could send her the report directly. She thanked him and put the phone back in its cradle.

"Okay," she whispered, "that was odd."

She picked up the phone and called Detective Hanks.

"I got an interesting call from a lab in Arizona," she said.

"Oh? What about?" he asked.

She first explained to him about Marcella's expertise in North American aboriginal pottery. Then she explained about the bone-tempered pottery of the late-prehistoric sites in Texas that Marcella had studied. She explained that Marcella had used a lab in Arizona to analyze protein antigens in the pottery samples to find out what species of animal contributed their bone to the pottery. She debated whether to explain why archaeologists wanted that data, but decided that would be too much information.

"She sent them some pottery sherds she found in Georgia. I'm assuming at her place, but the lab didn't know specifically where the sherds were found. When they ran their test, it came up with human antigens," she said.

Just as she had, Hanks remained quiet for a long moment. She assumed he was trying to figure how the heck to process that bit of information.

"She sent them pieces of broken pots that had human bone crushed up in them? Who would do that?" he asked.

"Pottery made in the late-prehistoric period had a tempering substance added to the clay to keep air bubbles out and keep it from breaking while it was being fired. The additive was usually grit, fiber, shells—stuff like that. Some peoples in Texas used animal bone. Marcella apparently found some pottery sherds in her yard and recognized from their appearance that they were bone tempered. Her daughter said that whoever the artist was who lived in the house at one time was a potter, according to Marcella, and used methods similar to the ones used by prehistoric Indians." Diane was wondering if she was making any sense at all to Hanks.

"Okay, this is now officially the weirdest case I've ever worked on. I confess, I don't know what to make of this new information. Were the pots made by the person who lived in the house immediately before Dr. Payden?"

"I don't think so. The potter's shed had fallen into disuse. But I don't know how long the house sat empty, or the line of ownership of the house, or who lived there before Marcella."

"I can get ownership records from the county courthouse," he said. "We can probably track down some answers about who lived there when. But does this new stuff help us in any way?"

"I have no idea," said Diane. "It doesn't appear that any pottery was made there in recent years before Marcella moved in. It would seem to be too long ago to be involved in what happened to Marcella, but who knows? At any rate, I asked Justin Ambrogi at Archaeo-Labs in Arizona to send you the report. He also faxed a copy to the museum."

"The museum?" said Hanks.

"Yes, Marcella works for us doing pottery sherd analysis."

"Oh, yeah, that's right. What a twisted case this is. I'm inclined to think this bone pottery thing, although an odd thing for sure, is not related to her attack. But like you said, who knows? We may be looking for a frustrated artist. A mad potter."

Diane laughed. "Perhaps," she said.

She hung up the phone and stood thinking for a moment. It was a bit of information she didn't know where to put. After a moment, Andie stuck her head in and said goodbye.

"Bye, Andie. See you tomorrow."

Diane gathered her things together and started for the crime lab, hoping her crew would be there and not out somewhere working on a murder. Halfway there, she got an idea and took the elevator down to the basement where the DNA lab was located.

Jin was there. So were the twins, Hector and Scott Spearman. They were dressed in jeans and pin-striped shirts with pointed collar flaps open at the neck, revealing gold chains. Hector's shirt was yellow and Scott's was green. She knew it was Hector because Hector was the older twin and he always wore a shirt color with a higher wavelength than Scott.

Hector and Scott started talking immediately. They always appeared as if they were never let out of the lab and had to jump at any opportunity to talk with anyone other than Jin.

"Hello, Dr. Fallon," said Scott. "We were just discussing . . ."

"The merits of using junk DNA . . . ," said Hector.

"For ancestry testing," said Scott.

When they were excited they spoke in that alternating way. She thought she might actually get dizzy listening to them, moving her head from one to the other. She understood how it might drive Jin crazy on occasion. They expounded on the disadvantages of using particular strands of DNA often referred to as "junk" because they no longer seemed to serve an active purpose.

"I'm sure Dr. Fallon didn't come down here for that," said Jin. "What's up, Boss?"

"I was wondering if you could analyze the DNA in pieces of pottery," said Diane.

That stopped the three of them. They stood for several moments just staring at her with completely blank expressions.

Finally Hector spoke. "It has to be something that was alive."

Diane laughed. "I'm sorry, I started in the middle of a thought." She laughed again. "The pieces of pottery were tempered with human bone."

"Who would do that?" said Jin.

"And why?" asked Scott.

Diane gave a minilecture on what little she knew of pottery making, similar to the spiel she gave Hanks.

"I honestly don't know why the aboriginal inhabitants in Texas used bone for tempering. Nor do I know why the person who once inhabited Marcella's house did. But do you think you could get any usable DNA out of it?" asked Diane.

"The firing would have destroyed any DNA," said Jin.

"They were fired in a bonfire kiln, which has a much lower temperature than a regular kiln," she said. "I know it's still a high temperature, but I was just wondering."

"You know," said Scott, "if the bases of the pots were thick—wouldn't they have to be thicker than the sides?" He shrugged. "Anyway, if we could find some very thick pieces that just happened to be at a place in the fire where the temperature was lower . . . like sitting on the ground . . . I'm just thinking here."

"Yes," said Hector, "perhaps the thick pieces might contain some strands that survived. Of course we would have . . ."

"To use Jin's protocol for shed hair," said Scott.

They looked at Jin.

"What do you think?" Diane asked Jin.

"It never hurts to try, but I don't really hold out any hope. But we may get a paper out of it." He grinned. So did Hector and Scott.

"I'll send you some samples," said Diane. "Thank you."

"By the way," said Jin, "I've done some analysis on our evidence. That large stain on the floor near the table was a combination of urine and feces, just as you said. Probably the spot where she died."

Diane nodded. "Thanks, Jin."

She left them and rode the elevator up to the third floor and walked over to the crime lab.

Neva, David, and Izzy were there. They were getting a lecture on handwriting analysis from a member of the museum archives staff. The sample under discussion was the writing on the back of Marcella's desk drawer.

Chapter 19

"I personally think that you can't tell much about what slant means in the young," Lawrence Michaels, one of the museum's archivists and their only handwriting expert, was saying when Diane walked into the dimly lit lab. "Children, especially early teenage girls, experiment with different handwriting on a whim—for fun. However, in the adult . . . Ah, Dr. Fallon. Good to see you. I was just explaining that I get a bit of mixed messages from the handwriting on the desk drawer."

Michaels was a middle-aged man with striking silver hair. He always dressed in a suit and tie, clothes he apparently found comfortable. Occasionally he wore a bow tie, which Diane thought gave him an entirely different persona. Today he had on a dark brown suit, a light pink shirt with a tie that was a dark shade of pink decorated with small brown fleurs de lis. Diane pulled up a chair and sat down beside David.

"This is a woman's hand," Michaels continued. "She is intelligent and creative—as suggested by the rounded *w* and the one *u*. These coiled shapes and counterstrokes that curve in what we might call the wrong way, suggest a self-centeredness. The closed *a*'s and *o*'s suggest that she is hiding something."

He indicated each of the characteristics with a laser pointer that jumped quickly from character to character, making lightning zigzags of neon red on the dry-erase board where he had projected the image of the note.

"The characters are largest in the middle zone—the ascenders and descenders don't go much above or below the baseline. This suggests immaturity—could be young at heart. Immaturity doesn't always have to be a bad thing. The way the letters slant in different directions is a little disturbing. Bottom line, I'm not really sure what you have here. Perhaps an intelligent, creative, selfish, and childishly disturbed woman with something to hide. Or maybe not. This isn't an exact science. I hope this helps." He grinned at his audience.

"No offense," said Izzy, "but I could have gotten most of that from the words she wrote. What adult, but a disturbed one, writes a message like that on the bottom of a drawer? Who did she expect would find it?"

Michaels shrugged. "The handwriting is consistent with the message. I can say that," he said.

"Thank you, Dr. Michaels," said Diane. "Quite possibly, it does help. What would really help," Diane said to all of them, "is if we could get an approximate date for when the message was written."

"Okay," said Michaels. "There is one other thing. See the double *s* in the word *missing*—how the first *s* is like an *f*, only backward? That's the way kids were taught to write about a hundred years or so ago. That's called a leading *s* because it is the first *s* in the sequence."

"Now, see," said Izzy. "That's helpful. You should have said that right off."

"Sorry," Michaels said, grinning. He dusted off his hands as if he had been using chalk instead of a laser pointer.

"Well, I think it's neat," said Neva. "Thanks, Dr. Michaels."

Neva escorted Lawrence Michaels to the door that was the threshold between the dark side, the crime lab, and the museum proper.

"I couldn't help but notice," David said to Diane when Neva returned, "that you said that quite possibly it does help. What is it you know?"

The others looked at David in surprise. Apparently they hadn't taken note of what Diane said.

Diane explained about the phone call from the lab in Arizona and what they had discovered about the sherds Marcella sent them. "I don't know that those were sherds she found in her yard, but for now, let's suppose they were."

"Okay," said Izzy. "That's a sign of a disturbed person.

Crushing up human bones to make pots? It's downright spooky. Maybe the handwriting guy had something after all."

"Yeah," said Neva. "We have a creatively disturbed, immature woman—writing a secret message on the bottom of drawers doesn't seem to be a sign of maturity. I think we ought to find out who she is."

"What we need," said Diane, "is a list of all the people who ever lived in the house. We can start with ownership records."

"That ought to be easy," said Neva. "I'll go down to the courthouse and do a search."

"Hanks mentioned that he would do it, but if we do it, it will save him time. I don't think this is a high priority with him, and it shouldn't be. It's unlikely to be related to what happened to Marcella."

"Except," said David, "they did steal objets d'art."

Diane nodded. "The paintings they took were hidden in the wall for no telling how long. Even though the pottery they stole was Marcella's own work, the thieves may not have known that."

Neva rubbed her hands together. "I like this."

David rolled his eyes. "She's become Nancy Drew. You know we solve crimes all the time, don't you?"

"I like this old stuff," she said. "It's interesting. I can see the attraction to archaeology—lots of old mysteries there."

"Okay, then," said David. "Like Diane said, the thing we need to find out is how old the note is, and how old the pottery is."

"I'll go down to the courthouse first thing and search the property records," said Neva.

Izzy stood, hitching up his pants as he stretched and yawned. "Tell you what, Neva, next time you decide to have a speaker, let me know so I can maybe sleep in or go wash my car."

"You didn't find that fascinating?" said Neva.

"I think it's voodoo," said Izzy. "It's like them profilers. I don't buy them either. Have you ever heard them?"

Diane smiled to herself.

"I noticed you didn't give him a sample of your handwriting," said Neva.

"Yeah, well, like I was going to let him say a bunch of gobbledygook about me and have you guys never let me live it down. I'm smarter than that." Izzy grinned at Neva.

Diane noticed that Izzy smiled and even laughed more and more since he had started to work with them. His good friend Frank Duncan had noticed it too. The crime lab had been good for Izzy—oddly enough—even with all the death they dealt with. It was catching the evildoers with proof of their evil deeds that did it for him. Izzy's son had been killed in a meth lab explosion. Not a meth lab of his making, but he and thirty fellow students died not knowing that someone was cooking meth in the basement of the house they were partying in. It wasn't fair and it hurt Izzy to the core. Izzy needed to do something that worked, something that he could see would put bad people in prison. He decided that maybe the crime lab would be that place where he could make a difference. So he eased his way in. So far it seemed to be working for him and for the crime lab.

"I'm going home, folks. See you tomorrow," Izzy said.

"I'm going home too," said Diane. "You guys do the same."

It was dark when Diane got in her SUV. She drove home thinking about Harmon Dance. His daughter was exhumed today. She wondered whether it was just more pain, or a relief that he might find out something better than what he had been trying to live with. Lynn Webber would probably carry out the autopsy right away. They might know something tomorrow.

Diane drove home to Frank's house. It had taken a while for her to call it home. In the beginning, it was a temporary arrangement until she found a house of her own. It turned out to be more comfortable than she thought it would be, and a lot easier than her apartment with her bizarre neighbors had been. Of course, they all thought she was the bizarre one. It was why they asked her to move. She couldn't blame them. There was an awful lot of havoc surrounding her when she lived there. Not so much at Frank's. Perhaps it was because he was there. She was not alone. She was not as easy a target.

Diane pulled into the drive. The lights were on in the house, but Frank's car wasn't there. The lights were controlled by a timer so that it always looked like they were home in the evening. She walked up to the steps just as a car pulled in behind hers. It startled her for a moment. She turned the key in the lock, ready to bolt inside if she had to. The headlights went out and she heard a car door open.

"Hi, Dr. Fallon. I hope I'm not disturbing you. It's Mark Tsosie. Jonas told me how to find your house. I was going to call when I got close, but with my cell phone I couldn't get service until I was in your drive. I wanted to talk to you about the police here, if you think they are doing everything—"

Diane's phone rang.

"Excuse me a moment," she said.

She pulled the cell phone out of her pocket and answered it, listened a moment, said a few words, and flipped it closed.

"That was Paloma," said Diane. "Marcella is awake. We can talk on the way there."

Chapter 20

Marcella lay so still in bed, it scared Diane. Her skin was almost as pale as her pillow. Her head had been shaved and bandaged. There were dark circles under her eyes. Diane glanced at the monitor beside her bed. It was calming to see the iconic heart flash with the steady beat of Marcella's pulse.

Paloma said her mother didn't remember anything about the day of the attack. She didn't even know why she was in the hospital. She did remember she wanted to speak with Diane. The original need to speak with Diane obviously occurred a day or more before Marcella was attacked.

Diane pulled up a chair by her bed. The nurse told Diane she had five minutes for the visit, no more.

"Hello, Marcella. It's good to see you awake," said Diane.

Marcella opened her eyes. "Strange," she whispered.

"What is strange?" asked Diane.

Marcella moved her eyes to Diane. "Desk," she whispered.

"We've seen the desk. The writing on the back of the drawer," said Diane.

Marcella nodded. The movement of her head was barely perceptible. "The pottery. Bone."

"Yes. Is that the pottery that was in your workroom?" said Diane.

"Yes. Sent samples," she said.

"The lab called," said Diane.

"What?" asked Marcella.

Diane didn't quite know what to do. She knew Marcella

was asking what species, but she was afraid the answer would be too disturbing.

"Species," whispered Marcella. It came out as almost a command, even in her quiet voice.

"*Homo sapiens*," said Diane. Somehow the genus and species designation seemed more academic and less disturbing than calling it human.

Marcella closed her eyes for several moments.

"Strange. Look in pitcher."

"The ones that were hanging in the living room?" asked Diane.

Marcella closed her eyes again and shook her head. "No. Pitcher. Water. Face."

"The piece of pottery you were gluing back together?" said Diane.

"Yes. Examine?" she said.

"Have I examined it?" asked Diane. "No. I packed up your work and took it to your office in the museum."

"Good. Examine face inside," she said.

"Look at the back of the face?" said Diane.

"Yes. Strange. Sherds too. Look at them," Marcella said.

"You need to leave," said the critical care nurse who had hovered nearby during what had to be a weird conversation.

Diane smiled at Marcella, squeezed her hand, and stood up. "I'll come back," she told Marcella. "Get better."

Marcella smiled faintly and nodded.

Diane started out the door and Marcella called behind her. She barely heard her.

"Artist," she said, and she drifted off.

Diane looked at the monitor of the vital signs. Everything was still steady and regular. She left the room.

"She seems to be doing well," Diane said.

Paloma and Mark stood with Jonas, who had come while she was with Marcella. He looked as anxious as Marcella's daughter.

"The doctor said he is hopeful," said Paloma.

Diane wondered whether she knew she was wringing her hands.

"She made a lot of sense when she spoke to me," Paloma said. She looked at Diane and Diane could see that Paloma desperately wanted her to agree.

"She did," said Diane. "She was weak, but we managed to carry on a conversation. She gave me instructions."

Paloma smiled and looked at Mark.

"See." He hugged her. "You see. I told you she was going to be fine."

"Jonas. I'd like you to help me look at some of her work tomorrow," said Diane.

"Be glad to, but surely she doesn't want to work on her sherds?" he said. His expression said that kind of dedication to work would be going beyond reason.

"No. She wants me to see something she found," said Diane. "The desk was one of the things that concerned her, but the sherds she was gluing together are another."

Diane decided not to mention that the pottery Marcella was finding around her home was bone tempered. She remembered she hadn't told them about the desk either. She would put that off. They didn't need to have on their minds what it all might mean.

"Does this stuff she wants you to look at have anything to do with what happened to her?" asked Paloma.

"I don't know," said Diane. "I wouldn't think so, but it was something that seemed to concern her. Most of Marcella's side of the conversation was one or two words."

Paloma nodded. "That's the way it was with us. Still, she made sense."

That was a concern for Paloma, Diane could see—that her mother would still have her brain function and that she would still be her mother.

"Yes, she did," Diane agreed. "She seems very coherent."

Mark drove Diane home. She hated for him to leave Paloma in the hospital, but they both seemed better now that Marcella was awake.

Frank's car was in the drive when Diane arrived. She said good-bye to Mark and went into the house. She was too tired to eat much. She drank a handheld soup and took a warm shower. When she came out she lay on the bed and Frank massaged her back—something he did very well. She was enjoying his hands on her bare skin when the phone rang.

"Don't answer it," she said.

Frank did anyway. "She's here," he said, and handed the phone to her.

She turned her head and made a face at him. He grinned and continued stroking her back.

"Diane, I thought we were beginning to have a good working relationship."

"Detective Hanks?" she said. "I thought we were too." *So why are you calling me this late?* she thought. "What's up?"

"Why didn't you call me when Marcella Payden woke up?" he asked.

"I thought you had left word with the hospital to call you. I assumed you were informed." *It's not my job to inform you*, she thought.

Her muscles must have tensed, for Frank increased the pressure on her back, kneading her muscles with his fingers.

"If I had been thinking, I would have called," she said. "But I've had a long day and was tired." Making efforts to soothe over Hanks' hurt feelings was a lot easier when Frank was there to rub her back.

"What did she say? The doctor wouldn't let me in until tomorrow," Hanks said. "Her daughter told me that Dr. Payden didn't remember anything about the attack."

"She was concerned about the pieces of pottery she'd found on her property. As we figured, she recognized they were bone tempered. Marcella was letting me know she had sent samples off for analysis. She also wanted to tell me about the desk. I told her I'd seen the message. Marcella told me to examine the pottery myself, but she didn't say what I was to be looking for. Her side of the conversation was mostly just one or two words at a time."

"Do you think this pottery business has anything to do with her attack?" asked Hanks.

"I don't know," said Diane. "I wanted to ask her how old she thought the pottery was, but she was very weak and not up to it. Her nurse ran me out."

"I suppose she has no idea who attacked her, or why?" said Hanks.

"She didn't even know why she was in the hospital. Tomorrow when you speak with her she may be more clearheaded. But she probably will never remember the events surrounding her attack."

Hanks seemed mollified when Diane hung up. She was

trying to keep a good working relationship with the police and detectives, but sometimes they didn't make it easy.

She turned over to face Frank. "No more answering the phone."

"Absolutely not," he said.

Next morning, Diane met Jonas in his museum office. Together they pulled out the boxes from Marcella's that Diane had packed. She gently took the ceramic mask out and set it on the desk facedown, cushioning it with batting. She twisted Marcella's work lamp over the piece of pottery and began examining the back side with a magnifying glass. She saw immediately what had disturbed Marcella. She turned the mask over and looked at the front.

"What?" said Jonas, who had pulled up a chair beside her.

Diane turned the mask over and looked again. "Marcella told me to look at the sherds with it too. We need to pull out the other boxes. Damn."

Chapter 21

"What are you seeing?" said Jonas, bending over and peering at the mask.

"The inside of the mask has the imprint of eyelashes, eyebrows, blemishes. This was made on a human face," said Diane.

"That's not really all that unusual," said Jonas. "Why is that a big deal?"

Diane turned the face around. "The nose and mouth area is solid, no breathing holes. I know they could have been sculpted shut afterward, but Marcella would have realized that too. There was some other reason she wanted me to look at this. She also said to look at pieces she hadn't put together yet."

"Are you saying this might be a death mask?" said Jonas. He put his hands on his hips and looked at her with a great deal of skepticism. "You know, she may have just been worried about preserving her work. Marcella is very dedicated."

"I know she is, and I'm not saying this is a death mask. I'm just saying Marcella wanted me to take a look," said Diane. "If she were concerned only that her work was being cared for, she would not have asked me to take a look. I know nothing about pottery. I do know about other things, and I believe that's why she wanted me to look at it."

Diane began pulling out all the boxes that held the pieces she assumed belonged with the mask. Jonas helped her clear space in the office to work, piling some of Marcella's books and papers on the floor beside her desk.

"I called it a mask," said Diane, "but according to

her notes, Marcella thinks the piece might be a stylized pitcher—the liquid would be poured out of the eyes. Not a functional use, I imagine."

"But interesting symbolism," commented Jonas. "Especially if . . ." He let the sentence hang.

Diane carefully lifted out the potsherds still resting on their backing of paper.

"These single pieces were surrounding the face in the sandbox on her worktable. Marcella placed them on this paper and drew an outline around each piece. Presumably they are all part of the same set," she said, looking at Jonas.

"Okay, let's see what we have here," said Jonas. "She'd have sorted and examined all of them first. You may find more information in her computer. She has a pretty sophisticated three-dimensional program she uses to assist in reconstructing pots."

"Do you know how to use the program?" asked Diane.

"You want me to take a look?" he said.

"Would you?"

"Sure," he agreed. "I imagine you guys have one similar to it up there." He looked up with his eyes, indicating the crime lab on the floor above.

"I have one in the osteology lab for skull reconstruction," Diane said.

As she conversed with Jonas about the merits of computer programs, Diane examined the sherds. A few had imprints reflecting irregularities similar to what might appear on the back of a shaved human head.

In the second sample she unpacked were three pieces that immediately caught her eye—broken fragments, each with a protrusion. She picked them up and examined them and then fit them together. Diane had made many casts of skulls for her forensic cases and she recognized what she was looking at—the cast of a sharp-force-trauma wound.

"Well, damn. This is what Marcella was concerned about." Diane showed it to Jonas and explained what it was.

He examined the piece under the light and with the microscope, then stood up. "This is terrible, just terrible. Couldn't it be something else?" he said.

"I don't know. Maybe," said Diane. She looked at all the

broken pieces laid out on the table. "It looks like the potter sculpted the clay around a head. How did he get it off?"

"Cut it in half," said Jonas. "Artists sculpting in clay will often create a work, then cut it in half so they can scoop out the center clay. Thick pieces of clay tend to blow up or crack in the kiln, so they scoop out the inside to make it hollow and then they put the pieces back together and sculpt over the seam. This artist could have sculpted the clay around the head to get the form he wanted, then cut the clay into pieces to remove it from the head, and then put the pieces back together to make the piece whole again."

"I see why this was on her mind," said Diane, almost to herself. "It may not be involved in what happened to her, but it still needs to be looked into."

As Diane was leaving the hospital room, Marcella had said the word *artist*. Diane assumed she meant "Find the artist." She wondered now if Marcella meant she had already found the artist? Could these pieces be younger than they thought? She would get Hanks to ask Marcella.

"Do you think you could reconstruct the whole pot—pitcher—whatever it is?" she asked.

"Sure," he said.

"First, let me take some photographs," said Diane.

She studied the face again. Even up close and even speckled with the bone inclusions, it was a beautiful face. She traced her finger along the curve of the lips and chin. The clay represented the elastic skin of youth, nothing sagging, nothing lined.

"I asked Jin to try to extract DNA from the bone in the pottery fragments. Hector and Scott suggested some strands might have survived in a very thick piece of the pottery. Could you select a piece that can be destroyed and is thick?" asked Diane.

"I can, but a bonfire kiln heats up to about thirteen hundred degrees Fahrenheit. Can DNA withstand that kind of heat?" asked Jonas.

"No, it can't. I'd probably just be wasting their time," she said.

"What exactly did they have in mind, if you don't mind my asking?" said Jonas.

"They were hoping we might luck up and get a piece that

was in a cooler place in the fire, and look to see if any DNA strands in the middle of the fragment were protected. They were going to use a protocol some friends of Jin worked out for analyzing the DNA of shed hair."

"I didn't think shed hair had DNA," said Jonas.

"It has such a small amount that it gets destroyed using traditional methods of extracting DNA. There's a method in which processing takes place on the slide that can save what little DNA exists. It would be a long shot anyway, but if bonfires get that hot, there would be no place cool enough for DNA to survive," said Diane.

"Might be worth a try anyway," said Jonas. "You know, in case it does work."

"I'll put it to them and let Jin and his crew make the decision," said Diane.

"How are the Elvi working out?" asked Jonas, grinning broadly.

"Their work is very good." Diane smiled back.

"I think they are a hoot. I've talked with them. They aren't nearly as far-out as they put on."

"I sort of suspected that," said Diane. "You know the thing about the shirts, don't you?"

"Color wavelength," said Jonas. "They're just showing off—making everything a puzzle. They're kids really. Of course, most of the people around here are kids to me. You're a kid to me."

Diane laughed.

"Tell me, can we find out how old these pottery sherds are? How did Marcella know they are modern?"

"Context, for one. She found them in a pit mixed with bottles and cans. The cans were pretty well rusted out. The bottles were dated to the fifties," said Jonas.

"Context? Is that it?" asked Diane. "Couldn't this be much older and have gotten mixed in somehow?"

"No evidence of any mechanism for strata getting mixed. Remember, the pottery sherds she found were of pots she could put back together. All the pieces were there. They were probably broken in situ. Also, we pretty well know all the prehistoric ceramics. Even something this unusual in Georgia would have been known long before now."

"Really, nothing left to discover?" said Diane.

"I didn't say there is nothing left to discover, but we're not going to find any lost civilization of bone-tempered face-pot people. It's like mounds," said Jonas. "People are always telling me they have an Indian mound in their field, and I tell them no, they don't. We know where all of them are. What I'm trying to say is that we know an awful lot about the prehistory of Georgia. Yes, we still have questions, but none so profound as lost civilizations of mad potters."

Diane smiled. "That's what Hanks called this unknown artist—a mad potter."

"He did, did he? Then I guess he isn't completely off his rocker," said Jonas.

"So you think these pieces date from the fifties?" said Diane.

"I think so. I didn't help excavate, and she hasn't said a lot about them. I didn't know they were bone tempered, for instance. She just mentioned to me the context she found them in."

Diane used the phone on the desk to call David and asked him to come down and photograph the sherds and the face when he had free time. She briefly explained to him what she had discovered.

"I need some high-contrast pictures," said Diane. "I need to see the topography of the sherds."

"Sure thing," he said. "Spooky case."

"No kidding," said Diane. "If you could hook up Marcella's computer, that would be helpful too. The one we found in the house."

She hung up the phone and turned to Jonas. "I appreciate your help in this."

"We should all get a chance to work on the dark side. Lawrence Michaels is just all tickled to have been asked to lecture on the other side." Jonas laughed.

"I need to give everyone in the museum a tour of the crime lab so they won't think it is so mysterious."

"It won't help. What you do there is mysterious by definition," said Jonas.

Diane shook her head and sighed. "I'm going up to call Hanks. I need to keep him apprised of the latest developments. He's going to love this one."

Diane left Jonas working in Marcella's office. She didn't get up to her own office as quickly as she would have liked. Too many people stopped her to ask questions. Docents stopped her to introduce her to the group they were giving a tour to. She happened across one of the curators, who wanted to know the status of a requisition. Diane did eventually make it to her office, but not to her phone. Ross Kingsley was waiting for her.

"I thought we could go interview some of the people Stacy Dance talked with during her investigation," he said.

"Sure," said Diane. She could call Hanks on the way.

She turned to Andie, who sat behind her desk putting together budget reports for the upcoming board meeting in a few days.

"When is Kendel going to Australia?" Diane asked.

"Tomorrow. She got the call from the museum today. She was very excited. She said they have a collection of really neat dinosaur species we don't have."

"Tell her I'll call her tonight," said Diane. "I'm going back to Gainesville. Call my cell if you need anything."

Chapter 22

They drove back to Gainesville in Ross' silver Prius. Diane's mind was not on Kingsley's case, but Marcella's. She had tried to call Hanks, but he hadn't answered his cell. She left a message telling him she would call back.

"I interviewed Stacy's boyfriend and her band members," said Kingsley, when he got on the interstate.

"What kind of band did she have?"

"Rock . . . and a little bit of everything. They seemed to be trying to find themselves."

"How did it go?" she asked.

Kingsley changed lanes a little too abruptly for Diane and she had to hold on to the handle at the ceiling to keep from leaning hard against the door.

"There is a problem establishing a solid alibi for any of them, since the ME gave only a ballpark time of death. Doppelmeyer decided Stacy did this to herself, and he just didn't do a proper autopsy. I don't suppose your friend Lynn can determine the time of death," he said.

"No, not now," said Diane.

"Besides Stacy, there were four members of her band, including the boyfriend. A female drummer, the boyfriend, who is the keyboardist, and two singers—a female and a male, who also plays the guitar. Stacy was a third singer. All had alibis of sorts. Which means the alibis aren't solid by any means."

Kingsley had a turnoff coming and he eased over into the right lane. This time Diane didn't have to hold on to the handle.

"I couldn't find any motive for any of them. I spoke

with the father again and he said they had all been friends since high school. Two of them were students at the community college with her. If they are involved, we need something to come out in the evidence, because I couldn't detect anything."

"Who found her?" asked Diane.

"They were thinking about inviting another member into the band, a girl who they said is really good on the guitar. She's the drummer's cousin. The cousin and the drummer came together to talk to Stacy about it, and found her. That's another discrepancy. The police report said the cousin was the one who found her. The father and the others said it was the two of them," said Kingsley. He shook his head and took the off-ramp. "Perhaps I should go practice psychology. I'm not really cut out for investigation."

"What do your psychologist's sensibilities say about them?" asked Diane.

"That they are telling the truth. I've checked all their backgrounds. None have any known involvement in drugs. But I've been fooled before. They practiced in the garage, so Stacy's father saw them frequently. He doesn't remember them ever arguing about anything serious. At most, a disagreement about what songs to sing at an event."

"You think her death has something to do with her brother's case, don't you?" said Diane.

Diane didn't like being a passenger. She'd rather be driving. There was a kind of helplessness about being a passenger.

"Yes. You think I'm making the same mistake as Doppelmeyer? I've made up my mind and I'm dismissing all other possibilities?"

"No, not really," said Diane.

"But just a little?" he asked.

"No, but I do think the temptation to go in that direction is very strong. We just have to keep an open mind and follow the evidence. Were there any jealousies? Sometimes people don't need a really big motive for murder. Small, petty ones will do."

"I asked about that. I interviewed each one separately. From what I can tell, Stacy and the boyfriend seemed pretty solid. I didn't see any jealousies about who gets to solo, or who gets top billing. Stacy wasn't even the lead singer; the other girl was."

"Did they have a lot of gigs? Did they make money?" asked Diane.

"Not really. They mostly played at school dances, bar mitzvahs, weddings, county festivals, that sort of thing. They've never played a club. The boyfriend said they were discussing doing a CD. These days you can apparently make them yourself. Don't know about distribution, though. He seemed to think they could sell enough from their Web site to get a following. What struck me about all of them is that they were having fun. They didn't see themselves as struggling musicians; they saw themselves as already having made it and were just looking to make it bigger. Stacy's death is a blow to them. Their grief seems genuine."

"Have you seen the Web site?" asked Diane.

"Yes. Nothing stands out. It introduces them, has a sample of their music, has a short video. It has a nice memorial for Stacy. Which, I should add, tells the world that she was murdered, not that she died by accident."

"Did any of them know anything about the investigation she was doing?"

"That was an odd thing, at least to me. No, they didn't. They said Stacy kept the business about her brother private. She didn't even confide to her boyfriend about the investigation. Her friends thought she needed a place where concerns about her brother and his problems didn't exist—and that was with them and the band. I think we're here," he said, turning onto a road that introduced itself as Georgia Heritage Estates.

The neighborhood Ellie Rose Carruthers had lived in was quite different from the one Stacy Dance and her brother, Ryan, grew up in. This place was far from the industrial district. It was an upper-middle-class neighborhood of doctors, lawyers, and upwardly mobile professionals. The yards were neatly manicured. There was no house that needed a coat of paint. One thing for sure, Ryan's car would have certainly stood out in a neighborhood filled with the higher-end cars she saw parked in the garages and driveways. Kingsley drove to a large two-story brick house and parked in the drive.

"The house across from this one belongs to the family of Ellie Rose Carruthers," he said. "This is Kathy Nicholson. She was the main witness who put Ryan in this neighborhood. Stacy came to see her three days before she died. Kathy Nicholson's husband died five years ago. He owned three hardware stores around Gainesville, and she lives alone," he said.

"Does she know we are coming?" asked Diane.

"No. This is a surprise," he said.

"Oh," said Diane.

They walked up to the house and knocked on the large, ornate oak door. Diane could hear footfalls almost immediately. The door was opened by a woman, slightly heavyset, dressed in brown slacks with a brown and cream striped blouse with a soft satin sheen to it. Her hair was ash brown with blond highlights and cut in a short, modern style. Kathy Nicholson had smooth skin, pretty features, and dark brown eyes. Right now she wore a cautiously pleasant look on her face. Diane saw her eyes dart to the car, then to the two of them—Kingsley in his casual sport coat and slacks, Diane in her Ann Taylor camel-colored jacket and pants. Kathy Nicholson seemed to relax. Diane knew it would be only for a moment.

"Can I help you?" she asked.

Kingsley took out his private investigator's license and gave it to her. None of the flash-it-in-front-of-her-in-hopes-she-doesn't-look routine.

"Mrs. Nicholson, I'm Dr. Ross Kingsley and this is my associate, Dr. Diane Fallon. May we speak with you? We can talk over at that lovely table you have in your side yard if you like," he said.

"Doctors. I hadn't realized that private investigators have such high standards, or are times just hard?" She smiled at the two of them, but it didn't show in her eyes.

"It's the firm I work for," said Kingsley, grinning at her. "They like educated investigators. My doctorate is in psychology. I was previously a profiler for the FBI."

Kingsley was really rubbing the education in a bit, thought Diane.

"And what about you?" she asked Diane. "What's your doctorate in?"

"Forensic anthropology," said Diane.

"That's about bones, isn't it?" she said. Diane nodded. "What do you want?"

She was suspicious now, Diane could see. Probably thinking about the visit she had about five weeks ago from Stacy Dance. Too many people coming around doing detective work—about one of the worst things to happen in her nice, pretty neighborhood.

"It's about Stacy Dance," Kingsley said.

The woman's smile disappeared. "I told that young woman what I saw. I'm sorry it was her brother. I know she was just a girl at the time and I understand that she believes him to be innocent. I told her if it were my brother, I probably would too, but I saw what I saw. I'm not going to help you get that monster out of jail." She handed Ross back his ID and started to close the door.

"Stacy was murdered," said Kingsley before she got the door completely closed.

The woman stopped and stared at him through the six-inch opening in the door.

"Murdered?" she whispered. "I don't want anything to do with this."

"We just want a few minutes of your time to ask you about Stacy," said Kingsley. "Her father is our client. His daughter is dead; his son is in prison. I would like to find out what happened so he can have some measure of peace."

She relented. Diane could see it in her eyes first, the softening around the corners. Kathy Nicholson stole a glance across the street, then opened her door.

"Come inside. It's too cold to be outside," she said.

Chapter 23

Kathy Nicholson ushered them into her living room, a roomy space with a large picture window. It was a formal living room with traditional furniture—a gold brocade sofa, matching accent chairs, highly polished coffee table and end tables. A portrait of her and her husband when they were young hung over the fireplace. She had a cream carpet throughout that was spotless.

Mrs. Nicholson was a good housekeeper. There was no dust, nor any clutter. The room also presented a starkness, like a place where no one lived. Perhaps it was because it was a room rarely used. Diane could see through a doorway into the dining room—a room that also had everything in its place. Mrs. Nicholson may have had a den or TV room tucked away that looked more lived in, but what she showed to the world was neatness and order.

Diane and Kingsley sat on the sofa, their backs to the window. Kathy Nicholson sat on one of the chairs. She didn't look comfortable, but Diane didn't think it had anything to do with the chair.

Mrs. Nicholson didn't offer refreshments. Diane and Kingsley weren't guests and were not under the protection of hospitality. They were intruders, people who had come to tear at the heartstrings and bring back bad memories. Perhaps even to affront those memories.

"It's kind of you to speak with us," said Diane.

"Yes," agreed Kingsley. "What we are trying to do is retrace Stacy's steps before she was killed."

Kathy Nicholson said nothing, offering no information. They were going to have to ask for everything.

"Will you tell us what you spoke with her about?" asked Kingsley.

She was silent a moment. Then she looked resigned.

"She wanted to know about my testimony. She started by telling me that she knew her brother, and that he was kind." She rolled her eyes and looked past them at the house across the street. "I simply told her what I saw."

"Was she upset?" asked Diane.

"Of course. But I don't know what she expected. That now I've had nine years to think about it, I made a mistake? Well, I didn't."

"Tell us what you saw," said Diane.

"I thought you were here about Stacy. I've told you, I'm not going to help you get that monster out of jail," she said.

"I'm asking questions that I know Stacy probably asked you," said Diane. "We would like to know her frame of mind. We would like to see if there was anything she heard that might have sent her in some direction that we could follow. This is not about Ryan Dance. It's about Stacy. We are trying to get into her head—a big part of what was in her head was her brother."

"We have spent nine years in this community trying to get over it," she said.

"You never get over something like this," said Diane. "You can only try to deal with it in some way that doesn't drive you crazy. I would like to think that for you that would mean helping us bring a little peace to another grieving father."

Kathy Nicholson nodded. "I had no quarrel with Stacy Dance. She was a young kid at the time of the trial. I remember her outside the courtroom. Her father wouldn't let her come in and she would wait out in the hallway with a relative. I could see she wanted to put her family back together. There was nothing I could do about that. The day I saw him—the day El went missing—he was driving an old gold Chevrolet. It was a large gaudy thing with rust spots all over it. It wasn't a car that we see here. Arlo Murphy's father down the street had a rusty old Ford fishing truck, but that's all he used it for—to go fishing. This car drove past El's house going too slow, like someone looking for an address."

"Where were you?" asked Kingsley, turning to look out the window.

"I know what you're thinking. It's too great a distance from here to the road. Well, I wasn't in the house looking out the window. I was in my garden. It's not there now. I quit gardening when my husband died. My garden was close to the road. I saw him clearly. His window was rolled down. His arm was resting on the door, half out the open window. I saw the snake tattoo he had on his forearm. I wrote down the license plate number. I was president of Neighborhood Watch then and I wrote down suspicious tags. Are you going to tell me that it wasn't his plate number?"

"No," said Kingsley. "We're just trying to get at what you told Stacy you saw. Surely she asked you questions, like was he looking at Ellie Rose Carruthers' house when he drove past?"

She was silent for several moments, her mouth set in a frown, her hands clutching the arms of the chair.

"I told her I saw him," she said.

"Did he turn his head in your direction?" Kingsley pushed her. His voice was calm, but he was pushing. Diane thought Stacy probably had pushed too. If the person was looking at the Carruthers' house, his face wasn't turned toward Mrs. Nicholson in her garden.

"Which way was he going?" said Diane.

"What do you mean?" Mrs. Nicholson asked.

"Which direction was he driving when you saw him?" she said.

"I was standing in my garden. Looking across the street at him. He was going north—to my left." She gestured with her arm.

"This street isn't a dead end, is it?" asked Diane.

"No," she said.

"Did he come back and look again?" asked Diane.

"I didn't see him if he did," she said.

"How long were you in your garden?" Diane asked.

"From nine in the morning until eleven. That's when I

worked in my garden," she said. "And my eyes are good. I have reading glasses now, but my eyes were twenty-twenty then."

Diane had read Kathy Nicholson's statement to the police, as well as her court testimony. It was in the file Kingsley had. Diane was willing to bet it was in Stacy's file too, the one that was missing. In Nicholson's first statement she emphasized the car, the plates, the Atlanta Braves cap, and the tattoo. Not the face. In court she said she recognized him. She pointed to him sitting beside his counsel. But the trial was held after Ryan Dance's face had been all over the news. The documents didn't say anything about a lineup.

Diane was willing to bet the first information Nicholson gave was the truth. Truths are often put forth first by witnesses because they are what is actually in the memory. Only afterward, when the pressure is on—from family, victims, police, prosecutors—do witnesses start saying things that are not exactly the truth, but could be. After all, it was so clear—the car, the hat, the tag, the tattoo. It was easy for Kathy Nicholson to say she saw the face and believe she had seen it, after she had been questioned by so many people who wanted her to be a good witness. She lived across the street from a grieving family who wanted the man put in jail. Pretty intense pressure.

"Was there a lineup?" asked Diane.

"You sound like you are trying to prove that monster was innocent," she said.

"Didn't Stacy ask you these questions?" said Diane.

"She asked me some of them. She didn't hammer at me the way you two are doing." She glared at them. "I told her I picked him out of a collection of photographs the police showed me," she said. "And I did."

"In the photo array, which one was it?" asked Diane.

"I don't remember," she said. "It was nine years ago."

"Yes, nine years ago at one of the worst times in your life and the lives of everyone around you. Was it the first one or the last?" said Diane.

"The first one, I think," she said. "I think you'd better go now. This has not been pleasant."

"I know," said Diane. "And you have been far more cooperative than we had a right to expect. I thank you."

Kathy Nicholson straightened up a little, then stood up. "I'm sorry for Stacy and her father." She paused. "Do you think her murder had something to do with her brother?" she asked.

"We don't know," said Kingsley. "That's one theory, but we have to wait for all the evidence."

"How could it? I saw what I saw. I wasn't mistaken," she said. "It wasn't someone else."

"We don't know why she was killed. It may have had nothing to do with what happened here nine years ago," said Kingsley. "It may be just a big coincidence."

She showed them out the door, and Diane and Kingsley walked to his car and got in. He started it up and drove out of Kathy Nicholson's drive and onto the street and stopped.

"Chilly," said Kingsley. "I'm glad we didn't have to do this outside."

"Me too," said Diane, looking out the window at the Carruthers' house.

"I would have helped ask questions," said Kingsley, grinning, "but it looked like you were on to something. Did you notice something?"

"Two or three things jumped out," Diane said. "If he was looking at Ellie Carruthers' house, why would he drive only in this direction?" Diane pointed in the direction Kingsley's car was headed. "He would have to look out the passenger window to see the house. Much easier to look out the window on the driver's side. So why didn't he case the house coming from the other direction? He could have seen more."

"Perhaps he did, but that was the only time he was seen," said Kingsley.

"Could be. I also noted that she did her gardening at the same time every day. If you needed a witness to be in a specific place in front of the victim's house, she would be your witness. And everyone in the neighborhood probably knew her schedule."

Kingsley nodded. "That's true. What else? You said maybe three things?"

"The tattoo. She saw it because he had his arm hanging out the window," she said.

"And?" he asked.

"It would be his left arm she saw, the arm that wasn't on the steering wheel. When you drive with one hand, which one do you use?"

"I'm left-handed, so I drive with my left hand," he said.

"Ryan Dance is left-handed too," she said.

Chapter 24

"We left-handed people are pretty good with our right hands, living in a right-handed world as we do," said Kingsley. "Just playing the devil's advocate."

"I know. All of these things I mentioned are tiny and can't remotely be used to benefit Ryan or get justice for Stacy. They are just interesting, small bits of information. They probably mean nothing. But when small pieces start adding up, sometimes you get a whole pot."

"A whole pot of what?" he said.

"I'm working on something else that has to do with broken pottery," she said. "It's on my mind."

"Her identification of Ryan gave me pause," he said. "I don't believe she saw his face."

"Neither do I," Diane said.

"So, did she call the Carruthers' house right away?" said Kingsley.

"Of course," said Diane.

"Do you think they will see us?" he asked.

"I believe so. There is a neighbor going over to her house now. I'm willing to bet it's for moral support."

"Why do you think they'll talk to us?" said Kingsley.

"They want to find out what we are up to—if they need to mount an effort to keep Ryan in prison. They want to scope us out to see if we are the kind of people who are up to the task of perhaps getting Ryan out of prison," said Diane.

"You don't think Kathy Nicholson believed we are only interested in Stacy Dance," said Kingsley.

"Nope. They can't afford to believe that," said Diane.

"I agree. You're not a bad profiler," he said.

"I thought you didn't believe in profiling?" said Diane.

"Slip of the tongue. I meant psychologist," he said, and put the car in gear to drive across the street to the Carruthers' house.

The door was opened as soon as they rang the doorbell by a woman perhaps in her early fifties, in shape, and tanned. Her dark brown hair was cut in a sort of a graduated pageboy style with blunt bangs. She wore a white blouse and dark gray slacks. She wasn't Marsha Carruthers. She was the neighbor Diane had seen walking over at a hurried pace. *Perhaps I was wrong*, thought Diane. *Perhaps she was called over to be gatekeeper.*

"Can I help you?" the woman asked.

Kingsley gave her his ID and explained what they were doing there, just as he had with Kathy Nicholson. The woman glanced at it and gave it back.

"I suppose you know this is a cruel intrusion," she said.

"It's certainly not our intention to be cruel," said Kingsley. "My client's daughter was murdered in a terrible way. We know she came to visit here a few days before her death. We were hoping Mrs. Carruthers would help. May we see her?" asked Kingsley.

She opened the door and stepped aside. "I'll be here with her," she said.

"Of course," said Kingsley. "A good neighbor is a priceless treasure."

The woman looked startled for a fraction of a second. She was probably not expecting him to quote Chinese proverbs. As Diane recalled, that was in his fortune cookie the other evening.

She led them into yet another formal living room. This one was not as bright and sunny as the one across the street. The dark, wine-colored drapes were closed. No outside light came in. The only illumination was from several lamps around the room. This living room was furnished with dark leather furniture, wood and glass tables, and a Persian carpet on a hardwood floor. The centerpiece of the room was the portrait over the mantel: a beautiful oil of Ellie Rose Carruthers—forever young, with long, wavy blond hair and blue eyes.

"Mrs. Carruthers." Kingsley held out a hand to a woman seated in one of the leather chairs. She didn't reach out to take it and Kingsley let it drop.

She had blond hair—bleached, but bleached well. She was too thin. Diane thought she probably had been too thin for several years now. She didn't smile at them. Her face, strained, lined, looked like carved stone. She sat in the brown leather chair wearing a brown dress with brass buttons. She made Diane think of a chameleon, as if she could easily blend in with the chair and disappear altogether.

"Thank you for seeing us," said Kingsley.

He and Diane stood waiting for an offer to sit, which never came.

"Why have you come to dig in my wounds?" she said. Her voice sounded like pieces of gravel rubbing together. The other woman, the neighbor, stood at her chair like a handmaiden. She put a hand on Marsha Carruthers' shoulder. Marsha reached up and touched it.

"We haven't come to cause pain," said Kingsley. "We're investigating the murder of Stacy Dance. We wanted to talk with you about her visit."

"Why do you say she came here?" said Marsha Carruthers.

Diane noted that they weren't surprised at the word *murder*.

"We are retracing her steps," said Kingsley. "Can you tell us what she talked about?"

"Do you think her death had anything to do with her investigation?" asked Mrs. Carruthers.

They weren't getting anywhere. They were answering each other's questions with questions. As they sparred, Diane had been observing the room. The chair Marsha Carruthers sat in seemed out of place in relation to the rest of the furniture. Then she saw the indentations on the Persian rug. The chair usually sat facing the fireplace. They had swung it around to face outward. It usually sat where someone could sit and look at the painting of Ellie Rose. Was that how Marsha filled her days, sitting in front of her daughter's painting? Or perhaps it was Ellie Rose's father who sat and looked at his daughter when he came home from work. Diane wanted to cry.

"That's our best working theory at the moment," said Kingsley.

"So you're thinking that wretched excuse for a human sitting in prison is an innocent victim?" Her mouth curled into an ugly shape.

"No, I don't think that," said Kingsley. "We are investigating Stacy Dance's death. Will you tell me what you talked about?"

"You don't know that her death had anything to do with—with this," she said. "You know where those people lived. How do you know the sister wasn't like the brother—into God knows what, probably drugs or something just as vile? That's the life they lived, and I resent your implying that she died because she discovered that piece of human garbage is innocent," she said.

"Mrs. Carruthers, Stacy Dance was a very nice girl. She took care of her neighbors, drove the elderly to their doctor's appointments. She was in college—"

"College? The University of Georgia is a college. Bartrum is a college. That place she went to is just a glorified tech school. She was nothing like my Ellie Rose."

Marsha looked back and forth from Kingsley to Diane as if daring them to defend Stacy again. The grief had sucked all kindness and love from her. She was empty of everything but hate.

"You're wrong about Stacy," said Diane. "And about Gainesville Community College for that matter, but especially about Stacy. She was kind. I understand—"

"Don't!" Marsha Carruthers' face hardened to granite. "Don't you say you understand how I feel. You can't possibly imagine!"

"I wasn't going to say that," said Diane, trying to keep calm in her own voice. "And no, I don't know how *you* feel, but I know how I felt. My daughter was murdered. She was the best part of me. She was my heart. I know how I felt when she was murdered, and it is indescribable. I live every moment with her loss and the knowledge that I failed to protect her. I also know that if I lose my humanity, I lose her again, I fail her again, and I couldn't bear that. Ariel was not yet six years old when she was killed, but she was a bright shining soul and I cherish every single memory of her. So don't tell me I can't possibly imagine." Diane unconsciously put her hand on her neck where she wore a locket with Ariel's photograph.

All of them fell into a shocked silence. The neighbor had a tear running down her cheek. She looked away and wiped it with her hand. Diane was sure this was more than she bargained for when she came over to give her friend moral support.

"I'll give you some unasked-for advice," said Diane. "You are in danger of losing the love you felt for your daughter. You are so overwhelmed with anger and grief that that special feeling you had for Ellie Rose is going to get lost in the abyss. Stacy was Harmon Dance's daughter and he loved her too. We just want to know what she talked about and if she said where she was going afterward."

Marsha sat very still. Her face hadn't changed, but there wasn't an angry comeback on her lips and Diane thought she saw them quiver. The neighbor squeezed Marsha's shoulder.

"I was here when Miss Dance came by," the neighbor said. "My name is Wendy. I live next door. She asked about whom Ellie was dating at the time, who her friends were. I told her we weren't going to tell her people's names so she could go pester them. I don't know where she went when she left here. Neither of us does," she said. "Honestly, we didn't tell her much. Do we look particularly cooperative to you?"

There was a rustling in the entryway and a young woman bounced in. She looked to be seventeen or eighteen. She was dressed in pink bell-bottoms with a wide white belt. Her pink T-shirt had a picture of an electric guitar outlined in rhinestones. Her long hair was black with a lock of pink on one side going from her forehead to her shoulders. Her eyes were outlined with black liner and she wore false eyelashes and bright pink lipstick. She had a diamondlike jewel on the side of her nose.

"Mom. Oh. Sorry," she said.

She stood still and looked into the living room. Diane and Kingsley turned to look at her. She looked so very much like Ellie Rose in the face that it startled Diane.

"Samantha, dear, why don't you fix your mother a glass of tea?" said Wendy.

Samantha looked at her mother. "Do you want some tea, Mom?" she asked.

"That would be nice, hon," she said.

Samantha skipped off to another part of the house.

"You have a very pretty daughter," said Diane.

"At least she likes pink," said her mother.

Diane thought she saw a hint that at one time Marsha Carruthers may have had a sense of humor.

"It was not our intention to cause you more pain," said Diane, "but it is important to find out what happened to Stacy."

She took a card from her pocket. She had brought the cards that identified her as director of the Aidan Kavanagh Forensic Anthropology Lab, the osteology lab she ran at the museum. It seemed a much better choice of card to give out with her name on it. Museum director would have been confusing, and director of the crime lab would be awkward, since she wasn't representing Rosewood. In her capacity as forensic anthropologist, she had much more freedom. Sometimes she felt like a con artist with all the different cards she had with different professions.

Kingsley handed her his card along with Diane's. "Please call if you remember anything that might help," Kingsley said. He nodded to Wendy. "We can show ourselves out." They turned to leave.

"Why haven't the police contacted us?" asked Marsha.

So they finally thought to ask, thought Diane.

Kingsley turned back to her. "I'm sure they will. Right now they may not know where Stacy's investigation led her," he said.

"I didn't think private investigators could investigate an open case," said Wendy.

Samantha came in with her mother's tea and gave it to her. Marsha gave it to Wendy, who took it to the liquor cabinet and set it on top, turned, and looked at Kingsley for an answer.

"That's a popular misconception," he said. "We just can't get in their way." Kingsley looked at each of them and nodded. He and Diane left.

"You finessed that well," said Diane when they reached the car.

"It wouldn't have done to tell them that, at the moment, the police are calling her death an accident," Kingsley said, almost absently.

He frowned and looked back at the house. Diane got in and closed the door.

"There's a note on your seat," she said when he opened his door to get in.

Kingsley picked it up and read it out loud. "*Lakeshore Mall. Cookie Company. Now. Please. Thanks.*"

"Not signed?" said Diane.

"It's from Samantha," said Kingsley. "Of course, when I met her, she was the drummer's cousin."

Chapter 25

Diane looked at him, perplexed. "She's Stacy's drummer's cousin?"

"She told the police she was. I think we need to go to the mall," he said.

He started to pull out of the drive just as a blue Volkswagen Phaeton pulled up, blocking them. A man jumped out, slammed his car door, and came marching up to the driver's side of their car. He looked in his late forties or early fifties. A slight bulge hung over his belt. He wore dark blue suit pants and a white shirt with the sleeves rolled up, and a light blue tie, loosened. He banged on the roof of Kingsley's car with his palms.

Diane got out of the car and looked over the roof at him. Kingsley got out on the other side. They stood face-to-face.

"What the hell do you think you're doing, coming around here harassing my family?" he said.

"We were not harassing," said Kingsley. "We were asking questions about a young woman who visited here about four weeks ago."

"You have no business here. I called the police to see what this was about, and they said the woman's death was an accident," he said. "So what are you playing at?"

His face was so red Diane was a little concerned. His comb-over fell into his face and he pushed it back.

"It wasn't an accident," said Kingsley. "But as to your complaint, we were not harassing your family. We were speaking with your wife in the presence of your neighbor."

"You aren't to set foot on my property again. Is that clear?" he said.

"We won't need to," said Kingsley. "The police will be handling it from here."

"If it wasn't an accident, the police would have told me. You think you know something they don't?" he asked.

"Dad, I need to go to the library." Samantha stood a few feet from him. A book bag hung on her arm.

A candy-apple red hardtop convertible, not there when Diane and Kingsley drove up, was parked in a small parking space just off the driveway. Diane assumed it was Samantha's.

"I can't get out," she said. "You're blocking the drive."

"Just a minute, Sam, honey." He turned to her. "Did these people upset your mother?"

"How could I tell?" she said. Her face looked both sad and a little angry.

"Sam, not now, and not in front of strangers," he said.

Kingsley and Samantha exchanged brief glances.

"Dad, you're always talking about me making good grades. Well, I need to get to the library," she said.

"All right. Do you have your cell?" he said.

"Always," she said.

"Don't be too late." He turned back to Kingsley and Diane. "I don't want you here ever again. I don't want you harassing my family, or my neighbors. Do you understand?"

"As I said, Dr. Carruthers, the police will be taking it from here. Now, we need to go, unless you intend to keep us here against our will," Kingsley said.

He backed off and raised his hands, palms outward, then walked to his car. "Just remember what I said," he yelled, getting into the driver's seat.

Kingsley and Diane got back in their car and Kingsley drove off. Diane saw the bright convertible behind them. Kingsley headed toward the mall.

"I certainly hope Lynn comes through," said Kingsley, "or I've just been bluffing."

"I said there's no guarantee she'll come up with murder," said Diane.

"But you think she will," he said.

"Yes. And with what we found in the apartment, I think the police definitely need to reopen the case." Diane glanced over her shoulder at the red convertible following them. "What is the deal with Samantha?" she said.

"I have no idea," said Kingsley.

"She was there when you spoke with the drummer, right?" asked Diane. "She looks a lot like her sister. You didn't recognize her?"

"We were in a dark café, and she has that pink and black hair and the weird makeup. No, I didn't recognize her." Kingsley glanced into the rearview mirror. "God. She found the body. What kind of hell is that?"

To Diane this was the hardest part of dealing with crime: the aftermath, the effect on the victims. Long after everyone thinks they should just get over it, the crime is always there inside them. Every day they wake up and it isn't a dream; it's a living nightmare.

"Are you okay?" he said as he turned on the Dawsonville Highway.

Diane nodded. "I wasn't very professional, I know. It's one of those characterizations that is likely to set me off—that I don't know the pain of loss."

Kingsley was acquainted with the tragedy Diane went through: the loss of her adopted daughter in a massacre in South America when Diane was there as a human rights worker.

"You may have done her some good. You let her know she isn't alone in her grief," he said.

"Maybe, but sitting in front of that painting day after day," she said. "If it was her and not the father."

"What? Did I miss something?" he said.

Diane told him about the indentations in the rug.

"I didn't notice. What made you look at the rug?" he asked.

"It was the arrangement of the furniture," she said.

"Do you have to be female to notice things like that?" he said.

"No." She smiled. "Just experienced at doing crime scenes. Little anomalies stand out. I can't imagine what it's like for Samantha."

He drove onto Pearl Nix Parkway and to the mall. Samantha wasn't far behind. They walked into the mall with her and sat down in front of the Cookie Company after Kingsley got each of them a rather large chocolate chip cookie and a drink.

"Are you going to tell my parents?" asked Samantha after she took a bite.

"How old are you?" said Kingsley.

"Eighteen," she said. "I'm an adult."

Diane had to smile. She tried to hide it behind her cookie.

"I take it you're not Jimmi's cousin," said Kingsley.

"No. We made that up for the police. I was so freaked out and Jimmi was, well, she was, I mean, Stacy was her friend since middle school."

"Why didn't you tell the police who you are?" asked Kingsley.

"I knew my parents would find out. I couldn't let that happen. They would take my car away. And Mother would have some kind of screaming fit if she knew I was hanging with Stacy Dance. I showed the police one of my fake IDs."

Kingsley rolled his eyes. "You what?"

Samantha reminded Diane of Star, Frank's daughter, the girl he adopted at sixteen when her parents, Frank's best friends, were murdered. Like Samantha, she had multicolored hair, was defiant, and used kid logic to make decisions.

"They didn't care. They hardly questioned me," she said. "I told them I lived in Ohio and was going home and that Jimmi could get in touch with me if they needed me."

"They bought that?" said Diane.

"I told you, they didn't care. They were like my parents. I'm invisible. I think it's my superpower," she said.

"Why were you hanging with Stacy? How did you meet?" asked Kingsley.

"Both of us were auditing a class at Gainesville State College. She wanted to transfer there and was trying it out. I'm going there until I can transfer to UGA. I recognized her last name, but there are lots of Dances, so I didn't think anything of it. Of course she recognized mine and kind of avoided me."

"How did you finally meet?" asked Kingsley.

"I found out she was in a band. A real successful band. They played lots of gigs, and people in class knew them. See, I play the guitar and I'm really good. I wanted to be in the band and they needed another guitar player. I talked to her and that's when she told me who she was. She was kind of freaked about it," she said.

"You weren't?" asked Kingsley.

"No. *She* didn't do anything to my family. And she said her brother was innocent and she was going to prove it," Samantha said.

"Did you believe her?" asked Kingsley.

"Why not? I've been blamed for stuff I didn't do. My parents still think I took money out of my aunt's purse when I was ten. It was my cousin who did it, but he's a really good liar. So why couldn't it have happened to her brother?" she said.

"What about all the evidence?" said Kingsley.

"Evidence doesn't mean anything. It can be anything people want it to be. I mean, look at *Jurassic Park*. The dinosaurs looked real to me," she said.

"It must be hard, living in a world where everything could be an illusion," said Diane.

"We all do. It just means we can make the world the way we want it. That's what Stacy's band did. They wanted to be successful and they are making it real. Or, they were," she said.

"You need to tell your parents you found her body," said Kingsley.

"They'll just yell," she said. "They'll tell me I betrayed El. You'd think they would want to be really close to me, with El gone and all, but they don't. All Mother does is sit in front of that painting. And Dad . . . he just pays lip service to telling me not to be late. He doesn't even know when I come home. He stays in his games. That's how he's remade his world," she said.

"Games?" asked Diane.

"*Warcraft* and *Second Life*. He fights demons, rescues princesses, and builds his own world to live in."

"I'm sorry," said Diane.

Samantha shrugged. "They gave me a cool car, clothes, telephones, and money. It's not so bad. I don't want that to stop. It's all I have."

"You need to talk to someone," said Diane. "The police are likely to be coming around and they'll recognize you. Your parents need to know what happened to you. Maybe this will jolt them into the real world. At least go to a counselor at college."

Diane took one of her cards and wrote her psychiatrist friend Laura Hillard's name and number.

"Dr. Hillard is a friend. Tell her I sent you. If you don't want to talk to her, she can send you to someone here who would be good."

"Shrinks can't take things out of your head," Samantha said.

"No, but they can teach you how to cope," said Diane.

"I cope," Samantha said in an uncertain voice, her eyes downcast.

"Are you having nightmares?" said Kingsley.

She nodded. "They've started back again. I had bad nightmares after El died," she said.

"Take Diane's advice. See someone, just to talk to, at least," he said.

"Maybe," she said, sticking the card in her purse.

"Have your parents been like this for nine years?" asked Kingsley.

"It comes and goes. It gets bad around Christmas and El's birthday. It's worse when Mother is drinking. Sometimes she takes a cure for a while, but sooner or later she goes back to it. She likes vodka in tea. Can you imagine? If she put it in orange juice, she'd at least get some vitamin C."

"By 'takes a cure,' what do you mean?" asked Kingsley.

"She goes to visit my grandmother for a while. They don't have any alcohol around and she stays in the house. Sometimes she goes to a clinic in Atlanta. She comes back and starts falling back into bad habits. I told them we should move, but they won't. They don't want to go to a house where El has never been. They think it'll make her disappear, and I'm like, hello, she's gone. She's already disappeared."

"You seem to have supportive neighbors," said Diane.

Samantha shrugged. "Kathy Nicholson is pretty nice. I go over to her house some. She gets kind of lonely. We talk about things. But it's not like she can do anything about my parents. Wendy Walters means well, but I think Mother wore her down. She used to try to discourage her from drinking, but now she just helps her. You saw when I brought the tea."

"Why did Stacy want to speak with your parents?" asked Kingsley. "If she knew you, you could give her a lot of the answers she wanted."

"Not really. I was nine when El died. I didn't know a whole lot that was going on in El's life. Stacy thought they could tell her about the day El disappeared. I didn't really know much about that. Except, I think my parents think it was my fault."

"How is that?" asked Diane.

"We'd been fighting that day and El said she didn't want to ride all the way to Grandma's house with me and she was just going to stay here. She wasn't home when we got back," she said.

"That wasn't your fault," said Diane.

Samantha shrugged again and took a sip of drink. "Maybe not, but still, if we hadn't fought . . ."

"You think she might have wanted to stay home for reasons of her own?" said Diane. "And the argument with you was just her excuse?"

Samantha raised her eyebrows and opened her mouth slightly. "I hadn't thought of that."

"Did she have a boyfriend?" asked Diane.

"She always had boyfriends. You saw her portrait. That's pretty much what she looked like. But it would have been in her diary," said Samantha.

"She kept a diary?" asked Kingsley.

Samantha nodded. "I loaned it to Stacy to copy."

Chapter 26

"Your sister kept a diary?" said Kingsley.

"Yes, like forever. I mentioned it to Stacy one time and she begged me to let her see it. I told her it wouldn't help. See, El caught Mother reading her diary when she first started writing one and she was really pissed. That's when she started writing in this code she made up. El was really smart. Mother wanted to read her diaries after she died, to be close, I guess. But she couldn't make heads or tails of them. Dad packed them in a box when he packed up El's room. Mom wanted to keep it the way it was, but it was a little too creepy for Dad. They saved her things in the basement. I took her last diary so Stacy could copy it."

"Did she copy it?" asked Kingsley. He leaned forward in his chair slightly. Diane knew what he was thinking. Diaries can be loaded with just the best clues.

"Yes," said Samantha.

So, the copies were probably in the file that was missing, thought Diane. "What happened to the diary?" she asked.

Samantha Carruthers hesitated and was quiet a moment. Then, quick as a mouse, she slipped her hand into her backpack, pulled out a book, and handed it to Kingsley.

"Stacy returned it to you?" asked Kingsley.

"No, not exactly. When I found her . . . like that, it was in her bookcase. The spine was facing out, but I saw it right away. So, well, I took it. After all, it was mine. Or, at least, my family's. I've been carrying it around, hoping maybe I could figure out how to decipher it," she said. "Jimmi said Stacy's dad told her Stacy's folder disappeared . . . the one full of stuff about her investigation. I figured something in the diary might be important."

The front of the journal had been découpaged with magazine cutouts from the television series *Charmed*.

Kingsley opened it up and he and Diane looked at the writing. It was a mixture of letters, numbers, and symbols.

"See," said Samantha. "You can't read it."

"Will you let us copy it?" said Diane.

"Sure. There's a place in the mall where we can go," Samantha said.

They took the last bites of their oversized cookies, washed them down with their drinks, and threw the trash away. Samantha led them to a Mailboxes Plus store where Diane copied the entire diary. When she finished, she handed it back to Samantha.

Sam stood for a moment, looking awkward. "You aren't going to call my parents, are you?" she asked.

"As you said, you are an adult now," said Diane.

"Yeah, but . . ." She hesitated, looking at her watch. "I guess I'd better get to the library."

"Thank you, Samantha," said Diane. "Seriously, you should talk to your parents. They need to know what's going on in your life."

"I'll think about it, but you don't know them like I do," she said.

"You may not know them as well as you think," said Diane.

Diane and Kingsley left the mall with Samantha. They watched her drive off before they got into Kingsley's Prius.

"She needs help," he said.

"Yes, she does. And her parents need to wake up and realize they have another daughter to care for. She's old enough to be out on her own. If she decides to make the break, it will be harder on all of them."

Kingsley glanced at the package of copies Diane held in her hand. "So, how do we go about deciphering that?" he said as he left the parking area and headed back to Rosewood.

"I'll ask Frank to do it," said Diane.

She removed the first several pages of the diary from the

store bag. The writing looked like gibberish to her—a lot of stars, squares, wavy lines, letters that didn't make sense, and numbers scattered throughout.

"He can do stuff like this?" said Kingsley.

"He and Jin too. They love codes, but—and if you repeat this, I'll have to kill you—Frank is better at it," said Diane.

Kingsley laughed. "He can really decipher that?"

"Sure. I'll have to see if he has time. If not, I'll ask Jin to do it," she said.

"I think the thing I appreciate most about working with you—aside from your brilliant mind, of course—is that all the people around you have such unusual talents that are terribly useful and interesting."

"That's true. I have a great appreciation of them myself," said Diane.

They rode in silence for a while, Diane still trying to make sense of the writing. She gave up and slipped the pages back into the bag. Her talents simply didn't run to encryption.

"You know I have to reinterview all of Stacy's band members," Kingsley said after a while. "I was completely fooled by Samantha and Jimmi. I thought they were telling me the truth."

"They probably saw themselves as telling you the truth. You heard her. Samantha makes her own reality. It's apparently the way she copes," said Diane. "It's apparently the way her parents are coping."

"Perhaps, but I'm a pretty bad detective when I can't tell if kids are telling me lies," said Kingsley.

"They aren't kids. They're nascent adults. They're always a challenge. But, yes, I agree you will have to talk with them again."

The rest of the way to Rosewood, they discussed what they had learned, which, other than the spectacular revelation that Samantha Carruthers discovered Stacy Dance's body, and that Ellie Rose Carruthers kept a diary, wasn't a lot.

They both believed that Kathy Nicholson, the neighbor across the street, did not, in fact, see the face of Ryan Dance. But at this point, she believed she did, and probably could not be shaken from that belief.

"Do you think the father, Dr. Carruthers, could have killed Stacy?" asked Kingsley.

"I don't know. He has a temper."

"Yes, but it was mostly verbal," said Kingsley.

"Mostly verbal? What about his charging up to the car and banging on the roof?" said Diane. "That seemed pretty physical."

"But when I was facing him, he could have been much more threatening and in my face, but he wasn't. I think he is basically a timid man. That's why he works out his bravery in the games. He never has to face anyone."

"What does he do for a living?" asked Diane.

"He's a podiatrist," said Kingsley. "Works mainly in sports medicine."

"Still," said Diane, "if he thought Stacy might be able to free her brother, what would he do? I think just the possibility of it might enrage both Samantha's mother and father."

"I don't know if the mere possibility would make him go over the edge," said Kingsley. "But I think the police should look at his alibi—assuming they reopen the case. I hope Dr. Webber comes through."

"I wonder how it's going. Lynn should have the body by now. . . . In fact"—Diane looked at her watch—"she should have had the body for several hours."

"If she finds that it's a homicide, my boss and I—he likes to be in on these things—will take the evidence you collected to the detective in charge and ask him to reopen the case."

"Then it will be out of your hands?" asked Diane.

"I think so. Stacy's father asked only that we determine if her death was murder. We'll have done that—provided Webber finds what we hope she finds."

They pulled up in the driveway and Diane got out. She bent down to talk to Kingsley before she closed the door.

"It's been another interesting day," she said. "I suppose we won't find out what Lynn discovered until tomorrow. If I hear from her tonight, I'll give you a call."

"Same here," he said. "Otherwise, I'll call you tomorrow."

Diane shut the door and went inside. Frank was already

home and had just gotten out of the shower. His salt-and-pepper hair was still wet. Diane gave him a kiss and headed for the shower herself. When she got out and went to the kitchen to find him, he had fried bacon and sliced tomatoes and lettuce to make BLT sandwiches. And he had heated some tomato soup. Comfort food. It smelled good.

"This is nice," said Diane.

She sat down and they ate sandwiches and drank soup out of large bowls with handles and talked about music. Frank told her *Stomp* was coming to the Fox Theater and that he would like to take her, Kevin, and Star. Kevin was his son by his first marriage and Star was his adopted daughter. Kevin was in high school; Star was a student at Bartrum. Diane thought they both would enjoy *Stomp*. She would too.

"How are you on free time?" asked Diane.

"What is it you want me to do?" He grinned at her.

Diane got up and retrieved the copied pages of the diary. "This is the journal written by the girl who was murdered nine years ago. Any chance you could decode it?" she asked. She handed him the pages.

Frank studied them for several minutes, now and again taking a sip of his soup and a bite of his second sandwich.

"Sure," he said.

"If you don't have time, I can give it to Jin," she said.

"Is that a challenge?" he asked.

Diane grinned. "No. I just don't want to impose."

"It won't be that hard. Didn't you say she was fifteen?"

"Yes. But I have no idea what could be the key." Diane had learned from a previous case where decoding was involved that you need a key to decipher it.

"I doubt there is one," he said. "This is something she would have a facility for. She would want to write it as fast as if she were writing normally. I believe it's a combination of rebuses and simple substitution."

"Oh," Diane said. "I couldn't make anything of it." She paused. "Okay, this is embarrassing. What's a rebus? I know what substitution codes are."

"Words and parts of words are represented as pictures." Frank waved a hand. "For example, the phrase 'I cannot' might be represented by pictures of an eye, a tin can, and a rope tied into a knot," he said.

"I knew you could do it," she said.

"When I can't break the code of a fifteen-year-old, I'll pack it in." He grinned at her.

After dinner Diane called Kendel, the assistant director of the museum, and they discussed Kendel's upcoming trip to Australia. Afterward, she and Frank spent the remainder of the evening watching TV, a luxury for both of them. It was a nice end to a day filled with reliving other people's tragedies. She wondered what the Carruthers' evenings would be like from now on.

Diane awoke early, but Frank was already up. She heard his footfalls on the hardwood floor. He came in the door to their bedroom carrying a tray with orange juice and cereal, and with the morning paper under his arm.

"Breakfast in bed?" she said, looking quizzically at him as he put the bed tray over her lap. "Is one of us dying? Is it an anniversary I forgot about? Were we fighting last night and I didn't realize it? I know you are very low-key sometimes." She grinned at him.

"No. I just wanted you to start your day off well," he said, and gave her a crooked smile, his eyes twinkling.

"Why? I mean, why today especially?" she said.

He laid the newspaper on the tray beside her silverware. "Because I think today may be one of those days where the shit hits the fan."

Chapter 27

Diane eyed him and picked up the paper. There on the top banner, the place on the page giving the reader a teaser for what is to come inside, was a school picture of Stacy Dance and a short paragraph with the caption: HOW WE TREAT CRIME VICTIMS WHO AREN'T AFFLUENT—WHY DO THEY FALL THROUGH THE CRACKS OF JUSTICE?

Diane looked up at Frank, who pulled up a chair, turned it around, and rested his arms on the back as he drank his own glass of orange juice.

"What is this?" she said. "Who?"

"You might want to get some food in you before you read any further," he said, smiling.

Diane took a drink of orange juice and opened the paper. The article started off about Stacy Dance, a college student who was trying to better herself. The article finessed the circumstances of her death, but said the death was ruled accidental by the medical examiner, Oran Doppelmeyer. It went on to say the ME had overlooked obvious signs that Stacy Dance was murdered, and suggested it was her socioeconomic level that drove the findings and not empirical evidence. The article had several quotes from Stacy's father, Harmon Dance, and told of his desire to find justice for his daughter.

Diane stole glances at Frank as she read. He merely grinned and sipped his orange juice. She recognized the style as that of Lynn Webber, even though the byline was of a journalist from the Atlanta newspaper.

"Lynn wrote this," Diane muttered. "She must have called Mr. Dance. What was she thinking?"

"Keep reading," Frank said.

The style of the article changed. Apparently the journalist had added her own observations. She mentioned the death of Ellie Rose Carruthers and said the deaths were similar—that Ellie Rose was strangled and her clothes were in disarray, like Stacy Dance. But the investigations were treated quite differently, again alluding to the higher socioeconomic level of Ellie Rose Carruthers. The article revealed that Stacy Dance had been trying to clear her brother of the conviction of Ellie Rose's murder, and the file in which Stacy kept all her evidence was missing. And the final provocative question: Could it be the real killer of Ellie Rose Carruthers also killed Stacy Dance in order to shut her up?

Diane looked up at Frank.

"I hardly know what to say," she said. "I told Ross she wouldn't go off half-cocked."

"At least she didn't use your name or mention the museum," said Frank.

"There is that. And she only mentions that Dance hired a private investigation firm, but not the name of it. Ross will be relieved. I think. But what the heck was she thinking?" Diane threw down the paper.

"Didn't you say she is inclined toward vindictiveness?" said Frank.

"Yes, but this is just going to alienate the detective in charge of Stacy's case, not to mention cause a political uproar. It might even hurt Lynn," said Diane.

"I'm surprised she made a comparison with the two murders. My impression is they were not alike at all," said Frank.

"They aren't, and she didn't. I think Lynn presented an article to the journalist and asked her to publish it under her byline. The journalist—what is her name?" Diane looked at the paper. "Meryl Babbitt. She—as is her right, since it's under her name—added details of her own. She probably saw they were both strangled, and ran with it from there."

Diane poured the milk over her cereal and took a bite. "At least no one will be calling me at the museum—except maybe Ross Kingsley. His wife will have to scrape him off the ceiling first. Jeez, I can't believe Lynn did this."

Diane finished her cereal and took the tray back to the kitchen. Frank was collecting his things and was about to head out the door.

"I'm going to take the diary pages with me," he said.

"Sure. Thanks for doing this," she said.

"No problem. I'll enjoy it. But I'll have to work at it in free moments," he said.

Diane kissed him good-bye and changed out of her nightshirt into black slacks, a white shirt, and a dark red jacket. She drove to the museum, parked on the crime lab end of the building, and went up the private elevator to the lab. David was there alone. The others hadn't arrived yet. He was at the round debriefing table reading the newspaper.

"Isn't this the case you are working on?" he asked.

"Yes," she said. "And before you ask, I don't know . . . well, yes, I do, but I don't know why she chose such a forum."

"What are you talking about?" asked David.

"Lynn Webber." Diane explained about the history of Lynn Webber and Oran Doppelmeyer.

"So, a little public humiliation for Dr. Doppelmeyer, then," said David.

"It would seem so. At least she didn't mention my name." Diane sat down at the table with David. "You know how you've been wanting to do a study of methods for finding buried human remains?"

"Marcella's yard?" said David. "I've been thinking about that very thing."

"I'm going over to the hospital to see whether Marcella's daughter will give us permission," said Diane.

"I'll ask Jin to let me borrow Heckle and Jeckle," said David. "He should be glad for the opportunity to work alone for a while."

"They aren't so bad," said Diane. "They enjoy research, so I'm sure they will be glad to help with the project." She stood up. "You clear it with Jin and I'll get Marcella's permission."

Diane drove to the hospital. As she parked, she toyed with the idea of going down to the morgue to speak with Lynn Webber, but decided against it. She wasn't sure what she would say to her. No doubt Lynn was getting quite a few calls anyway. Diane went up to the ICU waiting room. She found Paloma and her husband sitting on one of the small sofas. Both were reading paperbacks.

"Oh, hi," said Paloma.

Diane greeted them, pulled up a chair, and sat down. "How is your mother?" she asked.

"Much better. She's speaking more easily. We are waiting for the next visiting time," Paloma said.

"No more one-word sentences to decipher," said Mark.

"That's good. Have you spoken with Jonas, by any chance?" asked Diane.

"Yes, he visited with Mother late yesterday. She thinks someone may be buried in her yard. Maybe the woman who lived there—she wasn't real clear," said Paloma. "I was afraid she may be, well, you know."

"Frankly, we didn't give it much credibility," said Mark, "but Jonas seemed to agree with her." He cocked an eyebrow at Diane. "Is it possible?"

"Possible, yes," said Diane. She explained to them about the research project she would like to do in Marcella's yard.

"Mother would love it," said Paloma. "Look, why don't you go in at the next visiting time?"

"I don't want to take away from your time," said Diane.

"That's all right. She'll enjoy your visit. Mark and I can go down for some breakfast," she said.

Diane agreed and went in at the next scheduled visiting period. Marcella looked considerably better than she had the last time Diane saw her. She had more color in her face and her eyes looked brighter. She was sitting up, sipping broth through a straw. She smiled when Diane entered the room.

"I want to thank you for your kindness to Paloma and Mark," she said. Her voice was weak, but Mark was right; her sentence structure was much better.

"I'm glad to be able to help," said Diane. "I came to ask your permission to carry out an experiment in your yard."

Marcella smiled. She clearly liked the idea of experiments.

"That sounds delightful," she said. She took a sip of broth. "Jonas told me you found the sherds I was concerned about," she said.

"We did. That is what spurred the desire for the experiment," said Diane.

"Do you think someone is buried in my backyard? The note . . . I wondered if whoever wrote it was, well, murdered. I think there was some deranged artist living in the house and he may have done away with someone. What do you think?"

"I think I'd like to take a look in your yard. We are always looking for better ways to detect buried human remains. David has wanted for a long time to have a place to take soil samples to run a chemical analysis to see if he can pinpoint locations where remains have been buried. He wants to try other methods too—resistivity, seismic—and make comparisons. I wanted to ask your permission," said Diane.

"Yes, I think that is an intriguing idea. We can perhaps solve my little mystery and get some scientific information to boot. A good plan," she said.

"Tell me," said Diane. "How old do you think the writing on the desk is?"

"The desk was under a lot of junk that hadn't been moved in a very long time. I had an antiques dealer look at it. He thinks it is a handmade desk from the 1930s. If it helps, it had a buffalo nickel dated 1920 in one of the drawers. It was worth two dollars." She grinned and took a sip from a cup of coffee on her tray. "I hadn't finished looking into the pedigree of the house. I went to the historical society and spoke with a few old-timers who worked there. They weren't much help remembering, but they gave me a computer printout of a picture of the front of the house from about fifty years ago. It hasn't changed much. I was going to the courthouse next."

"I have someone searching the courthouse records," said Diane. "Tell me about the three paintings on the living room wall."

"That was the most fun thing. I was knocking out a wall upstairs, and there they were. Very nice, I thought. They seemed like they fit the house. I hung them in the living room," she said.

"Were they signed?" Diane asked.

"In a way. There is a picture of a bird in the lower-right

corner of each one. A black-and-white bird. I thought the artist might have a bird name, like Finch, Crow, Sparrow—there are any number of surnames that are birds. That's a thought," said Marcella. "Perhaps there is something in the paintings that we can date."

"The thieves took the paintings," said Diane.

"Why would anyone steal those old paintings?"

"That's one of the things we hope to find out. They also took your pottery that was in the living room hutch."

"I don't know what the paintings were worth, but they are going to be sorely disappointed in the pots. They aren't real artifacts," said Marcella.

Marcella pronounced each word with a short pause. Diane noticed her voice was fading quickly.

"What did you make of the subjects in the paintings?" asked Diane.

"One was a young woman, another was a young man—actually, they looked more like teenagers. The background of both was woods. Very wistful faces. The third was a woman, perhaps in her thirties, sitting in a chair."

Marcella stopped talking and her eyes suddenly grew wide. Diane was alarmed that she might be feeling ill.

"Well, why didn't I notice it before?" Marcella said. "She was sitting on a chair at a desk—the desk I found in the potter's shed."

Chapter 28

Marcella leaned back and put a hand to her head and took a deep breath.

"I'm afraid I'm tiring you out," said Diane.

"It's this damn headache that comes and goes that tires me out," she said. "It's good for me to think. I need to be able to think."

"Your thinking is just fine. Thank you for allowing us to experiment in your yard."

"My pleasure," whispered Marcella. "Experimenting is good. I have always liked the University of Georgia motto—do you know what it is?"

"No, I confess I don't." Diane grinned. "I don't even know the motto of Bartrum University."

"Georgia's is *Et docere et rerum exquirere causas*," Marcella said slowly.

Diane's Latin was terrible, unless it had something to do with anatomy. She merely raised her eyebrows.

"To teach, to serve, and to inquire into the nature of things. I love inquiring into the nature of things."

"That is a nice motto," said Diane. She squeezed Marcella's hand and started to leave.

"Bartrum's," whispered Marcella, "is *Quaerite et invenietis*: Seek and ye shall find."

"I'll remember that," Diane said.

Paloma and Mark were gone when Diane came out of the ICU. Diane guessed they were in the cafeteria. She punched the elevator button and waited. The doors opened and Lynn Webber was standing in front of her, managing to look stylish in her bright white lab coat. Diane got on the elevator.

"Were you looking for me?" asked Lynn.

"No," said Diane. "I have a friend in ICU."

Lynn looked very uncomfortable and it was all Diane could do not to smile.

"You do? I'm so sorry. I hope they are doing well," Lynn said.

"She is improving," said Diane.

"I read an archaeologist was attacked in her home. Is that your friend?" she asked.

"Yes, it is. Marcella Payden," Diane said.

Lynn was standing in front of the elevator buttons. She made no move to push them.

"I'm going to the lobby," said Diane. She pointed to the elevator buttons in front of Lynn.

"Well, hell," said Lynn. "Have you read the newspaper or not?"

Diane smiled. "Yes, I have."

"I suppose you're mad?" said Lynn.

"No, not particularly. I'm rather concerned about the political fallout for you."

"That reporter went way beyond what I wrote," Lynn said.

"I thought I recognized a shift in writing style," said Diane.

"I called her and asked why in the world she said the things she did about the two crimes being similar. She said it's her style to write what seems reasonable and let the facts shake out. If they are wrong, people will correct her." Lynn threw up her hands. "That's how she gets at the truth? Can you imagine that logic? What kind of epistemology is that?"

"Have you had many calls?" asked Diane.

"I probably have. My assistant is answering the phone. I've been out of the office," she said.

I don't blame you, thought Diane.

Lynn punched the button for the lobby and the elevator moved with a lurch. "Are you parked in the parking garage?" asked Lynn.

"Yes," Diane said.

"Me too. Have you heard from Ross?" asked Lynn.

"No. I expect to," said Diane.

"I hope this won't make his job more difficult," Lynn said.

The elevator doors opened onto the lobby. They stepped out as several people brushed past them to get in. Diane and Lynn headed for the exit to the parking garage.

"I take it from the article that Stacy was murdered," said Diane.

"Yes. A first-year student could have made the call. Hell, anyone who watches forensic crime dramas could have seen it was murder," she said.

A great many people were going to be unhappy with the findings, especially the way in which they were announced. Probably the only satisfied person at the moment was Harmon Dance. And quite possibly, the reporter.

The exit to the parking garage was just off a small hallway. Diane pushed on the large gray door. Just as they were outside, a man approached. Lynn started to speak, but stopped.

"You vindictive bitch. You stupid, vindictive bitch." The man was taller than either of them, but wasn't quite six feet. He was slim, but pudgy, had a round face and a head of thick, wavy, reddish brown hair. His eyes were close together and he had a cruel twist to his mouth. He held a newspaper in his right hand and was hitting the palm of his left hand with it.

"Oran Doppelmeyer," said Lynn. "I see you hate having your incompetence revealed. And after you have made such efforts to hide it."

"You think you can get away with this pathetic stunt? It's only going to show you up for the pissy little amateur you are." He stopped in front of Lynn and reached for her arm. "Don't think . . ."

Lynn's jaw clinched. "Get your hand off my arm," she said.

Diane could almost hear Lynn's teeth grinding.

"You need to go somewhere and calm down," Diane said to him.

He turned toward Diane without letting go of Lynn. "Who the hell are—Ow!"

Lynn had karate-chopped the arm that held her. Before he could react, Diane shoved her Rosewood identification in his face.

"Stop, or I'll place you under arrest. You think the newspaper makes you look bad now, wait until it gets the story that you attacked Dr. Webber. You won't be able to spin yourself out of it. Back off now and calm down." *Before Lynn beats you up*, she felt like adding.

He stared at Diane's identification for a long moment.

"What's this?" he said. "Crime lab?"

"Yes, and I can arrest if the need arises. Lynn, why don't you go on to your car?"

"And leave you alone with this maniac? No." Lynn was in a fighting mode.

Jeez, thought Diane. *They're both maniacs*.

Diane started to tell Lynn she needed to go first and let him save some face, but she could see Lynn wasn't in the mood to allow any face-saving measures for Doppelmeyer. The door opened and several men filed out, heading to their cars. They eyed the three of them as they passed. The heavyset men wore beards and overalls and clearly made Doppelmeyer uncomfortable.

"You need to go get in your car and go somewhere and chill," Diane said to Doppelmeyer. "No good can come of your staying here."

He glared at Lynn and pointed a finger. "We aren't finished."

Lynn pointed a finger back, punctuating her words. "Yes, we are."

He backed away, not breaking eye contact with Lynn. Unfortunately, Lynn wouldn't break eye contact either. She stood with her arms folded, staring. Doppelmeyer was at his car. He either had to break contact first, or stand there looking as stupid as Diane felt for standing there with the two of them.

His solution to his dilemma was to give Lynn the finger. There were some things Lynn wouldn't do and, happily for Diane, returning the gesture was one of them. He got in his car and left.

"Okay," said Diane. "Just what high school do you two go to?"

Lynn looked over at her sharply, then shrugged. "Oh, I suppose you're right. He just brings out the worst in me."

"I can see that," said Diane. "He's acting dangerous. I

think you ought to ask security to walk you to and from your car."

"He's all talk. He doesn't have the guts to do anything," she said.

"Grabbing your arm wasn't all talk. I'm serious. He looks like he's not finished. It won't hurt to get security to escort you to and from your car," she said. "They'll like the idea."

"I suppose you're right," said Lynn. "That lie he told about me those years ago still follows me. Whenever I go to a professional conference, invariably, someone brings it up. I needed something big to finally blow the ugly thing out of the water."

Diane wasn't sure whether the ugly thing Lynn referred to was Doppelmeyer or the lie. Lynn was still watching where he had left, as if he might return, backing up, to give her another piece of his mind.

"Besides," Lynn said, turning back to Diane, "everything *I* said in the article was true and it is a terrible miscarriage of justice."

"Just be careful," said Diane as she went to her vehicle.

She started up her SUV and waited until Lynn drove out of the parking garage to be sure she didn't have Doppelmeyer following her.

Diane drove back to the museum. She went to Andie's office first. Kingsley was there waiting for her. It was getting to be a habit of his, dropping by without calling first. He probably figured it was the most reliable way of getting to see her. Perhaps it was. She couldn't help but notice he had a copy of the newspaper with him.

"Hello, Ross," she said, smiling. "Andie, anything urgent?"

"Nothing urgent. Kendel got away okay. I drove her to the airport this morning early. I asked her to bring me back an Australian. I love their accents. I put the mail on your desk. Jin called for an appointment."

"Jin called for an appointment?" said Diane. "Since when does Jin call for appointments? Did he say what for?"

"No, but I know what it is. You want me to tell you?" said Andie.

"No, I want to stand here and guess. What does he want?" said Diane.

"He wants to go to a conference in the Netherlands.

They're teaching some cool stuff in DNA analysis. But that's just a guess. I think he's going to present it all formal-like so you'll say yes."

Diane called Jin on her cell. "Jin," she said when he answered, "if you are comfortable with leaving Hector and Scott in charge, you can go to the conference."

There was silence for a moment before Jin spoke. "How did you know?" he said.

"It's my job," she said. "How is the analysis coming of the evidence we collected in Gainesville? I have a feeling we are going to need it soon."

"I'm working on it. I'll be done today. Thanks, Boss," he said.

"Sure."

She turned to Ross. "You're here about Lynn Webber," she said.

Chapter 29

"I thought you said Lynn Webber wasn't a loose cannon," said Kingsley as he sat down in the leather chair across from Diane's desk.

Diane was glad to see him grinning broadly. She realized just how much she had dreaded trying to explain how a person whom she vouched for had screwed up his new job.

"Normally, she's not a loose cannon," said Diane. "I didn't know the impact their history had on Lynn's psyche. She's apparently been waiting a long time for a chance to pay Doppelmeyer back. And I'm afraid she's unrepentant, especially after the reaction she got from him."

"Reaction?" Kingsley said.

Diane told him about the parking garage encounter with Doppelmeyer at the hospital.

"You can arrest people?" he said when she finished.

"I have the authority, but I don't have restraints or a gun, so it would have been hand-to-hand combat. Fortunately, it didn't come to that," she said.

"Fortunately." He laughed.

"Which reminds me, I need to call Garnett. Excuse me a moment," she said.

Diane got Chief Garnett on the phone and told him about the incident at the hospital.

"Oran Doppelmeyer seemed out of control to me," she told Garnett, "and I had the feeling Dr. Webber didn't take it seriously enough. Can you have someone keep a lookout for her, or at least notify hospital security?"

"Sure," Garnett said. "Lynn's an officer of the court. What Doppelmeyer did was to commit a physical assault on her while she was on duty. And he made verbal threats against her. I'll make some arrangements. This is about that article in the paper?"

"Yes." Diane made a face. She hoped he wouldn't ask too many questions. She didn't particularly relish explaining the entire situation to him.

"The chief of police had a phone call from his Gainesville counterpart this morning," said Garnett. "The chief naturally didn't know what to say. He tried to reach Dr. Webber, but she's been in meetings all morning. Who exactly does she meet with?"

"I don't know," said Diane. "She likes to keep on good terms with the hospital administration, since her offices are there, so . . ." She let the sentence hang.

"Is there anything I should know about?" he asked.

Apparently her nonanswer hadn't been as subtle as she'd hoped. *Well, damn.*

"It depends on how you feel about plausible deniability," said Diane.

She heard him sigh. "How deep are we in this thing?" he asked.

"At the request of a private investigator, and on my own time, I reworked the Stacy Dance crime scene," said Diane. "It had been released by the Gainesville police more than a month ago and the case closed. Based on what I saw at the crime scene and in the police report, I suggested that the private firm currently involved in the case arrange for a new autopsy. At the father's request, the court order was obtained. The victim's father was very eager that this be resolved. He never believed it was an accident. Lynn was brought in to redo the autopsy. Jin helped with collecting the evidence and he is readying it to give to the Gainesville police when they call."

"Was Rosewood's crime lab involved in this?" he asked.

"You forget, I have labs and fancy equipment all over this building," said Diane.

"All right, then. Is this thing going to bite me in the ass?" he asked.

"I think it will turn out to be a good thing," said Diane. *Eventually*.

Garnett didn't ask any more questions, such as how did

the newspaper get hold of the story? He probably thought Mr. Dance called them. Diane was happy Garnett didn't ask. She might fudge a little when telling him certain things, but she was very careful to protect the honest relationship they had.

Garnett ended the conversation and Diane hung up the phone. She frowned at it a moment before she turned back to Kingsley.

"Is her article a problem for you?" she asked.

"No, not really. But I don't understand why she said some of the things she did," he said.

"The reporter added a lot of her own thoughts about comparison of the two murders," said Diane.

"That explains a lot." Kingsley steepled his hands. "Actually, it might shake up things enough to cause the killer to react," he said.

"Shaking things up is what the reporter said she was trying to do. I'm not sure I approve of the shaker method of finding the truth," said Diane.

Kingsley gave a noncommittal shrug of his shoulders. "You're probably right. But you never know."

"The article made the Gainesville police look bad. That's not a good thing," said Diane. "Maybe they did miss the boat, but they were kind of broadsided on this."

"Not really," said Kingsley. "Dance has been calling them every other day trying to get the case reopened. They should have known something might be coming their way."

"I've noticed you have a lot less sympathy with the authorities now that you've made a career change," she said.

"I guess I've been seeing a little more of the other side," he said. He put the tips of his fingers in the fountain on her desk. "Nice. I like the way you did the rocks." He took his fingers out and patted them on his jacket. "Did Frank say he could decipher the diary?" he asked.

Diane nodded. "Frank said it should be fairly straightforward. He may have even used the word *fun*."

"I've never quite understood how deciphering works," said Kingsley.

"It helps that there's always a pattern," said Diane. "Seriously, what did your employers say when they saw the newspaper?" she asked.

"They were sorry they weren't mentioned by name," he said, and gave her a rather lame smile. "What can I say? It's about business. However bad the article looked to the police, to my bosses it showed the effectiveness of their firm—and the speed with which we can determine the truth."

"Is that what we did, determine the truth?" said Diane.

"Part of it. Didn't we? The rest is up to the Gainesville police now. They will be wanting the evidence you collected. I'm going to suggest they send someone over here to sign for it. My bosses wanted to personally deliver it to the Gainesville PD, but I told them we need to have a simpler chain of custody from one official agency to another, and they agreed."

"All right. Jin is working on the analysis. I'll find out when he expects to finish. We'll hand over the evidence and the analysis. I suppose Mr. Dance is satisfied. Have you spoken with him?"

"Yes. He's very pleased that we have cleared his daughter's name. He's not happy that we have to turn the evidence over to the Gainesville police. He doesn't trust them. I told him the news media will be keeping an eye on them. He said it shouldn't have come to that; they should have done the job right the first time."

"I agree," said Diane. "However, things are how they are." She stood up. "I need to give some instructions to David and meet with a few of my curators, so I'm going to run you off."

Kingsley stood up. "I understand. If I stay much longer, I don't think you could get me out of that chair. You have a very comfortable office. Though I find the photograph of you hanging over that chasm a little disturbing every time I look at it."

Diane smiled. "A lot of people do." She said it as if it were a strange thought. Diane loved caving and she particularly liked vertical-entry caves. There was something quite exciting about repelling down an open chasm.

She walked out with him on her way to the crime lab. "Are you going to just let the police reinterview Stacy's band members?" asked Diane as they walked down the hall to the lobby.

"I think they'll do a better job. I'm sure they're scarier than I am," he said.

Diane started to leave him to go to her appointments, when she spotted three women at the information booth. She knew them. So did Kingsley.

"Well, hell," they both whispered together.

Chapter 30

Diane stood looking at Kathy Nicholson, Wendy Walters, and Marsha Carruthers as they turned in her direction. It was obvious they were being directed to Diane's office. The three of them spotted her and Kingsley. For a moment, Diane had the urge to run and hide behind the mammoth in the Pleistocene room.

Their faces ranged from grim to angry. As the three women approached, Diane wondered which office would be better for whatever was about to happen: her osteology office in her forensic anthropology lab with its cold, spartan decor, or her more comfortable museum office with its Zen-like qualities. She opted for Zen-like. That office was closer.

Marsha Carruthers looked much as she had when they interviewed her. She wore another dark dress. This one was gray with black buttons and a white collar and cuffs.

"I'm glad both of you are here," Marsha said. "We intend to speak with you."

Diane supposed it was only fair, since she and Kingsley went to their homes intending to speak with them, and did.

"Very well. We can talk in my office," said Diane.

She retraced her steps to her office, opening the doors to the administrative wing of the museum for her guests. She led them down the hall into Andie's office, where she found Jonas Briggs waiting for her.

"I thought I would escort you to the staff meeting," said Jonas. He smiled cheerfully, probably relieved that Marcella was doing so much better than the doctors had expected.

As Diane attended to Jonas, the three women waited impatiently. Kathy Nicholson spent the time scrutinizing Andie's seating area, a room Diane thought would be good for entertaining Peter Rabbit's mother, with its cottage-style overstuffed chairs and sofa. The room's colors of pink, blue, and green, and the floral design, were repeated in a porcelain grandfather clock. A rag rug in matching colors sat underneath a dark cherry pie-crust coffee table. Kathy Nicholson's gaze shifted from one item to the next, lingering on a crackled figure of a rabbit sitting on the coffee table beside magazines about museums.

The other two women simply stood, frowning and waiting. Diane didn't introduce anyone. It didn't seem appropriate and she didn't think the three women would appreciate it.

"Change of plan," said Diane. "Andie, you are taking my place at the meeting."

Andie's eyes grew wide. "What? Me?"

"You know the curators and the issues. You have the budgets. And you've been wanting to be more involved at a higher level," said Diane.

"Yes, but, I mean, they are all college professors, and I'm, well, me," she said.

"Ah," said Jonas, putting an arm around her shoulder, "but you sit on the right hand of the queen herself. Just remember that. And also that underneath their clothes, those college professors all wear Underoos."

Andie laughed.

"You'll do fine," said Diane. "They are all excited about the webcam project. If anyone gives you trouble, you can send them to me."

"See there?" said Jonas. "That'll put the fear of God into them."

After Jonas and Andie left, Diane ushered her three visitors into her office. Kingsley helped Diane pull up enough chairs to her desk. Diane thought about taking them into her sitting room but decided she wanted her desk between herself and the women. Kingsley was on his own.

"I'm sorry, but I have to make a call first," said Diane before anyone spoke. She walked behind her desk, sat down, and dialed David's number. "We have permission for the research project," she told him.

"Great. I thought we would. Marcella loves research. How is she?" he asked.

"She seems much better," said Diane.

"Good. Jin loaned me Hector and Scott. So, okay, what's the deal? Hector's the older twin, right? And there is something about his shirt?" said David.

"The color is a longer wavelength than Scott's," said Diane.

"Yeah, that's it. God, I hope this isn't a mistake," he said.

"They'll do fine," she said.

"They have improved the research design. We are going to collect samples using a smaller grid system—collect more samples—to determine the least number of samples needed for accurate results."

"They enjoy research," said Diane. "You shouldn't have any problems."

"Oh, and I've lined up some archaeology students to excavate, in case we find anything," said David.

"Just remember, if you locate anything, you have to call the coroner before you take anything out of the ground," said Diane.

"I've informed Whit, so he knows we might call," said David.

"Then you are good to go," said Diane. "Keep me informed."

She hung up the phone. They were all staring at her, the three women and Kingsley. She supposed at this end it was a strange conversation.

"Now," said Diane, "what can I do for you?"

"You can recant what you said to the newspaper," said Marsha Carruthers. "You aren't getting that trash out of jail. He killed my daughter." She leaned forward and repeated her plea. "He killed my daughter."

Diane guessed that Marsha's other daughter hadn't confided in her, or she would have mentioned it first thing. She hoped Samantha didn't wait too long. Diane didn't want the police to be the ones to tell the Carruthers it was their daughter who found Stacy's body.

"You told me you were not interested in getting that monster out of jail," said Kathy Nicholson. "But it's obvious you lied."

She pulled the newspaper article from her purse and tossed it on the table. It was the one Diane had already read.

"Neither I nor Dr. Kingsley had anything to do with the article in the paper," said Diane. "And we are not trying to get Ryan Dance out of jail."

"Then where did the newspaper get this information?" asked Wendy Walters.

"I've not talked with the reporter. I don't know her," said Diane.

"You told me you worked for . . . or are the director of"—Kathy pulled Diane's card out of her purse and read from it—"the Aidan Kavanagh Forensic Anthropology Lab. But it turns out you're a museum director." She tossed the card on her desk with the article. "Why would you deceive us in this way?"

"How is it you're qualified to say anything about how that woman died?" said Wendy. "People are going to believe what they read in the newspaper and there is going to be a call for the Dance boy's release, and the police are going to be chasing a wild goose, because . . ." She threw up her hands. "This is just stupid. Are the two of you scam artists? Is messing with people's lives how you get your kicks?"

"I am director of this museum. I'm also director of the Aidan Kavanagh Forensic Anthropology Lab, which is part of this museum. And I'm director of the Rosewood Crime Lab," said Diane.

They stared at her for a moment. Wendy spoke first. "What does Rosewood have to do with any of this? It's Gainesville's jurisdiction."

"I wasn't representing Rosewood when I spoke with you or when I investigated the scene of Stacy Dance's death," said Diane.

"Then you were using your employer's time and facilities for personal gain," said Wendy.

"No, I was not," said Diane. "First, my work was pro bono; second, I didn't use Rosewood's facilities or their time . . . even though I could have. You see, our crime lab does forensic analysis for jurisdictions all around the world, not just Rosewood. I'm still not understanding why you are here and what you hope to have me do."

"Is it true you said that woman was murdered?" said Marsha.

"Stacy Dance," said Diane. "Yes, she was murdered."

"We discovered that our medical examiner said she died by accident in a rather perverted and disgusting fashion," said Marsha. "What we want you to do is to recant what is in the paper. Our police aren't stupid. Neither is our ME. You have no business contradicting them. All it's done is get people to wondering about Ryan Dance. People have called me. People are saying we are rich and we have railroaded some poor boy." She stopped and her lips quivered. "And my baby did not die in the same disgraceful way that woman did."

"I know the circumstances of your daughter's death and those of Stacy's death are quite different," said Diane. "Neither of us is responsible for the reporter saying they were similar. But we do know how Stacy died, and she did not die by her own hand. She was killed somewhere else. Her body was staged in that embarrassing way. It was not her doing."

"It's your word against our law enforcement people," said Marsha. "They are good at what they do. They would not have said it was an accident if there was any evidence it was murder."

"My husband knows two members of the museum board," said Wendy. "Thomas Barclay and Madge Stewart. He is going to call them and tell them what you've been doing."

"That's fine," said Diane. "Call away. I can't change my findings. But you need to stop and look at the situation. You seem to be under the impression that it's easy to get someone out of prison. It isn't. Nothing in what we have discovered can in any way be used to get Ryan Dance's sentence overturned, or even reviewed, for that matter. And, certainly, the inaccurate reporting in a newspaper can't do anything for him."

"And," added Kingsley, "it is out of our hands. As you point out, the matter falls under the jurisdiction of the Gainesville police. It's their investigation now."

The three of them sat for a moment looking at one another, as if groping for something else to say. Finally they stood up. Marsha Carruthers leaned her hand on Diane's desk.

"I won't forget this. Ever. I won't forget."

Diane wanted to tell her to spend her energies on her living daughter. She wanted to tell her to do something to keep the good memories of Ellie Rose. She wanted to tell her she was so sorry that this terrible thing happened to her and her family. She didn't say any of those things. Instead she stood up, and she and Kingsley escorted them out of her office.

As Diane watched them go down the hallway toward the lobby, she wondered whether they would have been such good friends had the tragedy of Ellie Rose not bonded them together. Diane and Kingsley walked back into her office to debrief.

"Something was off. Something happened that they didn't mention," said Diane as she sat back down at her desk. "Or was this not strange to you?"

"I got the same impression. It was probably the article. If the Carruthers family have been getting crank calls, it would put them on edge. You know how disturbing such things can be. Especially if you are being called a criminal, and the man who killed your daughter is characterized as an innocent victim," said Kingsley. "I think Marsha is afraid of everything being in the news again, bringing back the intensity of those raw emotions. She is afraid of reliving the nightmare of her daughter's death again every day and is fighting those who would revive it."

"It looks to me as if she already relives it every day," said Diane.

"Privately," said Kingsley. "Not publicly. That's what she dreads. Funny, I was watching them. Marsha and Wendy were inside themselves, completely absorbed. I doubt they could even give a general description of what your office looks like. Kathy Nicholson was the only one of them interested in the things around her—your assistant's office, your office. While we were getting the chairs, she was looking at your Escher prints, your photographs, the fountain. I got the impression Kathy hadn't wanted to come. I think she would like to break her bond with the other two."

"What implications does that have?" said Diane.

"I have no idea. Just throwing stuff out. Like you, something bothered me too. But I can't put my finger on what exactly," he said. "Maybe it's that they seemed like the three witches from *Macbeth*. Okay, that was unkind, but I find them just a little spooky."

"Do you think Marsha or her husband could have killed Stacy?" said Diane. "You see how angry both of them are at us. What emotions must Stacy have brought out in them, poking around in their daughter's death?"

"I think it's a possibility the police should look at, but I'm not sure they will," he said.

He didn't say the two of them should look into it, but she felt that was what he was thinking. Perhaps she should have asked Marsha what she was doing the day Stacy died. Maybe dug a little deeper. But Diane had wanted to get them out of her office. Marsha Carruthers wouldn't have answered anyway.

Kingsley left and Diane looked over some budget requests before she headed for the crime lab. She thought about looking in on the meeting of museum curators, but decided she would let Andie handle it. If she were present, it would completely change the dynamics of the meeting.

Diane stopped at the information desk to speak with a docent, when someone touched her arm. She turned to greet them with a smile.

"Kathy Nicholson," Diane said, trying not to let the smile freeze on her face. "Did you forget something . . . or perhaps remember something?"

Chapter 31

Kathy Nicholson, sans Marsha and Wendy, stood beside the information desk with her purse on her shoulder. She had on a light wool jacket she hadn't been wearing in the meeting.

"No, I didn't forget anything," she said. "I'd like to speak with you." She looked around as if she were being watched, or on the lookout, lest she be seen by someone she knew.

"Let's go to my office," said Diane.

She told the docent she would see her the next day and led Mrs. Nicholson back to her office and closed the door. Diane didn't sit behind her desk, but pulled up a chair and sat across from her.

"May I get you a drink?" asked Diane. "I have a refrigerator in the next room with cold sodas."

"No, thank you, no," she said. "I have a friend meeting me in your museum restaurant a little later. She said it's very good."

"It is," Diane said.

Diane waited for Kathy Nicholson to speak. Kathy looked at her well-manicured hands a moment and back up at Diane.

"You must be wondering why I'm here," she said.

"I am," said Diane. "I hope you don't intend to try to persuade me to recant, as Mrs. Carruthers put it. It's not just my findings regarding Stacy's death, but those of our medical examiner as well."

"No, I haven't come for that, but the others think I have," she said.

"Oh?" said Diane.

"Do you really have all those jobs?" Kathy asked.

"Yes, I do. The forensic anthropology lab is part of the museum. The crime lab is housed here and I run it. I used to be a human rights investigator," Diane said, hoping that might help Kathy to understand her qualifications.

"They—we—weren't always like this. We were very happy people. You wouldn't have known Marsha ten years ago. Wendy either. Ellie Rose's death changed so much for us. But nine years is a long time, and I am so tired."

"Of what?" said Diane, gently.

"That's a good question. Marsha's grief, I guess. That's a terrible thing to say, I know. And I know you don't ever get over something like her daughter's tragic death. My husband died of cancer and I miss him every day. But . . . but I don't"—she frowned as if searching for the right word—"I don't cover the world with it. I don't walk through it as if it were syrup. I don't know." A small sigh escaped her lips, as if she gave up looking for the right expression. "Wendy told me what you said yesterday—about Marsha losing what it felt like to love her daughter, or something like that. She has, I think. That desperate anguish she felt when they found Ellie Rose's body is still fresh in her now, just like it was then."

Diane wondered why she was telling her all this. But she didn't say anything. She just listened. Her former boss at World Accord International always said the ability to listen is one of the most powerful tools one can have.

After a moment's silence, Diane spoke. "Why do you think Marsha has not healed?"

"I don't know. At first, Wendy and I tried to help Marsha cope. But after a while, Wendy just went along with her, and I stayed across the street with my husband more and more. We quit having the neighborhood barbecues we used to have when the children were small. I have a son, Colton. He's in California now at Berkeley studying political science. He's getting a master's."

"Do you see him much?" asked Diane.

"Not a lot. I go out there some. I'm thinking about moving," she said.

Diane smiled.

"My son doesn't like to come here anymore. I don't

blame him. Bad memories. Wendy's son, Tyler, is in law school at UGA now. He doesn't come home much either. So much has changed. I sometimes resent Marsha and her family. I think Wendy does too. I know that's unfair and cruel."

"But understandable," said Diane. Kathy obviously wanted to talk. Diane wondered whether she had been frank with anyone about this.

"Colton was a year younger than Ellie Rose. He and Tyler are the same age. We were so happy then. There were lots of kids in the neighborhood. Several people moved away after Ellie Rose's death. Even though Colton was a boy, I was afraid after El's death. You never know why someone kills children, or if yours might be next. All of us parents were afraid. Many distanced themselves from the Carruthers. Others, like Wendy and me, tried to help. But as I said, there was no helping her. I don't know what it would have been like if it had been my child. Wendy said your child was murdered," she said.

"Yes," said Diane. "I don't talk about it much."

Kathy nodded as if she understood. "What did you think of us?" she asked, suddenly.

"The three of you are very sad, especially Wendy and Marsha. They have turned very much inward. The whole time the three of you were here, you were the only one who seemed to be aware of your surroundings."

"Yes, we are different," she said. "You noticed that?"

"Yes, I noticed it. What I don't understand is why the three of you came here today. Did Marsha actually expect to have me say that what I found really wasn't true? Does she honestly think there is a chance Ryan Dance could get out of jail based on my findings about his sister's death?"

"Yes. Both of them think that. Marsha got some pretty mean calls that upset her after the article came out. And her daughter Samantha moved out. She is beside herself about that. But she never paid any attention to the poor girl. What did she expect? She wanted her family nearby, but out of her way. She never used to be so self-absorbed. Honestly, that's true. She was just the nicest person. Ellie Rose was a nice girl too. Always cheerful, always had something sweet to say. Her death tried my faith. It did. I think it tried Marsha's and Wendy's too."

"Samantha moved out?" said Diane. "I'm sorry to hear that."

"She is eighteen. And, frankly, I think it's a good thing. She was being smothered in that house. You were there. Could you live there?"

No, Diane couldn't have, but she didn't say it. Instead she gave Kathy a prod. "Is there something you wanted to say to me?"

"I wanted to ask you: Are you sure, are you really sure, that Stacy Dance was murdered?"

"The Gainesville police will be receiving all the new evidence soon and they will decide how to proceed and what to divulge. So I can't go into any specifics. However, I can tell you I have no doubts whatsoever, and neither does our medical examiner, that Stacy was murdered. And we both have had a lot of experience in what we do."

Kathy Nicholson's eyes teared up. Diane reached for a tissue and handed it to her.

"Are you afraid Marsha Carruthers or her husband might have done something to Stacy?" asked Diane.

Kathy was quiet for several moments. "I would never say that. Never," she said at last.

"But you might worry about it?" said Diane.

Kathy said nothing.

"Is there anything you know that bothers you? Anything you've seen?" asked Diane.

"It's just the anger. We drove up here together. It was just terrible. Wendy drove and Marsha sat in the front seat. I sat in the back. We discussed strategy. It was all so—so frenetic. Marsha was so angry. I think it was equating the manner of Ellie Rose's death to Stacy's that got to her. Wendy called the police and they told her what Stacy was supposed to have died from. For some reason, Marsha was angry with you in particular. I think it was the things you said to her. I suppose she saw you as trying to rob her of her grief. It's all she thinks she has."

"I'm sorry I upset her," said Diane.

"Wendy looked you up on the Web and discovered

you are the director of the museum," said Kathy. "We all thought you had deceived us about who you are."

"She didn't find the other positions I hold?" said Diane.

"No. I think the first item she found was the museum and she stopped there. It had your picture. That was the only listing we knew for sure was you. You aren't the only Diane Fallon in the world."

"That's true," said Diane, smiling.

"We didn't quite understand why you would have anything to do with a crime investigation. Frankly, I thought you and the gentleman with you were frauds. I thought you had lied to me."

"Didn't you look up the name of my osteology lab—the one on the card?" said Diane.

"We didn't think of it. When we found you, we thought that was it; we had found you out. None of us know very much about computers, really. I know everyone does these days, but we don't. Wendy used Marsha's husband's computer. She knew how to use Google. I always thought it was simply a very large number," she said.

Diane smiled. "I take it you don't follow the stock market either," said Diane.

"No," she said, and almost smiled. "I was amazed at all the information on your Web site. All the things about the museum. Wendy found the museum board of directors and discovered that both her husband and father-in-law, Everett, were on a couple of charity boards with two of the members. Wendy will make good on her threat to have them make calls about you. Her father-in-law is a type A personality, if you know what I mean. He'll pressure the board members to do something about you if Wendy asks him."

"Wendy will be sorely disappointed," said Diane. "It isn't a governing board. It's an advisory board."

"Oh, she will be disappointed," said Kathy.

"Tell me, why is Wendy so involved in Marsha's life?" asked Diane.

"Same reason I am. We are neighbors and friends. We go to the same church. We got caught up in trying to help Marsha with her grieving process and were kind of pulled into it. Over the years it became our life. It's not this bad all the time. We go though long periods of normal. Then something happens and Marsha will start drinking. It's gotten a lot worse since Stacy Dance spoke to her. And when you and that man—Kingsley—came into our lives and that newspaper article came out."

"I'm sorry our visit had that effect," said Diane. "Has Marsha been to grief counseling?"

"Yes. It hasn't worked—or it will work for a while until something happens," said Kathy.

"What triggers her relapses?" asked Diane.

"Lots of things. My husband's cancer and death were one thing. Wendy's husband is head of the oncology department at the hospital, so all of them were there for us during the process. When Samantha reached the same age Ellie Rose was when she died, it set Marsha off. As I said, Stacy's visit upset her. Sometimes a report in the news about some teenage girl who died would be enough to upset her again."

"You said they think you are here to talk me into recanting my findings. Why do they think that?" asked Diane.

"When we went outside to get in the car, I commented that maybe if we had been friendlier we might have gotten somewhere. Marsha turned on me and started to yell. She's been doing that more frequently. It made me mad and I almost told her that maybe I would be the one to recant my story. I came that close." Kathy stopped and took a deep breath.

"I wouldn't," she continued. "I saw what I saw. But I was so angry that she'd turn on me after everything. I made up my mind I wasn't going to ride back with them. I have a friend here in Rosewood, and I can spend the night with her and we can go shopping together tomorrow." Kathy wrapped her jacket closer to her as if she were cold.

"Wendy said she thought I was right," Kathy continued, "and if I came in to speak with you alone, I might get somewhere, or at least find out what you were really up to. I agreed. I just wanted to get away from them. Wendy is real good with Marsha. I'm not. Marsha agreed that it might be a good idea too, and she apologized to me for the things she said. But, you know, I'm tired. I'm tired of living in her world."

"What will you tell them?" said Diane.

"I'll tell them about your qualifications—about the human rights work," she said. "And that you said again that you aren't trying to get Ryan Dance out of prison. That's what Marsha is really concerned about."

"I'll repeat, just for clarity, the finding that Stacy Dance was murdered is not in any way related to Ryan Dance. Suspicious circumstances aren't proof of anything. Even if you were to recant your story about seeing Ryan Dance that day, it would have no effect on his status. There was too much physical evidence implicating him."

"But sometimes evidence is thrown out. People get released, even though everyone knows they are guilty," said Kathy.

"Very rarely," said Diane. "I haven't read the transcripts of the trial and I'm not a lawyer, but from what I understand, the police had probable cause to search Ryan's car, even without your testimony, so the incriminating evidence that convicted him would have been found anyway. The only way I can see him getting out of prison is if he really is innocent and the police happen to find indisputable evidence that identifies the real guilty party. I don't see that happening. If Marsha needs comforting on that point, have her talk to the district attorney or a defense lawyer. I'll bet you have one in the neighborhood."

Kathy gave Diane a faint smile and nodded. "That's what I'll tell them."

She gathered herself together and stood. Diane stood with her.

"But you do seem to know about Ryan Dance's case," she said.

"A little. But not for any other purpose than to understand where Stacy Dance was coming from," said Diane. "Much like Marsha's obsession, Stacy had her own obsession involving Ellie Rose's death and her brother's conviction. Something Stacy did may have gotten her killed, but it may be coincidental to her investigation. We just don't know."

Kathy Nicholson nodded and Diane walked her through Andie's office to the door and let her out. The woman had been forthcoming, but Diane was suspicious of her as much as she was of Diane. What if the three of them had killed

Stacy? she thought. What if she and Wendy had been so sucked into Marsha's world that they had formed a kind of vigilante cabal? The thought made Diane shiver. Other than the profound sadness, the three of them looked so normal.

Chapter 32

All in all, Diane had a good ending to a not altogether pleasant workday. After Kathy Nicholson left, Andie came back from the meeting with the curators and gave Diane her report. Diane told Andie to write it up and she could present it to the board.

Frank called and said he would be late coming home, probably very late. Diane grabbed an apple and cold drink from her refrigerator and called it dinner. She sat down on the couch in the sitting room off her office, put on a CD of classical music, and cleared her mind of anything to do with murder or death before she left the museum.

Diane drove out to Marcella's house before she went home. When she arrived there, Marcella's yard was lit up. David had brought the lights they used for night work. Why, she wondered, were they working at night?

A police car was parked in the drive. A patrolman sauntered up to her car.

"I hope there's not another problem," said Diane, getting out of her SUV.

"No, ma'am. David Goldstein asked a couple of us to come down and stand guard. He didn't want a repeat of the other night," he said.

"Good move. How is Patrolman Daughtry doing?" asked Diane. "His leg healing up?"

"Leg's doing good. Got in a bit of a dustup over his gun. I guess you heard," he said. "I don't think it will amount to much. He's off work now with his leg up, watching football reruns, so I guess he's doing great. You really think those punks will come back here?"

"I don't know. It was pretty stupid of them to come the first time," said Diane.

"You're right about that. Can't account for stupid. We'll keep a lookout. We got a little drive we can circle that takes us around to the back where they came in the first time. They try to park there again, we'll get them."

"Thank you, Officer," said Diane. She went around back and spotted David standing at a plane table tripod looking at aerial maps. Hector and Scott were making a grid of Marcella's yard with string and stakes.

"Are you camping here?" said Diane.

David gave her a look somewhere between a grin and a frown. "Looks like it. It was Scott's idea. He and Hector are all over the experiment thing. We'll probably be able to write a paper entitled 'The Best One Hundred Ways to Find a Buried Body in the Woods.' Seriously though, they did come up with some good ideas."

"Why not start in the morning?" she said, looking out over the lit yard at the busy Spearman twins.

David followed her gaze. "I see why Jin hired the two of them. They work very efficiently together." He looked back at Diane. "We started right after I spoke with you. It gets dark so early these days, Scott thought it would be a good idea to work after dark setting up grid lines so we can start taking samples in the morning. So far it seems to be going well." He grinned. "They haven't started singing 'Kum Ba Yah' yet. That's a plus."

"Wait until bedtime," said Diane. She looked around the yard. "Where are your tents?"

"Marcella's daughter and her husband came by the house. They told us to just bed down in our sleeping bags in her mother's living room. They are very nice people," he said.

"They are. Did she say how Marcella is?" asked Diane.

"Doing better, tires easily. She said she seems to have clarity of thought. I think Paloma was more worried about that than anything else," he said. "Neva is coming tomorrow to help. I think she said Mike will come too. That will be good."

"That's right—Mike is due back from Africa," said Diane.

Mike Seger was the museum's geology curator. He also worked for a pharmaceutical firm, collecting extremophiles from around the world, a job that allowed him to bring unique specimens back to the museum's rock collection.

"Due back tonight," said David. "This grid part isn't going to take as long as I was afraid it would. However, running the samples will take some time. Do you really expect to find bodies?" he asked.

"I'm not sure. It's a gut feeling. The bone came from somewhere," said Diane.

"A lot of strange stuff going on around here," said David. "Somebody was crazy for yard ornaments. We've found a ton of them just lying around. Lots of gargoyles. Apparently they haven't kept away the evil spirits," he said.

"They aren't on guard," said Diane, smiling and looking up at the roofline of the house.

"I suppose that explains it," said David. He gestured toward the porch where Daughtry fell through the rotten boards. "The policeman said Daughtry was suspended for a couple of days. The chief of police wasn't upset that he dropped his gun, but that he didn't report it. I personally think they're being a little tough on him. But it does look like Ray-Ray What's-his-name was shot with Daughtry's gun."

"Does Hanks know anything more about that?" asked Diane.

"If he does, he's not talking. I think information primarily goes one way with him. He's really trying hard to keep control of the case," said David.

"I'm not taking it away from him," said Diane. David grinned. "Don't you dare say, 'Not yet.' "

"Hanks did tell me he got a list of places that employ day laborers, and he's questioning people Ray-Ray worked with," said David. "I don't know if he's found out anything of value. What I wonder is why they shot Ray-Ray. Maybe he was just a day laborer in the burglary. Maybe he wasn't needed when it was finished."

"Could be," said Diane.

"Or maybe they just shot him because his name was Ray-Ray and they got tired of saying it over and over again.

Who would name their child Ray-Ray?" David threw up his hands.

"Have you been able to separate any of the footprints connected with Marcella's attack from the later ones that were left when we were attacked?"

"I have several prints on top of one another. I think most of the secondary prints were from the paramedics and Jonas Briggs. Izzy collected the shoe prints of the paramedics, so we have those, and I got Jonas to give me his. I've got the computer working on separating the images. I don't hold out a lot of hope. There's a lot of smearing. So far, the boot prints I told you about earlier are the only ones we've found that are clear enough to match with a specific shoe—if we find the shoe."

"Where is Neva on her search of the courthouse records?" said Diane.

"I don't know. She had to go out on a couple of murders over in Jackson County. She's working on the courthouse project between jobs," he said.

"What do you have here?" Diane gestured toward the map.

"Aerial maps taken in the area over the years. I'm looking for some common points we can mark with stakes. We're going to do an overlay when we get the data on the chemical makeup of the soil and see what ground features correlate with what chemical characteristics. Too bad we don't have any infrared photos."

"It looks like you have everything under control," she said.

"It's coming along. Hope we don't have any more surprise intruders," he said. "I got backup just in case. A couple of patrolmen wanted to earn overtime for the holidays coming up. It's all working out for everyone," David said.

"I met one of them coming in. They seem to have a plan for securing the property," said Diane.

"I walked them over the area when they got here," David told her.

It seemed to Diane that everything was going well here. If she hurried, she could make it home before it got too late to call Kingsley to fill him in on the latest about the three women from Gainesville. It would be interesting to see if he was as suspicious as she was about them.

"I'll be going," she said. "Call if you need me for anything."

"Will do." He grinned. "By the way, one of the things Paloma wanted was a copy of our research design for her mother. Seems Marcella is very excited about it. I never knew we had so many people around who are data wonks like I am."

"Yes, it's a scary thought, isn't it?" she said. "Who would have imagined—"

Diane was cut short by a loud cry coming out of the darkness.

Chapter 33

David and Diane jerked around and stared into the dark in the direction the cry came from.

"David! Help me! It's Hector, help! Oh jeez, help!"

Scott was perhaps two hundred feet from them. The lighting hadn't quite illuminated that far and all that was visible of him was a dim reflection of light from his lab suit and his face. He was kneeling on the ground in heavy undergrowth.

Diane hadn't heard a gunshot. That's what she'd feared. She and David ran toward Scott, jumping and skipping over piles of rocks and broken concrete, trying not to get tangled in the string, or trip over the stakes. Out of the corner of her eye Diane saw the bobbing flashlight of one of the policemen running through the woods in their direction.

"He's hurt," said Scott as they drew near.

"How?" asked Diane, breathing hard from the obstacle course she had just run.

"Hector was standing here. There was a noise, and he suddenly threw up his hands and just disappeared," he said.

"Scott, what do you mean?" asked David.

"Hector, can you hear me?" yelled Scott.

Diane heard a groan. She looked down at her feet and saw that she was standing on the edge of a wide, dark cylindrical hole in the ground, maybe six feet in diameter. Hector was somewhere below in deep shadow.

She knelt beside Scott, feeling in her pockets for a flashlight.

"Anyone have a light?" she asked.

"No," said David. "Damn. I don't. One of the policemen is coming. He has one."

"Oh jeez, Hector, say something," said Scott.

Diane put a hand on Scott's arm. "Stay calm. We'll get him out."

"What is this? Some kind of animal trap?" said Scott. "Who would do this?"

"It's an abandoned well," said Diane.

The patrolman had arrived and shined his light down into the opening.

"Well, hell," he said.

The bad news was Hector was lying at the bottom of the well. One leg was bent under him. Rotten boards and dirt half covered him. The good news was he was not far down—about ten, maybe twelve feet. Not far at all. But Diane worried about the walls of the well.

She took the flashlight from the policeman and handed him her keys.

"Go to my SUV. In the back is a bag with a rope in it and a backpack. Bring them. Hurry. And call the paramedics."

He nodded and headed off immediately through the dark in the direction of the driveway. Diane shined the light down the hole at Hector.

"Hector, can you hear me?" she said.

He moved. "Yeah. What the shit is this?" he said. His voice had a pissed-off, whiney tone, but it sounded strong.

"You fell down an old well," said Diane. "We're going to get you out. I need to know how you are. Are you hurt?"

He moved and yelped. "I think my leg is broken," he said.

"Just one?" Diane asked.

"Isn't that enough?" he yelled back.

Diane and David briefly smiled at each other.

"Are you hurt anywhere else?" she asked.

"It's kind of hard to tell. I'll try to stand," he said.

"Not yet. Stay still," she said, a little too sharply.

"Why? What else is down here—snakes?"

"Hector's afraid of snakes," whispered Scott.

"I heard that," yelled Hector.

"It's a little too late for snakes. It's too cold for them," said David. "I think," he added, under his breath.

"Okay," Hector said. Then after a moment he asked, "Where do they hibernate?"

"Rock outcrops," said David. "In the cracks. Not here."

Diane suspected David was spinning Hector a yarn. She didn't think he knew anything about snakes.

As David spoke to Hector, Diane examined the well with the flashlight. The debris piled around and on top of Hector indicated the well had been capped with a wooden platform that was covered in dirt and leaves with grass and briars growing over it. The rotten wood had collapsed under Hector's weight when he inadvertently stepped on top of it, not knowing it was there.

The sides of the well were lined with varied sizes of chiseled stone blocks held in place with very old mortar. The mortar had cracks and looked weathered. Sections had already crumbled and other blocks looked ready to fall. There was no way to know what kind of stress might make the walls collapse. But they had to do something.

Besides Diane, there were David, Scott, and two policemen. Enough to pull Hector out. More than enough. She guessed it would take only three of them for a vertical pull—maybe four, depending on Hector's weight.

"How much does Hector weigh?" Diane asked Scott.

"He won't say," said Scott, "but I weigh a hundred and sixty-four."

She did the math again. Three ought to do it. They only had to pull him up close enough to grab him once his arms and shoulders were within reach.

"Hector, you are not that far down," said Diane. "So, don't worry."

"Okay. I won't worry."

Hector groaned. Diane could see him struggling to move.

"What are you doing?" she asked, with some alarm.

"I'm trying to get my leg out from under me," he said. "I need to see how bad it is. And to do that, I need to move some of these damn rotten boards and crap on top of me."

"Be careful," said Diane.

"I will, but you need to tell me what you are worried about if it isn't snakes," he said. "So I can be careful with some effectiveness."

Diane hadn't wanted to panic him, but she didn't want him bumping against the precarious wall and causing the heavy stones and earth to collapse on top of him. If that happened, he would suffer truly serious injury and could die from the trauma or suffocation before they could get him out.

"I don't know how stable the wall is," she said. "It's very old."

"Oh. Oh jeez."

Diane could hear him breathing harder.

"You need to fight the panic," she said. "Don't worry. I've pulled people out of holes before. Piece of cake. We just need to be careful."

"Okay. No worry. Eat cake. Got it," he said.

"Are you all right?" asked Diane.

"He's okay. He thinks he's funny," said Scott. "I've tried to tell him he's not."

They heard another yelp.

"It's okay," he yelled. "I have my leg uncovered now. I need to see what kind of—" Hector screamed. "My leg, my leg! I can see the bone. Oh God. Oh God."

Compound fracture, thought Diane. *Damn. That means he's bleeding.*

She refocused the light, trying to avoid his eyes. Hector was sitting with his back to the wall with both legs now straight out in front of him. A piece of wood fell from above onto his legs and he yelped again.

"Move the wood out of the way," said Diane, gently. "Let me see your leg."

"You need to get him out of there," said Scott.

"I need to see how badly he's hurt," said Diane. "It will affect how we get him out."

"Oh God, my leg bone came out!" he screamed.

David and Diane looked at each other, a mixture of alarm and bewilderment.

"I've never heard—," began David.

"Wait a minute. False alarm," yelled Hector.

"Hector, this isn't funny," yelled Scott. "You are scaring us."

"No. I'm not being funny. I've got good news. I've found the buried bodies we're looking for."

Chapter 34

"What?" said Scott. "There's a body down there with you?"

"Not exactly—well, I guess, yes, exactly. But it's all bones," Hector said.

Diane heard Hector rustling around at the bottom of the well.

"Hector," said Diane, "don't move around so much."

Using her flashlight she examined the walls of the well and the area around the surface again. There were several trees nearby and one fairly close to the well, not a large tree, its trunk perhaps as big around as her leg. No large roots had worked their way through the cracks between the stones forming the wall, but smaller roots had, and the chances were good that tree root systems were pressing the wall in the direction of collapse. Where was the policeman with her rope?

Diane heard the rustling of someone walking through the leaves and brush and saw the play of a light. She looked up, expecting the policeman. It was Neva, and she had Mike Seger with her. Mike had Diane's rope bag and backpack.

Mike, the museum's geologist, was one of the best caving partners Diane had ever had. She was glad to see him there with Neva, another caving partner. Neva wasn't as experienced as Mike, but she was a reliable and skilled caver. Mike put the bag and backpack down on the ground.

His short brown hair was longer than when she last saw him. His lean features had developed a weathered look since he'd taken on his job visiting the world's most extreme environments. He usually had a serious look on his face. Here in the dim light his face looked to be carved out of stone.

"Hi, Doc. Good to see you." Mike's stern expression broke into a smile.

Diane grinned back. "Just the right people at the right time. We need to get Hector out of this well," she said. "I take it you saw the policeman?" She gestured at her caving gear.

Neva nodded. "Two of them. They stayed to direct the paramedics," said Neva.

She and Mike squatted down and looked into the well.

"What do we have here?" said Mike. "Hector, buddy, what the hell you doing down there?"

"Falling down a well seemed like a good idea at the time," Hector said.

Mike felt the ground around the top of the well. "Pretty firm," he commented. "But some collapse at the edge."

Diane explained the situation and the dangers and what she wanted to do.

"Let's get to it, then," said Mike.

David and Scott moved one of the battery-powered lights closer so they could see what they were doing. Diane and Mike opened the rope bag, basically a large tarp with grommets. It held Diane's caving rope. Diane took good care of her rope because it was literally a lifeline. She kept it clean and always took out any knots she had tied while caving. It was good rope and a lot of it.

"Do you think we can use that tree over there, the one closest to the well?" she asked Mike.

"Yeh, it looks good," said Mike. "We only have a what, ten-foot drop? It'll be over in a few seconds."

Neva took off her suede and faux fur jacket and hung it over a bush. She began rolling up her designer jeans.

"You warm enough?" asked Diane, looking at the thin sleeves of Neva's silk blouse.

"I'll be fine. You know, I'm like you. I don't know why I bother to dress up," she said. "Our lives are always on call for some death-defying adventure or another."

"At least you don't have on sequins," said Diane.

Diane began tying the handholds and a foothold in the rescue rope. Neva took the tarp and laid it over the edge of the well to reduce the crumbling of the edge when they pulled Hector out. Mike wrapped and tied off one end of a length of rope to the nearby tree at a height a couple of feet off the ground. The other end he tied into a half-hitch knot at a distance that allowed the rope to reach to the center of the well opening when the rope was fully extended from the tree. He took a rescue pulley from Diane's backpack, laid the long rescue rope in the pulley, and attached the pulley to the end of the shorter rope by means of a metal alloy snaplink. This arrangement would suspend the pulley and rescue rope midair over the center of the well as they lifted Hector out.

Mike, David, and Scott were going to do the pulling. Mike gave them instructions as they took up their places six feet or so back from the well on the side opposite the tree. The three of them gripped the rope firmly. Diane dropped the other end of the rope down the well to Hector.

"Hector, I want you to listen to me," she said.

"I'm listening."

"Put your good foot in the loop nearest the end of the rope. Use the other loops as handholds. Don't try to help us by putting your hands on the wall; it's much too unstable. Just hold on to the rope. Your leg is probably going to hurt, but you have to ignore the pain," said Diane.

"How do I do that?" asked Hector.

"You just do it," she said. "Scream if you have to, but don't thrash about, just hold on to the rope. Let us know when you are ready."

"You know," he said, "I've been thinking about the physics of hauling a weight up, and—"

"Hector, we have the math worked out. Just concentrate on hanging on to the rope," Diane said. "Remember what I do in my leisure time."

"Fishing?" he said.

Diane smiled. She watched him as he struggled to stand and she wondered whether she needed to go down into the well to help.

"You doing all right?" she asked.

"It's not so bad. I can do it," he said.

She winced as he held on to the side of the well to steady himself.

Hector got his foot in the loop and held on. He started to say something when a stone dislodged from near the top edge and fell with a crash as it hit the rotten wood.

"You all right?" she said. "Were you hurt?"

"No," he said in a voice that could be called squeaky at this point. He definitely sounded scared. "But, I'm ready to get out of here—now. Just don't drop me, okay?"

"You're going to be fine. You're in good hands. Here we go."

Diane signaled for them to pull. They leaned into the rope as if they were in a life-and-death tug-of-war, and Hector rose toward the surface, screaming at the top of his lungs. When his shoulders cleared the top, Diane and Neva pulled him to the edge and dragged him over the tarp and onto solid ground.

Scott ran over to him. "Hector, are you all right? Are you in pain?"

Hector lay on the ground breathing hard.

"I'm fine. Not much pain, really. It's just that, when Dr. Fallon suggested it, screaming seemed like such a good idea."

Diane opened the blade of her pocketknife and ripped Hector's jeans while David held the flashlight. His skin was bruised and swollen, but it wasn't an open fracture. What was most noticeable, however, was the broken tibia he held next to his chest.

"You brought a bone up with you?" said Scott.

"Well, hell, yeah. I wasn't going to have all that be a wasted trip. What is it, Dr. Fallon? Tell me it's not a deer or a dog," said Hector.

"It's not. It's human," said Diane. "It's relatively small, but judging from the epiphyseal union, I'd guess it was from a teenager."

"Dang," said Scott. "Wow." And then the realization: "A small teenager. Dead. In the well."

They heard the siren come up the driveway and stop in front of the house. David had cleared a path to the well by taking down some of his string and stakes. The two policemen led the paramedics around the back of the house to the abandoned well. The local firemen arrived with them.

The paramedics set the stretcher down and began attending to Hector.

"We were thinking," said one of the paramedics as he began taking vitals, "that maybe we would just drop by here every morning and evening. Save a lot of time."

They were the paramedics who had taken Marcella to the hospital, as well as Officers Hanks and Daughtry, and the late Ray-Ray Dildy—and now Hector. They probably decided the house was cursed.

"His vitals are good," he said.

"My granny always said this old witch house is haunted," the young paramedic said.

"You know this house, then?" asked Diane.

"A little. Granny says when she was a young girl, some crazy rich woman, an artist I think she said, lived here. She had all these demon creatures all over the roof," he said, as he immobilized Hector's leg.

"Gargoyles," said Diane.

"Is that what they were?"

"Supposed to ward off evil," said Diane.

"I'll have to tell Granny. From our workload over here the last few days, they needed to be working overtime. Okay, we're ready to go. Don't you worry, fella. You're going to be fine. But these old wells are a bitch, aren't they?"

Hector groaned.

"Do you know her name?" asked Diane.

"The crazy lady? No, but I imagine Granny does. I'll ask her," he said.

Diane reached in her pocket and handed him one of her cards.

After the paramedics took Hector and Scott to the hospital, one of the firemen, a tall, sturdy guy who looked as if he could have just reached down and hauled Hector up with one hand, began lecturing Diane about doing the rescue herself.

"One of you could have ended up in the well with him," he said. "Or made the whole thing fall in."

"I take your point," said Diane. "But Mike Seger and I are certified in cave rescue and we've had a lot of experience. We were aware of the dangers in this situation, and we took steps to make it as safe as we could. Our biggest concern was to get Hector out before the walls caved in on him. After he fell through the top, the sides were unstable and began to fall in before we started pulling him up."

The fireman paused a moment and looked into the well before he spoke. "Okay, then," he said. "I'm glad you've some experience and that everything worked out. Some people attempt a rescue and have no idea of the things that can go wrong."

"Thank you for coming," said Diane. "All of us appreciate it."

The fireman looked at all the string he had to step on and over to get there. "What you people doing here?" he said.

"This is a crime scene," said Diane. "We're searching for buried human remains."

"Crime scene? Don't you guys use yellow tape?" he asked.

"Sometimes. This is . . . was . . . a search grid," she said, indicating the layout of strings and stakes.

He squinted at Diane. "You're the crime lab lady," he said.

"Yes." But Diane wasn't sure about the lady part.

The fireman left and Diane went to the front porch to sit down and rest. David, Neva, and Mike went with her. David turned on the porch light and they pulled up chairs. Neva sat on the glider with Mike, who put his arms around her to warm her.

"What are you guys doing here?" Diane asked the two of them. "Shouldn't you be out to dinner or something?"

"Andie said you and David were here," said Neva. "I need to tell you some odd stuff about the crime scene I was just on."

"And the other thing," said Mike.

"Yes. I'm not sure, but I think I'm being followed," Neva said.

Chapter 35

"Followed?" said Diane. "Neva, someone is following you?" Diane gripped the arms of her chair and leaned forward.

"I think so," said Neva. "I may be wrong." Neva frowned in a way that put a crease between her eyes at the bridge of her nose, a small expression of insecurity that she made when she was undecided or afraid to commit to her own analysis.

"But you may be right," said Mike, urging her to talk.

"I noticed it yesterday. I feel really silly. It's just that I kept noticing the same vehicle, a black SUV with tinted windows. I know, that sounds so clichéd. I've tried to get behind it and check out the license plate, but I haven't been able to. It looks so easy in the movies." Neva brushed a strand of brown hair out of her eyes and smiled weakly.

"When were you first aware of it?" asked Diane.

"I think it was after I visited the historical society yesterday morning. That's down the street from the courthouse. After I looked up some records in the courthouse, I walked down to talk to them," said Neva. "Nice place. It's run by volunteers. I'd never been in it in all the years I've lived in Rosewood."

The two policemen David had enlisted for security had been standing by their car, smoking cigarettes. They threw the butts down and approached the porch.

"Hi," one said. "We were just wondering if you still need us tonight—since things kind of went in another direction." He laughed nervously.

"Now that we've found human bones in the well," said

Diane, "we need someone to keep the area secure. Can you stay?"

The men looked relieved. Diane guessed they were counting on the extra income.

"Oh yeah, that's fine," said the other policeman. "We're just going to check the back road." He moved his hand in a circle, indicating the route. "The whole trip won't take five minutes. We want to make sure nobody's parked back there like before." They went back to the patrol car and drove off down the driveway.

Diane looked at Neva. "Did you discover anything at the historical society?"

"Not really, but this is where it gets . . . well, it's one of those coincidences that makes David nervous," said Neva.

David tended to be paranoid and was very proud of it. He said it kept him prepared. His paranoia had been proven justified on too many occasions, which made him a trifle arrogant, but did keep them all primed for any eventuality.

"The crime scene I worked after lunch today—Mary Phyllis Lassiter. She was an older woman, about seventy, who was strangled in her home sometime last night. The creepy coincidence is . . . she was a volunteer at the historical society and she was there yesterday when I was there, though I didn't speak to her directly."

"How do you speak with someone indirectly?" asked David.

Neva made a face at him. "The woman I spoke with asked Ms. Lassiter whether she knew of an artist who might have lived years ago in Pigeon Ridge. That's this community. Apparently, Ms. Lassiter lived here as a girl," said Neva, "before she moved to Hall County."

"Did she know the artist?" asked Diane.

"She said no. She was knitting and didn't even look up. Which was kind of strange, because until then, she watched and talked like a magpie to everyone who came in," said Neva.

"You were followed and she was murdered?" said Diane.

"Yes," said Neva.

"You're right," said David. "That's the kind of coincidence that makes my scalp tingle."

"You didn't work the crime scene alone, did you?" said Diane, frowning.

"No. I know your rules. Izzy was working it with me. One thing caving taught me is to follow protocol," she said.

"Yes!" shouted Mike. He pulled Neva to him and kissed the side of her head.

Diane laughed. "It does that."

Diane's phone rang as she was about to ask Neva another question. She took the phone from her pocket and looked at the display. It was Izzy.

"Hello, Izzy. What's up?" she said.

"A little interesting turn of events," he said.

"Are you in the crime lab?" asked Diane.

"Yeh, I'm working on the evidence Neva and I collected today. The wife has one of her Mothers Against Drugs meetings. They meet here in the museum and I like to stay late and work when she's here."

"What's the interesting turn of events?" asked Diane. She didn't particularly like the word *interesting* used in that context. It usually meant something unpleasant.

"The shoe print we collected from the Lassiter murder today was made by the same hiking boot from the Payden attack. Think we got some punks targeting little old ladies?" he said.

"That is a surprise," Diane said. "Have you processed any of the other evidence?"

"Yes, but the print is the only really valuable thing I've found. It was a fairly clean crime scene. Like someone slipped in and out without touching much."

"I need to call Hanks," said Diane. "I'm glad you called me with this. Oh, before you hang up, Neva might be being followed by someone in a black SUV with tinted windows." She stopped and looked over to Neva. "Did you get the make?"

"Cadillac Escalade," said Neva.

Diane told Izzy the make. "Have you noticed anyone following you?" she asked.

"No, but I'll be on the lookout. Escalade. That's kind of

expensive, isn't it?" he said. "I'll watch for a tail. Did she get the license number?"

"No," said Diane.

"Like I said, I'll keep a lookout."

After she hung up with Izzy, Diane told the others about the boot print.

"You're kidding," said Neva. "The same person as here?"

"What do you think?" said David.

"Izzy was wondering if it might be someone targeting elderly ladies, but I don't think he knows about the historical society connection. Marcella went to the historical society too, when she was looking into who owned the house. She was asking about the artist who lived here, as well. That seems to be a key—"

Diane's phone rang again. This time it was from an unknown wireless caller. She answered.

"Yes?"

"Is this Dr. Fallon? This is Delbert Griffin, the paramedic who keeps showing up." He gave a little laugh. "I asked my granny about that woman's name, and she doesn't remember. She said she thought it was something like a bird, but that didn't sound right to her either. She said it's been more than sixty years. She and her friends just called her the 'rich witch.' Knowing my granny, she might have had another word in there too, that rhymed. Granny was somewhat of a rascal when she was young."

"Did she say how old the woman was?" asked Diane.

"I asked her if the 'witch' was real old. She said at the time she thought she was, but she was a teenager, and everyone over thirty looked old. Now that she looks back, she thinks she wasn't all that old. Granny's in her seventies, so I don't know what 'not all that old' means to her. I suppose anybody younger than she is."

"You and your grandmother have been very helpful," said Diane. "Thank you for calling. If the name comes to her, please let me know."

"I will. You know, when somebody is asked to come up with those old memories, they don't come to the surface right away. It might be that she'll wake up in the morning and it'll come to her," he said.

"I hope so. Is Hector doing okay?" asked Diane.

"He's in pretty good shape, really. He and his brother are a hoot," he said.

Diane agreed, thanked him again, and hung up.

"Marcella told us the signature on the paintings was a drawing of a bird," said Diane, after she told the others what the call was about. "It looks like the artist we are looking for had somewhat of a reputation at one time." Diane stopped and stared at Neva.

"What?" asked Neva.

"What you said about the Lassiter woman talking like a magpie. A magpie is a bird."

The three of them looked at Diane with a great deal of skepticism.

"That's a stretch," said David. "It doesn't even make sense."

"No. The word just reminded me of something. Initials. The first three letters of magpie are *m-a-g*. What if she used the bird drawing as a kind of symbolic representation of her initials?"

"Who?" said David. "What are you talking about?"

"The writer of the note on the bottom of the desk drawer," said Neva. "MAG. Remember? So, she was the artist?"

"Maybe," said Diane. "It's just a thought."

"A good one," said Neva.

David still looked skeptical, but relented that it was a possibility.

"I need to give Hanks a call. He needs to know about the connection between the crimes so he can coordinate with Hall County."

Diane started to key in his number when headlights came up the drive.

"That must be the policemen coming back from their rounds," she said.

"No," said David, standing up. "Everybody in the house! Now!"

Chapter 36

They didn't linger. All four of them jumped to their feet and headed for the door. David was the closest and reached the door first. He opened it and pulled everyone in, turned out the lights, and locked the door.

"Everybody stay away from the front windows," he said in an urgent half whisper.

"Okay," Diane whispered back from the darkness of the dining room. "Why are we here?"

"Those headlights aren't from the police car," said David. "They're set too high."

He stood near the doorway trying to see out the window. The lights went dark and they heard a door slam. Diane's heart beat faster. Neva, next to Diane, had her hand under her coat, ready to pull out her off-duty weapon. Diane could see Mike looking around the room, probably searching for a possible weapon. Knowing him, he probably didn't really believe anything was wrong, but he wouldn't be taking any chances.

"You mean like an SUV," said Neva.

"Yes," said David, "just like an SUV."

Diane had to admire David for noticing. She hadn't. *Well, hell.* She was about to assess what weapons they could lay their hands on, when a loud banging on the front door interrupted her thoughts. All of them stood stiff, waiting.

"What the hell are you guys doing in there?"

Detective Hanks.

David turned on the light and found all of them staring at him. He winced and rubbed his hand over his balding head.

"Well, I'm not right all the time." He shrugged. "I never said I was. Sometimes paranoia is just that. Besides, had it been the bad guys, we would be safe."

Mike visibly relaxed his tense body. Neva shook her head and opened the door. Detective Hanks was standing on the porch looking puzzled. He wasn't wearing his neck brace, but his arm was still immobilized in a sling and he favored his wounded leg.

"What was that all about?" he said. "I drive up and all of you make a mad dash for the house and turn off the lights?"

Diane smiled at him. "You have a new haircut," she said, and invited him into the house.

He stroked his short hair. "When your arm's in a sling and you're limping from being shot in the leg, you can't afford to have your hair standing up on end or blowing in the wind like a wild man," he said. "Now, what the heck . . . ? You guys looked like you were running for your lives. Who were you expecting?" He had the twinkle of amusement in his eyes.

Diane explained about the possibility of Neva being followed.

"My SUV's not black," he said.

"It's pitch-dark out. You can't make out colors in the dark," said Diane. "And your headlights were blinding."

"But that's still quite an overreaction," he said.

"Not considering we were shot at and a man was killed last time we were here," said Diane. "You aren't going to let us live this down, are you?"

"Not on your life. You should have seen you guys." He grinned. "And who are you? Just so I can get the story right," he asked Mike.

Diane introduced Hanks to her geology curator. They shook hands and Mike grinned at him. Mike often said it was entertaining to be with Diane and her team. He looked very entertained at the moment.

"And what are you doing out here?" asked Diane.

"I was at the hospital with some pictures for Marcella to look at. I hoped she might recognize some of Dildy's day laborer friends as people who might have worked on her house. She didn't. As I was leaving I saw the paramedics who brought me to the hospital the other day. They told me they had another run here tonight. Said something about some bones being found? Is that right?" he asked.

"We have several things to tell you," said Diane, "so you'd better sit down."

"Does Neva being followed have anything to do with this?" he asked.

From the set of his jaw, Diane could see he had gone from being amused by them to being suspicious again that Diane was leaving him out of the loop. He was probably wondering why she hadn't called him.

"We believe it might," said Diane. "The case has taken an unusual turn. And there could be someone after her."

They started to sit down when a pair of headlights suddenly shined in the window, blinding them for a moment.

"Well, shit," said Hanks. He unholstered his gun and went to the door and waited.

Diane and the others stood back with their arms folded. They heard two car doors slam. In a minute or so, they heard footfalls on the porch and a knock on the door.

"Everything okay in there?"

Hanks opened the door to the two policemen. Diane rose to greet them.

"We're fine," she said.

"Hi, Detective Hanks. Saw your vehicle. Guess you heard about all the excitement," said one of the policemen.

Hanks nodded.

The policeman looked at Diane. "All clear around the road. Nothing going on. We'll be out here making our rounds around the property," he said.

Diane could see the two of them were trying very hard to be conscientious. Probably sitting in their car and making an occasional circuit would be fine.

"Thanks," she said. "We'll be here for a little while."

He touched his hand to his hat and the two of them left.

Diane closed the door and grinned at Hanks. "It could happen to anyone. Want to renegotiate the thing about not letting us live that little episode down?"

Hanks smiled back. "I'm sure I wasn't as energetic as all of you were in jumping to conclusions."

"Perhaps not, but we sometimes exaggerate." She smiled sweetly at him.

He laughed. "That sounds like blackmail."

Thankfully, Hanks did seem to have a sense of humor and it seemed to have mellowed him again.

"I was just about to call you to tell you about the latest developments, when you showed up," Diane said. "Have a seat and I'll go through all of it with you."

"Should we be using this woman's house?" he asked.

"Marcella's daughter gave my team permission to camp out in her living room while we carry out our experiments," said Diane.

"Experiments?" he asked, laughing. "You're conducting experiments? That sounds ominous."

He chose a large leather chair to sit in. He stretched out his bad leg and shifted until he found a comfortable position. Diane was sure it was a relief not to have to wear the neck brace, but trying to go through a daily routine while your arm was in a sling and your leg hurt had to be difficult.

Neva sat leaning against Mike on one end of the sofa. David sat cross-legged in his sock feet on the other end. Diane chose the other stuffed chair, settled in comfortably, and started telling about the mask Marcella had been piecing together.

"When I saw her in the hospital, she told me to look at the inside of the pieces. I did and saw they had been molded over a human face."

"You mean like a death mask?" he said.

"Could have been, but we didn't know that. It could have been a life mask. But Marcella also told me to look at the sherds," Diane said.

"You keep using that word, *sherds*. You talking about broken pieces of pottery?" he asked.

"Yes, exactly," said Diane.

"Okay," he said. "Just making sure I understand. Go ahead."

Diane started to speak when he interrupted again. "Should he be here?" Hanks pointed to Mike. "No offense, buddy, but you're a civilian."

"Mike does consulting with the crime lab because of his knowledge of rocks and soils," said Diane. "He helped rescue Hector from the well. And the experiment we are working on involves soil samples."

Mike didn't even blink. Diane didn't tell Hanks that she hadn't actually talked to Mike about the experiment. But she didn't want to send Mike to wait outside. And it was true, after all, he did know about soils.

"Okay, go on," said Hanks.

"Marcella told me to look at sherds she had assembled from the back part of the mask. I did, and found what looks like a cast of a sharp-force-trauma head wound," she said.

"Now that's interesting," said Hanks. "So, the artist, or whoever, put the clay on over a head wound?"

"It looks that way. Some of the etching suggests the head was also shaved before making the mask," said Diane.

"This is getting weird," he said.

"We haven't even gotten to weird yet," said Diane. "Marcella, Dr. Payden, is an expert in pottery. She's creating a reference collection of pottery sherds and thin sections for the museum. A thin section is a very thin slice of, in this case, a pottery sherd, mounted on a microscope slide to be examined under polarized light so that its various constituents can be identified. Before she came here, her work involved prehistoric pottery from Texas that was tempered with animal bones. She was surprised to find that the pottery she found buried here in her yard also had been tempered with bone."

"I don't get it. Are we talking about this being an archaeology—what do they call it—site, an archaeology site? A dig? Why are you telling me this?" he asked without rancor, but with a lot of curiosity.

"No. There is no bone-tempered pottery in the prehistory of Georgia," said Diane.

She explained about what tempering is, how it gives a distinctive look and characteristics to pottery, and that in Georgia, common prehistoric tempers were fiber, shells, and grit.

"But this is not prehistoric. We are talking about modern pottery here. Are you with me?" she said.

"Not yet, but keep going," said Hanks. "This is like

watching the Discovery Channel. And I'm anxious to hear how your guy Hector got in the well. This is where all this is leading, right?"

Diane smiled. The others had been silent throughout her narration. It was the first time they had heard all of it. Mike hadn't heard any of it.

"Marcella used a lab in Arizona to analyze her Texas pottery sherds to identify the species of animal bone used for the tempering. It's a thing archaeologists like to know," Diane said. "She sent samples of the pottery she found in her yard here to the lab to find out what species of animal was used in it. The lab called me at the museum when they couldn't get in touch with Marcella. She was in the hospital. They were quite disturbed to discover that the species was human. I believe they faxed you a copy of their report."

"Well, yeah, but I couldn't make heads or tails of the damn thing." Hanks leaned forward, openmouthed. "Are you telling me those pots she found were made out of human bone? Now, that is spooky."

Out of the corner of her eye, Diane could see the surprise on Mike's face. Neva smiled at him and patted his thigh.

"The clay used to make them had human bone mixed with it for temper. Yes," said Diane.

Hanks put his hands on his face and rubbed his eyes. "You people know how to do weird. I'll give you that," he said.

"After discovering those two things—the sharp-force trauma and the human-bone tempering—it was incumbent on us to search for human remains on the property. I decided we would conduct a study David had been wanting to do. It involves developing quicker methods for finding buried human remains. Starting in the backyard, he and two technicians from the DNA lab were using stakes and string to grid the property into squares. They would then take soil samples at defined increments and analyze them for their chemical constituents. Decomposing remains leave chemical signatures. We don't know the range of the affected area for soil conditions in this region. The study was designed to answer some of the questions we don't yet have answers for, and to locate any remains that are here." Diane stopped to let it all soak in.

"Couldn't you use cadaver dogs?" he asked.

"We suspect the remains could be decades old. The context in which Marcella found the broken pottery suggested the 1950s," said Diane.

"Okay, so I take it your . . . experiment worked," he said.

"In a rather serendipitous way," said Diane. "While they were putting up stakes and strings for the grid, Hector fell into an abandoned well. It had been capped with wood that was covered in dirt and vegetation and had rotted over the years. The bone he discovered was at the bottom of the well. We suspect there are more," said Diane.

"Couldn't the bone be from a deer or something?" said Hanks. "People do throw dead animals down dry wells to get rid of the carcasses."

Diane was surprised at how often she was asked that question. Even Frank had made a similar query at one time. She wondered whether they really thought it was hard to tell the difference between animal and human or if they thought the skull was required in order to make a positive species ID.

"No," she said simply.

"Seriously, should we get the medical examiner to take a look?" he said.

"You can if you want," said Diane. "But it's a right human tibia of someone in their teens. Possibly female, but that's not certain. What is certain is that it is human."

"I take it you've done this before," he said.

Diane found it hard to believe that he didn't know. But he was relatively new to Rosewood and apparently knew her only as the director of the crime lab and the museum.

"I'm a forensic anthropologist," said Diane.

He winced and saw that David, Neva, and Mike were grinning at him. "Okay, I wasn't aware. Do you know how long it was in the well?" he asked.

"Probably more than fifty years. There is a particular smell the marrow leaves that lasts for decades in buried bone. That was gone. The bone had taken on the color of the surrounding soil, indicating it had been buried for most of its tenure in the well," she said.

"Where is it now?" he asked.

"In my car, wrapped in newsprint. We'll have to get

someone out here to stabilize the sides of the well so we can get the remaining bones out."

"So, now you don't have to complete your study," he said.

"Oh yes," said Diane. "Just because we found bones in the well doesn't mean the yard isn't full of buried bodies."

Chapter 37

"Oh, I see," said Hanks. "So we could have lots more bodies?" He stared at Diane. "Are you serious? This could be a . . . some maniac's burial ground?" He shifted in his chair, winced suddenly, and rubbed his shoulder. "Damn it," he said. "Sorry."

David got up and went to a cooler he had tucked in a corner of the room and brought everyone a cold drink. Diane took a long sip. It was a cool evening, but the ice-cold drink still tasted good.

"Any idea who this serial killer is? We are talking about a serial killer, aren't we?" he said. "And as wildly interesting as this is, it looks like it all happened a long time ago. Does it have anything to do with the here and now?" He took a drink and held the cool bottle on his collarbone.

"Some kind of killer," said Diane. "At best, someone who illegally disposed of a body. I don't know that we have a whole yard full of bodies. We may have only the one in the well. As for a player in this, we have a few ideas. We think the ceramic artist might be the same one who wrote the strange message on the bottom of the desk drawer, and the one who did the paintings that were stolen." Diane pointed to the wall over the sofa. David, Neva, and Mike turned to look at the blank wall as if a shadowy image might remain.

"Why the pictures?" he asked. "They were painted by this Mad Potter?" Hanks asked.

"I don't know for sure," said Diane. "We do know the pictures were signed by the artist with a drawing of a bird. The paramedic's grandmother—"

"Wait, you lost me. The paramedic's grandmother? What paramedic? The ones who came here?" said Hanks.

Diane explained that the paramedic who tended to Hector was familiar with the place, and his grandmother had knowledge of the house from when she was a teenager.

"Humph, small world," Hanks said, and took another drink.

Diane found that explaining the whole train of thought out loud, paired with what evidence they had and didn't have, was helpful to her understanding. She hoped Hanks found it illuminating, but he seemed more entertained than anything else.

Diane mentioned her thought that the initials MAG in the signature on the desk drawer might be symbolized by the picture of a bird. Hanks wasn't impressed with that. She didn't blame him. It sounded rather silly when she repeated it out loud to a skeptical ear.

"I get that, because the thieves stole the old paintings, it looks like the attack on Dr. Payden and the theft could have something to do with the old bones—and where the bones came from. But, frankly, that bird thing is a stretch," he said. "The whole past-present thing is a stretch." He brought the hand holding his drink up to his face and rubbed his eye with a free finger.

"There's also Marcella's pottery that was stolen," said Diane. "We speculated the thieves thought they were taking valuable Indian artifacts. But consider that Marcella's pottery and the pieces found here on the property were all fired on a bonfire kiln, which gave all of them the same distinctive appearance. The thieves might have been after pottery made by the Mad Potter, as you so colorfully call him or her, and took Marcella's pieces by mistake."

"Perhaps, but that connection is so tenuous, it really doesn't bear spending time on, really. No offense. Not that we don't need to find out who might be buried here, but, like I said, it looks like it was a long time ago and doesn't have anything to do with the attack on Dr. Payden. And I'm more concerned about that. I'm sorry, but there it is," he said.

Diane smiled at him. "So it would seem. But here's the kicker." Diane leaned forward, resting her forearms on her knees. "Neva has been tracing the ownership and history of this house—retracing Marcella's steps as she tried to discover the home's pedigree. That search took them both to the courthouse and the historical society. Yesterday at the historical society, Neva met a volunteer named Mary Phyllis Lassiter," Diane said.

"That name sounds familiar," Hanks said.

"You may have heard it on the news. Neva and Izzy processed her crime scene today. She was strangled in her home overnight," said Diane.

He looked startled. "Okay, I'll grant you, that's an interesting coincidence," he said.

"More than coincidence. Izzy called just before you arrived," said Diane. "He's working late at the crime lab processing the evidence. At the Lassiter crime scene they found the same expensive hiking boot print that we found here when Marcella was attacked—not just from the same kind of boot," said Diane. "The same boot."

Detective Hanks sat in stunned silence for a moment.

"You know, you could have started out with this information," he said.

"Perhaps," said Diane.

"Did the Lassiter woman live in Rosewood?" he asked.

"Hall County. Just over the line. You'll need to speak with Sheriff Braden," said Diane.

"You say Izzy Wallace is processing the evidence now? Can I see it?" he asked.

Diane shook her head. "Telling you about the boot print is a courtesy. The sheriff gets to see his evidence first," she said.

Hanks nodded. "I can respect that." He paused, staring at the blank wall behind the sofa, looking deep in thought. He shifted his position again, and again winced in pain. "Then what do we have here?"

"I don't know," said Diane.

Hanks looked at Neva. "What did the Lassiter woman say to you?" he asked.

"Nothing to me." Neva explained the interchange at the historical society. "I think you need to speak with Marcella and find out if she met Ms. Lassiter when she was there."

He nodded. "Are there any other surprises you have to spring on me?" he asked Diane.

"No. That's about all we know," she said.

He laughed. "I hope we aren't dealing with a league of Mad Potters trying to keep their ceremonies and history a secret."

"That would surprise me," said Diane. "I have no explanation. It could be that, unknown to us, the paintings *are* valuable, and the attack on Dr. Payden was simply about money. I have no idea if anything was stolen from Lassiter's house, but if it happens she had paintings by the mysterious artist . . . Well, it would be worth finding out. In the museum we have paintings by an unknown artist and we were unaware for a long time that they are extremely valuable. So it's not unheard of.

"Or," suggested Diane, "Marcella's attacker could be trying to prevent us from uncovering an old crime. The perpetrator could still be alive, though up in years, I would imagine. Or it could be a big coincidence, and what we first thought about Marcella's attack was correct—they just didn't know she was home, and got caught in the middle of a robbery."

Hanks flexed the hand that was in the sling back and forth, exercising it. "You've given me a lot to work with, I'll give you that. I haven't made any headway talking to Ray-Ray Dildy's associates. He was just a two-bit petty crook. No one I've spoken with knows what he was up to lately. But, basically, he was a loser to the end."

Diane saw the subtle frustration in Hanks that he hadn't been able to solve this crime—the eye tic he had frequently rubbed, the clinching of his jaw. He needed to prove himself. She understood that. Rosewood's previous chief of police had been murderously corrupt, and Hanks had been one of his last hires. Even though Hanks wasn't known to have done anything wrong, there was the taint of association. For the chief of police to have hired him, he must have thought him corruptible. How did anyone fight that? Hanks wanted to solve this, and do it himself. The fact that he had shared a little of his investigation tonight was a sign that he might be mellowing a bit where Diane was concerned.

"Do you know Sheriff Braden in Hall County?" asked Diane.

"We haven't met," he said.

"I'll call and tell him you're coming, if you like," said Diane. "I can send Izzy over with the evidence at the same time."

Hanks nodded. "Sometime tomorrow, late morning would be good."

"I'll give him a call in the morning," said Diane.

"I appreciate that." Hanks rose from his seat. "Well, I'll say this. This has been interesting." He finished the rest of his drink and looked around for a garbage can. David got up and took the bottle from him.

Diane left shortly after Hanks. On the way home she tried to call Frank on the home phone. No one answered. His car wasn't in the drive or in the garage when she arrived. She opened the front door and went inside. On the answering machine she found a message saying he wouldn't be home at all. He and his partner were going to Nashville, Tennessee, on a case—but only for a day—he thought.

She felt a little dispirited as she listened to the message. She had looked forward to seeing him. She wondered whether he had found time to look at Ellie Rose Carruthers' diary pages. Probably not.

She took a shower and got into bed. Tomorrow was going to be a big day. She had to excavate a well.

Chapter 38

The well was simply too unstable and dangerous for Diane to work in without structural reinforcements to hold back the crumbling walls. Mike called in an engineering consultant from Bartrum University who designed a liner for the well consisting of ten-foot steel chain-link fencing reinforced by steel posts, straps, and bars. It took two days for Mike to locate a contractor, collect the materials, and get the job done.

Thick cotton batting and wire mesh were laid over the debris in the bottom of the well and a temporary wooden platform was built over that to protect the remains lying beneath the rubble. The entire steel structure was assembled aboveground and lowered with extreme caution into the well by use of a construction crane. Inside the well, the liner was expanded outward against the stone wall and locked in place with reinforcing steel braces. All this was done without ever touching the bottom of the well or the delicate matter that lay there.

Mike attached a ladder to the side of the reinforced well. He and Scott strung the wiring for the work lights and removed the temporary platform, the wire mesh, and cotton batting from the bottom of the well. On the surface, the crew used wooden posts and beams to build a hand-operated winch above the well. They wrapped Diane's rescue rope around the hoist and attached a five-gallon bucket to the end of the rope for lifting debris out of the well.

Paloma said her mother was greatly frustrated not to be there. An excavation in her own backyard and she, an archaeologist, was stuck in the hospital. Andie came up with the idea of using a webcam down in the well. Marcella could watch the excavation, the crew at the top of the well could keep track of what was going on down below, and Andie herself could watch from her office. Andie saw it as an opportunity to conduct research for the webcam project she was working on with the curators. Diane thought it was a great idea. She got permission from Chief Garnett. David helped with the technical part. The webcams were attached to the wire liner near the work lights that illuminated the bottom of the pit.

"I love it," Mike said with obvious pride, looking down into the well at the finished construction. "I would trust my life with that, Boss." He grinned at Diane.

"Well, that's certainly reassuring," she said. She looked into the lighted well. "I'll have to give you credit. It does look safe and functional." But what she was thinking was how foreboding it was. She had the feeling she was looking into the mouth of something very dark and evil. She put on her caving hard hat with a light on it and lowered herself down the ladder.

Before she started excavating the bones, Diane had to clean out a lot of debris—pieces of the rotted wooden well cap, rocks, leaves, and surface vegetation that had fallen in with Hector. She filled the bucket time and again and the top crew hoisted the bucket loads out of the well using the winch. It didn't take as long as she feared to clear the bottom of the well. But it was tiring.

So now Diane was at the bottom of the well, kneeling over her real work. Marcella, Andie, Garnett back in his office, and her crime scene support up top were watching via Web video as Diane's hands brushed debris off the dome of a skull.

The rule of excavating is to work from the known to the unknown—start with bone you can see and follow it into the debris, inch by inch. Diane's tools were a trowel, a brush, and wooden tongue depressors so as not to harm the bone. It was slow work, but the ground was relatively soft clay, silt, and sandy soil. Fortunately, it was a dry well and had been for many years. Otherwise, they would be dealing with a whole other problem—a body that had decomposed in waterlogged soil. If she were dealing with a body that had become adipocere rather than skeletonized, it would be another whole level of unpleasantness.

The bones were a gray-brown color—the same as the surrounding soil. They stood out in relief like a piece of artwork. She brushed off a last clump of dirt and took a photograph. Diane moved to the edge of the well where she knelt and took several more photographs of the bones.

She asked for the basket, which David immediately lowered down to her on the end of the rope. She removed the skull first. She turned it over and brushed the dirt off it. What caught her eye at once was the cut in the back of the skull. There was little doubt in her mind that it would fit the pottery cast. Diane set the skull on batting in the basket and signaled for David to pull it up.

The vertebrae snaked from where the skull had been lying on its side, curving before terminating at the sacrum. When they winched the basket back down, she picked up the vertebrae one at a time and put them in the basket in order, along with the pelvis. It was a female pelvis, from a teen. She signaled David to hoist them up. Next she sent the ribs.

The rest of the bones were in disarray. Diane stopped and sat back on her haunches. The angular rocks behind the wire bit into her back. She folded her arms and sat for several moments, glad the webcams weren't aimed at her face. She took several deep breaths.

When she worked as a human rights investigator in South America, there was a nun in the mission where they were housed who was forever giving them advice that sounded like Zen koans. Once when Diane and her crew became disturbed over a mass grave, she said, "In order to get close to them, you must get far away from them." It was a concept they all knew and relied upon, but when Sister Margaret said it, it took on a more spiritual essence. Diane often had to stop and find that faraway place to put her emotions.

The remains had been butchered. Of course, she knew they would have been, if, indeed, these were the bones that were ground up for temper. But being confronted with the jumbled, cut bones was far more disconcerting than the intellectual knowledge of what had theoretically happened.

The arm bones were behind the body, upside down, as if someone threw them down the well after the torso was thrown in. They were broken—some from the falling rock, or the falling Hector, and some from the butchering. The shoulder blades were nothing more than spines of bone. The bodies of the scapulae were gone; only jagged edges remained. Scapulae were relatively thin. Probably they were easier to grind down than the heavier bones. She took several more photographs.

She picked up one of the long bones of the arm to place it in the basket. Under it lay another. That made three humeri. The minimum number of individuals in the well went from one to two. The bones represented at least two bodies. She placed the bones in the basket and watched as they were raised to the top.

"You want to take a break?" David called down.

"Not yet," she said. "Send down some small boxes."

She collected the hand bones, tiny pieces that belonged to the wrist and hand. Again there were bones that represented at least two people. She rough-sorted them into left and right and size. One of the individuals was larger than the other. Most of the hand bones were missing. There were not four complete sets. Maybe they were yet to be uncovered. Maybe they too had been ground into temper.

A piece of something caught her eye. It had been under the arm bones, and like the bones, was similar in color to the earth. But this object was not bone. She began gently teasing and sweeping the dirt away. She found the edges. It was something rolled up. She believed it was leather. Once she had outlined it in the soil and excavated a few inches under it, she carefully picked it up. It was surprisingly heavy. Something was wrapped inside it.

As she put it in the basket, the object came apart and two hammers fell out: a large iron mallet and a smaller hammer with a broad face. She paused again and wiped her forehead with the back of her hand. *Damn it.* She knew what it was. The bone hadn't been ground; it had been pulverized. Bones had been put in the leather and pounded with the hammers. First the large hammer to break it up, then the smaller one for finer work. She sent it up and then she climbed the ladder to the surface. She needed a break.

Up top, Detective Hanks had been watching the computer screen with Mike. It looked as though Mike had been giving him a lecture—probably on soils, or Blue Ridge geology. Neva was wrapping the bones and packing them in boxes. Scott was helping. Topside around the well looked like a scene from *Road Warriors*—all scaffolding and cables that had a jury-rigged quality to it. Sparks popped from the flames of a wood fire that was burning for warmth.

When David helped her off the ladder, he stared at her face. She knew what he noticed. He'd seen it in her many times, as she in him when they were working on mass graves. That forlorn, hopeless look. The knowing that even if you brought the perpetrators to justice, it wouldn't balance the scales, because you hadn't prevented those victims from suffering; you hadn't stopped the killing. David put his arms around her and hugged her. The others looked up, a little alarmed, as if she might be hurt.

"Are you all right?" said Neva.

"Sure," said Diane. "I'm just taking a break." She tried a weak smile.

She greeted Detective Hanks as David put a cold bottle of water in her hand.

"Have you been here very long?" she said.

"Not too long. I've been working with Sheriff Braden. Thanks for the introduction. He's been easy to work with," he said.

"That's good. The county sheriffs don't always welcome Rosewood detectives," she said, grinning at him. "I assume my crew has been bringing you up to speed on what we're doing?"

"I've been watching you on the laptop. I'm not sure it's helped very much. Kind of like watching paint dry, if you know what I mean. No offense. Mike's been telling me about . . ." He looked at Mike. "What was that word?"

"Inceptisol," said Mike.

Mike grinned and winked at Diane after Hanks turned back around to her. He had probably been purposely pedantic—something Mike enjoyed doing to unsuspecting people.

"Yeah, which, as I understand it, is dirt—that, soil horizons, and nice rocks. Like I said, it's like the Discovery Channel around you guys." He took Diane's arm. "I thought I'd fill you in on what Braden told me."

Chapter 39

They sat on Marcella's front porch. Diane took her helmet off and set it down by her feet. She hugged her brown nylon jacket around her against the cool breeze. Hanks gestured toward the helmet.

"Neva and Mike tell me that all of you explore caves together," he said.

Diane nodded. "We do, as often as we can. I particularly enjoy mapping unexplored caves," she said.

"Is that dangerous?" he asked, staring at her hard hat.

"It can be," she said, "but we practice safety."

Hanks nodded, looking back at Diane. "Mike talks a lot about rocks," he said. "Tell me, do women really dig that?"

"They do, but I think it's the whole package they like," said Diane, smiling. "Mike is one of our more popular continuing education instructors."

He shook his head and Diane waited for him to get around to what he wanted to talk about. A lot of Detective Hanks' small talk revolved around trying to understand the people around him. It was as if he found Diane and her crew a complete mystery. Of course, nearly everyone she knew, including Frank, found her love of caving a mystery.

"Sheriff Braden is a stand-up guy," Hanks said. "He was surprised about the overlap in our cases. Wasn't sure what to make of it either. He spoke with Lassiter's friends, but didn't discover much. She lived alone and had no family. Never married, as far as they knew. She worked as a secretary all her life in a family-owned office supply company. She retired eleven years ago and has done volunteer work since. The woman lived a very quiet life. She was known as an expert knitter and taught a few classes at a local knitting shop. This is not the resume of a woman who would have enemies. It looks like a burglary-homicide."

"What was taken?" asked Diane.

"Her purse and jewelry box for sure. Not valuable items. Braden thinks she may have been killed because she wouldn't reveal the whereabouts of valuables they may have thought she had. I asked him about artwork. He said he didn't know of anything missing. We went to her apartment together. There was nothing that we could see missing from the walls or from display cabinets. Her neighbors said she didn't have anything like pottery in her house. She liked porcelain figurines of fancy-dressed ladies that she bought from TV shopping networks, but all of them seemed to be there and, frankly, I can't see anyone stealing them. The boot print is all we have that connects these two crimes, and neither of us have any answers. The sheriff hasn't found any witnesses in her neighborhood who might have seen anyone near her home."

"What about the people at the Rosewood historical society?" asked Diane.

"Miss Lassiter did secretarial work for them three days a week. She would also come in just to visit on days she wasn't working," he said. "They knew who her friends and neighbors were and a little bit about all of them. She was a woman who offended no one and enjoyed her retirement."

"Had Marcella spoken with her?" asked Diane.

"Yes. I talked with Dr. Payden before I came here. She asked the people at the historical society, Miss Lassiter included, about the owners of this house here in Pigeon Ridge. She particularly wanted to know whether there was an owner who was an artist. Dr. Payden had a list with her of previous owners that she had gotten from the courthouse records. She said Miss Lassiter had a vague recollection of the house, but couldn't tell her anything."

"Maybe the attack on Marcella and Miss Lassiter's murder had nothing to do with what happened here years ago. Maybe someone who visited the historical society targeted both of them for some other reason. Perhaps their attackers thought they had money," said Diane.

"Maybe. But as you pointed out, stealing pottery and old paintings wouldn't seem to be a fast track to riches. Miss Lassiter's friends said she didn't have any valuable jewelry. They seem to be the most stupid thieves I've run across. It doesn't look like they are getting anything of real value."

"Did Neva or Marcella give you the list of previous owners of the house?" asked Diane.

"Neva did." Hanks took out his notebook and flipped through the pages. "Original owner was Edith Farragut, then Maude Saxon, Kenneth Northcutt, Jonathan Ellison, and Marcella Payden. From the dates we estimate for the artist, Edith Farragut would have owned the house at that time. The only specifics I have about her are that she built the house at the turn of the last century and maintained ownership until 1959, when it was sold to Maude Saxon. I've got someone looking for a death certificate for Ms. Farragut, and census records to see who might have lived here with her. I think she would have been too old in the 1950s to be the Mad Potter. This would have been a younger person's occupation. At any rate, she certainly would be dead now if she was an adult buying property at the turn of the century," he said. "She'd be well over a hundred and . . . What?" he said, staring at Diane.

"How absentminded of me," Diane said. "I have a friend who might have known the family. The paramedic said his grandmother referred to the woman who owned the house as being rich. Wealthy people in a small town like this would know one another," said Diane.

"Who are you talking about?" asked Hanks.

"Do you know Vanessa Van Ross?" she said.

"The mayor's mother?" he said. "You know her?"

"She's the real power behind the museum," said Diane.

"And here I was given to understand that you are the queen of the museum," he said.

"Not at all. I'm just the viceroy," she said, smiling. "What made me think of Vanessa was your mentioning age. You know Vanessa's family is filled with centenarians and supercentenarians, don't you?" she said.

"Actually, no I didn't," he said. "What's a supercentenarian?"

"Someone more than a hundred and ten. Vanessa's

grandmother died not long ago at the age of a hundred and fourteen," said Diane. "Her mother lives with her and is approaching a hundred. Vanessa is around the age of the paramedic's grandmother. Between her and her mother, she might know something."

"Is her mother, ah, clearheaded?" he asked.

"Sharp as a tack," said Diane. "So was her grandmother up until the time of her death."

Diane fished her phone out of her jacket pocket and selected Vanessa's number. The call was answered by the housekeeper.

"Mrs. Hartefeld, this is Diane Fallon. May I speak with Vanessa?" she asked.

"Of course, Dr. Fallon. Anything to get her out of my hair this afternoon," she said.

Diane heard Vanessa in the background. "Oh, for heaven's sake, Harte, give me the phone. And you are going to help me with these photographs? Hello, Diane, dear. How are you?"

"I'm well," said Diane.

"From what I hear, you are in a well. Is that where you are calling from?"

"Almost. I'm topside now. How do you get your information?" she said, smiling into the phone.

"I visited Marcella and she was having the most wonderful time watching you excavate her well on a computer," she said. "I do hope that young man who fell in is doing all right."

"Hector Spearman is doing fine," said Diane. "Recovering from his injuries, and irritated at having to be off work, but other than that, he's good. What I was calling about is this house." Diane explained about the paramedic's grandmother knowing the place from when she was a girl. "The courthouse records show the owner at the time was Edith Farragut. Did you know her?"

"Edith Farragut. That name does sound familiar. Edith Farragut," she said again. "I didn't go to high school in Rosewood. Most of my teenage and young-adult years were spent in Switzerland and other parts of Europe. However, Mother might remember the woman," said Vanessa.

"She or someone in the house was an artist," said Diane. "Did pottery and painting, I believe. This would be before 1959."

"You say the people who lived in that house were wealthy? That wasn't a particularly wealthy section of Rosewood. It may have been a rental and someone else entirely lived there," she said.

Diane hadn't thought of that.

"I'll ask Mother and get back to you. She's napping now, so it will be later on this evening. I'll speak with her when we are having our cocoa."

"Thank you," Diane said.

"You're welcome. I quite like the webcam proposal," she said. "I should very much like to have a setup in my house. I can be, what do they call it, one of your beta testers," she said. "Too bad we didn't think of this when we were putting the dinosaurs together. What fun the schools would have had with that."

"I'll set you up first thing," said Diane. She flipped her cell closed. "Vanessa's going to speak with her mother this evening," Diane said to Hanks, then relayed to him the rest of the conversation.

"That might be the break we need. I didn't think about it being a rental," he said.

"Neither did I. I think it's because stuff belonging to the occupant is still here—the desk, the paintings," said Diane.

"I suppose," he said. "What have you found in the well, speaking of stuff they left behind?"

"I've found the bones of at least two individuals, so far. One is a teenage female who was killed with a sharp blow to the head. She had been butchered and some of her bones crushed, perhaps for pottery temper. I found a large piece of leather and iron hammers that may have been used for crushing the bone, but I won't know for sure until we examine it."

Hanks let out a long breath. "Man, that's cold-blooded and gruesome."

"It is," said Diane.

"If you will, keep me informed. Garnett gave me the old case too, even if it's not related to the attack on Dr. Payden," he said.

"I will," she said.

Diane stood up. Rest over. It was time to go back in the well.

Chapter 40

Diane worked in the well past dark. The temperature dropped and her hands got stiff and cold. Her support crew up top were no doubt getting uncomfortable too, so she quit for the night. She had revealed most of a second skeleton. It was in a similar condition to the first—sharp trauma to the head, butchered. The bones belonged to a male in his teens. He was a little larger than the female but not much older. Diane covered over the remaining bones with black plastic and climbed out of the well.

Neva and Scott had taken the excavated bones and other evidence to the lab earlier. Diane asked Neva to use the skull to start a facial reconstruction with the 3-D laser scanner and software. Neva was an artist and Diane taught her how to read a skull to visualize what the face would have looked like. This enabled her to enhance the computer drawing to give her pictures a more realistic quality. She also taught Neva how to make a cast of the skull and do a sculpted representation of the victim. Neva turned out to be very skilled at artistic reconstruction.

David decided to camp out at the well. Marcella again volunteered her living room and the policemen were again on guard, happy for the overtime. Diane fervently hoped there were no more surprises awaiting on Marcella's property.

"Why don't you let me finish the excavation?" said David as Diane was climbing into her SUV. "I'm perfectly capable."

"Of course you are, but I want to finish it," she said. "It's almost done. Tomorrow morning ought to finish it."

"If you change your mind, call," he said, patting her shoulder and closing the driver's-side door for her.

He motioned to her and Diane rolled down the window. "Is Frank home yet?" he asked.

"Sometime tonight," she said. "Call if anything happens."

David laughed. "What's left to happen?"

"Who knows?" she said. "Alien abduction?"

"I'll be sure to call if it happens. You'd like that."

Diane smiled, waved good-bye, and drove home. Frank's fraud case in Nashville had taken longer than he expected, but he assured her when she spoke with him earlier that he would be home late this evening and if he could leave early, he would. He also told her he was working on Ellie Rose's diary and that he was sorry he wasn't there to see her down in the well.

Diane parked in the drive and went into the house. It was quiet. Frank had a quiet house. She liked that. Quiet was soothing. She locked the door and walked up the stairs to the bedroom, undressed, and ran a hot bubble bath. She reluctantly took her cell phone with her and laid it on the floor next to the tub. She showered first, scrubbing the dirt off her body, and washed her hair. Then she got into the warm, scented bubble bath, leaned her head against the back of the tub, and closed her eyes. Quiet and peaceful, that's what she liked. She could just sleep here for the night and let all the strain and soreness soak out of her tired muscles.

The sound of the doorbell brought her out of her comfortable stupor, but she didn't move. It rang again. Anyone who would come to her for an emergency would call her cell. So it was probably not any of her crew or anyone at the museum. It wouldn't be Garnett, Hanks, or Kingsley. They had her number. So did Star, Frank's daughter. Frank wouldn't knock; he had her cell number and a key. They all had her number. It probably wasn't a neighbor with some emergency. There were closer houses than Frank's to run to. Same for a road emergency. There were closer houses to go to for help. Frank's house was in the middle of a double lot with lots of trees.

It wasn't anything she needed to attend to. They would just have to return during civilized hours to ring the doorbell. Diane closed her eyes again.

The doorbell rang again. This time they leaned on it. They banged the door with their fist.

"Okay, this is obnoxious," said Diane. She submerged a moment, then came up and rubbed her hands over her hair, squeezing the water out of it.

It must be a drunk, she thought. Or someone who had the wrong address. Or maybe it was a process server for some unknown thing someone was suing her for. Whatever it was, she decided not to face it naked. She got out of the tub, dried off, and slipped on underwear and sweats. She dried her hair with a towel. All the while, whoever it was banged on the door and rang the bell. *Damn it. What the hell?*

She slipped her feet into her fleece-lined house shoes and walked into the bedroom. The ringing stopped. Great, she should have waited longer. She started for a front window to see if she could get a glimpse of a car. The outside security lights came on in the yard on the bedroom side of the house.

The pissant was coming around the house. She turned out the light in the bedroom, walked to the stairs, and peered down to the foyer. She heard someone rattle the back door. Time to call the police and ask them to send a car.

She nearly fell down the stairs when the gunshots were fired. Someone was breaking into the house with a very large gun. Diane didn't hesitate. She ran to the chest of drawers in the closet and got her gun and ammunition clips. She carried them and her cell up to the attic. She closed the door at the top of the attic stairs and pulled a large chest in front of it. Light from the security lamps shined through one of the dormer windows, giving the attic a spooky glow. She called 911 and explained to them what was happening. She held the phone to her ear with her shoulder, shoved a clip into the butt of the gun, loaded a round into the chamber, and clicked on the safety.

"Stay on the line, ma'am," the operator said.

"Can't. I think he is in the house. I'll call back when I can."

"Ma'am, stay . . ."

Diane hung up and called Chief Garnett for good measure.

"I'll make sure they are on their way," he said. "You have a gun?"

"Yes. I'm holed up in the attic. This is some bold home invader. He must know the police are about to come," she said.

She listened for footfalls. Frank's house didn't have carpet. He had polished wood floors and sound reverberated off them. She heard the footsteps downstairs. Diane took up a position behind a large trunk near the wall. She knew it was filled with Frank's old *National Geographic* magazines. They ought to be a fairly decent bullet stopper. This vantage had a view of the door but was not in front of it. If he came up the stairs and began blasting through the lock and moved the chest of drawers, she would have time to shoot before he got to her. It seemed like a good plan.

Only now did Diane notice that her heart was racing and she was sick to her stomach. She heard footsteps on the main stairs. Maybe he wouldn't find the attic stairs. They were hidden in the bedroom closet.

Her cell rang. Damn, she forgot to put it on vibrate. She answered with a whisper.

"Diane, are you all right? You sound hoarse. This is Vanessa. Mother remembered—"

"Can't talk now, Vanessa. I'll call back."

A booming gunshot slammed against the attic door.

"Is that gunfire?" said Vanessa.

"Yes. Got to go."

Chapter 41

Diane dropped the cell, rested her shaking arms on the trunk, and aimed the gun at the doorway. If he came straight through the doorway, he might not think to turn to the right until it was too late. He would have to lean into the door to move the chest. He would be off balance. That would give her time—if she was lucky. He hit the door with another earsplitting shot. What if there were more than one of them? Damn, she hadn't thought of that. Why hadn't she thought of that?

The chest jumped as another bullet slammed through the back. It sounded like an elephant gun, it was so loud. Diane checked to see if the safety on her gun was off. It wasn't. *Shit.* She would get killed if she didn't start thinking. She moved the switch with her thumb.

Sirens whined in the distance. *Hurry. Please, hurry.*

The intruder shot the door twice more. The sound was so loud the entire neighborhood should have heard it. She thought she could hear him reloading—*clink, clink.*

The chest began to inch forward. He was pushing on it now. Diane steadied her gun. He apparently put his shoulder into it, for the chest moved forward at least three feet and he stumbled into the room—facing Diane. He raised his shotgun toward her as she fired three times and ducked behind the trunk. She felt the floor shake when he fell. At the same instant, a blast from his shotgun shook her eardrums and the wall behind her exploded, debris falling over her. Diane lay still a moment, stunned. When her head cleared, she wanted to peek over the trunk, but she was afraid it was a trap. What if he was playing dead? What if he had backup? She was stuck. She crouched behind the trunk and listened to his breathing. It came in gasps, sounding real enough, but she didn't believe it.

"Help me," he whispered.

She was too scared to move, too wary to trust. She tried to think what to do, but her brain was too panicked.

Damn, she thought. *I've been in bad situations before. Why am I suddenly such a coward?*

She stayed low and moved slowly to look around the side of the trunk next to the wall. There was a six-inch opening between the wall and the trunk she could have seen through, if it weren't so dark. The only significant light reflected through the windows from the security lamps. They had suddenly gone dark. The motion detector outside had timed out. Only dim light from the floor below seeped up the stairs and through the open doorway. It did little to illuminate.

The sirens were louder. Help was coming. But the sirens were too loud. She wouldn't hear him if he moved. Diane stayed still and listened hard through the noise. She stared through the space beside the trunk until her eyes became adjusted to the darkness. She saw a booted foot moving, trying to get up. She shot at it and he yelped.

She heard him whimper and mutter something she couldn't make out. He seemed to be down, but Diane didn't trust him. She waited, tempted to shoot him again.

Get some backbone, she told herself.

She heard banging on the door downstairs. The police. But what if it was Frank? He wouldn't know what he was walking into. She rose slowly, keeping her back flat against the wall, and surveyed the darkened attic. She saw the dark form of the intruder squirming on the floor. The shotgun was within his reach. She aimed her gun at him and made her way slowly to the downed form and kicked the shotgun aside. She stepped over to the door, keeping him in sight, keeping her gun trained on him, and flipped the light switch.

The sight startled her. The man on the floor looked like Ray-Ray Dildy. No, it looked like a slightly younger and different version of Ray-Ray Dildy.

What is this, some kind of maniac crime family?

"Police!" Muffled voices came from downstairs.

Diane walked around and picked up his gun. She looked down at his face. He was scared and suffering. She could see he was wearing a bulletproof vest, but one of her bullets had managed to hit him through the arm opening and another in his leg.

"Help will be here soon," she said, and walked out of the room, down the attic steps, and out to the stairs. She stood his shotgun in the corner of the stairwell.

"I'm up here," she called.

She heard running through the house from the rear. They had found the broken back door. She walked down the stairs, her hands held high where they were clearly visible to the police. The first person she saw was Douglas Garnett. He met her at the base of the stairs.

"The intruder is wounded on the attic floor," she told him.

Diane sat on the living room couch, leaning forward with her head in her hands while the police secured the house. The intruder had wanted her to answer the door. He was going to shoot her and walk away. Frank would have come home and found the door open and her lying on the floor, dead. She took a deep breath and stood up when she heard the paramedics coming down the stairs with a stretcher. They were the same ones who had been making the runs to Marcella's house.

"Didn't we just take this guy last week . . . and wasn't he dead?" one of the paramedics asked Diane as he and his partner passed with the stretcher.

"Must be the same family," she muttered.

As they went out the front door, she thought she heard one of them mumble that he was going to write a book.

Frank came in a moment later, alarm and bewilderment on his face. Diane looked at him with tears in her eyes. He had gotten away early. What if he had arrived when the intruder came blasting through the door? She put a hand over her mouth, trying to gulp back the fear.

"Sweetheart, are you all right?" He ran over to her and she hugged him hard.

"There are a couple of doors you're going to have to fix," she said.

"What happened?" he asked.

Garnett came down the stairs with the police officers. He stayed inside and sent the other officers to search the grounds. Garnett, Diane, and Frank sat down in the living room.

Diane sat trembling on the sofa. "Jeez," she said, "I can't seem to stop shaking."

Frank put an arm around her shoulders and pulled her to him.

"Can't say as I blame you," said Garnett. He was wearing a suit. She wondered what he was doing in a suit this late. He should be in pajamas. He handed her her cell phone. "It was on the floor."

"Oh God, Vanessa," she said. "She must be worried sick. She called just before . . ."

She dialed Vanessa's number. It was picked up at half a ring.

"Diane, are you all right? We could hear the gunfire. Harte is here with me," she said.

Diane remembered now. She had dropped her phone as the intruder came into the room. Vanessa must have heard most of it. *Damn.*

"I'm fine. I had an intruder, but he's gone now," said Diane. "The paramedics took him away."

"You had an intruder? Dear, it sounded like a firefight."

"There was an exchange of gunfire, but I'm okay. I'm sorry to have hung up on you," she said.

"I think you need a good stiff drink, girl. You are sounding way too calm, and that's not good," said Vanessa. "What? Just a minute. Harte is mumbling something." She paused. "Harte says she will bring you one of her special tonics if you need it. I can recommend them."

Diane smiled. "Thank her for me. I'm fine. Just rattled. Did you say your mother remembered something?" Diane asked.

"Yes, but I can talk to you later about it. I'm sure the police are there," said Vanessa.

"They are, but I'd like to give them the information," she said.

"Okay. Mother remembered Edith Farragut. Farragut

was the woman's maiden name. Mother didn't know her well. My grandmother said the family were merchants, and she didn't associate much with them. Grandmother could be a bit of a snob. Anyway, she also said Edith's husband gave her the creeps when she saw them in church—just something about him. She didn't say what. She also said he had a lot of pride. The whole family did. I'm not sure what she meant by that either. They divorced, but the two of them lived near each other for a long time. They didn't live in Pigeon Ridge, but in Rosemont, near here. They purchased the old Gutemeyer estate. Mother said they had a daughter named Maybelle Agnes Gauthier."

"Maybelle Agnes Gauthier," repeated Diane. MAG.

"Mother said the daughter was an artist," continued Vanessa. "She may have lived in Pigeon Ridge—in a sort of artist's cottage. Mother didn't know Maybelle very well, even though they were contemporaries. She said she was a strange girl, but painted very well indeed. Mother thought that at one time she may have had a painting of hers. A landscape, she thought. She said if you go to the courthouse, in the corridor where all the portraits of Rosewood politicians are hanging, you can see one of her paintings. She signed with the picture of a little bird. Mother has no idea why."

"Do you know what happened to her?" asked Diane.

"Mother didn't know. We lived in Europe for a while, so we didn't know about a lot that went on in Rosewood. When we came back in 1957, Mother said that Edith Farragut had died and the Gauthiers were gone."

Chapter 42

Diane hung up with Vanessa, but not before Vanessa again told her to get herself a good stiff drink. From the way Diane felt at the moment, anything in her stomach wouldn't stay down. She sat quietly, collecting her senses before she spoke. Garnett didn't push.

"I guess you need my gun," she said, gesturing to the weapon lying on the coffee table. "I shot four times."

Garnett nodded. "Just procedure," he muttered, and took possession of the gun.

There was a jumble of things going through her mind, but what rose to the surface at the moment was the thought that if she had waited any longer to get out of the bathtub, she would have gone though all this naked. "Hell," she muttered.

"Can I get you something?" said Frank.

"Vanessa recommends Irish whiskey or Kentucky bourbon. I think I'll pass for now," she said. *You never know when I may need a steady hand and good aim.*

Garnett asked her what happened and she gave him a description of the evening's events.

"Why did he target me?" she asked.

"That's the question, isn't it?" said Garnett. "If he had been successful, the investigation into the attack on Dr. Payden would have gone on. The well would have still been excavated. I don't know what was supposed to be accomplished."

"From his looks, he might be related to Dildy," said Diane.

"He won't be talking for a while and I can't make a positive ID until we check his fingerprints, but I'm pretty sure he's Ray-Ray's cousin, Emory," said Garnett. "We don't know of any criminal activities connecting them. The two sides of the family don't get along and haven't since Raymond and Emory were kids. If it is Emory, he's been a petty crook all his life, just like his cousin. They just ran in different circles," said Garnett.

"How could they run in different circles?" said Diane. "Rosewood isn't that big."

"Emory is from Atlanta," said Garnett.

"Ray-Ray's name was really Raymond?" said Diane. "I'm glad to know his mother didn't name him Ray-Ray."

"Just as bad, if you ask me. His legal name was Raymond Raynard Dildy," said Garnett. "Kind of runs in the family. His cousin Emory's first and middle names are Emory Emanuel. I'm at a loss to explain how Emory escaped the moniker M&M."

Garnett's phone rang. He hadn't chosen a piece of music for his ringtone, but had just an old-fashioned ringing sound. He flipped it open.

"Garnett."

From his conversation, Diane guessed it was the policemen who had gone out to check the grounds, and they had found something.

"They found what they think is his vehicle parked beyond the trees in back of the house," he said. "It's a beat-up green Toyota registered to a Rick Gomez. It was reported stolen yesterday. We'll leave it where it is until your people go over it. I'll have my people watch it and your house."

When Garnett left, she called David and asked him to finish the well excavation.

"I'm going to sleep in," she said. "I'll be out late morning."

"What's happened?" he said.

Diane hadn't wanted to tell him, but he needed to be alert in case some maniac came to Marcella's place. She gave him a brief description of the evening's events. She tried to play it down, but the facts of the incident being what they were, it was hard to put a no-big-deal face on it.

"Diane, my God, why in the . . . ," he said. "Are you all

right? What the hell was that about? You say he's related to the guy who was killed here?"

"I don't know what it's about, and yes, they're apparently related. I'll talk to you about it tomorrow. Right now, I'm going to bed to get a good night's sleep. Tell the policemen there to keep a lookout. And David, be careful. Be extra paranoid."

"Sure thing," he said. "You know how I am."

"This is just crazy," said Diane when she hung up. "I don't know why I was a target. It solves nothing for anyone, unless it's some kind of revenge thing."

"Revenge? Who?" Frank asked. "And for what?"

"Maybe it was just a coincidence Emory turned out to be related to Ray-Ray. Emory is from Atlanta, which is a straight shot down the interstate from Gainesville. Perhaps Marsha Carruthers and her husband are behind it. Perhaps it's some kind of revenge for stirring up the tragedy in their lives."

As she said it, it didn't seem right. The kinship thing between the two men was just too much of a coincidence. She was getting a major headache.

"Why don't I heat up the leftover pizza?" said Frank. "We'll have pizza and red wine. You know how you love leftover pizza."

"Sounds good," she said.

While they waited for the pizza to warm in the oven, Frank boarded up the back door so it wouldn't open at all.

"I'll have it fixed tomorrow," he said. "I'll call my partner and tell him I'm taking the day off."

"I'm sorry you have to do that." Diane felt guilty on top of everything else. She had brought this to his house. Maybe it wasn't her fault, but it was about her.

"They could have been after me," said Frank. "After all, had I been here, I probably would have been the one to answer the door. I do have Atlanta connections who might want some revenge."

Frank had a strange habit of reading her mind sometimes. But she probably wore her feelings on her face. She was a terrible poker player.

"Ray-Ray after Marcella; his cousin after you?" She

shook her head. "That would be too much of a coincidence."

They ate and drank and Diane began to feel better.

"I finished the diary," he said.

"Oh? Was it hard?" asked Diane.

"Very easy really, once I got to know how Ellie Rose's mind worked. She must have been a neat kid. Very clever code for a kid."

"How did it work?" asked Diane.

"She had symbols for diphthongs and consonant blends—letter combinations like *oo*, *ou*, *th*, *st*, *ious*—that kind of thing. For other letter combinations she drew doodles that represented the sound—like in a rebus puzzle. For example, for *air* she drew three curled wisps."

Frank got a piece of paper and drew the doodle for her.

"The symbol for the consonant blend of *st* is a star. So if she wrote the word *stair*, it would be a star and these little wisps." He drew it for Diane.

"If she had to use a letter, she would go two up in the alphabet," he continued. "So *a* would be *c* and *z* would be *b*. The consonant blend *th* is the numeral three. The word *the* would be written as the numeral three with the letter *g* immediately following it." He grinned. "She was a good little doodler."

He took several bites of pizza and a sip of wine.

"There was a little complication, in that sometimes she would change how she wrote a word. For example, the symbol for the suffix *er* was a drawing of an ear. *Mother* was sometimes *oq*, with the numeral three immediately following, and then the drawing of an ear. And sometimes it would be a drawing of a moth and an ear."

"That seems like it would take a long time to write," said Diane.

"Not really. The drawings were doodles, stylized versions of what they represented. If you're going up the alphabet only two letters, you can work that out pretty fast," he said.

"I'll call Ross Kingsley tomorrow. He'll be happy you were able to decode it," said Diane. "I got the impression he thought it would be impossible."

"You know, I kind of got to know her. Not just reading

her diary, but seeing the way her mind worked, examining her whimsical creativity."

He stopped for a moment and took a drink of wine. Diane thought for a second he was going to tear up. She put a hand on his and he smiled at her.

"As I said, she was a neat kid," he said.

"Anything in her diary that would shed light on anything?" said Diane.

"Most of it was normal kid stuff. Talk about school, friends, boys she liked, teachers. There are a couple of drawings that occurred several times that I can't decipher."

He drew one for her. It was a triangle over an elongated diamond shape with slightly curving sides and what looked like horns.

"It looks kind of like a snake with scales and horns," said Diane.

"That's what I thought," he said. "I can't come up with a rebus or anything else that makes sense. I think it's a person, but that's as far as I got, except that it's clear she didn't like him. If I had a list of names of people in her circle, I might be able to decipher it."

"What was the context?" asked Diane.

"Dread seeing 'blank.' 'Blank' has changed since 'blank.' The second blank is the other doodle I can't figure out." He drew it for her.

"These are almost like Rorschach tests. The identification is in the eye of the beholder," said Diane. She examined the last drawing. "It looks like a ruin or a broken brick wall. What do you think?"

"I thought it looked kind of like a broken igloo," he said. "These look like blocks. Notice that the scales in the snake-like figure are similar to the bricks or ice blocks in the other figure."

"Something to sleep on," said Diane. She finished her pizza and upended her wineglass. "Vanessa will be disappointed we didn't have Irish whiskey," she said.

Diane got ready for bed as Frank went around and checked all the doors and windows in the house. If they were willing to shoot off the locks with a big gun, doors were useless, she thought.

She was sitting on the bed in her nightshirt when he came into the room.

"You know, I was really terrified," she said.

Frank sat down beside her and took her hand. "It's completely normal that you were."

"No, I mean I was really terrified," she repeated.

"And it's really normal," he said, grinning at her.

"You know I've been in a lot of dangerous situations. I was never this scared," she said.

Frank was silent for several moments. "Over the past few years you have been getting happier," he said. "It's taken a while since Ariel's death, but gradually your grief has made room for other emotions—like love and friendship. You've built a lot of that here in Rosewood. I'm not saying your life now means more to you, but you feel like you have a lot to lose, and it scares you. I believe that's part of it. And there was also the overly violent nature of the attack. It was designed for terror. But you did well. You won."

Diane leaned against him. "I'm going to find out who did this to your house," she said. "And to me."

Chapter 43

Diane had hoped to get out to Marcella's house by late morning, but she had to go to the police station first to make a formal statement. She wrote out an account and signed it before she went to Garnett's office, hoping it would save time. It didn't. She had to speak with Internal Affairs. It wasn't pleasant, mainly because the incident wasn't pleasant. But it wasn't that bad either. They weren't hostile, really. Stern, but not particularly aggressive. The prevailing culture in Rosewood was, if a man shot his way into your house, you had the right to shoot back. After she spoke with IA, she went to Garnett's office.

"Sorry about all this," said Garnett. "You know. Procedure. Hanks will join us shortly. We had a discussion with Emory in the hospital and we thought you would be interested in hearing about it."

Diane was relieved that he was still alive. She didn't want to have killed someone. "How is he?" she asked.

"Critical but in stable condition," said Garnett. "Only two of your bullets did any damage. The other two were stopped by his Kevlar vest. One bullet went in the arm opening of the vest and found the radial nerve but managed to miss the artery. Doctor said his right arm's going to be paralyzed. His right little toe was mangled by the bullet to his foot. They amputated the toe. Still, he's a lucky guy. Don't go wasting your time feeling bad for him. You know what he had planned for you. If he had got you to open the front door, he was going to blow your head off."

Diane shivered. She did know that.

Detective Hanks came in and pulled up a chair. He

stared at her as if looking for signs of the previous evening, or maybe signs of a nervous breakdown.

"Are you all right?" he asked.

"I'm fine," said Diane. "Just bewildered. Did he say what this was about?" she asked.

Garnett snorted and nodded to Hanks, who gave her a grim smile.

"He was talkative," said Hanks. "Said he had a contract to kill you."

"A contract?" said Diane. "Someone put a contract out on me? Why?"

"We don't know. He said he doesn't know who or why." Hanks smirked and looked at Garnett. Diane had the feeling he was trying not to laugh. "Emory said he received an envelope in the mail with two thousand dollars and your picture and address in it. He thought it was some kind of mistake until he got a call that evening. A man claiming to know his cousin, Ray-Ray, told him he'd sent it as a good faith payment. That he was looking for a good man to do some wet work for him."

"Wet work? He actually said that?" said Diane.

"Yeah," said Hanks, grinning. "He actually said those words."

"The man asked him if he was up to it. If he was, he would get another fifty grand. The man said that he'd tried to use Emory's cousin, but he was a disappointment, and he wanted to know if Emory was going to be a disappointment too."

"Emory asked what would keep him from just holding on to the two grand and doing nothing," said Garnett. "The man told him nothing was to stop him, but if this went well, he would use him again. That is, if he didn't mind doing a little traveling, like to Las Vegas and places." Garnett gave a derisive chuckle. "Las Vegas." He shook his head.

"Emory said the caller told him that from time to time he would receive an envelope, just like the one he'd received about you, with information and money in it," said Hanks. "If he did well—get this—the man would open him an offshore account for the money to be deposited directly. Emory thought he'd made the big time."

"Are you saying that some kind of organized crime people have put a contract out on me?" said Diane. "Are you serious?"

"Believe me," said Hanks, "no serious crime organization would hire this guy for anything. He was being played, big-time. No fifty grand would be sent to him after—the deed."

"But we don't know who hired him," said Garnett. "His phone records show the call came from a throwaway cell. We are going to assign a couple of men to you until this is over. We do take this seriously, no matter what kind of buffoon this Emory is. Someone out there knew he would be a good fall guy. He told Emory to make it quick and violent. If you wouldn't let him in the door, he was to, quote, 'blow the door off its hinges.'"

"Emory may be a moron," said Hanks, "but the man who hired him isn't. He knew how to con Emory into doing what he wanted him to do."

"How do we find this guy?" asked Diane.

"We don't know that yet," said Garnett. "We're going to start with Emory's family. There's a chance he made all this up and it's actually the family taking revenge because of what happened to Ray-Ray. Maybe they weren't as estranged as they led us to believe. But if that's the case, we still have the question, why you? Why not Hanks here, or Daughtry? They were the two officers most closely connected to Ray-Ray's death."

"I have to call my security," said Diane. "The way things are, I can't use my museum office. I won't bring a maniac into the museum after me. Until we catch this guy, I'll use my office in the crime lab. Analyzing the evidence from Marcella's may be the best way to find the answer to all this."

Garnett nodded in agreement. "It's a reasonable course of action," he said. "That's all we have at the moment. We keep running into dead ends. Whoever the mastermind is behind this, the guy is good at covering his tracks."

"Please keep me informed on what you discover," said Diane to the two of them. "Knowledge is what will keep me safe."

"We will," said Garnett.

Diane nodded. "Did you tell Hanks about my talk with Vanessa?" she asked Garnett.

"We talked about it this morning," Garnett said.

"You think this woman, this Maybelle Agnes Gauthier, is our Mad Potter?" asked Hanks.

"Mad Potter?" said Garnett.

"What else would you call someone who made pots out of human bones?" said Hanks.

"I guess that's what I would call them," Garnett said with a laugh. "Just don't let the press get hold of that."

"She may have been," said Diane. "But, so far, we only know that she was a painter."

"At least we have a name," said Hanks. "Easier to ask around about a person if you have a name. I was thinking I might send someone over, one of the girls, uh, women, over to the retirement homes to ask around. Some of those old-timers might remember her."

"Good idea," said Diane, rising from her chair. "If I'm finished here, I am going to the lab. I'll be either there or at the house."

She left the building, followed by her two bodyguards, and drove to the crime lab.

When Diane put the crime lab in the west wing of the museum, she added an outside elevator that went only from ground level to the crime lab on the third floor. She also added a small room, a lobby and guard post, at the ground-level entrance to the elevator. It was comfortable and had its own facilities. There was a receptionist and a permanent guard on duty. Diane invited the policemen to stay there. The crime lab was secure, she assured them.

"What about the entrance to the crime lab through the museum?" one of them asked.

"There's a guard on duty there as well. It also has reinforced doors and locks."

Diane left them in the elevator lobby and rode up to the crime lab. Izzy was there, holding down the fort while David and Neva were at the crime scene at Marcella's house.

Izzy looked at her wide-eyed when she entered the lab. "Are you all right?" he asked when she walked in. "Jeez, what the hell happened? I've been hearing some strange stuff. The news and some of my buddies said someone shot his way into your house."

Diane explained the events of the previous evening and her visit to the police station.

"Those IA inquiries," he said, "don't worry about them. They have to do that. Nobody's going to fault you for shooting some son of a bitch in your house. Jeez, he shot through the back door."

"It was very violent," said Diane. "I intend to find out who sent him and why."

"This case has been strange from the beginning," said Izzy. "Attacking Dr. Payden and making off with only a few paintings and a little pottery—what is that about? And that crazy writing on the bottom of the drawer. You know, at first it sounded like the writer was the victim, but now it looks like she might have been the perp. I don't know what to make of it. And what about that poor Lassiter woman? None of it makes a bit of sense."

"No," said Diane. "But it will soon. I won't have people coming after me and messing up Frank's house like that," she said. "I'll be in my office in the osteology lab. There are two policemen downstairs assigned to watch over me."

Diane went to her office and called her chief of security and told her what was going on. Diane told her she wanted to make the office wing off-limits to all but museum personnel until this was solved. She then called Andie, her assistant.

"Dr. Fallon, I heard on the news. Was it true? Are you all right?" she asked.

"I'm fine," said Diane. "I'm working from my osteology office, for the time being. I want you to work from the office up in archives."

"Why?" asked Andie.

"Because you are in my office and I don't want anyone in there. I've instructed security. And please, don't talk about this. Just have your workstation routed up there," she said.

"Sure. You think someone will come here?" she asked.

"I don't think so. The guy who broke into Frank's house is in custody. But someone sent him and we don't know who yet. I just want to be extra cautious and make sure everyone is safe," she said.

"Sure, I'll do that. I'm really sorry this is happening," she said. "You know, people are just crazy."

"That seems to be the general consensus," said Diane.

After her talk with Andie, Diane donned her lab coat and walked into her osteology lab. The lab was a large room with bright white walls, white cabinets, and plenty of overhead lighting. It was a bright room and cheery in its own way, with its shiny tables, sinks, and microscopes.

Neva had been working on laser mapping the skull. Her computer drawings were spread out on the counter. They showed a pretty girl. She looked so young. Too young to be dead.

The ceramic mask and sherds had been brought up from the archaeology lab and were lying on another table. The bones excavated from Marcella's well were in plastic containers sitting on one of the metal tables. Diane started laying them out in anatomical order on two tables—one for each skeleton. They were broken skeletons with missing parts. It was a sad group of bones.

She examined the skull of the female. It was small with nice, even teeth, but they were starting to decay. Without intervention they wouldn't have stayed nice for very much longer. Was she homeless? Poor?

Diane fit the mandible, the lower jaw, to the maxilla, the upper jaw, and held them together with one hand. She placed the reconstructed ceramic mask over the face.

It was a perfect fit.

Chapter 44

Diane set the mask aside, a mask she strongly suspected was made of clay tempered with the crushed bones of its subject. When she had first seen it sitting in Marcella's workroom, she was struck by its beauty. She saw now that the beauty was in the young girl. The mask was simply the product of a cruel and arrogant mind.

As she was about to lay the mandible aside, Diane's eye stopped on a disfiguration showing through the dirt stains. It was a healed fracture—a disturbing sign, evidence of an older severe injury. She laid the young girl's mandible on the table and turned the skull over in her hands and looked at the back of it. The cut extended vertically across the parietal and occipital of the skull. It looked to have been made by a heavy bladed weapon, most likely an axe or a hatchet. From the size and depth of the cut, it was clear the sharp edge of the weapon would have gone into the brain. There was no doubt this wound would have killed her.

Diane picked up the broken pieces of pottery containing what appeared to be an impression of the head wound. Accounting for the thickness of the skin and tissue on the skull at the time the clay was applied to the head, the mold looked to be a fit. At this point she could not say with certainty that the pottery sherds were or were not impressions of this skull wound. A microscopic examination of the pattern of the mold and the wound would be more definitive.

She photographed the skull and the mask to show the direct comparison. Next, she photographed the healed fracture on the mandible. After that, she did the measurements of the skull at all the craniometric points, recording each. Doing the measurements provided some momentary relief to Diane. The math helped her keep the objectivity and emotional distance she needed in the face of the terrible cruelty she saw in the bones.

When she finished examining the skull, she placed it on the table with the rest of the brown-gray stained skeleton. These bones had a sad story to tell, aside from the terrible trauma of the fatal head injury and the severed limbs. There was the healed fracture of the mandible. Three ribs had been broken and healed. Both the left and right radii of the arms contained healed fractures caused by the young girl's arms being twisted. The femur had been broken and healed in her lifetime. The femur was a big strong bone, not easy to break. If it was broken, it was because it met with a sizeable force. The young teen had been abused for years before she was murdered. Diane wondered whether she ever had any joy in her life.

As Diane finished and packed up the first set of bones, David, Neva, and Scott came in with the remaining contents of the well.

"You doing okay?" David said.

The three of them gathered around her as if there were something they could discern in her appearance if they looked closely enough.

"I'm fine," said Diane.

"I heard the other guy's not doing as well," said David.

Diane frowned.

"I see Garnett sent guards," said Neva. "They're downstairs in the lobby."

Diane nodded. "Until they find out who sent him—and why—I'm using the office here," she said.

"Good idea," said David. "It's more defensible."

"David said the guy last night is related to what's his name—that Dildy guy," said Neva. "Why are you being targeted?"

"I don't know," said Diane. "It makes no sense. But I intend to find out. I just don't know how, right now."

"If the answer lies in Marcella's well," said David, "I think we may be able to crack it."

"Oh?" Diane pulled off her gloves and washed her hands. "Come into the office and tell me what you found."

Diane's osteology office was more spartan than her museum office and it was a good deal smaller. The walls were painted an off-white cream color that she had hoped would give the room a warm glow. It hadn't. The floor was green slate. She hadn't wanted the static electricity or fibers that a carpet would generate. The desk and filing cabinets were a dark walnut. The comforts in the room were a long burgundy leather couch that sat against one wall, a matching chair, and a small refrigerator in the corner. A watercolor of a lone wolf hunting was the only decoration.

Scott looked around the room. "This is nice," he said, sitting down on one end of the sofa. David sat on the other end and Neva took the chair.

Diane got everyone a drink from the fridge before she sat behind her desk.

"How's Hector doing?" she asked Scott.

He bobbed his head up and down. "He's doing okay. He's learning to maneuver on crutches and thinks he can now come back to work. I think he needs a few more days' healing. They had to put a pin in his leg." Scott screwed his face into a painful-looking grimace.

"The tibia is a long, thin bone," said Diane. "It needs the support. Tell him we are all thinking about him."

"He sure hates to miss all the work," he said.

Diane could see he meant it. Hector and Scott apparently loved work.

"So," she asked David, "what have you found? Smoking gun? Fingerprints?"

"Funny you should mention that," he said. "Under the remaining bones we found several items of interest. You know how there were two hammers—a large one and a smaller one? There were two axes, actually an axe and a hatchet."

"Possibly the murder and dismembering weapons," said Diane.

"That's what we think," said Neva.

"They are rusted, and the wooden handles are mostly rotted away, but we may be able to do something with them," said David. "But what was under the axes is really great," he said. "We found a zippered case with sculpting tools in it. Because they were closed up, the wooden handles are in better condition. They have dark stains that I think are blood and—drum roll, please—there are fingerprints in the blood."

Diane opened her mouth in surprise. "Fifty-year-old fingerprints? Are you serious?"

"It gets better," said David. "They also threw unused clay down the well. You know how clay is. Think about those little bull figures from Çatal Höyük in the Old World archaeology section of the museum. They have those ancient fingerprints all over them. Clay is really good for that."

"That's a gold mine," said Diane. "That's amazing."

"We think so," said Neva. "They just threw all the incriminating evidence down the well and covered it over. We can do a lot with it."

"Well-done," said Diane.

"The credit goes to those who tried to get rid of the evidence," said David. "I wish all our perpetrators were so accommodating."

"It's almost as if they put the evidence in a time capsule," said Scott. "We're going to try to get DNA from the blood. No guarantees, but if we do, it will be a good paper. Speaking of which, there is just no DNA in the pottery sherds. Even in a bonfire kiln, it's just too hot," he said.

"I didn't think it would work, but I appreciate your trying," said Diane. "You never know until you try."

Just as she was about to heap more praise on them, the phone on her desk rang.

"Yes," she said.

"Diane, this is Ross. I know this is short notice, but Detective Fisher from Gainesville, who was the detective in charge of the Stacy Dance case, wants to come over and have a look at the evidence. He wants to bring the medical examiner, Doppelmeyer, and he wants Dr. Webber to be there."

"Is that all?" said Diane. "Does he want dinner?"

"Just about. He's bringing his supervisor and he wants your supervisor to be there too. I tried to explain that this doesn't have anything to do with Rosewood, but he wouldn't listen."

"I see. I wonder if Vanessa's free. She would find it interesting," said Diane.

"Funny. I'm sure he meant Garnett," said Ross. "Is that a problem?"

"No problem. He'll just have to be disappointed. Garnett has nothing to do with it. I won't have the mayor or the parks director here either, because they didn't have anything to do with the Stacy Dance case either," she said. "I will ask Jin to join us. He's analyzed all the trace evidence."

Kingsley laughed. "Okay. I can handle that. I hope Detective Fisher can."

"He'll have to," said Diane. "Have you called Lynn?"

"Yes, she's willing. A little too willing if you ask me," he said.

"When do they want this to take place?" said Diane.

"This evening, they said. After work."

"Good, I'll be able to get some more work done before then."

She had already hung up before she remembered that she didn't tell him that Frank had translated the diary pages. She could tell him later when she saw him.

She called the restaurant and ordered steak dinners to be delivered to the lobby of the crime lab for her two security guards. Then she dialed the DNA lab and asked for Jin.

"Yo," he said.

"What is the status of the Stacy Dance evidence?" she said.

"Done. I put it in the evidence vault in the crime lab. We ready for a transfer?" he asked.

Diane explained about the meeting. "Can you attend?" she asked

"Sure, Boss. Glad to," he said.

She looked at her watch. She'd have time to get started on the other set of bones before the meeting.

Chapter 45

The teenage male skeleton looked similar to the female skeleton as it lay on the paper atop the metal table. It was stained the same earth-toned colors. It had similar wounds in the skull—sharp-force trauma to the back of the head. His limbs had been removed from his body, not with any surgical precision, but with an axe, and evidenced all the clumsy damage that came with a coarse instrument.

Looking at the arms that had been severed, the sliced head and trochlea of the humeri, Diane wondered whether the woman, MAG, could have been the artist who created the bone-tempered pottery. Could she have dismembered these bodies by herself? No, she would have needed help. Lynn Webber needed a diener to grapple with the cadavers, put them on the table for autopsy, arrange them for photographs. Most medical examiners did. The deadweight of a human body would have been extremely hard to move around. There had to be at least two perps—or one burley man. It would have been next to impossible for one woman to do this. Especially at a time when women were not as buff as they are now.

Perhaps it was a true artist colony and several people lived in the house. Maybe the message on the desk drawer meant MAG knew what was going on and she was afraid for her life. She or her mother was the landlord. Why didn't she move in with her parents? Or get them to throw the others out? But sometimes it isn't that easy. Bullies can intimidate some people into emotional paralysis. And the writing on the drawer came from an emotionally distraught person.

Diane had finished with the measurements of the skull when she heard raised voices coming from the crime lab. She took off her gloves, washed her hands, and went out to see what was happening now.

David, Neva, and Izzy were at the round debriefing table with Jin. David was pointing to evidence envelopes laid out in front of them. He was arguing with Jin, gesturing to a report he had in his hand. Neva stood by with a frown on her face. Izzy just looked puzzled.

"What's going on?" Diane asked. Her people rarely argued.

"Jin has mixed up the evidence," said David. "It's all compromised. Marcella's and the Dance case from Gainesville you are working on."

"What?" said Diane. She did not want to hear that, not with a crowd of law enforcement and forensic people on the way to examine the Stacy Dance evidence. "Jin?"

"I didn't, Boss. I don't know what he's talking about. You know I don't mess up," he said.

Diane turned to David. He looked tired.

"What's this about, David?"

"This evidence he's about to give away to Gainesville. Some of it is the evidence we collected at Marcella's. I don't know how, but somehow when he was working on the Gainesville stuff, it got mixed up. I don't see how we can use any of it now."

"No, Boss, I've been trying to tell him," said Jin. "I don't know what he's talking about. I worked on the Dance evidence in my lab. You know that."

Jin stood with his arms crossed, glaring at David, who glared back.

"Let me see," said Diane.

She read the Stacy Dance evidence report, flipping through the pages, looking at the photographs Jin had taken of the evidence.

"What's the problem?" said Diane.

David tapped the paper in her hand. "The evidence Neva and Izzy collected from Marcella's is mixed in with the Dance evidence. Jin must have been working here when we were, and he grabbed the wrong evidence."

Diane had collected much of the evidence from the

Stacy Dance crime scene, and she recognized it in Jin's report and photos.

"Are you saying this is the evidence collected at Marcella's? Have you looked in Marcella's container?" said Diane.

"I was about to get it to see what kind of damage has been done," said David.

Diane looked at the jumble of shoe prints Jin had separated out using the computer software. "The shoe prints too?"

"Yes," said David, "especially the shoe prints."

"You're saying this is the boot print collected at Marcella's?" Diane asked David again, pointing to a photo.

"I had to work on it to get it clear," offered Jin. "There was a jumble of shoes on the electrostatic lifting film. I had the software separate out some of the prints from one another."

David pointed at the photograph. "This is the hiking boot print from Marcella's. Yes."

"In that one, the heel was showing good," said Jin. "I tried to filter out the other overlapping shoes from the rest of the print, but the heel is really clear."

"The heel is all you need for an identification," said David. "That's how I know it's the same. See these two chips in the heel? . . . Wait. Are you saying this isn't a mistake?"

"I don't see how it could be," said Diane. "You think Jin took the evidence out of the bags and relabeled them?"

"No," said David, "but I thought he was here when we were processing Marcella's, and—"

"You had already processed Marcella's evidence before we collected the Stacy Dance evidence," said Diane. "I collected these shoe prints at the Stacy Dance scene. David, you owe Jin an apology. It's the same print as the one from Marcella's because the same boot was at both places."

"What?" at least three of them said in unison.

All four of them looked at Diane as if she had said Kendel had just returned from her trip and had brought them a unicorn skeleton.

"What are you saying?" said David.

"She's saying you need to apologize," said Jin. "Hey,

you mean it's the same guy, don't you? Jeez, Boss, that's weird."

It had taken a few seconds for it to dawn on all of them.

"But this would connect with the Lassiter crime scene too," said David. "The same boot print was there. I don't understand it. The MO is too different. They don't look anything like crimes done by the same perp. Wasn't there a lot of postmortem staging and cleanup in the Dance murder? Didn't it have a definite sexual aspect to it?"

"Yes," said Diane. "So it appeared. That's what drew the Gainesville detective to the wrong conclusion."

"Well, the attack on Marcella and the murder of the Lassiter woman had no sexual component. And not much evidence of planning at all. They look like crimes by an amateur looking for loot."

"They would appear that way," said Diane.

"Do you think the Gainesville guy may have thrown away the boots by the side of the road or something and the Rosewood guy found them?" said Jin.

"This makes no sense," said David.

"I agree," said Diane. "It doesn't seem to. We also collected evidence of rope and other fibers in the Stacy Dance murder. The rope is the same too?"

"According to Jin's report, it's made of the same material," said David.

Diane again read through portions of Jin's evidence report on the Stacy Dance crime scene.

"I've read Marcella's evidence report," said Diane. "I've seen the blowup photographs of the fibers and read the chemical analysis of them. These fibers from the Stacy Dance scene are the same—the same dyed black wool and Manila hemp fibers. Granted, there are lots of ski masks like that and lots of rope. But you said, David, it was as if the masks and the rope were stored together. Could it be that . . ." She threw up her hands. "I can't explain it. But this evidence described in Jin's report is the evidence I collected at the Stacy Dance crime scene. He did not make a mistake."

"You going to apologize?" said Jin.

"Sure," said David. "Jin, I'm sorry. I shouldn't have jumped all over you like that."

"I understand. I would have thought the same thing," said Jin.

Neva rolled her eyes.

"I'm not sure I'm getting this," said Izzy. "Did the same guy do all three crimes? Or are we looking for somebody who fished clothes out of the trash in Gainesville and used them in two more crimes down here? Or are we looking at some bang-up-big coincidence?"

"I don't know," said Diane. "But if we can find Marcella's attacker, or the Lassiter murderer, we can ask them where they shop. In the meantime, I guess I need to ask Hanks to come to the meeting too."

Diane set up the meeting in the basement conference room near the DNA lab. She was holding it away from the crime lab to distance her involvement in Kingsley's case as far as possible from the jurisdiction of Rosewood. The conference room had a large round table with a white quartz top and comfortable chairs. Jin had picked out the furniture for the room. She wasn't sure why he wanted white, but it was a pretty table—one that King Arthur would have liked.

Diane asked her policemen bodyguards to be present. She didn't quite trust Oran Doppelmeyer to remain civilized. There must be more to their history than Lynn Webber had told her. The policemen seemed pleased to actually be involved in what was going on, rather than just sitting on the sidelines in case something should happen. They were also pleased with the food Diane had sent them. The way to a policeman's heart.

She called Hanks and told him about the boot print. He was as mystified as she and her crew were. He seemed to like the scenario that the boots were thrown away and retrieved by someone else—the ski masks too. That was how the rope fiber got on them. The masks were near the rope, picked up the transfer, and when Marcella's attacker used them, the fiber was transferred again. It was the only scenario that made sense.

Diane put the Stacy Dance evidence in the DNA lab. Her bodyguards were in comfortable chairs near the door, and now she waited for the others to arrive. She was not looking forward to this evening. She'd rather be at home with Frank.

Chapter 46

Diane asked museum security to post someone at the information desk to greet her guests and bring them downstairs to the DNA lab. Ross Kingsley arrived first, looking, as usual, professorial. Lynn Webber came shortly after, looking rather stunning in a black gabardine suit with an olive silk taffeta blouse. She was dressed to be a presence in the room. Her black hair had a lustrous sheen and her makeup was perfectly applied.

Diane wondered whether she had remembered to run a comb though her own hair.

Sheriff Braden, who was in charge of the Mary Phyllis Lassiter investigation in the neighboring county, arrived shortly after Webber. He hadn't changed from his sheriff's uniform. Jin was already there, working in the DNA lab. Detective Hanks arrived after Braden. Now it was only the Gainesville contingent who had yet to arrive—Detective Ralph Fisher, Chief of Detectives Nancy Stark, and Medical Examiner Oran Doppelmeyer.

When Diane called Sheriff Braden, she had asked him to sit on one side of Lynn Webber. Diane was going to put Detective Hanks on the other side. Diane told Braden about her encounter with Doppelmeyer in the parking garage at the hospital and that she didn't want him to get aggressive. Sheriff Braden, of course, was outraged. He was known to be fond of Dr. Webber ever since she arrived in the Rosewood area. Putting her between Hanks and Braden was to protect Webber from herself as much as from Doppelmeyer. Diane had a gut feeling that Lynn wasn't ready to turn loose of him yet.

Diane mentally went over her ducks and calculated whether or not they were in a row. Close enough. The only problem she had with the meeting was any fallout for the Rosewood PD. Gainesville PD assumed that Rosewood had butted into their jurisdiction. She could see how that would piss them off. She hoped refusing to have Garnett there would reinforce her message that Rosewood wasn't involved.

Diane served coffee, and as they waited she told Kingsley about the diary.

"He translated it?" Kingsley seemed surprised.

"He said it was pretty easy," said Diane. "I don't have it with me, but you could come over tomorrow, or this evening, and Frank can go over it with you."

"Anything of interest?" asked Kingsley.

"There were a few entries about people she described as creepy. It's hard to say who they were because proper names were harder to decipher. Frank can tell you about it."

The people from Gainesville arrived. They didn't look happy. Chief of Detectives Nancy Stark wore a plain brown suit and white blouse. It was wrinkled, as if she'd had it on all day and then had to drive here in it. Stark's short dark brown hair was just beginning to gray. Her dark blue eyes looked suspicious as Diane made introductions. The detective, the one who closed Stacy Dance's case as an accident, was in his mid-fifties. He had a thick shock of white hair and black eyebrows. He frowned at all of them. From the way Doppelmeyer glowered at Lynn, he was as angry now as during their run-in at the hospital. This was going to be a fun meeting. Diane ran her fingers through her hair.

They all did shake hands. That was a start. She and Lynn managed to avoid Doppelmeyer's handshake. Not hard, since there were so many people. Diane directed them to the table and offered coffee. They declined. Perhaps later, she thought. Right now they probably felt that Rosewood was telling them they did a piss-poor job of investigating one of their own crimes. Diane understood their anger.

Chief Stark turned to Hanks. "You are Ms. Fallon's supervisor?" she asked.

"No, ma'am. I don't think she has one." He laughed.

If he was hoping to relieve the tension, he hadn't. Rosewood's inside jokes didn't play to a Gainesville audience. However, Kingsley smiled, as did Lynn.

"Your counterpart, Chief Garnett, is my supervisor when I work for the City of Rosewood," said Diane. "In the Stacy Dance death, I am not working for Rosewood. I am a consultant to the private firm of Darley, Dunn, and Upshaw, represented here by Ross Kingsley."

"What are they doing here, then?" Stark asked of Detective Hanks and Sheriff Braden.

"They are working on cases that have a certain overlap of evidence. I thought it would benefit everyone for them to be here," said Diane.

"You shared our evidence with them?" Fisher said. It was more of an accusation than a question.

"It's my understanding that the Stacy Dance case is closed. This is evidence we collected at the behest of her father. As yet, it isn't your evidence," said Diane.

"What are the patrolmen doing here?" said Chief Stark. "Why are we in Rosewood's lab?"

"This is the museum's DNA lab," said Diane. "As for the patrolmen, they are bodyguards assigned to me by Chief Garnett."

"That's an insult," said Fisher, in a voice louder than he meant. The acoustics of the room were quite good. His white hair highlighted his reddened ears and face. "I know there've been some accusations thrown around. I believe Dr. Doppelmeyer here, that he's behaved with the utmost propriety. However, if you need calming down, you have my guarantee you are safe from him."

"Detective Fisher," said Diane. She kept her voice calm and even and maintained eye contact with him. "Here in the museum, the DNA lab, and crime lab, we place a particular importance on the difference between what we believe and what we know. I know that Dr. Doppelmeyer accosted Dr. Webber in the parking garage. I know, because I was there. I understand that you believe he did not. I hope you understand that, logically, I can't accept your guarantee."

"Jesus save us," he mumbled, turning his face away.

"I understand that sometimes in a darkened garage, perceptions might not be as accurate as we like," said Chief Stark. "I agree with Detective Fisher. Bodyguards are an overreaction to the situation, one that insults us and our integrity."

"They were assigned to me because last night a man was sent to my home to kill me. He shot his way into the house. I fled to the attic where he followed and shot his way through that door also. He was about a second away from shooting me, point-blank, with a shotgun blast. Fortunately, I shot him first. We don't know who sent him. The guards will be with me until we find out and the situation is resolved."

Kingsley looked at her openmouthed. "Are you all right? How's Frank?"

"He wasn't home. I was alone," Diane said, still looking at Stark.

"I heard something about a home invasion in Rosewood," said Stark. "That was you?"

"Yes," said Diane. "You will forgive me if, today, I am a little cranky."

"You think it was me?" said Doppelmeyer. "I had nothing to do with it."

"I don't think you did. I really don't. I think it had something to do with another case I'm working on. But that's what I believe. I don't know." She turned back to Chief Stark. "I understand that some people are panicked when confronted, even in a mild way, in the dark confines of a parking garage. That's not true of me or Dr. Webber," said Diane. "We viewed the situation accurately."

"So did the security cameras," said Lynn Webber. "Hospital security can make them available if you want to see them."

Doppelmeyer looked at Lynn and snarled. "You vindictive freaking bitch."

Both Fisher and Stark jerked their attention to him. She could see they were surprised by his vehemence—and his inability to keep his temper in check.

Sheriff Braden stood up and faced him. "I don't know where you were raised, but here we don't talk to a lady that way."

Diane was suspecting that there was something more to Doppelmeyer and Lynn's enmity than what Lynn had described. She was willing to bet that Lynn had rebuffed his attentions and that was a large part of what led to him getting her fired.

"You know," said Ross Kingsley, "normally in these kinds of meetings, we try to break the ice with small talk and jokes. And I'm ashamed to say that I find this more entertaining, but we have some evidence we would like to show you."

"That's why we're here," said Stark.

Jin had been standing by a credenza with the box of evidence on top of it. He came over with the box and set it between Diane and Ross.

"This is Deven Jin," said Diane. "He's the director of the DNA lab. He was formerly on my crime scene team. He helped gather the evidence and he processed it."

"Hi." Jin grinned, as if they were all good friends.

"Dr. Webber has her autopsy report that she will go over with you," said Diane.

"Let's get it over with, then," said Detective Fisher.

Chapter 47

Diane put a diagram of Stacy Dance's room on the table. She had marked where all the evidence was found. She turned the map to face toward Fisher, Stark, and Doppelmeyer. She also placed their own photograph of Stacy next to the map.

Kingsley explained his firm's involvement first. Diane noticed he tried to keep all words out of his narration that might in any way suggest that their guests had bungled the case. He used a lot of passive voice and weasel words. He was far more tactful than Diane would have been.

"Her father, Harmon Dance, left her room intact," Kingsley said. "That's why I was able to have Diane examine it." He nodded to Diane and they gave her their strained attention.

"When someone is strangled, they often evacuate their bladder and bowels," began Diane.

"Oh, here we go, Pathology 101," said Doppelmeyer.

"Oran, let's listen," said Chief Stark. Her voice was quiet, but it held her authority.

Doppelmeyer sat back in his chair, his ears turning red. "We know this," he said.

"I was just introducing the evidence," said Diane. "I meant no disrespect." She pointed to a marked place on the diagram that was in the living room area of Stacy Dance's apartment.

"This is where she was strangled. We found her urine and feces here and it covered a wide area. It had been cleaned up, but there was enough left for Jin to positively identify it as belonging to Stacy Dance," said Diane.

"What about the bed?" said Fisher. "Did you check it?"

"Yes. It was negligible. The amount was what you might get from transfer," she said.

Diane put a photograph of the rope in front of them.

"This was around her neck. Notice that it is tied with a granny knot. If you are involved in cutting off the blood supply to your brain for fun, it's important for the knot to be easily released when you want it to be, or you lose consciousness. You use a knot that lets the rope slip, or you use a knot that can be released by a pull on the end of the rope. You don't use a granny knot. Granny knots are incorrectly tied square knots that are notoriously hard to untie, and they don't slip. Look at the picture. There is no way she could have gotten out of this. She would have lost consciousness in as little as four seconds after the knot was pulled tight, and death would have followed within minutes."

"It could have been suicide," Fisher shot back.

"Have you ever in your experience seen a suicide like this?" said Kingsley. "Has anyone committing suicide ever attached clothespins to their nipples?" Fisher didn't say anything. "This was staged to humiliate as well as to deflect the manner of death."

"You know about knots?" Stark asked Diane.

"Diane is an expert in knots," said Kingsley.

"She is," said Lynn Webber. "I hadn't heard of a forensic knot expert until I met her. Let me tell you, when we had those hanging victims, she made sure my diener and I were really careful with the knots. She read those knots like a book."

"How do you get to be a forensic knot expert?" asked Fisher.

Diane could see the skepticism in his face. But she saw interest too.

"Study and experience. My interest began when I became a caver. In caving, your life often depends on your knowledge of rope and knots. Then I had my first case involving ropes, and it grew from there," said Diane. "Knots carry unique information. They tell you things about the person who tied them. It's often not a great deal, but it can be a critical piece of information. I can look at a set of knots and tell you if the person is a caver or a rock climber, a boater, or a hauler. I can also tell you by looking at their rope if they are careful or reckless."

"Huh, interesting," said Stark. "So this is not a knot someone would use in this situation?"

"Not like this. In this situation, if a granny knot is used at all, it would be to tie a small loop to stick the end of the rope through to make a loop around the neck that would release."

Diane watched their faces to see if she was winning them over. She couldn't tell. They had far better poker faces than she did. Except Doppelmeyer. And he was not ever going to be won over. But he didn't need to be. Nancy Stark was their audience. She was the one who needed to be convinced.

Diane showed them another photograph of the rope. "This part of the rope—the opposite end from the noose—has Stacy Dance's epithelials and blood on it for a length of a little more than eighteen inches. She was strangled with this end." Diane looked to Kingsley.

"We also found other evidence, which we will discuss in a moment," said Kingsley. He nodded to Lynn Webber.

Lynn placed her autopsy photographs of Stacy's neck on the table beside the photograph they took of Stacy as she was found. She handed them her report. With her well-manicured fingers, Lynn pointed to Stacy's neck in their photo. Lynn didn't use nail polish. She buffed her nails to a shine and kept them short. Her nail beds were long and made her nails look longer than they were. She had pretty hands that were a contrast to the difficult photographs she was showing.

"This ligature here," she said, pointing to a reddened line across the neck, "it's the same line here on your photo. This is the mark left when she was strangled, as evidenced by the deep-cutting indentation of the rope and the characteristic perimortem color and pattern of the tissue damage."

Stark nodded. "Go on."

"This ligature"—she pointed to a second indentation around the neck—"is where the rope was later tied around her neck—the way she was found. If you look at your photograph, you can see some of it where the towel sort of lifts the rope a little."

She handed them a magnifying glass. Stark and Fisher picked up the photographs and examined each.

"Notice the different color," Webber said. "See that the bruising did not spread through the tissues from the site of the rope. She was already dead when this was tied around her neck."

Chief Stark had a copy of Doppelmeyer's autopsy report. She read it over several times.

"Oran, you don't mention two strangulation ligatures," said Stark.

Detective Fisher took the report from her and read it.

"It means nothing," Doppelmeyer said. "I told you she's incompetent. This is not an original photograph. She probably Photoshopped this."

"This is a copy of the photograph from your file," said Kingsley. "If you compare it with the original in your file, you'll see that it hasn't been changed in any way. If you don't believe the photographic evidence, Stacy Dance hasn't been reburied yet. You can have a third ME look at her."

They were silent for several long moments. Diane could now see the doubt in both Stark and Fisher. Doppelmeyer saw it too.

"You're not buying this crap, are you?" he said.

Neither answered him.

"What is the other evidence you mentioned?" asked Detective Fisher. "The evidence that involves their cases." He wagged his hand between Detective Hanks and Sheriff Braden.

"The hell with this," said Doppelmeyer. "If this is all you have, I have important work to do. What a waste of time. I'm glad I drove." He got up to leave.

Diane asked one of the policemen to show him how to get to the first floor. She then turned to Hanks and nodded. He and Braden told them about Marcella Payden and Mary Phyllis Lassiter. Hanks told them about the fiber evidence and he told them about the boot print.

"The same boot print showed up at the Stacy Dance

scene," said Hanks. "We don't know why. The crimes were completely different. Not just the age of the victim, but"—he threw up his hands—"all of it. With Payden and Lassiter, it was like a smash and grab. Very quick and violent. With Miss Dance, it was staged and slow. It's possible the same person was involved in both. Or it's possible your guy threw away the clothes he used and our guys found them."

"When Diane told us about the evidence connection," said Sheriff Braden, "we looked for some connection between our victims and yours. Couldn't find any. Not that we had a lot of time to look—this evidence just came to light—but still, nothing so far."

"If you get a suspect, we'd like you to allow us to watch the interrogation. We'll do the same," said Hanks.

Both Braden and Hanks had been very matter-of-fact, assuming that Gainesville PD would reopen the Dance case. They didn't know anything about the politics or the biases that closed it in the first place. They were just looking at the evidence. Diane suspected Stark and perhaps Fisher noticed that about them, the lack of guile.

"All right," said Chief Nancy Stark. "We'll take another look. I'm not making any promises."

"There's something else," said Kingsley.

"What's that?" asked Stark, frowning.

"I almost hate to say, because it's going to turn someone's world upside down," said Kingsley. "But she knows it's coming. You know the young woman who discovered the body of Stacy Dance?"

"The gal from Ohio, cousin to the drummer?" said Fisher. "I suppose I need to get her back here."

"She's not the drummer's cousin," said Kingsley. "Her name is Samantha Carruthers. She's the sister of Ellie Carruthers—the teenager Stacy Dance's brother was convicted of killing."

"What?" said Fisher. "The hell you say. You are not serious?"

"Unfortunately, yes," said Kingsley.

"What the hell was she doing hanging out with the Dance girl?" Fisher said.

"Several reasons," said Kingsley. "Among them, I suspect Samantha Carruthers had doubts about the identity of her sister's murderer. I think it was something subconscious, but I believe it was there."

"How did they get together?" asked Fisher.

"They were in the same college class," said Kingsley. "Stacy had a band. Samantha played the guitar and wanted to join the band."

"How did you find out?" he said.

"I was retracing Stacy Dance's last days. I spoke with her band members. Samantha Carruthers was there, but she was introduced to me only as the drummer's cousin, visiting from out of town. I went to meet with the Carruthers family, as Stacy had, and Samantha showed up at home—literally walked in through the front door—while I was interviewing Mrs. Carruthers. 'Hi, Mom. Hi, dear.' Imagine my surprise."

"Damn, imagine *my* surprise," said Fisher. "Why didn't she tell me when I interviewed her? Why the fake name?"

"She said she didn't want her parents to know. You can imagine what their reaction would be. I didn't give her away. I knew something must be up. She met with Diane and me later and spilled the beans. Samantha's moved out now. I'm not sure where, but the drummer probably knows. I told her you would be finding out. Your showing up won't be a surprise to her, but it will be to her parents. Like I said, I hadn't wanted to turn her world upside down. I still don't."

Kingsley didn't mention the diary. It had more to do with the Carruthers murder, and the Gainesville visitors wouldn't have wanted to revisit that. If the diary came up later, he told Diane, he would give it to them. Diane thought they were about ready to go. Then Stark spoke up.

"What about that newspaper article?" said Stark. "That has been very uncomfortable for us, and unfair."

Diane was hoping they wouldn't mention it.

"I sympathize," Diane said. "As I am director of the museum, newspaper articles have been the bane of my existence lately. We didn't have anything to do with the article."

By *we*, Diane meant Kingsley and herself. They would assume, however, she also meant Webber. If Lynn wanted to come clean, fine, but Diane doubted she would. Too much to lose.

Stark nodded. "It had a lot of inaccuracies," she said.

"I agree," said Diane.

The meeting broke up and Diane called Frank and asked if he felt like having a guest. She knew he had been busy all day repairing the house. She wished she had been there with him.

"Sure. I'll order Mexican," he said. "And I have an idea about the names I couldn't decipher."

Chapter 48

Diane cleared the table after the dinner of enchiladas, Spanish rice, and chiles rellenos Frank had ordered, and brought out fresh brewed raspberry-chocolate coffee. Frank was laying out the decoded diary pages on the table and explaining to Kingsley what they meant.

"You've impressed me," said Kingsley. "You talk like this was easy."

"It was fairly easy," said Frank. "Just a little time-consuming. Fortunately, there's not much to do in a motel room."

"That's right, you just got back from, where was it, Nashville? I'd think there would be a lot to do in Nashville," said Kingsley.

"I'm not much into nightlife," said Frank. "Ben, my partner, and I are pretty boring."

Frank gave Kingsley a code sheet with all of Ellie Rose's little doodles and what they represented. He had another sheet with symbols for proper names that he couldn't translate.

"Most of the names were friends from school, judging from the context," he said. "If I had a list of her friends, I could figure out who she was talking about in each instance. Most of what she wrote about was related to the normal concerns a girl her age would have. Lots of drama, but nothing serious. It's these two names that are the ones of interest." Frank pointed to two doodled symbols in the list. "They are the only ones she seemed to be truly wary of."

Frank showed Kingsley larger drawings of the two doodles. "Diane and I thought this one looked like a stylized snake with scales and horns. And the other one looked like some kind of a masonry ruin—bricks or something. I thought maybe it looked kind of like an igloo—at least, the blocks reminded me of ice blocks. At any rate, the jagged outline looks like something broken," said Frank. "Note that the snake scales in the first symbol are small versions of the larger blocks in the other symbol."

"You said you had a flash of what they might mean?" said Diane.

"If they are names, what if the outline represents the first name and the inside pattern represents a last name? That would make these two symbols represent two people who share the same last name. For example, Ellie Rose might have represented my name by using a hot dog with small doughnuts inside it, and my daughter's name would be a star with doughnuts inside."

"Doughnuts?" said Diane and Kingsley together.

"I don't get it," said Kingsley.

"You know, Dunkin' Donuts. That's one type of coding Ellie used—a kind of rebus soundalike: Duncan—Dunkin'."

Diane laughed.

"Like the Brick twins, Snake and Jagged," said Kingsley, grinning.

"Sort of," said Frank.

The phone rang. Diane rose from the table, carrying her coffee with her, and answered the phone.

"Diane, uh, Thomas Barclay here. How are you? Read in the paper you had some kind of dustup at your home."

Dustup? Yes, that's what it was, a dustup. Diane frowned and sat down in the living room and took a sip of hot coffee. Thomas Barclay was one of the museum board members, one whom she struggled to get along with. He was a bank president with a forceful personality.

"Yes, there was an incident here. A man shot the lock off the door and forced his way in with a gun and tried to kill me. I'm fine. I was able to shoot him before he shot me," she said. She realized she sounded sharp, but calling what happened to her a *dustup* pissed her off.

There were several moments of silence.

"My God, a home invasion—here in Rosewood. What were they after?"

"Me, apparently," said Diane.

Barclay seemed to be at a loss for words. "Do the police have someone watching your house?" he said.

"Yes, they've had someone with me all day."

"Good, good," he said. "The reason I called is—well, I got a curious call from a friend. A man I serve with on a board of directors in Atlanta. Name's Everett Walters."

"The name sounds familiar," said Diane. She waited for him to get to the point.

"He's a good man. Usually very sensible. He said his son over in Gainesville has a very good friend and neighbor that you've been harassing. Of course, I told him that was unlikely. But the thing is, the thing that makes it difficult is, he insists that the board, the museum board, get rid of you. Says your behavior is casting a bad light on the museum. I told him we don't have the power to fire you. He said we need to do something, that his son's friends suffered a terrible tragedy and now you are causing them immeasurable suffering on top of it, and you have to be stopped. What's this about?"

"It's not about museum business and I'm sorry that a member of the board was dragged into it. You need not worry about museum involvement. You can tell your friend, Mr. Walters, that the Gainesville police will be handling things from here on out," she said. "We've turned everything over to them."

He was quiet again. Apparently Barclay had never been on an advisory board before. He much preferred making policy, rather than merely expressing his opinion. He would have liked very much to be able to fire Diane, or at least to curtail her powers. Not being able to do either, he made an effort to be polite.

"All right. I'll tell him the police will be handling it. I'm sure that will be a comfort," he said.

"I'm sure it will. You said he is usually very sensible," said Diane. "How well do you know him?" Diane thought it very odd that he would call with such a vehement request. She could see him asking Barclay to look into it, or to find out what was going on. But to request that she be fired? That was a little over-the-top. Had Wendy leaned hard on him for Marsha Carruthers' sake?

"Oh, we go back," said Barclay in his best bank president's voice. "He owns several businesses in Gainesville and Atlanta." He said it as if that were Everett Walters' measure of worth. She supposed that for Barclay it was.

"Everett Business Supplies, Walter Ace Parcel Delivery, Night Couriers. His son is chief of oncology at the big hospital in Gainesville and is being looked at to run for a congressional seat. Has a grandson in law school. Good solid family. His father was the one who started the family business. Good tradition. Everett's not given to histrionics—I wouldn't have thought."

Apparently Walters' call sounded a little over-the-top to Barclay too. That was interesting.

"It's unfortunate he bothered you with this," said Diane. "I assure you, he has exaggerated to the point of absurdity. There is no reason to worry. I hope the rest of your evening is uneventful."

"Yes, ah, yours too. Terrible about the home invasion. Just terrible. Here in Rosewood you don't expect that kind of thing. Well, good-bye, Diane."

Diane bid him good-bye and hung up the phone. She took the phone to its station and went back to the table.

"What was that?" asked Frank.

"Thomas Barclay, from the bank—a member of the museum board. Wendy Walters' father-in-law is calling museum board members. Or rather, he called Thomas Barclay, at any rate, and asked him to fire me for harassing Marsha Carruthers and her family."

Kingsley looked at her with an expression of puzzlement. "You're serious? He did that?"

"That's what he said."

"It sounds like the Carruthers are using their neighbors to put pressure on you to stop the investigation," said Frank. "A little late for that."

Diane didn't say anything. She was staring at the drawings.

"Diane? Are you there?"

It was Kingsley's voice. But Diane didn't say anything. She barely heard him, she was so interested in Ellie Rose's doodles.

Chapter 49

"Diane," said Frank, "you thought of something. I can tell by the trance you're in."

Diane didn't answer. She walked over to one of the bookcases in the living room and pulled out a desk encyclopedia and flipped through the pages. She was coming to understand how Ellie Rose's mind worked too. Diane put the encyclopedia back and pulled down a travel book, thumbed through it, and replaced it. She pulled out a geography book and looked through it. It had the picture she wanted. She grabbed a bookmark from the basketful Frank kept on the shelf and marked the page. She took the book to the table, sat down, and pulled the drawings over to her and studied them.

"Did Ellie Rose ever truncate a name in her representation of it?" Diane asked Frank.

"What do you mean?" he asked.

"For example, if she were writing about me, might she use a drawing of dice, or rather one die, to represent the syllable *Di*, rather than symbolizing the whole word *Diane*?"

"Sure. The symbol she used for *Atlanta* was a sun with squiggly rays," Frank said.

"I don't get it," said Kingsley.

"Hotlanta," both Diane and Frank said together.

"Oh, of course." Kingsley grinned.

"Okay," said Diane, pointing to the drawing of the snake. She paused, trying to organize her thoughts. "We called this a snake because this top triangle looks kind of like the head of a snake, and the elongated, curved diamond shape below it looks like the body of a snake—and maybe she did that on purpose—making a symbol with a double meaning. But this drawing could also represent a tie," said Diane.

"A tie?" said Kingsley. "Like neck ornamentation?" he said, pulling at his own brown and tan striped tie.

"It could," said Frank.

His eyes twinkled. Diane could see he loved decoding things. Actually, it was kind of fun.

"Okay, now look at this other one—the jagged outline that we interpreted to mean something broken or in ruins. But look at this." Diane turned to the page she had marked in the book and pointed at the photograph. Look at just the outline of this face of Mount Everest. The shape is the same as her symbol. Notice that her drawing of the jagged shape is always the same. It wasn't a generic jagged-shape thing she was representing. It was this particular thing: Mount Everest."

"You're right," said Frank. "It's the same outline. Okay, we have Tie and Everest. You are suggesting that those are the first names, right?"

"Sort of," said Diane. "You said you think the pattern inside the symbol is the last name. The crosshatches look like scales on the first symbol because we identified it as a snake. On the second symbol, I called them bricks in a broken wall. I think I was right, at least about the wall part.

"When we think about drawing something that represents a generic wall, we don't draw something made out of stucco or drywall—we think of bricks in a wall. The bricks mean *wall*. So, what we have is Tie Wall and Everest Wall, or rather, Tyler Walters and Everett Walters. Those are the names of Ellie Rose's neighbor and his grandfather—the man who is trying to keep me busy with something other than investigating this case."

Kingsley and Frank both sat back, silently looking at the drawings.

Kingsley nodded and stroked his short beard. "I'll buy it," he said.

Frank looked up from the drawings to Diane. "Is that what the call was about just now? This Everett Walters?"

"Yes," said Diane. "He called Thomas Barclay. They serve together on some board in Atlanta. He wanted Barclay to fire me. Maybe he thought I'd be too busy trying to save my job to pursue this case."

"Thomas Barclay. Isn't that the banker who gave you a hard time about the Egyptian artifact scandal?" asked Kingsley.

"The very one," said Diane. "Even Barclay thought Everett Walters was a little too dramatic in his demand. Walters must have been very insistent."

"Well, that's interesting," said Kingsley. "Very suggestive. What was it again that Ellie Rose said about them in her diary?"

He rustled through the papers on the table until he came up with the diary translation Frank wrote.

"If we put the names in place of the symbols, it reads: Dread seeing Tyler Walters. Tyler Walters has gotten mean since Everett Walters came into his life. Tyler Walters is just too creepy. Everett Walters scares me." Kingsley put the list down. "Tyler lived next door to Ellie Rose Carruthers. You don't think . . ."

"You know," said Frank, "just because Ellie Rose was put off by them doesn't mean they killed her. I know that's what's running through your minds right now. And not to put a damper on things, but we don't know if Diane's decipher of these symbols is correct. I think it is, but we don't know for sure."

"I know," said Diane, "but here's the clincher. Barclay just told me that one of Everett Walters' businesses is Walter Ace Parcel Delivery. If I'm not mistaken, that's the company Ryan Dance worked for, and it was in their secured parking lot that he parked his car—the car with all the evidence in the trunk that he claims someone must have planted. You have to admit, it's worth looking into."

"You're right," said Kingsley. "My God, you're right about that."

"So now you do intend to look into the Ellie Rose murder case? The one you assured those women in Gainesville that you weren't investigating?" said Frank.

"Yes," said Diane. "This may turn out to mean nothing, but it's really making the hair stand up on the back of my neck."

"Just checking," said Frank. "I find it a little chilling myself." He smiled. "I know I would follow up on it."

"It makes sense about Wendy Walters," said Kingsley. "It was obvious she and Marsha Carruthers are codependent. I could see what Marsha was getting out of the dependent relationship, but I couldn't understand what Wendy was getting. If she was trying to assuage her guilt, it would lead her to go way above and beyond the behavior of a good neighbor."

"Her guilt about what exactly?" said Frank.

"That's the question," said Kingsley, absently pulling at his tie. "Did someone in her family kill Ellie Rose, and did she know about it?"

"Jeez, it's beginning to sound like a Shakespearean tragedy," said Diane. She started to offer more coffee when the phone rang again. She left them at the table wondering if Wendy was some variation of Lady Macbeth and went to answer it.

"Diane, it's Vanessa. How are you?" she asked.

"I'm doing well. No real lasting effects. Frank replaced the doors today. You'd never know they had been shot up," said Diane.

"That makes me shiver every time I think about it. I don't know how you remained so calm during all that," she said.

"I wasn't really all that calm," said Diane.

"You did well. I'm very impressed. God forbid, if I'm ever in that situation, you are the one I want by my side to protect me. But the reason I called, Mother said she remembered getting letters about the Gauthier family when we were in Europe. She said the letters were from Laura Hillard's great-grandmother, Ernestina. She kept mother up-to-date on all the Rosewood gossip in those days," said Vanessa.

Laura Hillard, Diane's psychiatrist friend, and her family went several generations back as residents of Rosewood.

"Does she remember what they said?" asked Diane.

"No. She got so many letters during that time," Vanessa said. "When Daddy was ambassador, our life was a whirlwind."

"I don't suppose she saved the letters," said Diane.

"Well, that's the thing. She's insisting that Harte and I

go up in the attic and look for them. She can't remember exactly where they are stored, and you know how big our attic is. It's going to be like finding the lost Ark in the government's warehouse," said Vanessa. "Harte told me to use that analogy. She said, since you love science fiction, that you would understand it."

Diane laughed. "I do, and it's a good analogy."

"Oh, I'm glad. I know how you hate bad analogies. Poor Thomas Barclay still hasn't recovered from your scolding of him over the 'Where there's smoke there's fire' reference."

Diane smiled to herself. "Thomas called this evening. A man named Everett Walters is wanting him to dismiss me from the museum. Do you know an Everett Walters? He owns some businesses in Atlanta and Gainesville."

"Dismiss you? This person thinks he has a say in who is director of my museum? For what reason did he think you should be fired?"

Diane could almost see the look of indignation on Vanessa's face. She related the conversation she had with Thomas Barclay.

"I think Walters wants me away from that case in Gainesville. I won't get into that. It's a really long story," Diane said.

"I'll call Thomas," Vanessa said.

Nothing infuriated her more than people messing with the museum.

"Everett Walters? The name sounds familiar. Yes, the Everett Walters I know has a son, Gordon Walters, who, I believe, is a doctor. I've heard talk of him running for Congress. I don't know why he thinks that makes him qualified. Doctors can be so arrogant. Is that the same Everett Walters who called Thomas?"

"That's him," said Diane.

"I hope Thomas gave him an earful, but I doubt it. I'll let you know if we find anything in the attic," she said.

Diane looked at the clock sitting on the fireplace mantel. It was too late to call Detective Hanks. Besides, it would be better to wait and see if Vanessa found anything. She went back to Frank and Kingsley. They were still discussing possible scenarios for who killed Ellie Rose.

"Vanessa thinks she might find some more information about the previous owners of Marcella's house," said Diane as she sat down. "That's Detective Hanks' case—the one with the strange boot print connection to Stacy Dance's crime scene," she reminded Kingsley. "It was Vanessa's mother who remembered the name of the family who owned Marcella's house years ago. Vanessa said her mother just remembered that Laura's great-grandmother wrote letters to them while they were in Europe about the latest gossip involving the Gauthier family. Apparently they were . . ."

Diane stopped. Frank and Kingsley were staring at her, both with surprised looks.

"What?" she said.

"You don't speak French," said Kingsley.

"No. I'm not good with languages. I barely spoke enough Spanish and Portuguese to pass for the village idiot when I was in South America."

"The Anglicized name for Gauthier," said Frank, "is Walters."

Chapter 50

"Gauthier and Walters are the same name?" said Diane.

"Yes," said Kingsley. "That is, sort of. One is French and the other is English." He grinned.

"Can that be only a coincidence?" said Diane.

Frank didn't say anything for several moments. He studied the list of things Ellie Rose wrote in her diary about the two people she feared. But he didn't seem really to be looking at it.

"You know," he said at last, "this might explain the attack on you."

"How?" asked Diane.

"You are the only person investigating all three crime scenes—Marcella Payden, Mary Lassiter, and Stacy Dance. The perp might think that, if you were out of the way, then no one would make the connection between the Rosewood, Hall County, and Gainesville crimes."

It made chilling sense. But who was the *enginer* who threw a *petar* at her gate and blew it up? Did Everett Walters send the thug who shot his way into Frank's house? Did his son? His grandson? His daughter-in-law? Everett Walters called Thomas Barclay to have her fired. Did he think that would get her off the case? Did he perhaps take a less violent route, while some other member of the family took the more violent approach?

But that was not the first question she needed to answer. The first question was, were the Walters of Gainesville related to Maybelle Agnes Gauthier of Rosewood?

The ringing phone brought her out of her thoughts.

"Diane, this is Vanessa. I'm sorry for calling so late. I

just had a thought. It's silly really, but you know, it's one of those strange coincidences. Did you know that Gauthier in English is Walter? Isn't that interesting?" she said.

Of course, Vanessa spoke fluent French. It appeared that everyone except Diane was multilingual.

"Frank and Ross Kingsley just this minute pointed that out to me. We were marveling at the strangeness of the coincidence."

"I've found a trunk full of letters," said Vanessa. "There are probably more trunksful stuck in hidden places in the attic. Tomorrow we'll help Mother go through these. With a target date of 1957 or thereabouts, it'll be easier. Except that Mother will probably want to read them all."

"Thank you, Vanessa," she said. "You've been a really big help in this."

"Oh, good. I can get one of those patches, can't I?" she said.

"What patches?" said Diane.

"Oh, don't you know, dear? The museum staff designed a small patch to give to whoever does consulting with the dark side. They sew it on their caps or their jackets or whatever. Lawrence Michaels just got his for some kind of handwriting thing—he didn't reveal any details, so don't worry—and he's so proud."

"I was unaware of the patch," said Diane. She rubbed her forehead and pinched the bridge of her nose. The museum staff were always up to something, it seemed.

"They found letters," Diane told Frank and Kingsley when she hung up. "But I think it's going to be a while before they find the ones they are looking for. From what Vanessa says, Lillian Chapman, Vanessa's mother, never threw any of her letters away, and she's nearly a hundred."

"You know, that might be just what we need," said Kingsley. He gathered up the papers and put them in his folder.

"A lot of it will be gossip," said Diane.

"Maybe. But it may also contain leads." He put the file under his arm and rose. "I thank you for dinner and the illumination."

After he left, Diane pushed crime and murder out of her mind and practiced the piano. Frank had found her an intermediate-level version of Pachelbel's Canon in D that she was learning how to play. It was a nice way to end the day before going to bed. Frank always played the piano before he went to bed. He chose Diane's favorite Chopin nocturne.

Diane lay awake thinking about the Walters family. It would be more than a coincidence if they were related to the artist who disappeared more than fifty years ago. She kept going over scenarios for all that had happened. What if someone in the Walters' household killed Ellie Rose? Who would it be? Did Wendy know who it was? There was a good possibility that she would. Whom would she protect? Her son? Certainly. Her husband? Probably, but maybe not. Then again, many women would protect the father of their children in order to keep the stigma away from them. Her father-in-law? Less likely, but most people hate scandal. The son was the most logical. Mothers are driven to protect their children.

Diane had another thought. Kathy Nicholson, the neighbor across the street from the Walters, had a son the same age as Wendy's son. Did he know what happened? Was he involved? He did move far away from Georgia—as far as he could get without going into the ocean. He rarely came home. Curious.

"I know you have lots of questions." Frank's husky voice came out of the dark. "But you need to get some sleep."

Diane smiled to herself. "Was I thinking too loud?"

Frank gave a deep-throated chuckle. "I just know you." He leaned over and kissed her.

"What you need to be thinking about is how to get a judge to issue a search warrant for their cars and houses," he said. "Word games aren't going to convince any judge, and most aren't impressed with coincidences either. I don't know all the evidence you've collected, but I don't think any of it actually connects directly to anyone in the Walters family."

"It doesn't, and you're right. But I have some ideas," Diane said. She moved over to the crook of Frank's arm, snuggled against him, and went to sleep.

Diane's bodyguards followed her to work and took up their positions in the lobby of the crime lab. It was probably one of their easier assignments, thought Diane. At least it would be until something happened.

The crime lab was empty when she arrived. She went straight to her lab and began working on the remaining bones David had excavated from the well. She measured and examined each one, adding the new information to what she already had. She stood back and looked at the young male skeleton with its missing bones.

It would have been necessary to remove all flesh, blood, marrow, and sinew from the bones before they could be crushed to make the temper. Almost certainly, they were skinned and boiled. Not a pleasant task. Something you wouldn't want to do in your kitchen. In a shed, perhaps.

Diane cast her mind back to Marcella's place. There were two outbuildings—three, if the carport was counted. One of them, Marcella identified as a potter's shed. The other one, her daughter, Paloma, told Diane, was filled with junk from previous owners and should be torn down. Did it have a vent in its roof? A chimney? She didn't remember.

She did have a clear image of the yard filled with various items of decor. She wondered which owner had put them there. Did they have meaning? Were there any clues to be had from the concrete statuary?

But not everything was concrete. Diane remembered seeing a large cast-iron pot planted with flowers. It would have been perfect for boiling body parts. She would ask Marcella where she found it. Probably not in the yard, if it was old. She didn't think cast iron would last long out in the weather. Or would it? Perhaps it was in one of the sheds.

Diane repacked the bones, washed her hands, and put the paperwork on her desk. She called down to museum security to see if everything was calm. It was. No incidents whatsoever. That was a relief. Her team should be in the crime lab by now. She went to speak with them.

Neva, Izzy, and David were there working when she entered. Diane called them over to the round table and asked them for updates on the crime scenes they were working on.

"We almost don't have time for any more crime," said David. "We need to open a branch office. Not that I'm complaining. It's good for business. Never a dull moment." He gave a rundown on the various evidence they had in process, then turned to Marcella Payden.

"We've started the backyard research project again at Marcella's. Scott's been a big help. He's a little too careful where he steps—jumpy about the prospect of more abandoned wells—so he's slow, but I can't say I blame him. And the paramedics haven't made a run out to the house in several days. So things are good."

Diane smiled. "David, you speak French. Why didn't you tell me that Gauthier is the French word for Walters?"

David looked at her for a moment. "Why would I?" he asked.

"Oh," she said.

She realized they knew next to nothing about the Carruthers, Walters, and Nicholson families. They knew only about Stacy Dance and her crime scene. She gave them a brief description that turned to a long description when they started asking questions.

"Talk about your weird coincidence," said Izzy. "Jeez, this case is full of them. You think it's the same family—Gauthier and Walters?"

"I don't know," said Diane.

"You know," said Neva, "sometimes people change their names if they don't want to be associated with an infamous relative. Imagine how Jeffrey Dahmer's extended family must feel."

"Sometimes they do it because the old name is just too hard to pronounce," said David. "Or they don't want to sound foreign."

"It's probably just a weird coincidence," said Diane, "but I'd like to investigate the possibility."

"What you're thinking is that the Walters family doesn't want the connection made between them and their Mad Potter relative," said David. "Assuming the Mad Potter was a Gauthier, and the Walters are really the Gauthiers."

"I think it may be a possibility," said Diane. "The Walters are a prominent family. Gordon Walters, the oncologist in Gainesville, is testing the waters for a run for Congress. He, or his father, Everett Walters, might want to keep the skeletons in the closet."

"Who wouldn't want to keep these skeletons hidden?" said Neva. She shivered and pushed her hair back behind her ears. "I gave the facial reconstruction drawings to

Hanks. He's going to show them around some of the area retirement homes. He doesn't hold out much hope that anyone will remember them after so long, but there's always a chance."

"You did a good job on the drawings. I hope we get some hits," said Diane.

"You know," said Izzy, "I think we need to have our own Web site where we can post Neva's reconstructions. A lot of people have computers these days. Who knows? We might get some hits there."

Izzy wore jeans and a T-shirt like the rest of her team usually wore. He started out with slacks and button-up shirts. Diane was glad to see that he had adapted well to her team. Not that he should dress like them, but she wanted him to feel a part of the team, to identify with them. Not everyone could.

"Good idea," said Diane. "Would you like to do it?"

Izzy raised a hand as if shoving the idea away from himself. "I'm just learning about computers. But good ol' David here . . ."

"I think it's a good idea too," said David. "It wouldn't be hard. The hard part is to make it so people can find it. Your average person doesn't go surfing for missing persons. But we can give it a try."

"Okay, in your spare time, then, go ahead," said Diane. "Neva, I want you to remember everything you can about the black Escalade you saw. Did it have any stickers on it? Did it have a front plate that identified the dealership? Anything?"

"I've gone over it in my head," said Neva. "I believe it had a UGA parking sticker on the front window, but I'm not sure. It didn't have a dealer plate, or any front plate."

"Find out if anyone among the Gainesville families we discussed has a car like that," said Diane.

"Will do," said Neva. "I can probably get a list of Cadillac Escalades registered on the UGA campus. You want me to do a little investigating and see if the Tyler guy might be a hiker?"

"Yes," said Diane. "But would he wear his good hiking boots except when he was hiking? Jin doesn't."

Neva grinned broadly. "We start judging what perps

might do based on Jin's behavior and no telling what we might come up with," she said, and they all laughed. "If they're really comfortable, and I'm guessing they would be, then he might like them in a high-risk situation."

Diane nodded and turned to David. "Have you been able to identify any of the fingerprints you found on the objects in the well?"

"I haven't run them yet," he said. "That's on my schedule for this morning."

"Be sure to include the database of people who've been bonded," said Diane.

David put a hand over his heart. "Have you ever known me not to be thorough?" he said.

"Never," said Diane. "I'm just looking for reasons for a judge to grant a warrant."

"I hear you," said David. "We will scour the evidence."

Diane's cell vibrated in her suit pocket. She pulled it out and looked at the display. Detective Hanks.

"Hi," said Diane. "What's up?"

"You know I told you I was sending someone to retirement homes looking for people who remembered Maybelle Gauthier?"

"Don't tell me you found someone who knew her. That's great," said Diane.

"Nope," said Hanks. "We found *her*."

Chapter 51

Diane sat frozen for a moment. Speechless.

"I thought that would surprise you," said Hanks.

"Are you saying you've found Maybelle Agnes Gauthier? She's alive?" said Diane.

Diane wondered whether her face looked like David's, Izzy's, and Neva's did—wide-eyed, drop jawed. She didn't know why she was so stunned. Vanessa's mother was alive and she was about the same age as Gauthier.

"I'm going out to interview her late this afternoon," said Hanks. "I thought you would like to come along."

"Yes," said Diane, "definitely."

"She's alive?" David said when Diane hung up. "The woman who wrote on the desk drawer? Actually, do we really know that was her? What do we know about her? Do we really know she even lived in the house?"

"We are fairly sure she was an artist who did oil paintings," said Neva. "Vanessa's mother remembered her—right? We don't know if she was into ceramics or if she was a murderer. David's right, we really don't know much about her. We just suspect a lot. Do you think she's as clear-headed as Vanessa's mother?"

"No idea," said Diane.

"I really doubt it," said Izzy. "I've been thinking about that writing on the desk. You know, it's kind of crazy."

"You think?" said Neva.

"Okay, smarty, hear me out," said Izzy. "What if her family knew she was crazy and was going to come take her to the funny farm, and she got wind of it? Maybe she left the message so that, I don't know, her imaginary friends would find it and save her. I mean, who else did she expect would find it? I'm betting she's loony tunes."

"She might have been taking drugs when she wrote that," said David. "She was an artsy type. Maybe a member of the beat generation. Were they only writers, or could other artists claim membership?"

"Beat generation?" said Neva.

David shook his head. "I forget how many babies we have here. This was before you were born. Google it."

"David," said Diane, "it was before you were born."

"Yeah, maybe, but I have an old soul," he said.

A call came in about a crime scene and Diane sent Neva and Izzy out on the call. It was the kind of scene Diane hated—someone killed in a bar. It meant dealing with people who were intoxicated, belligerent, and evasive.

"Take backup," said Diane. "Call and ask that my bodyguards be assigned to you. I'm going out later with Hanks to the retirement home."

"Sure," said Neva. "Tell us all about it when you get back."

Neva and Izzy retrieved their crime scene kits from the locker and headed out. Diane asked David to look for a match for the fingerprints on the items retrieved for the well and to call UGA to get a list of Escalades with parking permits.

"I want to know as soon as you can find out. Neva may be busy for a while," said Diane.

She went back to her office to finish up her paperwork. Before she began, she called Vanessa.

"Diane, we must be psychic," said Vanessa. "I was about to call you to report our progress. We found a stack of letters from the dates you and I were talking about. We are just sitting down to begin reading them."

"That's good news, Vanessa. I called with some interesting news of my own. Detective Hanks found Maybelle Gauthier in a retirement home. We are going to see her late this afternoon."

There was a pause. "Did he, now? How clever of Detective Hanks. She's alive. I've been thinking that she was probably buried near that house. But she's alive—and retired? You say she is in a retirement home? I wonder what she retired from?" said Vanessa.

Diane could hear her speaking with her mother and she heard Lillian's clear voice say she wanted to go see her.

"I guess you heard that," said Vanessa.

"Yes, I did," said Diane.

She was about to say that it wouldn't be a good idea today; then she thought that perhaps it might. Lillian Chapman was a contemporary of Maybelle. There was a chance Lillian could get through to her whereas they might not. Diane had no idea what condition Maybelle Gauthier was in. Like Lillian, she was getting close to a hundred.

"Let me make a call," said Diane.

At four o'clock they were in Vanessa's limousine—Diane, Vanessa, Lillian, Detective Hanks, and Mrs. Hartefeld, who, Vanessa said, "insisted on coming to look after Mother." Diane knew better. Like the rest of them, Mrs. Hartefeld was overcome with curiosity.

She and Hanks sat on one seat, facing to the rear, Vanessa and the others facing forward. It reminded Diane of a stagecoach, only the ride was smoother. Vanessa served them orange juice from a small refrigerator. Diane had expected Hanks to say no when she called, but he too thought they might get more information if Lillian were there. Hanks seemed surprised that Lillian Chapman wasn't frail. Diane thought he expected her to be in a wheelchair. She was slim, had strength in her arms and legs, and had a sharp mind and a clear voice. She did not look like a woman in her mid-nineties.

Vanessa and her mother wore pantsuits. Vanessa's was a navy raw silk suit with a blue shirt. Her mother wore a turquoise linen suit with a peach blouse. Both had platinum white hair. Vanessa's was pulled back in a twist. Her mother's was short with a slight wave that reminded Diane of the twenties, but with a little more lift. Harte had on a black skirt and a pink sweater set with pearls. They looked like very unlikely sleuths.

Lillian was telling Diane and Hanks about one of the letters. Diane was particularly thrilled to hear what they had discovered among one stack of letters tied with a pink ribbon. It contained a piece of information she needed to go along with other evidence to present to a judge for a warrant.

"I knew Ernestina Hillard from childhood," said Lillian. "Poor soul died young. She wasn't yet eighty."

Hanks suppressed a smile.

"She wrote me while we were in Europe. My husband, Vanessa's father, was in the diplomatic corps and we traveled a lot in those days. Vanessa was schooled in Switzerland. I don't know whether that was a good idea or not."

Vanessa rolled her eyes. "*Mother*," she said.

"Be that as it may, there we were, and the only news we got from home was bits in foreign newspapers and letters from friends. Dear Ernestina was the most reliable. She wrote me about the scandals, in particular. I'm ashamed to say, I rather enjoyed them."

"Was there a scandal concerning the Gauthiers?" asked Hanks.

Diane thought Detective Hanks would be impatient to get to the point, but he seemed to be somewhat in awe. She got the sense that he enjoyed meeting Vanessa and riding in her limousine.

They passed through an area of road construction where the pavement was uneven and their orange juice almost sloshed out.

"Oh dear," said Lillian. "I didn't get anything on me, did I?" She looked down at her blouse. "You know, the older you get, the less you can afford to have food stains on your clothes."

Hanks laughed.

"You're fine, Mrs. Chapman," said Harte.

"Diane told you about the letters, didn't she?" asked Lillian.

"Yes," said Hanks. "People don't write letters much anymore, do they?"

"No, they don't, and that's a shame. But I have to tell you, I rather enjoy my e-mail," she said.

Hanks raised his eyebrows. He wasn't expecting that.

"Vanessa and Harte found so many of my old letters. Apparently, I had just dumped bundles of them in a trunk. But the one thing they found was just a wonderful surprise," she said.

"What was that?" asked Hanks. He knew, because Diane told him when they picked him up at the station. It was kind of him to let Lillian tell it.

"An unopened letter from 1957. I can't imagine a greater treat. Judging from the date on it, it must have arrived about the time we were packing to come home from Europe. We flew home, of course, but our trunks and the furniture were sent by ship. I guess I just stuck the letter in one of the steamer trunks with my other letters. I always kept my letters together with a pretty ribbon tied around them so they wouldn't get lost. In all the rush and confusion of packing and unpacking, I must have forgotten it was there. Travel in those days was quite a bit more involved than it is today, you know, particularly with a retinue as large as ours, and if you had an unmarried teenage girl under your arm. You would not believe those European men, their audacity." Lillian waved her hand as if to dismiss the thought. "But in any event, that which was lost is found again. And what a surprise when we found it. Vanessa, Harte, and I had a wonderful time reading it."

She took it out of her purse and handed the translucent blue pages to Hanks. He and Diane had to strain to read the spidery handwriting.

Dear Lillian,

Do you remember the Gauthier-Farragut divorce? Certainly you do, beautiful Edith Farragut in that big Parisian hat coming out of the courthouse dressed just like she did when she was a young girl. Here in North Georgia! She was a sight. Remember us laughing. We were awful.

Well, I have more news. You remember my telling you that three years ago her daughter, Maybelle Gauthier, just dropped off the face of the earth? Neither Edith nor Jonathan would talk about her. You wouldn't believe the rumors that were flying. Her father married her off to a prince. No one believed that one. For having such a beautiful mother, Maybelle was quite a gawky girl. The Barbers down the street said she committed suicide. She was over forty and never married, Mr. Barber said, so what else could she do? He always was a harsh judge of character. Some of the kinder folk said she went to Paris to study art. I think I believed that. She was such a wonderful artist. You remember the portraits she did—and the landscape your mother bought that time. It was beautiful. But I digress.

Here's the juicy bit of news I promised. Maybelle's father, Jonathan, took Everett (you remember Everett—Jonathan Gauthier's son by that new young wife he married seventeen years ago. Everett is about Vanessa's age, I think, maybe a bit younger) and his wife, and moved to Atlanta—and changed their name to Walters! Can you believe that? He changed his name! He didn't tell anyone. Virgil found out quite by accident when he was getting some legal work done. (They share the same lawyer. Virgil had no idea.) We still don't know what happened to Maybelle. Her mother lives in Marietta. As far as I know, she is still keeping with her maiden name, Farragut. Sarah tried to ask her one time about Maybelle, but Edith ignored her. I wonder what happened to that girl. And why do you think Jonathan changed his name? Strange, isn't it?

I'll be happy to see you safe at home. I just can't imagine living in strange countries all these years. Has Vanessa forgotten her native tongue? You're lucky she didn't marry a foreigner while you were there. I'll bet you'll be glad to get back to civilization.

Safe journey,
Ernestina

They arrived at the retirement home. The chauffeur pulled into a parking place near the door and stopped.

Chapter 52

"Oh my. This is a dreary place," said Lillian Chapman as she stepped out of the car and put a hand on Detective Hanks' arm.

"I would hate to live here," muttered Vanessa. "It looks so sad."

Diane retrieved a box and a file folder from the car, then turned and looked at the building. It was a one-story sprawling structure of concrete blocks painted a pale yellow. The grass in the surrounding yard had turned brown and dry with the coming of fall. The few scraggly trees had already lost their leaves.

"I appreciate your allowing us to come, Detective," said Lillian. "This is going to be interesting."

"I'm hoping she will respond to someone who once knew her," he said.

They entered the building and went into an office just to the right of the front door. A young woman with multicolored hair got up from her desk and came to the counter. She wore jeans and a sweatshirt that said I'LL TRY TO BE NICER IF YOU TRY TO BE SMARTER.

"Can I help you?" she asked with a bright smile. She quickly scanned the five of them and gathered up several forms. "You'll have to fill these out," she said before Hanks could give her an answer. The woman smiled at Lillian. "This is a real nice place."

"I'm sure," said Lillian. "Very nice hair extensions you have, my dear. I particularly like the purple and green together."

The young woman patted her hair. "Oh, thanks."

Hanks showed her his badge. Diane noticed he had taken off his arm sling and left it in the car. His movements were a little stiff, but he wasn't wincing in pain.

"We have an appointment to see Miss Gauthier," he said.

"The police to see Miss Agnes? Well, I hope she hasn't done anything wrong. It wasn't a bank job or anything, was it?" The young woman giggled at her joke.

"Please send them in here, Miss Jolley."

Jolley, thought Diane. *Her name is Jolley*. They went into the office of Ms. Christina Wanamaker, according to the name on the door.

"Please, sit down," she said. She was a woman in her early forties. She had dyed black hair pulled back in a severe French twist. Thick eyebrows and turned-down lips. She looked around for a moment, seeing that there were more people than chairs.

"Miss Jolley," she called, "could you bring two more chairs?"

The screeching sound of chairs being pulled across the tile floor split the air. Harte was nearest the door. She ran out to help carry them in. They sat down and Hanks made introductions as Ms. Wanamaker pulled a file out of her drawer and opened it on her desk.

"I'm hoping you know of family for Miss Gauthier," said Ms. Wanamaker. "We, of course, have a mandate to take care of the indigent, but the economy being what it is, we would welcome it if relatives could help with the expense of her care."

"We hope this leads to her relatives," said Hanks. "We have reason to believe it will."

"Do you have someone in mind?" she asked.

"We have some definite leads we are following," said Hanks.

Ms. Wanamaker's face brightened. "Are they in a position to help, do you think?"

"It's possible," said Hanks.

Diane could see he was walking a fine line between trying to keep to the truth and trying to keep Ms. Wanamaker cooperative. She referred to Maybelle as indigent. If Everett Walters was indeed her brother, he certainly could and should have been helping all these years.

"Can you tell us something about her?" asked Hanks.

"I don't know a lot," said Ms. Wanamaker. "As best I can determine, she's been in the system for more than fifty years. Over that long period of time there have been many changes in care, and most of her original records were lost. What I do have has been pieced together and is very sketchy. Miss Gauthier was first institutionalized in a clinic in the early or mid-fifties. I don't have an exact date. That facility was called the Riverside Clinic, in Rosewood. I believe there is now a museum where the clinic used to be.

Diane and Vanessa couldn't have been more startled if someone had thrown ice water on them.

"Is that your museum?" asked Hanks.

"Yes," said Diane. "What is currently the RiverTrail Museum building was the location of a clinic in the forties and fifties."

So, Maybelle Agnes Gauthier had been a resident of the psychiatric clinic that used to be in the building. When renovations of the building were under way in preparation for the opening of the museum, boxes of old records were discovered in the basement and subbasement. Diane wondered whether Gauthier's name was listed somewhere among them. She would ask her archivist to find out.

"Oh," said Ms. Wanamaker, "you know it, then."

Diane nodded. "Yes, we do."

"It closed down sometime in the fifties, as I understand," the retirement home director said.

"In 1955," said Diane.

"Miss Gauthier was moved to a retirement home in Clarksville after that. It burned, and that's where a lot of the files were lost. After the fire, she was in the hospital for a time, due to burns on her arm. She was not severely injured, but she was hurt badly enough that she needed care for a time. After that, she was in three other nursing and retirement homes before she came here. As I said, she has been in the system a long time."

"When she was first institutionalized, she would have been in her early forties," said Diane. "Do you know what she was diagnosed with?"

"We don't have the original diagnosis, but over the years she has been diagnosed with a list of things," said Ms. Wanamaker, picking up a piece of paper. "Everything from schizophrenia, delusional disorder, dissociative identity disorder, paranoid personality disorder, bipolar disorder, to Ganser syndrome. Personally, I don't think anyone knew. I don't know what symptoms she had when she was first institutionalized. Seriously, if she kept being shuffled from nursing homes to retirement homes, it couldn't have been that severe. She has always been coherent while she has been here. In fact, she is an artist. Did you know that?"

"Yes," said Hanks. "Painter, right?"

"She's done some wall murals for us, even at her age. They are quite good. She's also a very good potter." Ms. Wanamaker pointed to a shelf behind them. "She did that."

They all turned and looked at a ceramic pitcher formed in the shape of a beautiful girl with long curling hair. One lock of hair looped and curled, making the handle for the pitcher. The eyes were empty.

"Would you like to see her now?" she asked.

"Yes," said Hanks, "that would be good."

Chapter 53

The retirement home smelled like a prison to Diane. She didn't like it. She walked beside Hanks as Christina Wanamaker led them down a long hallway. Several wheelchairs were in the hall with elderly men and women asleep in them. No one was attending to them. Diane noticed a few visitors, but most of the residents were alone.

The walls of the facility were painted the same pale yellow as the outside of the building. The floors were a green tile. Bad elevator music was piped in from somewhere. The place was clean, but Lillian was right; it was dreary. It made Diane realize that the hardest thing in the world to be is old, poor, and alone. Time to find her inner objectivity. It wouldn't do to break down and cry here in the hallway.

Ms. Wanamaker led them to a large sunroom. One wall was painted with tropical plants, flowers, and birds. It was the cheeriest thing Diane had seen in the place. Gauthier's work, thought Diane, was still very good. At the far end of the room a woman, dark against the waning light, sat near a large picture window.

"Miss Gauthier," said the retirement home director, "you have visitors."

"Visitors," came a rough, halting voice. "I? Visitors? I don't believe I've ever had visitors before."

They approached the woman, their shoes clicking and echoing on the tile floor. Diane set her box and folder down on a nearby table and grabbed a couple of chairs. Harte helped her. They placed them near the woman. The director adjusted the window blinds to reduce the sunlight coming through. Now there was just the ambient light from the fixtures in the room, a harsher light. Diane, Vanessa, Lillian, and Hanks sat down in a semicircle in front of the woman. Harte sat back a little behind Lillian.

Maybelle Agnes Gauthier was a lanky woman. Even at her advanced age she did not look shrunken, but large boned and tall. Her hair, fine white wisps over the crown of her head, was thin and showing a pinkish scalp. Her face was crisscrossed with lines. Her lips had all but disappeared, they were so thin and lined. She wore a pink housedress, a gray bulky sweater, leggings, and house slippers. But most noticeable about her were her eyes. Diane had never seen eyes their color. They were a dark bluish color with flecks of yellow and light blue, almost like copper ore. The eyes followed each one of them as they arranged their chairs. They had a sheen to them as they moved, as if she had had cataract surgery.

"Maybelle," said Lillian, "it's been a very long time. The last time I saw you was at one of Rosewood's cotillions and we were young women dressed in white gowns and gloves."

"Cotillion. I haven't heard that word in a long time. Who are you? I don't recognize you."

"I'm Lillian Chapman. I used to be Lillian Egan."

"Lillian Egan? I don't remember. You say we knew each other? I didn't know many people."

"We did not know each other well," said Lillian, "but our paths crossed on occasion. My father owned the railroad that ran through Rosewood."

"I remember the railroad. I think my father probably hated your father." She gave a throaty chuckle. "He hated a lot of people."

"We would like to know about your life," said Detective Hanks.

"My life? You would like to know about my life? Why?" she said.

"We think it would be interesting," he said.

"Do you?" she said. "All of you people have come here thinking my life is interesting? Why is that?"

"You are a famous artist, for starters," said Hanks.

Gauthier was far more clearheaded than Diane thought

she would be. It frankly surprised her. She knew Lillian had a keen mind, but she came from a long line of people who aged slowly.

"And we have been digging in your backyard," said Hanks slowly.

She looked startled, almost confused. Then she said, "Young man, I don't have a backyard."

"You did a long time ago," he said. "Didn't you?"

"A long time ago, yes. That was so very long ago. Before . . . before . . ."

She let the sentence fade away without finishing it. She seemed to have withdrawn into herself.

"May we record our conversation?" said Hanks.

Silence.

He turned on the recorder anyway.

"You know, Maybelle, at our age," said Lillian, "there isn't much that can hurt us anymore. Sometimes it's good to tell people about our lives before everything is gone. I remember your mother and her large hats."

Maybelle smiled. "Those hats. As a little girl, I used to traipse around the house in those hats." She frowned. "Until Father came home. He was opposed to traipsing. My mother is dead. So is my father."

"We are very old," said Lillian.

"Yes. Very old," she repeated. "Why have you come?" she asked again.

"You asked us to," said Diane. "You said if you ever disappeared, come find you. You wrote it on the bottom of a desk drawer. It took a long time, but we are here."

She didn't say anything for a long time, just stared at Diane.

"I did, didn't I? I had forgotten. It was so long ago."

"Why did you leave your note on the bottom of a drawer?" asked Hanks.

"I didn't want my father to find it. He wouldn't know to look there. I thought Mother would."

"How did you come to be here?" asked Diane. "Why aren't you living in Pigeon Ridge? You did live there, didn't you?"

"Yes. My mother gave the house in Pigeon Ridge to me.

It was hers to give. I came to be here because my father put me away. Mother came to see me, but she couldn't rescue me like I thought she would. I have a brother somewhere. I don't think he knows where I am. He was a good brother. He must be dead too. Maybe I shouldn't tell you my story after all." She turned her head away, dismissing them.

"We know your brother," said Diane.

Gauthier jerked her head back around and looked at Diane.

"Your younger brother, Everett. Isn't that his name?" said Diane.

"You know him?" she said. "Does he know where I am?"

"We found you," said Diane. "He could have too. You would be proud of him. He has several businesses. He married and has a son. He has a grandson. His son is a doctor and is going to run for Congress. His grandson is a law student at the University of Georgia. He's going to be a lawyer."

Diane stopped and let it sink in. It didn't take long. She saw the change come over her eyes. Gauthier had been indigent, living in dingy retirement homes for almost sixty years, and her brother had prospered. The whole family had prospered.

"Is that the truth?" Gauthier said.

Diane had found a photo on the Internet for the occasion. It was an award banquet for Everett's son, Gordon Walters. The whole family was there, sitting around the table. Thank God for the Internet. She went over to Gauthier and handed her the photo.

"This is your brother here. Beside him is your nephew, Gordon Walters, his wife, Wendy, and your grandnephew, Tyler Walters," said Diane.

"Walters?" said Maybelle Gauthier. "Why is his name Walters?"

"Your father left Rosewood and changed his name," Diane said.

"Everett looks like Father," she said. "He looks like Father."

"Does he?" said Diane.

"He left me here and never looked for me." She looked up at Diane and her eyes were hard, like jet coal. "You came here for my story. Okay, I'll tell it. I'll tell you my story, all of it. There's not much they can do to me now."

Chapter 54

"Father was a hard man with no use for art, or daughters. But Mother was rich and she was strong willed. She protected me. I didn't have any pets growing up. I knew better. Father couldn't be trusted. He was mean and vindictive." Maybelle Gauthier looked at Lillian. "If your father was alive, he would tell you. My father ruined many men with lies. Lies were sharper than swords."

"I seem to remember Papa saying something about Jonathan Gauthier," said Lillian.

"Mother divorced him and lived on her own. She owned property in Pigeon Ridge and told me I could live there. Father tried to marry me off to one of his friends. I wouldn't have it. I was in love with someone else, an artist."

She shook her head and her eyes suddenly softened. She was quiet for a moment. When she spoke again, Diane almost jumped, her voice was so filled with venom.

"Father ruined him, ruined his family, and told me it was my fault. I heard he died not long after. I think he killed himself. He was sensitive. Not like me. I was as strong as my mother. Like her, I lived by myself. I lived on the money from my trust fund and my portraits."

The light filtering through the windows was fading and a kind of darkness settled over the room, even with the overhead lights.

"I didn't make any more friends. It was dangerous, because of Father. And after a while I grew too old to marry off. Father found himself a new wife, and they had a son. That was Everett. After that, Father left me alone. He had what he wanted. Then I got two ideas." Gauthier's eyes glittered with excitement at the memory.

"I had grown tired with painting and I wasn't selling as much as I used to. I always thought Father had something to do with that. It was like him. I still had Mother and my trust fund. I became interested in pottery. I'd see it in art shows in Atlanta and liked the idea of the clay flowing though my fingers. And I quite liked the symbolism of vessels. I didn't like the shiny stuff the other artists produced. I wanted something more earthy. I discovered how the Indians made pottery, and I liked that. There was a creek not far from my house that had an ample supply of clay. But I wanted to do something different."

She paused for a moment and licked her thin lips.

"And I wanted to ruin my father's favorite thing—his son. Everett was old enough to go about by himself. Children did in those days, especially boys. I invited him to come visit me. I showed him my art. I got to know him. He was a lot like Father—mean. But he seemed to like me well enough. I think because I was strong. Not many people stood up against Jonathan Gauthier.

"I had an idea for making my pottery come alive, in a manner of speaking. Making each piece have meaning greater than a mere pot. Make it a true vessel. I got Everett to bring me young people his age to model for live masks. I tempered my pottery with grit then and sold the pieces in Atlanta. Mine were unique and they sold well."

Diane hadn't seen Harte leave and didn't know she was gone until she came back with bottled water for everyone. Apparently she'd noticed Maybelle was getting hoarse.

Maybelle took a long drink before she continued. Diane was afraid she might change her mind and stop. Hanks thought the same thing, she guessed, for he frowned when he was handed his drink. But she didn't stop. She merely quenched her thirst.

"I took Everett to movies in Atlanta—violent movies. I could see by the look in his eyes he liked them. I'd drop little hints about Father—about people who crossed him, how some disappeared. Then I'd say it wasn't true. It wasn't, but I knew that denying it would make him believe it. He was so much like Father. I told him so, and he liked the idea. He wanted to be like Father.

"I'd been toying with the idea for a long time of trying out a new temper that would add more meaning to my work. I needed Everett to do it. I told him about bone temper, how wonderful it was, and how we needed bones to do it. Not just any bones, but human bones, the way the Indians did it, I told him. I gradually raised the idea in his mind of killing one of the people he brought home. Someone no one would miss. I could see the idea excited him. I coaxed him, we talked about it, and I asked him his ideas, until, after a while, he thought it was all his idea. But I told him how to do it, to use the small hatchet and do it quick and efficient. He did and he was good at it. The first one was a tramp."

Out of the corner of her eye, Diane could see that Harte was shivering. She pulled her sweater tighter around her and nervously fingered her pearls. Vanessa and Lillian were quiet and still, their faces blank masks.

"I sold a great many pottery vessels, each one with its own unique face—young, old, beautiful, harsh. Did you see the pitcher in Miss Wanamaker's office? That one wasn't special and is made with ordinary clay, but you can get the idea of what the others must have been like. Isn't it beautiful? All the pottery vessels I made after that had a special look about them. People in Atlanta told me they looked as if they could come alive. They were right. But they didn't know it."

She took another long drink and stared off into the distance. Diane thought they might be losing her. She got up and opened the box. In it lay the partial mask that Marcella had put together.

"We have one of your pieces," said Diane, handing it to her.

"Oh, it's the most beautiful one of all. And Father crushed it. You know, I like it like this. I like the lines formed where the pieces are fitted together. I hadn't thought of breaking it and putting it back together. That adds another symbolic dimension."

"Please go on," said Diane. "We want to hear about your art."

Maybelle Gauthier didn't take her eyes off the mask in the box as she spoke.

"I bought a cauldron and put it in the shed, and I boiled the bones down after Everett cut up the pieces that I needed. When the bones were perfectly white, I dried them and crushed them. They made the perfect temper for my clay. I used the face of each person as the form to sculpt the piece. When I finished and it was fired, it was the most beautiful work of art you have ever seen. There was nothing like it in the galleries. It had the rough look of Indian pottery but the delicate sculpting of modern work. Each piece had a spirit in it. People saw it, even if they couldn't put a name to it. I made a fountain for a man in Atlanta who loved the idea of water coming out of the eyes.

"Then Father found out. I don't know how. I suspect that he came to visit when I wasn't there and saw something he shouldn't. Everett told me they were coming after me. That's when I wrote the note. I was afraid. Everett helped me throw everything we could down the well. I hid all my work I had there. But when Father came, he found my pottery and crushed the beautiful pieces in front of my eyes and threw them in the fire pit. I hated him for that. He didn't find the portraits I did of them. I hid them in the wall, along with a portrait of my mother."

"What about the young victims?" said Lillian. "Didn't you feel bad for them?"

Diane thought Lillian probably couldn't hold it in any longer.

"Oh, they were far better off. The people Everett brought home had terrible lives. At least they could now live forever in art," she said. "And their suffering was over."

"So your father took you to a clinic," prompted Diane.

"Yes. What was the name? Something about a river. It was a huge Gothic building. Mother would come to visit me and she would cry. She told me if I got out, Father would see that I went to jail. This way, no one would ever know what I did, and one day I'd get out and could start over. Everett begged me not to tell on him and I didn't. I didn't even tell Mother about his part in it.

"The clinic was a terrible place. At night you could hear people screaming. I never knew what was happening to them. I was smart enough to stay quiet and be easy to get along with. That way they wouldn't increase my medication or do whatever it was they were doing to the other poor patients."

Diane shivered. She and Vanessa exchanged horrified glances. Diane didn't know very much about the clinic that once had been housed in the museum building. The docents made up ghost stories about the old clinic, but she never considered that strange and terrifying things really may have gone on there.

"They closed the place down in just a year," continued Gauthier. "Good riddance. I was taken to another place. I forget the name. I was there for, I don't know, but it seemed like several years. Mother would come see me, but then she died. She was my last hope. The doctors had to sedate me when I heard. I was still smart enough to be very good and they let me work in the office sometimes. It was there that I saw the surgery orders that my father had signed. He told them to give me a lobotomy. Do you know what that is?"

Diane nodded. "Yes," she said.

"They wanted to cut part of my brain out. I had been around patients who had lobotomies. I would lose everything. I would lose my art. My father would win. I had to do something. He came to visit one evening before they were to do the surgery. I'd planned it all. It was so easy, much easier than making my beautiful pottery. I got some chemicals from the janitor's closet ahead of time and stole an extra key they kept in the desk drawer of the receptionist's office. As I said, I had been on good behavior and they gave me pretty much free run of the place. It was as if I were invisible. My father and the doctor were in the doctor's office with the door shut. Before they knew anything was going on, I set fire to the outside office and locked the door. I left the key in the lock so the doctor couldn't unlock it from the inside. The office was away from the dormitories in a separate building. There was no one to know or to hear. I stayed there looking at my father and the doctor as they tried to escape. They couldn't get out the windows because they were barred. There was a glass window in the door, but it was double paned and had wire in between. And I watched them. I watched my father screaming at me. And I did this."

She pointed her middle and index fingers at her eyes, then pointed them at Diane. She did it over and over in a sharp, jerking motion, her brows knitted together, her eyes dark.

"He did that to me as a child when he wanted me to pay attention to him, to look him in the eyes, to let me know he saw me. I called it his devil look, and I did that to him. That was his last vision—me giving him the devil look. And I'm not sorry I did that to him."

Chapter 55

It was quiet in the room. The light from the windows was almost gone and only the harsh halogen light from the overhead fixtures was left. Diane didn't know what she thought she was going to hear from Maybelle Agnes Gauthier, but she was oddly stunned and affirmed by what she heard.

She picked up the folder again and took out the likenesses that Neva had created of the two skeletons from the well and handed them to Gauthier.

"Who are they?" Diane asked.

She ran her wrinkled hands over the drawings. "Lovely," she whispered. "Who did these?" She looked up at Diane.

"A woman who works for me," Diane said.

"I didn't name them. A name would have only diminished what I was trying to say," she said.

Diane took a breath. "What were their names before you met them?"

"Dust to dust," Gauthier whispered. "I was taking them back from whence they came. I crushed them to dust and re-created them into something more beautiful. Something their fathers couldn't hurt. See"—she looked at the mask still in the box in her lap—"even though my father crushed her, she's still beautiful."

"Who were they?" said Hanks. "We need to know who they were."

"It was a long time ago. I don't remember."

"Of course you do," said Lillian, her voice harsher than Diane had ever heard it. "You painted her; you talked with her as you were doing her portrait. What did you call her?

She told you about herself. You knew her father hurt her. What was her name?"

Gauthier didn't say anything. She stared at Lillian, but without anger. She gazed at the mask again, brushing it with her fingers, and finally spoke.

"Patsy. It seems as though I called her Patsy. The boy—I called him Steven because he reminded me of my Steven. He was quiet and sensitive. He sat so still as I painted him. He seemed to take joy in just sitting still. He liked Steven better than his name. I don't remember what it was," she said.

"Do you remember their last names?" asked Diane.

"No. I didn't care what their last names were. Those were their fathers' names," she said.

"Why didn't you change your name to Farragut?" asked Diane. "Why did you keep your father's name?"

Diane had caught Gauthier by surprise. She looked wide-eyed for a moment, as if trying to understand the question.

"I don't know," she said finally. "I don't know."

"Why did you use a drawing of a bird for your signature?" asked Hanks.

She smiled. "Mother used to call me her little magpie," she said, "and I lived in Pigeon Ridge. I liked the idea of being something that could fly away whenever I wanted."

Hanks looked at Diane and his lips twitched into a whisper of a smile.

"How many were there?" said Diane. "How many did you turn into art?"

"Not many. Not many. Ten, maybe. Perhaps fewer," she said.

"Where are they buried?" asked Diane.

"I don't know exactly. Everett handled that. Somewhere nearby."

Hanks rose to his feet. "Thank you for speaking with us."

He said it as if it were all he could do to say the words. Diane understood.

Hanks reached to take the box containing the mask from Gauthier. She snatched it away.

"Can't I keep it? It's mine."

"It's evidence, ma'am," he said, and took the box and put the lid back on it.

They left her there, sitting in the empty sunroom with the harsh light shining on her. No one spoke until they were almost to Rosewood. Lillian broke the silence.

"All that going on in Rosewood, and no one knew? Weren't those poor people reported missing?"

"They must have been," said Diane.

"The little boy she said liked to sit still. Poor little thing," said Harte.

"He was worked hard," said Diane. "The muscle attachments on his little bones were too developed. He'd led a hard life. He was undersized for his age. He wouldn't have looked like the teenager he was."

They were silent again until they were pulling up to the crime lab parking lot where Vanessa had picked up Diane and Detective Hanks.

"Is that what you have to deal with every day?" asked Vanessa before they got out.

"It's usually not this crazy," said Hanks. "No, I take that back. When someone gets stabbed for his shoes, or his lunch money, that's pretty crazy. But I don't usually deal with insanity on quite this scale."

He put his sling back on his arm. Diane saw that he was still in pain.

"I want to thank you for the ride," he told Vanessa. "I've never ridden in a limousine before."

"Everyone should have a limousine ride at least once," Vanessa said, smiling at him. "Thank you for putting up with us."

"You were very helpful," he said. "Mrs. Chapman, you made the woman connect with her past. I'm not sure I could have done that."

"I'm glad we could be of service," Lillian said. "It certainly gives one something to think about, doesn't it?"

Diane and Hanks got out and watched the limousine leave the parking lot.

"I'm sure there's fresh coffee in the crime lab if you'd like some," said Diane.

"Fresh coffee sounds good. Will your personnel be up there this late?" he asked.

"Are you kidding? They're waiting on pins and needles to hear the story," she said.

"That's the first time I've met Vanessa Van Ross," said Hanks. "You say she's the real power behind the museum?"

"Yes, she is," Diane said.

"An interesting family. I have a ninety-year-old great-grandfather and he has to have twenty-four-hour care. Mrs. Chapman is heading to a hundred, you say? I could invite her out for racquetball."

Hanks shook his head as he entered the lobby for the crime lab and nodded at Diane's bodyguards, who were playing cards with the crime lab guard.

"Interesting family," Hanks said again.

"The Gauthiers were an interesting family," said Diane.

They got on the elevator and rode to the crime lab.

"Interesting isn't how I would describe them," said Hanks.

Diane was right; her team were all there, including Jin—plus Frank. Diane grinned and introduced Frank to Detective Hanks.

"I thought you would be here soon, so I thought I'd take you to dinner in the restaurant," Frank said.

"Why don't we all order dinner?" Diane said. "We can eat it in my office and Detective Hanks and I can debrief with you."

"Let's," said Neva. "We are dying to hear about Gauthier. Could you get any sense from her?"

"That depends on your definition of sense," said Hanks.

"How was the bar fight crime scene?" Diane asked.

"Uneventful," said Neva.

"Yeah, the guy lying on the floor with a knife stuck in his gut kind of sobered them up," said Izzy. "We didn't have any trouble."

They ordered dinner. While waiting for it to arrive, Frank, Izzy, and David moved the round table from the crime lab to Diane's office. She, Neva, and Jin carried the chairs. Neva batted Hanks away when he tried to take one of the chairs.

"You have to be really sore," she said.

"It's not so bad."

"I don't believe that," Neva said. "We've all been hurt and it, well, it hurts."

"That's one of the things I miss around here," said Jin, "your way with words."

Neva hit him in the shoulder of his Hawaiian shirt. Even with the weather cooling down, Jin still wore Hawaiian shirts and Bermuda shorts when he was off duty. Diane thought it was funny that he was critical of what Scott and Hector wore.

They put the chairs around the table and Neva sat down. "Okay," she said. "Tell us all about it."

Alternately, Diane and Hanks told Maybelle Agnes Gauthier's story to an astonished audience.

"And I thought she was probably the victim," said Jin, "living with some guy she couldn't get away from who made crazy pots."

"Wait a minute," said Neva. "You mean she was here, when this was a clinic? She was an inmate?" Neva sat with one foot resting on the chair seat, hugging her knee to her.

"Yes," said Diane. "How's that for a really disturbing coincidence?"

"I don't think they called them inmates," said David.

"I'd say it's a good word," said Izzy. "I've lived in Rosewood all my life and I've never heard of these people."

"This whole thing goes way off the dial on my freak meter," said Neva.

"You should have been there with her," said Hanks. "She's got the strangest color eyes. Didn't you think so?"

Diane agreed.

"She had praise for your drawings," Diane told Neva.

"Oh, well, I'll just quit my job and take her letter of reference with me to New York," said Neva.

The buzzer rang on the museum side of the crime lab.

"Food's here," said Izzy.

He and Frank went to get it. They came back pushing the cart with their food. Frank handed it out and they settled in to dinner.

"David," said Diane, "you were quiet during the narration. What have you got up your sleeve that you haven't told us yet?"

"What makes you think I have something up my sleeve?"

"I know you," said Diane. "What is it?"

"Two things," said David. He turned silent as he slowly savored a bite of his salad with his favorite dressing.

"David," said Jin, "you don't have to make an entrance. What is it?"

He put his fork down. "UGA issued a parking sticker to Tyler Walters for a black Cadillac Escalade."

"Okay," said Hanks. "That's what I want to hear. You said two things?"

"I got a hit on the fingerprints from the potting clay we found in the well. First, let me say that the thumbprint in the dried blood on the sculpting tool matches the thumbprint in the clay. Second, when I ran the database for people who are bonded, the print came up a match for Everett Walters. Detective Hanks, I think you can get a warrant now to search the cars and residences of both of them."

Diane and her crew, Frank, and Detective Hanks discussed every permutation of possible solutions to the crimes, and she was sure one of them was probably correct. But sorting out which individual actually attacked Marcella, which one killed the Lassiter woman, and who killed Stacy Dance was impossible—or at least, beyond them for the moment.

"We'll probably wake up with a brilliant idea in the morning," said Neva.

"I'm sure," said Jin as the two of them helped Diane put the dishes back on the cart.

Frank and Izzy put the table and chairs back in their places and Diane told them all to go home. She knew David would probably go down to the basement where he had his own private office and work into the night on some project that involved some algorithm or database or other.

Diane followed Frank's car home and pulled up behind him in the drive. There was already a car parked over to the side of the driveway. Diane recognized it as Lynn Webber's black Mercedes SUV. Lynn was sitting on their doorstep looking up at the stars through the tall trees.

Chapter 56

"Lynn?" said Diane, as she and Frank approached the steps. "Have you been waiting long?"

Lynn stood up with a Coke in one hand and an envelope in the other. She was dressed for colder weather than the current temperature warranted—jeans, suede jacket, and boots. She looked stylish, as always, but she also looked to Diane like a kid about to run away to a colder clime.

"No, not long. I would have called, but sometimes it's better to just show up," she said.

"Hello, Dr. Webber. How are you this evening?" Frank took out his keys, opened the door, and stepped aside to let Lynn and Diane enter.

"I'm fine, and please call me Lynn, because I'm going to call you Frank," she said.

"Okay, Lynn," he said. "Would you like some coffee?"

She held up her plastic bottle of soda. "No thanks. Got caffeine here." She looked around at the decor. "This is a beautiful house," she said as she shrugged out of her coat.

"Thanks," said Frank. He led the way into the living room and offered Lynn a seat. Diane and Frank sat opposite her.

"I'm sorry it's so late. You must be wondering what I'm doing here."

Diane started to speak, but Lynn barely paused.

"I need to apologize. I'm aware of the care you used in selecting your words when you responded to Chief Stark's concerns about the newspaper article. I very much appreciate your discretion. I like my job here and I know what would happen if they knew it was I who initiated the article.

I wish I could say I'm sorry I did it. But I'm not. However, I am sorry I misused your trust in me to settle my grievance with Doppelmeyer."

Diane didn't quite know what to say, at least to someone who was currently a guest in her home. But it didn't matter, because Lynn wasn't slowing down.

"One reason I'm not repentant is because Doppelmeyer is a sorry excuse for a medical examiner. I know that sounds like I'm being tacky, but it's true, and he needs to be outed. If he doesn't do his job right, justice is not served. Innocent people can go to jail and the guilty are left to kill again. I know I can't travel across the United States and root out every bad ME. But I can this one." She took a deep breath.

"Well, in for a penny, in for a pound." She took the envelope and handed it to Diane. "I did some research. This is my way of making up to you and Ross Kingsley—and to, well, you'll see." She stood up. "I explained everything." She put her jacket over her arm. "I thought it would be colder out this evening. Can't count on weather forecasts worth a darn."

Frank and Diane saw her out to her car and watched her drive off.

"What the hell was that?" said Diane on the way back into the house.

"She certainly can talk when she gets going," said Frank. "Needs to work on her apologies, however."

Inside, Diane sat down on the couch, opened the envelope, and took out several typed pages. It was an analysis of an autopsy. Diane read the pages several times and put them back in the envelope. She felt strangely unsurprised, though she wouldn't have guessed. She could call Ross in the morning. Right now, she was tired and wanted to go to bed.

The phone awakened Diane out of a pleasant dream of swimming in an underground lake flanked with giant crystal formations. She looked at the clock. It was just past four in the morning. She reached for the phone but Frank got to it first. She held her breath. Early calls were never good.

"Hello," he said, and paused. "It's for you." He handed Diane the phone.

"I know it's very early," said the female voice, "and I'm so sorry to call you this early, but I need you to come to my house, please. I'm not sure what else to do."

"Who is this?" said Diane.

"I'm sorry. This is Kathy Nicholson. Could you and Mr. Kingsley come? My son is here. He needs to talk with you. Please come. We'll tell you about it when you get here."

"All right," said Diane. She replaced the phone, sat up in bed, and swung her feet around.

"Who was that?" said Frank.

Diane told him. "You think it's a trap?" she said.

"Don't know," he said. "I'm not sure what would be gained by trapping you at this point. The horse is out of the barn. Are you going?"

"I'm going to call Ross," she said. "If he can go, I will. If not, I don't know. Kathy Nicholson sounded frantic, and desperate."

Diane dialed Ross Kingsley's number. Lydia answered in a sleepy voice.

"Lydia, this is Diane Fallon. I'm very sorry to wake you up. I just got a call from someone Ross and I have been interviewing—may I speak with him?"

"Yes, just a moment."

Diane assumed they were replaying the same scene that she and Frank just went through. But she heard Lydia mumble.

"You know, if you and she would have an affair like normal people, I could get some sleep."

"Hey, Diane," Kingsley said. "What's going on?"

Diane apologized again for waking him and Lydia. Then she told him about the phone call from Kathy Nicholson.

"I can meet you there," he said.

There was no, "What do you think this is about?" Just, "Let's go," as if she had called him and said, "'Come, Watson, the game is afoot. Not a word! Into your clothes and come!'"

Diane got into her clothes. Frank came in with an instant breakfast and told her to drink it.

"Take your gun," he said.

Diane looked at him and sighed. He was right; she needed to take a gun. The gun issued to her by Rosewood hadn't yet been returned to her, but she had her backup gun. She slipped on the shoulder holster. It felt strange. She didn't think it would ever feel familiar. She put on a dark zip-up jacket and finished her breakfast, drinking the last of it down.

There wasn't much traffic in Rosewood that early in the morning, but by the time she got on the interstate, it had picked up considerably. At the turnoff to Gainesville, dawn had begun to crack enough that she could just see a line of light outlining the horizon. Kingsley had timed it just right. He pulled in behind Diane as she parked on the street in front of Kathy Nicholson's house.

It was still dark and the streetlights were on. Diane looked across the street at the homes belonging to Marsha Carruthers and Wendy Walters. All the windows were dark. Only the porch lights were lit.

"What do you think this is about?" asked Kingsley.

"Something to do with that house over there," said Diane, gesturing with her head toward the Carruthers' house.

The lights were burning inside the Nicholson residence. They walked up to the door and rang the bell. Kathy must have been waiting at the door, for it opened immediately.

"Oh, thank you for coming. I just don't know what to do and, and, well, you seemed so nice." She paused. "I hope it was the right thing, calling you, but . . ." Her sentence trailed off.

Diane could see Kathy had been crying. Her nose and eyes were red and puffy. She sniffed and put a tissue to her nose and led them to the living room, where a young man was standing near the couch that sat under the front window. He had been looking out. Even though the drapes were drawn, there was a slight part where he had held them open. He had been crying too. His tanned face was puffy like his mother's. Diane tried to remember his name—Colton.

Colton was a tall, lanky young man. Diane did the math. He would be twenty-three. He looked both younger and older. In his face and manner he could still be a teenager.

But not in his eyes. They were older. He had dark hair cut short, and light brown eyes. He wore jeans and a navy blue sweatshirt with CALIFORNIA BERKELEY printed across the front.

"Please, sit down. Can I get you something to drink? Coffee?" said Kathy.

Both Diane and Kingsley declined. They sat beside each other on the couch by the front window. Diane felt the pressure of her gun under her jacket.

"My son came in late last night. I didn't know he was coming until he called me to pick him up at the airport." Kathy Nicholson sat down in a chair with a sigh. Her son stood beside her and put a hand on her shoulder. "This is just the most, the most terrible thing. I don't know what to do."

"I do," Colton said. "I need to go over and talk to Marsha and her family. I have to do this, Mom."

"Why don't you tell us first," suggested Diane.

Colton nodded. "Okay." He pulled the other stuffed chair closer to his mother and sat down. "It's about El Carruthers. That guy in prison? He didn't kill her."

Chapter 57

Tears spilled onto Colton's cheeks. "I was only fourteen. Do you know how young that is?"

"He had just turned fourteen," said Kathy.

"Mother, please. This is hard enough," he said. "Tyler Walters was my best friend."

He stood up and walked around and rested his forearms on the back of the chair, as if he couldn't sit down, but needed to be propped up.

"Mother told me what happened with that girl, Stacy Dance, Ryan Dance's little sister. She told me how Marsha Carruthers has been acting—the anger and the drinking. I got afraid for Mother. She didn't know what really happened, and it's gotten so mixed up."

"Why don't you start from the beginning," suggested Diane.

He nodded. "I'm not sure what the beginning is anymore," he said.

His mother sobbed into her handkerchief.

"Just start from the first thing you remember," said Kingsley.

"I was in my room listening to NSYNC, and Tyler came to my window and knocked. I let him climb in. He was really upset. He kept pacing and saying, 'Oh, man, oh, man. I really did it this time.'"

Colton paused and looked away from Diane and Kingsley, his face screwed up into a grief-stricken mask.

"He was only a kid like me. He told me he had just killed El—Ellie Rose. I thought he was kidding. I mean, who comes in and says they just killed someone? He said he'd been wanting her for a long time but he couldn't get her alone. She kept avoiding him. He had told me already that one day he was going to jump her and I told him he couldn't do that. He didn't listen to me."

Colton Nicholson sat back down in the chair. His mother reached over and touched his hand.

"I'm sorry, Mother," he whispered. "Tyler said she started screaming and he put a hand over her mouth. Tyler was really strong. His grandfather made him work out all the time."

Diane thought that was a strange way of putting it, but she didn't want to interrupt him.

"Everett Walters, Tyler's grandfather, took him to some hookers as a birthday present when he turned thirteen," continued Colton. "Tyler said his grandfather told them to make a man out of him. After that, he was kind of crazy, if you know what I mean. At the time, I was really interested in hearing about his experience with the hookers, but it kind of scared me too. His grandfather scared me. He encouraged Tyler to be a bully at school. He got into trouble more than once for it. He kept telling Tyler he had to be a man. That's hard when you are just thirteen."

Colton paused again and put his head in his hands. He straightened up after a moment and continued. "He said he did it to her. He said his grandfather was right—she was better than a hooker. But she bit him and started screaming, and he choked her. He said she was in the woods in back of his house, that he had covered her body with branches. I told him he had to go tell his father. He shook his head and said he was going to tell his grandfather, that he would know what to do."

"Did he?" asked Kingsley.

Colton nodded. "Yes. When it was all done, Tyler was calm about it all. He said his grandfather fixed everything. He told me never to tell anyone. If I did, his grandfather would kill me. He wasn't threatening me or anything. It was just a fact. He said he didn't tell his grandfather I knew because he would have killed me. I believed him. I was scared."

Colton waited a moment. His eyes were glossy with tears. He had been living with this for nine years, dreading every time he came home. Diane couldn't blame him, even though he should have come forward much earlier.

"That man Dance is innocent. Tyler's grandfather, Everett Walters, framed him. Tyler said Dance was some no-account and it didn't matter. But Mother tells me that someone killed his sister, that she was trying to free her brother. I know it was Everett Walters who did it."

"What about Tyler?" said Diane. "You don't think he could have killed Stacy Dance?"

"El was an accident. He wouldn't kill somebody on purpose."

"He raped Ellie Rose on purpose," said Kingsley.

"Don't you think I know that? El was my friend too. I told Tyler he needed to talk to a counselor or something, but—he was all different after he met his grandfather. Tyler's grandfather wasn't always in the picture. He and Tyler's grandmother divorced when Tyler's father, Gordon Walters, was a kid, and she got custody and raised him in another state without Everett. Everett had businesses here in Georgia and didn't travel, I guess. Anyway, Tyler said Everett didn't try to see his son, Gordon, growing up and regretted it. Everett Walters sought his son out when Tyler was a kid—it was several years after Gordon Walters moved back to Georgia."

"Why did he wait?" asked Kingsley.

Colton shrugged. "I think Everett read something about Gordon in the newspaper—when he became head of oncology or something—realized that that was his son." He shrugged again. "Wendy hated Everett, but Gordon, Dr. Walters, was happy to have his father back in his life. Wendy said Gordon had blinders on when it came to his father. But she did too. She had no idea about the things that Everett was teaching Tyler. She sure didn't know about the hookers. She'd have had a fit. Tyler said that his mother and father argued about Everett a lot. Everett had no respect for women and that included Wendy. Gordon was so clueless about his father. But, to be fair, he did work all the time."

Colton talked to them for an hour. It was sometimes disjointed and Diane had to make the connections in the right sequence. She imagined he was about talked out. He and his mother had apparently talked all night. He stood and looked at his mother.

"I have to tell Dr. and Mrs. Carruthers what really happened. They deserve to know. Then I'm going to get you to move out to California with me. You don't need to live here any longer. Not across the street from the Walters. Not after today."

Mrs. Nicholson looked at Diane and Kingsley. "What will happen to Colton? What will the police do?"

"He will have to answer questions," said Diane. "Get a good lawyer to go with him to the police station. He was a minor and he was scared. He didn't have anything to do with what happened to Ellie Rose until after the fact. But he still needs to have a lawyer with him."

"Oh God," she wimpered.

"Mother, this has defined my life for nine years. My childhood ended that day. I can't have a relationship with anyone until I resolve this. Tyler won't like it, but he was a minor too. It's his grandfather they need to put in jail."

Light was starting to filter through the crack between the drapes. Daylight was finally here. Diane imagined that it was a long time coming for Colton and his mother.

He headed for the door.

"Colton, you need to call first," said his mother.

"No. I need to go over and do it. I need to get this done," he said.

"I'll go with you," she said. "Please let us go with you."

Kathy Nicholson had said *us*. She apparently wanted Diane and Kingsley to go along too. *Well*, thought Diane, *this ought to be fun*. She looked at Kingsley, who was getting to his feet.

"Son," said Kingsley, "you need to wait and do this another way. You don't know what Mrs. Carruthers' reaction will be. She probably won't believe you at first. She may blame you. She needs people around her when you tell her."

"I've thought it through. Marsha knows me. When I come home I always go see her. Samuel will be there. He doesn't go into his office this early. I know them. They need to hear this and I need to tell them, and I'm going to."

Ross sighed. "Very well," he said. "Then all of us will go with you."

The four of them walked over to the Carruthers' house. Colton Nicholson rang the doorbell. It took a couple of minutes before anyone answered it. Diane and Kingsley stood back so that whoever answered the door, or looked out the peephole, would see the Nicholsons first. Diane didn't think Marsha Carruthers or her husband would let them in otherwise.

It was Marsha who opened the door. She was in a robe. She didn't have on any makeup and her hair was up in a ponytail.

"Kathy? Colton?" she said. "I didn't know you were home. Is anything wrong?" Then she saw Diane and Kingsley. "You! What are you doing here?"

"I asked them, Marsha," said Kathy Nicholson. "Colton needs to tell you and Samuel something."

"This early? Can't it wait?" she said.

"No, Marsha, it can't," said Colton. "I should have come a long time ago."

"Honey, who is it?" Samuel Carruthers came to the door in a bathrobe. "Colton. It's been a while." He looked at Diane and Kingsley and pointed a finger at them. "I told you never to come onto my property again."

"Please, Samuel," said Kathy. "Please, let us come in."

Dr. and Mrs. Carruthers looked confused. They stood there making no decision for several moments. Then Marsha stepped back and let them come in. They all went into the living room, where Ellie Rose's portrait hung over the mantel. The stuffed chair was sitting facing it. An empty drink glass was on the side table where Marsha had left it the evening before. Diane wanted to go home and get into bed.

Marsha and Samuel sat in the leather chairs. Kathy and Colton sat on the sofa. Diane and Kingsley stood off to the side, near the wall. Diane hoped she blended into the wallpaper.

"What's this about?" asked Marsha.

Colton took a deep breath. For all his insistence on coming over right at this moment, he was losing his nerve. He blurted it out. No preamble or explanation, just, "Tyler Walters killed El. His grandfather framed that Dance guy. Tyler told me it was an accident."

Marsha and Samuel sat there as if they hadn't heard. They stared at Colton, then at Kathy, then at Diane and Kingsley.

"They told you to say this," said Marsha. "You sons of bitches."

"Marsha, I called them early this morning after Colton and I talked all night. I'd told Colton about the murder of Stacy Dance, and he got on a plane and flew here. These people had nothing to do with it. I called them, well, because they were nice to me and aren't the police—though I know we'll need to talk to the police after we talk to you."

"I don't understand," said Samuel. "Are you saying that Tyler Walters killed my baby girl? That he raped her? He was just a kid then."

Colton laid out the whole story just as he had for Diane and Kingsley.

Chapter 58

There were times when Diane didn't know if Marsha and Samuel Carruthers were actually hearing what Colton was telling them. Their eyes seemed out of focus. They looked dazed and confused.

"Did Wendy know?" asked Marsha.

Colton nodded. "She came home as they were moving the . . . as they were putting El into Everett's SUV."

Colton had sneaked glances at the portrait as he told his story. He looked at it now as if it were Ellie Rose herself looking down on him.

"Tyler said Wendy got hysterical there in the garage. His grandfather slapped her and she hit him back with a mop handle. Tyler said he had to get between them. He said his grandfather convinced Wendy that what they were doing was for the best."

"Best?" whispered Marsha. "Best?"

"Look, Mrs. Carruthers, I'm sorry. I'm sorry. I should have told you the truth years ago. But I was afraid. And then later, well, I couldn't bring myself to relive the whole thing. I just tried to pretend it didn't happen, until I had to come home. I only came forward now because of Stacy Dance. I'm really afraid that Tyler or his grandfather . . ."

Colton stopped talking because Marsha was up and going to the phone. They all watched as she dialed and waited.

"Wendy, I need you to come over." She replaced the receiver.

Diane didn't imagine, given their relationship, that Wendy thought the request was strange, or, in fact, much different from other summons she probably received over the years of Marsha's growing dependence on her.

Marsha sat down again. No one said anything. The quiet made Diane uneasy. She was sure they all felt uneasy, but emotions were too quiet, too under the surface. It reminded Diane of a volcano waiting for just the right pressure to build up before it erupted.

"Did you have anything to do with her death?" Marsha asked Colton after a moment. Her gaze bored into him with an intensity that seemed to literally nail him to his seat.

"No ma'am, as God is my witness, on my father's grave, I swear to you that I only found out after it happened, when Tyler came to my window and told me," Colton said.

While all their attention was on Colton and Marsha, Diane snaked her hand inside her jacket, took her gun from its shoulder holster, and put it in her jacket pocket. She wasn't sure why she felt she needed to do this, other than she had experience with the inconvenience of having a gun zipped up inside a jacket when she needed it—or rather, Frank had.

Her movement didn't go unnoticed. Ross looked over at her and gave her a quick smile with a twitch of his lips. He had felt it too. It was as if emotions were becoming a miasma settling in the room that could be seen and breathed in. Diane shivered. It was cold. If she believed in ghosts, she would have been convinced that Ellie Rose's spirit was in the room. She was glad she had worn the jacket.

Diane heard the door open and close. Wendy had arrived. Diane unconsciously slid closer to the tall parlor palm.

"Marsha, are you in the living room? Is something wrong? I saw those dreadful people's cars parked across the street.... Oh, Colton, dear. I didn't know you were home. How nice to see you."

Wendy had started talking before she entered the room and hadn't stopped once she was there. She looked much as she had when Diane had last seen her. Nice hairstyle, but sans makeup. She didn't come in her robe, but had slipped on emerald green slacks and a dark pumpkin sweater.

"I thought those awful people were back—" She stopped talking when she spotted the awful, dreadful people standing next to the wall. "What are you doing here? Marsha, we can get a restraining order."

Marsha stood facing her. "It was Tyler all along, Wendy. It was Tyler, and you knew." Marsha's voice was quiet and came out in a rasp.

"What? Marsha, are you all right?" said Wendy.

"Tyler killed my baby girl and you knew, damn you. Damn you to hell." Marsha's voice was loud now and shaking with anger.

Wendy looked as though Marsha had hit her in the stomach with a baseball bat. There it was, the knowledge she dreaded anyone ever knowing.

"I don't know what these people have been telling you," began Wendy.

"I told her," said Colton. "I'm sorry, Mrs. Walters, but Tyler told me when it happened and I've been carrying it with me all these years. With what's been happening, it has to come out. You know that."

"Why? Why did you cover it up?" said Samuel. "I thought we were friends."

"How can you ask that?" said Wendy. "It was an accident. Ellie was dead and nothing could bring her back. I didn't want Tyler's life to be ruined too."

"What? You didn't want your son's life to be ruined? What kind of self-centered," began Marsha. "I see it all now. You here all the time keeping me drunk so I would never suspect."

"Now, wait a minute. I did everything in my power to help you get over it," said Wendy. "I didn't mean—"

"Get over it? Get over it? You thought this was something we could just get over? You insufferable bitch!" Marsha stepped toward her. "You even have the gall to call it an accident? He raped her. Your son raped my daughter and choked her to death."

"He was just fourteen. She was fifteen," said Wendy.

Samuel Carruthers stood up and faced Wendy, balling his fists. "Are you saying this was our daughter's fault?"

Wendy backed up several steps. "No, really, I just, it's

just that Tyler was so young. He didn't know what he was doing," she said.

"Didn't know what he was doing? God, apparently you are as clueless as I've been these past years," said Marsha. "You didn't know that your father-in-law took Tyler to a brothel for his thirteenth birthday? He knew what he was doing, all right. He knew plenty what he was doing."

"What? What?" said Wendy.

"It's true, Mrs. Walters," said Colton. "Tyler told me about it."

Wendy put her hands to her face and screamed. For a moment Diane thought she was going to claw her own eyes out, the way she dragged her hands down her face, but she bent over and heaved.

Diane stepped forward. "There's something. . . ."

She didn't get to finish. She looked up and saw Tyler Walters standing in the doorway.

"Colton, I protected you from Everett all these years," said Tyler.

Tyler wasn't tall, but he did look in shape. Diane thought of the way Colton said that Tyler's grandfather made him work out. He had black hair like his mother and the strange dark blue–flecked eyes like his great-aunt. He could have been handsome, were it not for the curl of his full lips, and eyes that were a little too far apart. But perhaps he was considered handsome to young women nowadays. Diane didn't know. She found him creepy.

"I know, buddy, and that's why I texted you what I was doing. I thought you deserved a heads-up on what was coming down," said Colton.

Colton told Tyler what he was doing. Diane wanted to smack him. Colton was still fourteen where his friend was concerned. He still thought it was some kind of mistake. *Well, hell.*

"I left Athens as soon as I got your text message. I guess you've already told them everything," said Tyler.

"Look, Tyler, you'll have to admit, a lot of shit's been going down. This Stacy Dance thing, and Mrs. Carruthers has been treating my mother pretty bad. I had to do something."

Marsha cast a glance at Kathy Nicholson. Diane thought she saw a little regret.

"Tyler, I'm calling the police," Marsha said.

"No, Marsha, you're not." Tyler pulled a gun from behind him and pointed it at her. "I want everybody just to sit down and think things through."

Chapter 59

"Tyler," said Wendy, "what are you doing? Where did you get that?"

"Mother, will you stop talking to me like I'm twelve?" he said. "Now, everybody just sit down."

He looked over at Diane and Kingsley where they stood leaning against the wall. He stared at them like nemeses he'd longed to see in person.

"You, come over here and sit down on the couch with Colton and Kathy."

"Tyler, there's something you need to know," said Diane.

"Shut up. That's the last time I'm going to tell you. Talk again and I'll shoot you." He waved the gun at her.

Diane and Kingsley walked to the couch and sat down, Kingsley by Colton, Diane between Kingsley and the arm of the sofa. Diane tracked Tyler as he walked back and forth between her and Samuel Carruthers. Were it not for Samuel in the line of fire, Diane would shoot him, or at least shoot his leg. It was against what she had been taught—go for the midsection. Psychologically, Diane had a hard time with killing someone. But she could. She had.

"Marsha, sit down," he said, pointing the gun at Mrs. Carruthers, who shot daggers at him with her gaze as she took a seat.

"Mother, get that chair over there and sit in it. I'll just stand over here. Now, I need to figure this out." He wiped his hand over his forehead.

"Damn it, Colton, this would have been a lot easier if you had kept our bargain," he said, turning the gun on his friend.

Colton held his hands in front of him. "Look, man, this is wrong. This isn't you, Tyler."

"It's me, Colton. It's me." Tyler beat his chest with his free hand. "Get that through your thick head. This is me."

"Tyler, honey," said his mother, "stop this. You were so young at the time it all happened. This isn't you."

"Mother, will you please? What is it I have to say to get you to shut the fuck up, huh?"

His mother whimpered and covered her face with her hands. Diane wondered what the hell he was so intent on thinking through. Just how had he planned to get out of this?

Diane's cell phone binged the tones telling her she had a text message. Tyler looked over at her.

"Gimme that," he said.

As Diane removed the cell from her pocket she flipped it open and glanced at the message: *ug srchd bts Cqns shrd n clst.*

Tyler looked at the message. "What's this?" he said. "What does this say?"

"Gotcha," said Diane.

Diane saw it in his eyes before he raised his hand, the flare of anger, the emotional call to violent action. Her hand was still in her other pocket, on her gun. She aimed as accurately as she could under the circumstances, and shot through the jacket, hitting Tyler in the shin, shattering his tibia. Lucky shot. But then again, he was close. She was up and grabbed his gun as the others were still gasping. Tyler fell to the floor and held on to his leg, moaning.

"Tyler!" screamed his mother. "What did you do to him?"

"She shot him, you stupid bitch," said Samuel Carruthers, jumping from his chair. He grabbed Tyler by his shirt and hit him across the face. "You piece of crap. You piece of waste."

"Stop," cried Wendy. She jumped up and grabbed Samuel around the waist. "Stop it. You're a doctor; help him."

Diane gave Tyler's gun to Kingsley, took her phone, and started to dial the police.

"Stop right there. Just stop right there and put down that phone and those guns."

They all jerked their heads up at the sound of the different voice. A man in his seventies stood in the doorway to the living room, well dressed in brown slacks and matching sport coat, and holding a Glock 9mm. Diane guessed this was Everett Walters. *Well, great.*

Everett Walters may have been in his seventies, but he apparently took his own advice about keeping in shape. He was well built and tanned. He appeared strong and his gun hand never wavered.

"You, Samuel, get off my boy and wrap up his leg. Ty, wipe the blood and snot off your face and stop whining."

He looked at Diane. She expected his eyes to be the color of his sister's, but they weren't. They were a lighter blue, piercing, cold. She didn't look away.

"You," he said, gesturing his gun at Diane, "put your gun down on the table over there. You do the same," he told Kingsley.

The two of them laid down their weapons beside Diane's phone.

"Boy, didn't you check them for guns?" he said.

Tyler said something that Diane didn't understand. He was the kind of guy who was all bluster when he had the gun, but reverted back to being a child when someone took it away from him.

"Everett," said Wendy, "they know."

"Shut up, girl. They know nothing. It looks to me like the two of you came in and shot my boy here. That's what I see. What this Nicholson boy said means nothing. Hell, he might have been in on it with Ryan Dance. They can't prove anything. Everybody just keep your mouths shut and we'll all get out of this. These two are a couple of thugs. That's what we'll tell the police. Who's to say different?"

"Me," said Marsha. "Your boy, as you call him, raped and killed my daughter."

"Stupid woman, you're not going to believe what Nicholson said? Sit down and listen. I'll tell you how this is going to go down."

Apparently he had been listening at the door, thought Diane. Tyler must have called him.

"Now, listen here," said Samuel Carruthers. "Who the hell do you think you are, coming in here like this after what you've done?"

"I'm the guy with the gun. And I'll always be the guy with the gun. Listen here. What they've said is a lie."

"He admitted it," said Samuel.

"Did not," said Tyler.

"If you've finished tying up his leg, sit down," said Everett Walters. "Everybody sit down or I start shooting, and fuck the consequences."

Samuel had torn a piece off Tyler's shirt and tied it around his leg. He tightened it so that Tyler yelped and he sat back down in the chair beside his wife. Diane didn't think he really did much in the way of tending to the wound.

"We might just have a home invasion. Those are going around." Everett grinned at Diane with nicotine-stained teeth.

"Apparently," Diane said. "Sometimes, though, it doesn't play out the way you expect. You've made some assumptions that aren't supported by the facts. Now, you can tell me to shut up, like Tyler did. But I'm the one with the knowledge of all the crimes and what the police actually have. That's why you sent the assassin to my house, isn't it? To kill the person who could make the connection."

Diane heard someone suck in a breath.

"Everett," said Wendy, "this has gone too far. Look what you've done to my son. Don't you have any conscience?"

"Shut up, woman." He didn't even look at her when he spoke, but stared at Diane.

"She got a text message on her phone," said Tyler. His face was streaked with blood and tears, even though he made an effort to wipe it with his sleeve.

"Text message? Is that something we should be concerned about?" said Everett.

"There is so much you don't know," said Diane. "Yes, it is something you should be concerned about. But first, you need to tell Tyler how you played him. Tell him the truth . . . that he didn't kill Ellie Rose."

Chapter 60

Diane attracted all their attention, including Kingsley's. It was Marsha who recovered first.

"What? You mean Ryan Dance is guilty after all? After all this! Just what are you playing at?"

"Ryan is not guilty," said Diane. "What Colton said is true, to a point. I tried to explain, but Tyler threatened to shoot me if I spoke. Mr. Walters, you need to tell Tyler the truth."

Diane had a plan in mind. It wasn't a particularly good one, but it seemed like very few of her plans were, in this kind of situation. Rushing either one of them was out of the question, so she would try the old *divide et impera* approach. It had worked for the Romans.

"What?" said Tyler. He rocked back and forth, still holding his leg, trying not to cry.

"Tyler raped Ellie Rose," continued Diane. "He choked her to unconsciousness and she was badly hurt. She hit her head in a fall, I suspect, while Tyler was fighting with her. But then Tyler called his grandfather for help, and Everett Walters came, prepared with a hatchet, just in case he got the chance. And he did. When Ellie was trying to get up, he struck her down."

"Oh," whimpered Marsha. "Oh God." She put a hand over her mouth and rocked forward. Her husband reached out to her.

"When he got rid of her body," said Diane, "he struck her head against a rock to disfigure the wound—using blunt-force trauma in an attempt to hide the evidence of the sharp weapon that killed her."

Diane stared Everett in the eyes. "You tried to make it look as if her head were injured when Dance threw her body down the embankment. And fortunately for you, Gainesville had a brand-new medical examiner with a track record of making wrong calls. But another medical examiner recently analyzed the photos of the autopsy and saw the sharp cuts in the skull that you tried to obscure."

"You bastard," said Wendy. "You freaking bastard—all this time . . ."

"Just your ME's word against ours, seems like to me," Everett said. "Don't listen to her."

"Tyler needs to listen. He can redeem himself," said Diane. "It's not too late."

"You got nothing," Everett said. He pulled a straight-back chair from its place near the wall beside the fireplace, sat down, crossed his legs, and looked very smug.

"You saying I didn't kill El?" groaned Tyler.

"That's what I'm saying," said Diane.

"Don't listen to her, boy. She'd say anything," said Everett. "She's desperate." He grinned at Diane.

She could see her plan had little chance. Tyler was in too much pain, he was only half listening, and his grandfather had a big hold over him.

"What was the text message?" said Tyler. "What does it mean? Someone please get me some painkillers?"

"Please," said Wendy. "Samuel, you must have something. Give him something."

"He can take the pain for a little while," said Everett. "Just until we figure this thing out. Everybody stays in the room so I can see them."

"Pour him a drink," said Kingsley. He nodded toward the bar in the corner where Wendy poured Marsha's drinks.

Everett nodded and Wendy got her son a bottle of vodka and poured him a drink, which he downed in one gulp.

"Now, what's this about the text message?" said Walters. "The boy seems to think it's important."

"The Athens police department executed a search warrant on Tyler's residence. In the closet they found incriminating evidence."

"Of what?" said Everett. "They found nothing."

"A sequin that matched my dress," said Diane. "You

stepped on it when you attacked me at Marcella Payden's house and carried it back on the bottom of your boot."

"That's nothing," said Everett. "Just as I thought, you got nothing."

"Granted, the sequin alone, it could be argued, is just a coincidence. Even the matching fibers could be considered a coincidence. They're common. However, they also found a broken piece of pottery," said Diane.

Everett laughed. "You got nothing."

"On the contrary," said Diane. "You broke a pot on the way to your vehicle."

"A broken piece could have come from anywhere," said Everett.

"You stole pottery that Dr. Marcella Payden made. She does archaeological research. Do you know what a histological examination is? It's a microscopic inspection of stuff, like tissue, broken pottery kind of stuff. The point is, we can match that piece with the broken pieces of her property. We can place Tyler at Marcella's house at the time of the second attack." Diane stopped a moment to let it sink in.

"Tyler. Not me," said Everett.

Good, thought Diane, *be the self-centered bastard you are.*

"I don't have the results of the search of your premises yet," said Diane.

His eyes narrowed and his gun wavered in her direction. "You won't find anything," he said.

"That remains to be seen. You seem to be ignorant of how trace evidence works. Which brings me to boots."

Everett winced at her words. Diane could see he didn't like being called ignorant.

"Boots?" whispered Tyler. He moved toward the table.

"What you doing, boy?" said Everett.

"Getting their guns," he said, "so they don't make a grab for them. You said they're desperate. I see that guy, Kingsley, eyeing them."

"Good thinking, boy. We can figure this out. You just hang in there. Feeling that vodka yet?" said Everett.

"A little," he said. He groaned as he reached for the guns. He got hold of them, put them in his lap, and scuttled back, leaning against a wall. "Mom, throw me a pillow."

Wendy took a decorator pillow from the couch and tossed it to her son, who put it under his leg with a yelp. He took another swig of vodka.

"What about the boots?" said Tyler.

He looked pale and his leg was still seeping blood. She had better hurry.

"Your Garmont hiking boot," said Diane.

Wendy sucked in her breath. "I gave you some—"

"Shut up, you damn fool," said Everett.

Tyler set the bottle down and looked at Diane. "What about them?"

"We identified the make of shoe by the tread pattern that we collected from the floor at Marcella's house. We can match the boot prints to individual boots because of the nicks and wear patterns. We already have."

"Again, Tyler," said Everett.

"We have a warrant to look for your size ten and a half Oliver steel toe safety boots," said Diane, locking her gaze with his.

She had surprised him. He was startled, but recovered quickly and started to speak, but Tyler beat him to it.

"Put down your gun, Granddad, or I'll shoot."

Chapter 61

"What the hell you talking about, boy?" said Everett.

Tyler held the gun straight out in front of him, pointing it at his grandfather.

"I don't like the way you been saying that all the evidence is on me. Put it down or I'll shoot. You been telling me I need to be strong. This is me being strong. Put down the gun."

"I could shoot you before you could shoot me," said Everett.

"Go ahead, risk it." Tyler sniffed.

"That's liquor courage, boy. It ain't real," said Everett.

"It's real enough. Now put it down," he said.

"Better think about what you're doing, boy," Everett said. "We'll get out of this."

"I am thinking. I want to hear more about how I didn't kill Ellie Rose. All these years you been holding it up to me," said Tyler.

"Can't you see what she's doing? She's lying," said Everett.

"This is the last time. Put it down on the floor," said Tyler. "If she's lying and I sense it, you can have it back."

Everyone looked back and forth between them as if they were watching a tennis match. Tyler's hand wavered and Diane thought his grandfather was going to shoot him. Tyler steadied his hand.

"I could shoot you, boy," said Everett.

"I could shoot you, old man," said Tyler.

"It looks like we got ourselves a Mexican standoff," said Everett.

Wendy jumped suddenly with astonishing speed and tackled Everett, knocking him over in the chair.

Diane heard the gun fall but didn't see where it went. She started to rise.

"If anybody moves, I'll shoot," said Tyler. "You people better start taking me seriously."

Diane relaxed back in her seat.

Tyler's voice was high-pitched and strained, but his words weren't slurred. And although his skin was pale, his eyes were bright. For the short term, he was okay. For the long term, if they couldn't end this soon, he would pass out, which would be fine if Everett was disarmed.

Diane knew Everett had planned to kill them all and blame it on Tyler. She heard it in his talk, saw it in his eyes. He was thinking that all the evidence pointed to Tyler. He didn't quite believe the boot prints implicated him—or he thought he could get around it—perhaps by saying he gave them to one of Tyler's friends, some guy he didn't know—maybe Ray-Ray or his cousin. Diane needed Everett to see that his plan wouldn't get him off the hook. She needed to tell him how deep in alligators he really was. She didn't think Everett knew about the discoveries in the well. She doubted seriously he knew about their visit to his sister. It was time he knew.

The scuffle hadn't lasted long. From the look on Everett's face, it surprised him that a mere woman could overpower him. But he hadn't counted on the anger that the much-younger Wendy had toward him. Diane saw the gun. She saw Everett start to reach for it right before Wendy kicked it under the couch.

Now, instead of being in the clutches of both a madman and a wounded, intoxicated kid with no moral center, they were in the clutches of only the kid. Diane thought that was better. She thought Tyler could be reached.

"Now, Granddad, pick up the chair and sit down. I can shoot you before you make it to the door, and I will. Mother, thanks. You sit down too," said Tyler. "I want to hear more about my innocence. So that means I want all of you to put your hands in your lap and keep them there. If you so much as scratch, I'll shoot. I don't have a lot of options anymore and damn little patience."

"You do have options," said Diane. "We know that you were present at all the crime scenes, but not that you killed Stacy Dance or Mary Lassiter, or that you attacked Marcella Payden."

"What?" said Wendy. "Tyler, who are these people? I've never heard of them."

"Shut up, Mother." Tyler rubbed his eyes. "God, there's so much you don't know," he mumbled. "You and Dad are so clueless."

His grandfather was watching him, waiting for a chance. Diane stared at him a moment. He moved his right leg forward a fraction.

"Your grandfather has a gun strapped around his ankle," said Diane.

"I know," said Tyler, "but if he keeps his hands in his lap, it won't be a problem." He held out his gun toward his grandfather and took another drink of vodka.

"Very well, then, Tyler," said Diane. "Please, let me tell you what we have. You have a way out of this."

"That little creep doesn't deserve a way out," spat Marsha.

Diane locked gazes with her. "If he isn't at fault, he does deserve a way out," said Diane.

She hoped she could telegraph to Marsha to keep her mouth shut and not infuriate the little creep holding the gun on all of them. Her husband seemed to get the message. He reached over to her.

"I said not to move," said Tyler.

"I'm just holding my wife's hand," said Samuel evenly.

Diane saw him squeeze it and put his own back in his lap. Kathy Nicholson glared at her. She and Colton kept quiet.

"You see what they're doing, don't you, boy?" said Everett.

"Would you stop calling me *boy*? I've always hated that. Yes. They all want to live, with the possible exception of Marsha." He took another drink of vodka. "But that doesn't mean Fallon doesn't have interesting things to say. I'm a lawyer, almost, and I can evaluate it. You've never given me any credit. Now shut up." He coughed.

"Why would Granddad have killed El?" said Tyler, not taking his eyes off Everett. "Not to save me."

"Did your grandfather tell you why he wanted to kill Marcella Payden or Mary Lassiter? I'm sure you thought his killing Stacy was to hide what the two of you did to frame her brother. Stacy had Ellie Rose's diary pages and she was beginning to decipher them. But the other two must have mystified you."

Diane was careful to accuse Everett Walters of the killings, although she thought that it was Tyler who choked Stacy to death. That conclusion was based, weakly perhaps, on the fact that he had done it before, and that his overlapping boot prints were lifted from the spot where Stacy actually died. But right now, she wanted Tyler to believe that he could clear himself.

"Ellie's diary?" said Marsha. "She had Ellie's diary?"

"Yes. She was a musician and good at math," said Diane. Like Frank, she thought. "Stacy was probably translating the parts that told her how Ellie was afraid of Tyler and his grandfather. Did Stacy call you, threaten you?"

"She called Granddad," said Tyler. "Stupid thing to do."

"What about Lassiter and Payden?" asked Diane. "Weren't you curious why they had to die?"

"He said it needed to be done," said Tyler. "You haven't answered my question. Why would he kill Ellie Rose?"

Diane eyed Everett. He looked smug. He didn't know she knew about his sister. Showtime.

"Some killers get off on the terror of their victims," said Diane, not taking her eyes off Everett. "Sometimes it's a sexual-control thing. Is that right, Ross?"

"Often," he said.

"But not you," said Diane. "It was a god-control thing with you. I imagine as a boy staying over at your big sister's, playing among all the statues of fauns, gargoyles, and dragons, it was like a little kingdom, a little Olympus. And what you really liked to do, what really made you feel powerful and in control, was to sneak up behind the unsuspecting prey and strike them dead, like a god in his dark realm. They never knew it was coming. You had the power to snuff out their life, and just like that, they were no more."

Everett's face slowly dropped its smug expression. He looked worried. Finally.

"What?" said Tyler. "What the hell are you talking about?"

"Didn't he tell you?" said Diane. "Your grandfather is a serial killer from way back. Not the ordinary kind, I don't think. He had more control than others of his kind. He prided himself in that."

"Not all serial killers lack control or feel a compulsion to constantly seek out victims," said Kingsley. "Some are opportunistic killers. I suspect your grandfather is one of those." Kingsley looked Everett in the eyes. "You can go for years without killing, can't you? You're like the smoker who can just stop and not look back and not obsess about having another cigarette."

"But I'll bet Everett couldn't resist the possibility of killing Ellie Rose," said Diane. "It was an opportunity presented to him, so he brought the hatchet. It's not that easy for a fourteen-year-old, like you were, to strangle someone. He knew there was a possibility she was still alive. And the pull of nostalgia was just too great, even for a man of his control."

"Are you serious?" said Tyler. He briefly took his eyes off his grandfather, and Everett started to reach for his ankle gun. "Watch it, old man. Is this true?" he asked him.

Everett straightened up. "Rubbish. Fantasy."

"Not according to your sister, Maybelle," said Diane.

Everett looked sharply at Diane, his eyes wide with surprise. He paused for many long moments, staring at Diane.

"Mags has to be a hundred and ten by now," he whispered.

"Not quite a hundred. Ninety-seven, I believe," said Diane.

"Senile," said Everett. Some of his smugness came back into his face.

"Actually, quite lucid," said Diane. "Creepy as hell, but her story is consistent with what we found in the well."

The smug look was short-lived. His mouth turned down into a frown.

"You know," said Diane, "I'll bet when you had your fingerprints taken at the time you were bonded for your business, you worried. You worried if they were on the items you dropped in the well when your father was coming to take your sister away. It was a long shot that they would ever be found, but it had to give you pause. And then came Dr. Marcella Payden, archaeologist and curious homeowner. She was looking for the artist who had created the broken pottery that she discovered in the fire pit in her yard and painted the portraits she found hidden in the walls. What if Marcella found your sister, Maybelle, and she told about the well? There goes your reputation. And here your son is about to run for U.S. congressman. You couldn't do anything when your father sold the property—you couldn't tell him it should stay in the family because of what was in the well, but you could do something now to keep the current owner quiet. Had you planned to try and buy it back? Maybe clean out the well?"

Everett said nothing. He stared at Diane so hard, she thought he was trying to will her to shut up.

"What well? What's this about?" said Tyler.

"It's about why you are innocent," said Diane.

That kept his attention on her story. Tyler was looking for a way out. When he first came into the room, he didn't think there was a way out without more murder, and his having to leave behind everything he knew. He had hope now, and Diane was counting on his hope to get them out of this alive.

"At first I wondered about Mary Lassiter," said Diane. "How did she figure in this? Of course, when we found out that she worked at the historical society where Marcella Payden was asking questions about who lived in the house in Pigeon Ridge, I realized that Mary Lassiter was your age. You both were contemporaries in Rosewood. Marcella sparked a memory in Mary Lassiter. She knew something about an artist who disappeared when she was a girl. The artist had a brother, Everett. She remembered you. She probably looked you up on the Internet. People do that a lot these days, trying to get in touch with people they used to know. For her it was probably a lark, maybe a chance for a little romance late in life. She didn't know you would consider her to be a loose end to be tied up, along with Marcella Payden. That's why Mary Lassiter's purse was stolen when she was killed. You wanted her cell phone, but didn't want the police to focus on the phone. You didn't want them looking at her call records. But Sheriff Braden is very thorough, and he'll check the call records as well as the Internet history records where she worked at the historical society." Diane paused a moment, letting it sink in.

"You see, Everett Gauthier," Diane continued, "we've been really busy at the crime lab."

"Gauthier?" said Wendy and Tyler together.

"That was Everett's family name before they moved from Rosewood, before it was changed to Walters—the Anglicized version of Gauthier. Everett's father's attempt to hide the family skeletons, as it were, by changing his family's last name. Everett's sister, Maybelle, did to him what he did to your son. She hated her father and his new wife, and she decided to ruin her half brother, Everett. She turned him into a killer."

"No," whispered Everett. "No. My sister loved me. She wouldn't have said those things."

"Well, when she discovered that you lived in luxury while she lived as an indigent in insane asylums and nursing homes for almost sixty years, what did you expect?"

Diane looked at the others, then at Tyler.

"Everett's sister, Maybelle Agnes Gauthier, your great-aunt, had a unique way of making her pottery. She used human bone from people she enticed Everett to kill. The sixteen-year-old Everett chopped them up and boiled the parts so she could render the bones into dust to temper the clay for her pottery. Nice little family, huh?" said Diane. "We found some of the bodies in the well, along with Everett's bloody fingerprints on the tools and in the clay."

Everett Walters was shaking now. Diane couldn't tell if it was from anger or from the fear that came with revelation.

"That's what you brought into your house, Wendy," said Diane, "a monster who had access to your son. And he brought him to this. This is why I have sympathy with Tyler, Marsha. He didn't have a chance, under the influence of someone like Everett."

"Shut up. Shut your damn hole, you bitch. Shut your damn mouth." Everett was shaking his fist at Diane.

"You," said Wendy, "have the nerve to tell her to shut up, you monster. Look what you've done."

Everett ignored Wendy, but continued to stare at Diane. "I'll kill you, if it's the last thing I do. I'll kill you and you'll know it's coming. I'll chop you up while you are still alive. You'll feel everything. You bitch. You bitch. You'll feel every cut."

"See, Tyler, this isn't you," said Diane.

But Tyler had passed out.

Chapter 62

When Diane looked back at Everett Walters, he was pointing a gun at her.

Well, hell.

"Now it's time to pay the piper," he said.

"Oh God, Tyler," yelled Wendy.

She stood up and started toward her unconscious son. As she crossed in front of Everett, she didn't see the blow from the pistol butt coming to the back of her head. Wendy reeled forward and fell, crashing into the table, rolling off it onto the floor at Marsha's feet. For a moment, Diane thought Marsha was going to kick her. Wendy struggled to get to her feet. She looked seriously hurt.

"Just lie there," said Diane. "Until you get your breath."

Ross Kingsley stood and faced Everett. "This may seem like a good idea to you now, but you're very angry. I understand that. Take a moment and think about this. It will do you no good to cut off your nose to spite your face," he said.

"It won't be *my* nose I'll be cutting off," he said. "You and the woman are do-gooders. I know your type. You take care of people too yellow to take care of themselves. So this is why I'm going to tell you, I'll be shooting these other folks first. I'll shoot my worthless daughter-in-law right now unless you sit down. Do you understand what I'm saying to you?"

Kingsley hesitated a moment, then sat down. Diane guessed he was trying to think of something else to say. Right now, Everett wasn't in the mood to listen.

All the guns were across the room with Tyler, except the

one in Everett's hand and the one under the sofa. Diane tried to think of a plan to get her hands on one of them. She didn't see how she could do it fast enough.

But maybe Wendy could. She was still on the floor and Diane could see her looking under the couch. She saw the gun; Diane was sure. But the coffee table was between her and the sofa. Everett would cut her down if she tried. Maybe if there was a diversion.

"Apparently, it's me you want to, how did you put it, chop up in little pieces? Why don't you leave these people alone?" Diane said, standing up and facing him.

"All full of piss and vinegar, aren't you? Think you can make your move once we get away from these people here? I know how your mind's working." He tapped his finger on his temple. "It's not going to go like that. No, I'm not going to drop my guard. You aren't going to get off, not after what you've done."

"Don't like being outed as a serial killer?" said Diane. She stepped toward him.

"Shut up. When I tell you to shut that damn hole of yours, I mean it," he said.

He started backing slowly toward the entrance to the living room, pointing his gun at Diane's head.

"Any one of you so much as looks like you're going to stand up is going to get it. I can shoot her and any one of you before you dive for the guns. Now, we are going out. You try and follow, she's dead and I'll take my chances. Are we all on the same page?"

He looked back at Diane, who stood a few feet away from him.

"Still got that mind working, don't you, girlie? Thinking about doing a dive like Wendy?" he said.

Diane was thinking of something like that. Diving at him quickly, knocking him off his feet before he could shoot. But he was too alert to a move like that now. If he was taking her to another location, he had to get her out of the house, across the yard, and into a vehicle. He would have to let his guard down at some point.

"Don't do it," said Everett. "It won't work. Now, very slowly, I want you to step—"

Crash!

Everett fell to the floor, a pink guitar careening away from the spot where his head had been a moment before.

"That's for my sister," said Samantha.

She hit him again on the head with the solid hardwood guitar.

"That's for making me ruin my Fender Stratocaster guitar. I'll send you the bill."

She kicked him in the back.

"That's for ruining my family."

Diane grabbed the gun that had fallen from his hand.

"Play much baseball?" Diane asked Samantha.

"No, but I have a mean golf swing," she said, and hugged Diane.

Diane turned in time to see Kingsley on his feet, hitting Samuel Carruthers in the jaw with his fist. Kingsley knocked him against a hutch filled with china that crashed on the shelves. He picked up the guns and turned to face Carruthers, who was struggling to his feet.

"What happened?" asked Diane, keeping an eye on Everett Walters as she spoke.

"He was going after the gun," said Kingsley. "He was planning on shooting one of them. I've been watching him."

"You're crazy. I'm going to sue," Carruthers said. He stood, scowling at Kingsley, his bathrobe askew, showing his gray boxer shorts and T-shirt. He rubbed his jaw and ran a hand through his uncombed hair.

"I saw it," said Kingsley. "You telegraphed your intentions. You've been sitting there stewing over your helplessness. And now that everything's over, you were going to get a gun and shoot one of the people responsible for your daughter's death. Now that they were helpless and you could do it in safety."

"How dare you," began Marsha, retying her own robe. "You come in here and disrupt our lives."

Kingsley ignored her.

"If you want to be a man, take care of your family. The two of you have been self-indulgent so long, you've forgotten that you have another daughter. Get out of the computer games and quit sitting staring at your dead daughter's painting and drinking yourself into oblivion. Look at the two of you. Your daughter just came in and saved your sorry ass and all you can think of is how to make yourself feel like a man. Did either of you go to her just now? And while I'm at it, do you know she found Stacy Dance's body? Do you know what that kind of thing does to a person?" said Kingsley.

Marsha whimpered and looked at her daughter. "Samantha? How could she have found her? That doesn't make sense."

"There's going to be a lot in your world that doesn't make sense for a while," said Kingsley. "Start by getting sober and talking to your daughter like an adult. And thank her for saving us all."

"Well said," whispered Diane.

She started to say something, when she heard Kathy Nicholson yell at Wendy. Diane turned to find Wendy with a gun on them.

"This is just too much," said Diane. "Put down the gun."

Wendy had tears running down her cheeks and was rubbing the back of her neck with her free hand. She looked strange to Diane, uneasy on her feet. She tried to speak but collapsed on the floor.

Diane ran to her and felt her neck. Nothing.

"No pulse," said Diane.

"What?" said Kathy. "How?"

Samuel Carruthers came over to her and felt for a pulse himself. Then he felt the back of her neck. "She's gone," he said.

"The hit by Everett?" asked Diane.

Samuel nodded. "I think it broke her cervical vertebrae. When she started moving, the bones cut through her spinal cord."

Diane put a hand over her eyes. "God, this is just an awful day," she said.

"What was she trying to do?" asked Marsha.

"I think, save her son from us," said Diane. "I don't know."

"That man drove her crazy," said Kathy.

"Did anyone call the police?" said Diane.

"I did," said Samantha. "Before my big entrance."

Diane went back over to where Everett was stirring. "Just stay on the floor," she said.

"What are you doing here?" Marsha asked her daughter.

"I came in through the window upstairs to get some of my things. I was trying to do it without your knowing. Then I heard some crazy stuff down here, so I crept down with my guitar. Good thing."

Diane heard the police sirens. It was a happy song. She and Kingsley gladly gave long statements to the police that went well into the afternoon. It was dinnertime before she and Kingsley went to their vehicles.

"We've got to quit meeting like this," said Kingsley.

Diane put a hand on the handle of her car door. "I'm giving up private work. Don't call unless you want a tour of the museum. By the way, that was quite a lecture you gave the Carruthers."

"They needed it. It really pissed me off when he decided to do some man stuff after his daughter did all the rescue work," said Kingsley.

"Are they going to be all right?" asked Diane.

Kingsley shrugged. "Samantha will be. I don't know about her parents. Who knows? Sometimes near-death experiences can change people. Want to meet at the Olive Garden on the way out of town? I'm famished."

Epilogue

Diane wrote up the final report on all the crime scenes her crime lab team was involved in relating to Everett and Tyler Walters. The police turned up more evidence than they needed executing the search warrants. Everett Walters thought he was being so clever not leaving any evidence. He never checked his feet. They found two more pottery pieces and two burgundy sequins under the floor mat of his truck. Part of the rope he used to truss up Stacy Dance was in the pickup toolbox. His boots were in his office closet at one of his places of business.

Marcella Payden recovered and went back to Arizona for an extended visit with her daughter and son-in-law. She and Jonas Briggs were writing a paper on serendipitous archaeology. Marcella kept her house, even though David, Scott, and Hector turned up remains of nine more bodies. Marcella wasn't scared away. It was a home with history and she was an archaeologist. As far as she was concerned, it was the house and property that outed the villains.

Jin had gotten DNA samples from all the skeletons recovered—mostly from the roots of teeth, but some from inside the bones. Neva reconstructed all their faces. So far, they hadn't gotten any hits on who the victims might be. They had been dead well over sixty years. Diane didn't hold out much hope they would be identified.

Kingsley and his bosses went with Harmon Dance to take his son home from prison—and had a press conference there in the parking lot. Kingsley told Diane that Darley, Dunn, and Upshaw wanted to hire her. She said no.

Maybelle Agnes Gauthier celebrated her ninety-eighth

birthday at her retirement home. The authorities were still trying to figure out what to do with her. They no longer considered her a threat, but Diane told Hanks she was not so sure. He agreed.

Kathy Nicholson moved with her son to California. She wrote Diane that Colton was considering transferring to the University of Hawaii and they might move there. Diane guessed that the coast wasn't far enough away from their bad memories in Georgia. Kathy Nicholson had to come to terms with the fact that she had not seen Ryan Dance drive by, but her own neighbor, Tyler Walters. Tyler told the police in his statement that he and his grandfather knew Kathy would be working in her garden and all Tyler had to do was be in Ryan's car, wearing Ryan's hat, and hanging his arm out the window for her to see the fake tattoo—and never turn his face to her.

Tyler Walters recovered and was tried and convicted for raping Ellie Rose Carruthers, murdering Stacy Dance, which he finally admitted to, kidnapping Diane and the others, and conspiring with his grandfather to kill Mary Lassiter and Marcella Payden, and framing Ryan Dance. He received life in prison, and was given the possibility of parole after twenty-five years because he testified against his grandfather. Tyler's father decided not to run for office. Jonas Briggs said it was a good thing. With the potential candidate's father, son, and late wife—not to mention his aunt—in his bio, no one but Jeffrey Dahmer would vote for him, and he was dead.

Everett Walters went to prison for life without possibility of parole for killing Ellie Rose Carruthers, Mary Phyllis Lassiter, Ray-Ray Dildy, Stacy Dance, and Wendy Walters, and for framing Ryan Dance, and kidnapping Diane and the others, and trying to assassinate Diane. He confessed to none of it. Tyler said his grandfather shot Ray-Ray to tie up a loose end and liked the idea of using a policeman's gun to do it. Ray-Ray was a day worker at one of Everett Walters' businesses. Everett learned about his cousin, Emory, from him. Tyler said that Ray-Ray and Emory were the only two people his grandfather had hired to help with the dirty work and that he had planned to kill Emory after he'd killed Diane in the home invasion.

The authorities were still uncertain whom to charge with killing the eleven people from sixty years ago. The resolution was still undergoing legal wrangling. Everett Walters' lawyers were saying that because his fingerprints were only on sculpting tools and clay, the state had no basis on which to charge him. His lawyers also claimed that his sister's testimony was unreliable, since she had been diagnosed on several occasions as being of unsound mind.

Oran Doppelmeyer, Gainesville's medical examiner, was let go by the city, much to Lynn Webber's delight. Diane suspected that if Lynn had the opportunity in the future, she would mess with his life again.

Diane didn't know what Samuel and Marsha Carruthers were up to or how they were coping. But she and Frank went to hear Samantha and the band one evening. They weren't too bad and Samantha seemed to be doing well. She was still in school and she had dyed all of her hair pink. Kingsley had bought her a new guitar. Frank told Diane it was a very expensive guitar.

Diane sat in her office going over the budget reports when the phone rang.

"Diane Fallon," she said.

"Dr. Fallon. My name is Clara Chandler. I hope I have the right place. I copied the number off the TV screen and, well, my eyesight's not too good anymore."

"What can I do for you?" said Diane.

"My sister, Patsy Chandler, went missing fifty-six years ago and she looked just like the picture I saw on the news of a girl you found down in a well. You said her name might be Patsy. I hope it's her. I'd like to take her home. We thought our daddy kilt her and buried her somewheres. He was mean like that."

"Would you come in and give us a DNA sample?" asked Diane.

"What do I have to do?" she asked.

"Let us take a cotton swab and rub inside your cheek," she said.

"Oh, like they do on those crime shows?" she said.

"Yes," said Diane.

"I can do that. My son can bring me down there right

now. That would be wonderful if it's my Patsy. We were twins and I have missed her all these years."

"I hope she is your sister too," said Diane. "I would like to see her claimed by her family."

Diane hung up the phone and looked at the mask of Patsy Doe, as they had called her, that Marcella had completed. It sat on a shelf and stared into infinity with empty eyes. Diane was uncertain what to do with it. Marcella said to have it buried with Patsy's remains—after all, it was made with dust of her bones. Maybe Marcella was right: remains resting, reunited, in peace. Dust to dust.

The gray sky grew darker as Diane watched. The storm was coming fast. She tried not to show her unease as she listened to Roy Barre going on about his grandfather's collection of Indian arrowheads that he was loaning to the museum. The two of them stood beside the museum's SUV, the four-wheel-drive vehicle she had driven to his mountain home. Diane had the driver's-side door open, key in hand, ready to get in when he wound down, or at least paused in his narrative.

"So, you going to put a plaque up on the wall with Granddaddy's name?" Barre said. "He'd like that. He picked up arrowheads from the time he was a little boy. Found a lot of them in the creek bed. That big pretty one I showed you of red flint—he was crossing the creek, looked down, and there it was, big as life right there with the river rocks."

Diane had heard the story several times already.

"Yes," she said, "there will be a plaque. Our archaeologist, Jonas Briggs, will oversee the display."

Roy Barre was a tall, rounded, cheerful man in his mid-fifties, with a ruddy face, graying beard, and brown hair down to his collar. In his overalls and plaid shirt, he didn't look as though he owned most of the mountain and the one next to it. Even with the oncoming storm, had she consented, he would at this moment be showing her the property and the crisscross of creeks where his grandfather had found his arrowheads.

"Granddaddy didn't dig for them, even when he was a little boy—he knowed that was wrong. You know, some people look for Indian burials and dig up the bones looking for pottery and nice arrowheads. Granddaddy didn't do that. No, he didn't bother anybody's resting place. He just picked up arrowheads he found on the ground or in the creek. A lot of them was in the creek, washed from somewhere. He never knew from where. He just eyed the creek bottom and, sure enough, he'd always find something. He sure found some pretty ones. Yes, he did."

The trees whipped back and forth and the wind picked up with a roar.

"Roy, you let that woman go. I swear, you've told her the same stories three times already. A storm's coming and she needs to get off the mountain."

Holding her sweater close around her, Ozella Barre, Roy's wife, came down the long set of concrete steps leading from her house on the side of the hill.

"Listen to that wind," she said. "Lord, it sounds like a train, don't it?"

"Mama's right, Miss Fallon, you need to be getting down the mountain before the rain comes. The roads can get pretty bad up here."

"Thank you for your hospitality and the loan of your grandfather's collection," said Diane. "I'm sure our archaeologist will be calling to ask you to tell him your stories again. I hope you don't mind."

Mrs. Barre laughed out loud and leaned against her husband. "How many times would he like to hear them?"

"You know how to get back to the main road?" asked Roy.

"I believe so," said Diane, smiling. She got in the car before Roy commenced another story and started the engine. She waved good-bye to them and eased down the long, winding gravel drive just as the first drops of rain started.

Diane was the director of the RiverTrail Museum of Natural History, a small, well-respected museum in Rosewood, Georgia. She was also director of Rosewood's crime lab, housed in the museum, and a forensic anthropologist. It was in her capacity as museum director that she was in the mountains of North Georgia, arranging the loan of the substantial arrowhead collection. Jonas Briggs, the museum's archaeologist, was interested in the collection mainly because LeFette Barre, Roy's grandfather, had kept a diary of sorts describing his hunting trips, including drawings of the arrowheads he had found and where he found them—more or less. Jonas wanted to map the projectile points—as he called them—especially the several Clovis points in the collection. Unfortunately he was away, or it would be he, instead of her, up here in the North Georgia mountains trying to dodge the coming storm.

The mountain roads weren't paved, and they were marked by ruts and gullies. She should have left sooner. The storm brought the darkness too soon, and despite what she said, she was just a little uncertain whether she could retrace her steps back to the main road. She looked down at the passenger seat for the directions. They weren't there. *Well hell*, she thought. Probably blew out of the vehicle while she had the door open. *Just pretend it's a cave*, she told herself.

The trees looked frenzied, whipping back and forth against the darkening sky. Diane watched the road, looking for familiar landmarks. The rain began to fall harder. Diane turned her wipers up several notches and slowed down. With the heavy rain and fog, it was getting harder to see the road.

A tire slipped into a rut and spun, and for several moments she thought she was stuck. She pressed the four-wheel-drive button on the gearshift, and suddenly the vehicle lurched forward and was out. Just ahead, she recognized her first turn. That road wasn't any better. It had heavy gouges and grooves carved into it by years of wheels and weather doing their destructive work. Diane remembered the ruts from when she came up the mountain, but the only annoyance then was a rough ride.

"Doesn't anybody fix roads around here?" she grumbled to herself as she hit a deep pothole and again spun her tires.

So far, she was remembering her way back, but visibility was getting worse. She turned her wipers on the fastest setting. She would have liked to pull off the road and wait for the rain to stop, but she was afraid of getting stuck. She would be on foot if her vehicle became mired in the muddy shoulder of the road, and coming up the mountain, she'd discovered that the area had no cell service.

Diane hoped she wouldn't meet anyone trying to get up the mountain as she inched along the narrow road, looking for the next turn. She couldn't find it. *Well, damn*, she thought to herself. *Did I miss it?* There was no turning around. *At least if I keep heading down*, she thought, *I'll get to a main road sooner or later.* She kept going—and looking.

Then she spotted the road—she just hadn't gone far enough. She turned onto another dirt road, slipping in the mud as she did. Up ahead she saw a house that she remembered from her trip up. *Good.* She sighed with relief. She was on the right road.

The house was dark. Diane didn't think anybody lived in it. It was run-down and, frankly, looked haunted, with its gray board siding, sagging porch, and strangely twisted trees in the front yard. *Boo Radley's house*, she thought to herself as she approached.

A flash of lightning and a loud crack caused her to jump and slam on the brakes. The cracking sound continued, and with a sudden stab of fear, Diane saw one of the trees in the yard of the house falling toward her. She put the SUV in reverse and spun the wheels. The tree crashed across the front of her vehicle, and in the strobe of lightning flashes, she saw a human skull resting on the hood of her car. A skeletal hand slammed hard against her windshield and broke apart.

ABOUT THE AUTHOR

Beverly Connor is the author of the Diane Fallon Forensic Investigation series and the Lindsay Chamberlain archaeology mystery series. She holds undergraduate and graduate degrees in archaeology, anthropology, sociology, and geology. Before she began her writing career, Beverly worked as an archaeologist in the southeastern United States, specializing in bone identification and analysis of stone tool debitage. Originally from Oak Ridge, Tennessee, she weaves her professional experiences from archaeology and her knowledge of the South into interlinked stories of the past and present. Beverly's books have been translated into German, Dutch, and Czech, and are available in standard and large print in the UK.